Luxury ESCAPES

MAISEY YATES
ANNE McALLISTER
JANETTE KENNY

MILLS &
BOON

Published in Great Britain 2014
by Mills & Boon, an imprint of Harlequin (UK) Limited,
Eton House, 18-24 Paradise Road, Richmond, Surrey, TW9 1SR

LUXURY ESCAPES © 2014 Harlequin Books S.A.

A Mistake, A Prince and A Pregnancy © 2010 Maisey Yates
Hired by Her Husband © 2010 Barbara Schenck
Captured and Crowned © 2010 Janette Kenny

ISBN: 978 0 263 91129 9

010-0114

Harlequin (UK) Limited's policy is to use papers that are natural, renewable and recyclable products and made from wood grown in sustainable forests The logging and manufacturing processes conform to the legalenvironmental regulations of the country of origin.

Printed and bound in Spain
by Blackprint CPI, Barcelona

A MISTAKE, A PRINCE AND A PREGNANCY

MAISEY YATES

January 2014

January 2014

Maisey Yates knew she wanted to be a writer even before she knew what it was she wanted to write. At her very first job she was fortunate enough to meet her very own tall, dark and handsome hero, who happened to be her boss, and promptly married him and started a family. It wasn't until she was pregnant with her second child that she found her very first Mills & Boon® book in a local thrift store—by the time she'd reached the happily ever after, she had fallen in love. She devoured as many as she could get her hands on after that, and she knew that these were the books she wanted to write!

She started submitting, and nearly two years later, while pregnant with her third child, she received The Call from her editor. At the age of twenty-three, she sold her first manuscript to Mills & Boon and she was very glad that the good news didn't send her into labour! She still can't quite believe she's blessed enough to see her name on, not just any book, but on her favourite books.

Maisey lives with her supportive, handsome, wonderful, nappy-changing husband and three small children, across the street from her parents and the home she grew up in, in the wilds of southern Oregon. She enjoys the contrast of living in a place where you might wake up to find a bear on your back porch, then walk into the home office to write stories that take place in exotic, urban locales.

For Aideen and Ben
You're two of the bravest people I know,
and you've inspired me in more ways than you can
know. I'm your number one American fan.

CHAPTER ONE

"OH, PLEASE don't rebel on me now." Alison Whitman put her hand over her stomach and tried to quell the rising nausea that was threatening her with immediate action if she didn't get a hold of some saltine crackers or a bottle of ginger ale. Morning sickness was the pits, and it was even worse when it lasted all day. Worse still when you were about to tell a man he was going to be a father.

Alison put her car in Park and took a deep breath, almost relieved to discover a roadblock in her path. The wrought-iron gates that partitioned the massive mansion from the rest of the world looked impenetrable. She didn't know a lot about this man, the father of her baby; nothing really other than his name. But it was clear that he was way out of her league, both financially and otherwise.

Her eyes widened when she saw a man in a dark suit with security-issue sunglasses prowling the perimeter of the fence. Was Max Rossi mafia or something? Who had security detail in the middle of nowhere in Washington State?

The guard, because that's what he had to be, exited through a smaller pedestrian gate and walked toward her car, his expression grim. He gestured for her to roll her window down and she complied, self-conscious of the crank handle that she had to use to perform the action. Her car wasn't exactly a new, fully loaded model.

"Are you lost, ma'am?" He sounded perfectly pleasant and polite, but she knew that his right hand, which looked as though it was resting on his hip and was partly concealed by his dark suit jacket, was likely gripping a gun.

"No. I'm looking for Mr. Rossi. This is the address I was given."

The man's lips turned up slightly. "Sorry. Mr. Rossi isn't receiving visitors."

"I'm…" She swallowed. "I'm Alison Whitman. He's expecting me. At least I think he is."

The guard held up a hand, pulled a cell phone from his pocket and hit Speed Dial. He spoke rapidly in a foreign language, Italian, she guessed, before hanging up and turning his attention back to her.

"Go ahead and pull in. Park your car at the front." He walked to the gate and keyed in a code. The iron monstrosities swung forward and Alison pulled the car through, her stomach now seriously protesting.

She really didn't know Max Rossi; she had no assurance he wouldn't harm her in some way. Maybe she hadn't thought this through.

No, that wasn't true. She *had* thought this through. From every angle until she was certain she had no choice but to come here and see the father of her baby, despite the fact that she wanted to bury her head in a hole and pretend the whole thing had never happened. She couldn't play ostrich on this one, no matter how much she might like to.

The house was massive, its bulk partially concealed by towering fir trees. The intensity of the saturated greens surrounding her was almost surreal, compliments of the year-round rainfall. Nothing new to a native of the Pacific Northwest, but she rarely ventured outside the Seattle city limits anymore, so being surrounded by this much nature felt like a new experience. And seeing such a pristine, modern mansion set in the middle of the rugged wilderness was akin to an out-of-body experience.

Of course, the past two weeks had also seemed like an out-of-body experience; first with the positive pregnancy test, and then with all of the revelations that had followed.

She parked her ancient car in front of the house and got out slowly, really hoping she didn't lose her lunch in the middle of the paved driveway. Not exactly a way to make a good impression on a man.

The security detail appeared out of nowhere, his hand clamping firmly on her arm as he led her to the front door.

"I appreciate the chivalrous gesture, but I can make it through the door on my own," she said drily.

Her escort gave her a rueful smile, but loosened his grip and let his hand fall to his side. Although she noticed he was still ready to grab hold of her if he needed to.

He opened the front door for her and she had a feeling it wasn't good manners that made him allow her to go in first, but a desire to keep himself in the most advantageous position.

"Ms. Whitman." The deep, velvet voice held just a hint of an accent and the sound made her already queasy stomach turn, but not with nausea. This feeling was something she didn't recognize at all; a strange twisting sensation that wasn't entirely unpleasant. She put a hand to her stomach and tried to suppress it.

The sight of the owner of the amazing voice only increased the pitching sensation. She watched as he strode down the sweeping, curved staircase, his movements quick and smooth, masculine yet graceful.

He was the most handsome man she'd ever seen— not that she ever spent much time dwelling on men and their looks. This man, though, demanded admiration, even from her. He was just so masculine, so striking. He would turn both male and female heads wherever he went, that was for sure. And not just because of his arresting features and perfect physique. It was his air of authority, the absolute power that emanated from him. It was compelling in a way that captivated her.

His square jaw was set and uncompromising. Hard eyes, dark and fathomless, framed by a fringe of thick eyelashes, stared down at her. If not for the expression in his eyes, she might have called them beautiful, but the intense glare that he fixed on her put paid to that description.

He looked familiar, although she couldn't imagine where she would have ever seen someone like him. Such an example of masculine perfection hardly haunted the halls of the pro bono law firm where she worked.

She swallowed thickly and took a deep breath, hoping the infusion of fresh air would banish some of the nausea she felt. "Yes."

"You're from the clinic?" he asked, coming to a stop in front of her. His posture would make a marine envious. She had to crane her neck to look at him, his height topping her own five foot four inches by at least a foot.

"Yes…no. Not exactly. I don't know how much

Melissa explained when she called you." Melissa was one of her dearest friends in the world, and when she'd heard about the mistake made at the clinic she'd not only contacted Alison right away with Max's information—against the wishes of her boss—but she'd offered to be the one to contact Max, as well.

"Not a lot, only that it was an urgent matter. Which it had better be."

Not for the first time she contemplated just turning around and leaving, leaving the whole situation behind her. But that was the coward's way out. She didn't believe in leaving loose ends, and, unlike some other people, she didn't walk away from her responsibilities. Not ever.

"Is there somewhere we can go and speak privately?" she asked, looking around the cavernous entryway. No doubt the house had a lot of private rooms where they could sit and talk. Of course, the idea of being in an enclosed space with a man she'd never met didn't rank as a favorite for her. She was trained in self-defense and she had pepper spray on her key chain, but that didn't mean she wanted to get in a situation where she would have to use either one. Especially since she had a feeling neither one would prove effective against Max Rossi.

"I don't have a lot of time, Ms. Whitman."

Anger flared through her. *He* didn't have a lot of time? As if she had any spare moments just lying around. It was difficult for her to take any time off of work. Every case they handled was vitally important to the people involved. They were advocating for those who couldn't advocate for themselves, and by taking the afternoon off to drive up here and talk to him she was leaving her clients in the lurch.

"I can assure you that my time is valuable, too,

Mr. Rossi," she said stiffly. "But I need to speak with you."

"Then speak," he said.

"I'm pregnant," she said, wishing, even as she said the words, that she could call them back.

A muscle in his jaw ticked. "Am I meant to offer congratulations?"

"You're the father."

His dark eyes hardened. "You and I both know that isn't possible. You may not keep a record of your lovers, Ms. Whitman, but I can assure you I'm not so promiscuous that I forget mine."

Her face heated. "There are other ways to conceive a child than sexual intercourse, as you well know. When Melissa from ZoiLabs called she implied that I worked there but I'm a...I'm a client of theirs."

He froze, his expression hardening like granite, his jaw tightening. "Let's go into my office."

She followed him through the large living area of the house and through a heavy oak door. His home office was massive, with high ceilings that were accented by rich, natural wood beams. One of the walls was made entirely of glass and overlooked the valley below. There was nothing as far as she could see but pristine nature. Beautiful. But the view was cold comfort in the situation.

"There was a mistake at the clinic," she said, keeping her eyes trained on the mountains in the distance. "They weren't going to tell me, but one of my friends works there and she felt I...that I had a right to know. I was given your donation by mistake and there was no log of your...of your genetic testing."

"How is this possible?" he asked, pacing the room with long strides.

"I wasn't offered a specific explanation. The nearest thing to an answer I got is that your sample was mixed up with the donor I had selected because your last names were similar. My intended donor was a Mr. Ross."

Max gave her a hard look. "He was not your husband or boyfriend?"

"I don't have a husband or a boyfriend. It was all meant to be done anonymously. But…" She took a shaky breath. "It isn't that simple now."

His lip curled. "Not so simple now that you've found out the 'donor' for your child is a wealthy man? Are you here to collect some kind of prenatal child support?"

Alison bristled. "That isn't it at all! I'm sorry to have bothered you, I really am. I'm sure you didn't expect the recipient of your donation to show up on your doorstep. But I need to know if you underwent genetic testing prior to using the clinic."

"I didn't leave a donation," he said, his voice rough.

"You must have! She gave me your name. She said it was your sperm that was given to me by mistake."

A muscle in his jaw tightened and she noticed him slowly squeezing his hands into fists and releasing them, as if in attempt to gain control over his temper. "I had a sperm sample at the clinic, but it was not meant for anonymous donation. It was for my wife. We were having trouble conceiving."

"Oh." Alison felt all of the blood drain from her face, leaving her light-headed and dizzy. Now she really wanted to turn and run away. She'd read horror stories in the paper about couples involved in mix-ups, and people losing their babies. She clamped a possessive hand over her stomach. The baby was still hers, even if this man was the biological father. She was still the mother. No judge would take a baby from a competent, loving mother. And Max's wife wouldn't want a baby that didn't belong to her anyway. She couldn't.

"I just...I just need to know..." She took a breath. "I'm a nonaffected carrier of Cystic Fibrosis. The donors are all screened for genetic disorders before they're accepted. But your results weren't in the file. Melissa knew that I was concerned and she was going to get me the information about you, only it wasn't there."

"That's because I wasn't a *donor*," he said harshly.

"But have you been tested?" she asked, desperation clawing at her. She had to know. Watching her sister succumb to the disease in childhood had been the hardest thing Alison had ever endured. It had been the end of everything. Her family, her happiness. She had to know so that she could prepare herself for the worst. She wouldn't terminate her pregnancy. No matter what, she wouldn't do that. The memory of her sister, of that wonderful, short life, was far too dear to her to consider that. But she *did* need to know.

"I have not had that test done."

She sank into the plush chair that was positioned in front of the desk, her knees unable to support her anymore. "You need to get it done," she said. "*Please.* I need you to do it."

Maximo examined the woman sitting in front of him, his heart pounding heavily in his chest. He hadn't given a thought to the clinic in the past two years, not since Selena's death. When he'd received the phone call from the employee at ZoiLabs he had assumed it pertained to his sperm sample. They had called shortly after the accident to ask him if they could discard it, but he'd ignored the voice mail message. At the time he simply hadn't been able to deal with it. He hadn't imagined that these might be the consequences.

Now he was going to be a father. It was the most amazing and terrifying moment he'd ever experienced. His gaze dropped to Alison's flat stomach. She was so slender it was almost impossible to believe that she could be carrying his baby. *His* baby. A son or daughter.

He could easily see a vision of a dark-haired child, cradled in Alison Whitman's arms as she looked down at the infant with a small, maternal smile on her face. The image filled him with longing so intense that his chest ached with it. He thought that he'd let that desire go, the desire for children. He thought he'd laid that dream to rest, alongside his wife.

But in one surreal moment all of those dreams had been made possible again. And in that very same moment he'd found out that his child might have serious health complications. His tightly controlled life was suddenly, definitely, out of his control. Everything that had seemed important five minutes ago was insignificant now, and everything that mattered to him rested in the womb of this stranger.

But he could get the test. Find out as soon as possible if there was a chance their baby might have the disease. Having something to do, something to hold on to, real action that he could take, helped anchor the whole situation to reality, allowed him to have some control back. It made it easier to believe that there really was a baby.

"I will have the test done right away," he said. He hadn't been planning on going back to Turan for another two weeks, but this took precedence. He would need to see his personal physician at the palace. He wouldn't take any chances on having this made a spectacle by the press. They'd caused enough damage in his life. "And what are you planning if the test is positive?"

She looked down at her hands. They were delicate,

feminine hands, void of jewelry and nail polish. It was far too easy to imagine how soft those hands would feel on his body, how pale they would look against the dark skin of his chest. A pang of lust hit him low in the gut. She was a beautiful woman; there was no denying that. Much less adorned than the type of woman he was accustomed to.

Her face had only the bare minimum of makeup, showing flawless ivory skin, her copper eyes left unenhanced by colored eyeshadow. Her full lips had just a bit of pale pink gloss on them that wouldn't take long to kiss right off.

Her strawberry blond hair was straight, falling well past her shoulders, and it looked as if it would be soft to touch, not stiff with product. A man would be able to sift it through his fingers and watch it spill over his pillow. His stomach tightened further. It said a lot about how much neglect his libido had endured if he was capable of being aroused at this precise moment. And when had a woman ever appealed to him so immediately? When had lust grabbed him so hard? Never in his recent memory, that was certain. Guilt, usually easy to ignore after living with it for so long, gnawed at him, harder and more insistent than usual.

"I'm keeping the baby no matter what," she said slowly, raising her eyes to meet his. "I just need to be prepared."

Something about the way she said that *she* was keeping the baby, as if he, the child's father, had no place in its life, caused a torrent of hot, possessive anger to flood through him. It was so intense that it momentarily blotted out the lust that had just been firing through his veins.

"The baby isn't yours. The baby is ours," he said.

"But…but you and your wife…"

He froze, realizing suddenly that she didn't know who he was. It didn't seem possible. Her face betrayed nothing, not a hint of recognition or foreknowledge concerning what he was about to say. If she did know who he was, she was a world-class actress.

"My wife died two years ago."

Those exotic eyes widened and her mouth dropped. "I'm…I'm sorry. I didn't know. Melissa didn't tell me that. She didn't tell me anything about you but your name."

"Usually that's enough," he said ruefully.

"But then…you don't think I'm going to give you my baby?"

"Our baby," he growled. "As much mine as yours. Assuming of course that you're actually the mother and it wasn't some other woman who donated genetic material."

"No. It's *my* baby. Biologically. I was artificially inseminated." She lowered her gaze. "This was my third attempt. I didn't get pregnant the first two times."

"And you are certain it was my sample that took?"

"They were all your samples." She pursed her lips. "They made the mistake months ago. They only realized after the last time. The time that was successful."

Silence hung between them, thickening the air. Maximo felt his heart rate quicken, his blood pumping hard through his veins. He looked down at her, at those full pouting lips. In that moment his only thought was what a shame it was that he had not made three traditional conception attempts with this woman. She was incredibly beautiful—an enticing mix of strength and vulnerability that appealed to him in a way he didn't understand. He crushed the surge of almost crippling desire that was washing through him.

"So you're capable of having a baby with a man the usual way, and yet you chose to make one with a turkey-baster?" he said, his voice harsh.

Her lip curled in disgust. "That's horrible."

It was, and he knew it. Yet he felt compelled to lash out at her, at the woman who had walked into his home and tilted his world completely off its axis. He hadn't been entirely happy with how his life was, but he had come to the point where he'd accepted it. Now she was here, offering him things he had long since let go of. Only what she was offering was a mangled, twisted version of the dream he and his wife had shared.

"You're a lesbian?" he asked. If she was, it was a loss to his gender. A waste of a very beautiful woman, in his opinion.

Color flared in her cheeks. "No. I'm not a lesbian."

"Then why not wait and have a baby with a hus-band?"

"Because I don't want a husband."

He took in her business attire for the first time. The extreme beauty of her face had held his attention before, preventing him from examining the rest of her appearance too closely, and he hadn't noticed the neatly tailored charcoal pantsuit and starched white shirt. She was obviously a career woman. Probably intent on having day-care workers raise their child while she set about climbing the corporate ladder. Why have a baby, then? An accessory no doubt, the ultimate symbol of all she had achieved without the help of a man. Distaste coiled in his stomach, mingling with the desire that lingered there.

"Don't imagine for one moment that you will be

raising this child without me. We'll have paternity testing done and if it is in fact my baby, you may yet find yourself with a husband, regardless of your original plans."

He didn't want to get married again. He hadn't even been inclined to get involved in a casual relationship since Selena's death, but that didn't change the facts of the situation. If this was his child, there was no way he would be an absentee father. He wanted his son or daughter in Turan with him, not half a world away in the United States.

The thought of having his child looked upon as a royal bastard, illegitimate and unable to claim the inheritance that should belong to him or her by right, was not something that settled well with him. And there was only one way to remedy that.

The look of absolute shock on her face might have been comical if there were anything even remotely funny about the situation. "Did you just propose to me?"

"Not exactly."

"I don't know you. You don't know me."

"We're having a baby," he said simply.

"I fail to see what that has to do with marriage," she said, that luscious mouth pursed into a tight pout.

"It's a common reason for people to marry," he said drily. "Arguably the most common."

"I fully intended on being a single parent. I wasn't waiting around for a white knight to sweep me off of my feet and offer matrimony. This wasn't plan B while I waited around for Mr. Right. The baby was my only plan."

"And I'm sure the League of Women applauds your progressive viewpoint, Ms. Whitman, but you are no longer the only person involved here. I am, as well. In fact, you *chose* to involve me."

"Only because I need to know if you're a carrier for CF."

"Couldn't you have had the baby tested?"

"I want to know before the baby is born if there's a chance he or she might have the disease. It's something that would require a lot of emotional preparation. There's testing that can be done *in utero*, but they typically don't perform the test unless both parents are found to be carriers. I could have waited and said I didn't know the father and gotten prenatal testing done but there's a slight miscarriage risk and I just couldn't take the chance, not when I could just come and talk to you. "

"Or perhaps all of your feminist posturing is simply that. Posturing. You said you have a friend at the clinic, and I'm a powerful, wealthy man. It is not outside the realm of belief that you did not receive my sample by accident. How is it that my sample has been sitting there for two years and it suddenly got mixed up with the donor sperm?"

Maximo had seen people go to extreme lengths to get a hand on his money, to use his influence. Had this woman cooked up a scheme in order to net herself money and power? People had done worse for far less than he had to offer, for less than the mother of his child would stand to gain.

"I don't know why the mistake happened, I only know that it did," she said, her pretty white teeth gritted. "But don't flatter yourself by thinking I would go to such trouble to tie myself to you just to get money. In fact, don't flatter yourself by assuming I have any idea who you are."

He barked out a laugh. "It's hardly flattery to assume that a woman who is presumably well-informed and well educated would know who I was. Unless of course you're neither of those things."

Her eyes shimmered with golden fire, her finely arched brows lowered and drawn together. "Now you're measuring my intellect by whether or not I'm aware of who you are? That's quite an ego you have there, Mr. Rossi."

"I'd hate to confirm your take on my ego, Ms. Whitman, but my official title is Prince Maximo Rossi, and I'm next in line for the throne of Turan. If the child you're carrying is mine, then he or she is my heir, the future ruler of my country."

CHAPTER TWO

SUDDENLY it was horrifyingly clear why he'd looked familiar when she'd first seen him. He wasn't just Mr. Max Rossi. She *had* seen him before. On the news, in the tabloids. He and his wife had been media favorites. They were royal and beautiful, and, by all accounts, extremely happy. Then, two years ago, he'd been in the news for his personal tragedy. The loss of his wife.

She was thankful she was sitting or she would have collapsed.

His dark brows snapped together and she registered concern in his eyes before her vision blurred slightly.

"Are you all right?" He knelt down in front of her and put a hand on her forehead. His skin felt hot and his touch left a tingling sensation behind when he swept his hand down to her hair and moved it aside, exposing her neck to the cool air. She hadn't realized she'd been sweating until that moment.

"Yes," she said. Then, "No."

"Put your head down," he said.

She was far too sick to do anything but comply. He gently tilted her head down, his hand moving slowly up and down the curve of her neck, the action soothing, his touch shockingly gentle despite the strength of his hand. It had been a very long time since anyone had touched her. There had been handshakes, casual contact during conversations at work, but she couldn't remember the last time someone had put their hand on her with the intention to comfort. She hadn't realized how amazing it could feel.

But Maximo's touch was causing little rivulets of sweet sensation to wind through her, the slight rasp of his firm fingers against her skin a source of pleasure rather than the kind of anxiety she might expect. It was amazing how a man's hands could be so gentle, yet so firm and masculine. She looked down at his other hand, which he'd settled on her thigh. It was so different from hers; his fingers long and blunt with clean, square nails, his palms wide and strong.

She could feel the warmth from his hand seeping through her wool trousers and she was shocked at how comforting it felt. And something beyond comforting. Something that made her breasts feel heavy and the air seem thick. She'd thought she just wasn't the kind of person who responded to physical touch. She had never really been tactile or sexual, and that hadn't ever bothered her. In fact, it had been something of a relief. She had never wanted to have a relationship, had never wanted to open herself up to someone like that, to grow to depend on them. As a result she'd gone out of her way to avoid serious romantic entanglements.

Her reaction to Maximo was due to pregnancy hormones. It had to be. There was no other explanation for why a part of her left ignored for so long should suddenly come roaring to life.

"I'm fine," she said, her voice sounding strangled. She covered his hand with hers to move it away and the contact sent a shiver of something purely sexual through her. She jerked her hand back and stood up, ignoring the wobble in her vision. "Thank you."

"Are you sure you're healthy enough to sustain a pregnancy?" he asked, his voice full of concern, though for her or the baby she wasn't sure.

"I'm fine. It just isn't every day a girl finds out she's pregnant with the heir to the Turani throne."

Maximo knew there was no way Alison could have faked the way the color had suddenly drained from her face, no matter how accomplished an actress she was. And now, her golden eyes looked haunted, those pretty hands unsteady. After seeing the expression of pure shock on her face he couldn't really believe that she'd orchestrated anything. She certainly didn't look like a woman who was watching a carefully plotted scheme come to fruition. She looked like a hunted doe, all wide-eyed and terrified.

"It isn't every day a man finds out he's received a second chance to have a child," he said.

"You want the baby," she said, her voice hollow.

"Of course I want the baby. How could I not want my own child, my own flesh and blood?"

"If this is about producing an heir can't you find some other woman to…"

"Enough!" He cut her off, rage heating his blood. "Is that what you think? That it would be so simple for me to forget that I had a child in the world? That I could simply abandon him because he was not planned? Could *you* walk away so easily?"

"Of course I couldn't walk away!"

"Then why do you expect me to do it? If it is so simple, you have this baby and give him to me. Then have another one with a different man's *contribution*."

"You know I could never do that. I could never leave my baby!"

"Then do not expect that I could."

"This is… This is all going wrong," she moaned, sinking into the chair by his desk again and covering her face with her hands.

He swallowed. "Things in life don't always go as we plan. Things change. People die. Accidents happen. All that can be done then is the best thing possible with what remains."

She looked up at him, her eyes glittering with frustrated tears. "I don't want to share my baby with a stranger. I don't want to share my baby with anyone. If that makes me selfish then I'm sorry."

"And I'm afraid I can't let you walk away with my child."

"I didn't say I was going to walk away with your child. I understand that this is…difficult for you, too. But you weren't planning on having a baby. I was, and…"

"I planned on having children for years. It was denied me, first through infertility and then through the loss of my wife. And now that I have the chance again, you will not stand in my way."

He couldn't let her out of his sight, of that he was certain. And his course of action after that was still undecided. Marriage still seemed like the most viable of his options, the only way to prevent his son or daughter from suffering the stigma of illegitimacy. And yet the very idea of marriage was enough to make him feel as if his lungs were closing in. But in the meantime, this woman wasn't going to get any chances to escape from him.

"I have to fly back to Turan to see my personal physician. I'm not undergoing any medical testing in the U.S."

"You and your wife obviously did your fertility treatments here."

Yes, they had. Selena had been raised on the West Coast of the United States and they'd always kept a residence in Washington for vacations. It was the place they retreated to when they needed a break from the stresses of life under the microscope in Turan. That was why they had chosen the clinic in Washington to pursue their dream of starting a family. It was relaxing here…a place they had both felt at ease.

"Yes," he said drily, "but my confidence in the competence of your medical system has declined greatly in the past forty minutes, for obvious reasons. My doctor in Turan will be fast and discreet."

She nodded slowly, obviously not seeing any point in arguing with him. "When do you think you'll be able to have the test done?"

"As soon as I arrive. The health of my child is important to me, too."

She suddenly looked so desolate, so achingly sad, that it made him want to take her into his arms and just hold her, gather her fragile frame against him and support her, shelter her. The sudden, fierce need to comfort her shocked him. Was it because she was pregnant with his child? That had to be it. There was no other explanation for such a burning hunger to keep this woman safe from everything that might harm her. His child's life was tied to hers and that called to him as a man—as a protector—on the most primal of levels.

Alison herself called to him on an even more basic level. Was it some kind of latent male instinct to claim what now seemed to be his? The ache to take her in his arms, crush those soft breasts against his chest, kiss her until her lips were swollen, to thrust into her body and join them in the most intimate way possible, was almost strong enough to overtake his carefully cultivated self-control.

"I'm thinking of taking legal action against the clinic," she said softly. "I'm a lawyer and I'm certain we would have a case."

"I'm certain we would, too, despite the fact that I don't have a law degree," he said wryly. "That would mean a lot of press."

The media circus would be out of control. Sensational headlines for a world that loved nothing more than scandal. And his wife's fertility issues, his marriage, all of it would be thrust into the spotlight. It was the last thing he wanted, both for Selena's sake and his own. There was no point in tearing down her memory—not now that she was gone. Some things were best left buried, and the final months of his marriage were among them.

"You do tend to attract a lot of media attention, don't you?"

"I didn't think you listened to entertainment news."

"I don't. But I do stand in line at the grocery store on the odd occasion, which means I've seen the headlines. I just didn't pay close enough attention to recognize you on sight."

"Or by name."

She shrugged. "I only have so much room in my head for trivia. Then I start losing important information."

A reluctant laugh escaped his lips. He liked that she was able to take shots at him, even in the circumstances. It was rare that anyone stood up to him. Even Selena hadn't done that. She had simply retreated from him.

Maybe if she had been willing to come at him with her anger rather than keeping it all inside…

It was much too late for what-ifs. He pushed thoughts of Selena aside, choosing instead to focus on the problem at hand.

"I would like you to go to Turan with me."

Her thickly lashed eyes widened. "No. I can't. I'm busy here. I have a heavy caseload that demands a lot of my attention. Each one of my clients is extremely important and I can't put anyone off."

"Is there no one else at your office that can take care of that for you? You are pregnant, after all."

"There's no 'pregnant, after all.' I have responsibilities. Responsibilities that aren't going to take a holiday just because *you* want me to."

"I see. So your career is so important to you that you cannot manage to take time off to be there in person for the testing? For something that is so important to our child?"

She stiffened, her cheeks suddenly flooded with color, her pert chin thrust out at a stubborn angle. "That isn't fair. It's emotional blackmail."

"And if that doesn't work I'll resort to some other form of blackmail. I'm not picky."

Her lips were pursed again and he wanted to see her relax her mouth, wanted to enjoy the fullness, the temptation that she presented. It had been so long since a woman had tempted him he was enjoying the feeling. He extended his hand and rested his thumb on her lower lip. Her mouth parted in shock and heat shot from his hand to his groin when the action caused his thumb to dip between her lips and touch the wet tip of her tongue lightly.

Desire twisted his stomach. He wanted her with an

intensity that shocked him. And he wasn't certain the pregnancy had anything to do with that. He wanted her as a man wanted a woman. It was as simple as that.

Suddenly his left ring finger felt bare. It was a strange thing to be conscious of since he'd taken his wedding band off after Selena's funeral. He hadn't wanted to carry the reminder of his marriage with him.

"We have to work something out," he said softly. "For the baby's sake. That means compromise, not blackmail."

She turned her head and broke their contact. "Why do I get the feeling the commoner will be doing all of the compromising?"

His lips turned up. "Now, *cara*, you misjudge me. I'm a very reasonable man."

"I'll have to conduct an interview of the people you've had thrown in the royal dungeon once we get to Turan," she said, a slight bite still evident in her resigned tone.

"They aren't allowed to speak, actually, so your interviews will be short."

He could see a reluctant smile pull at the corners of her mouth. It made something that felt a lot like pride swell in his chest.

"I'll have to call the office to try to arrange for the time off." She took a shaky breath and pushed that lovely strawberry hair off her shoulders. "When do we leave?"

Alison regretted her decision to go with his royal highness almost the moment she agreed to it, but no matter how much she turned it over in her mind, no matter how much she wanted to run from it, she knew she couldn't.

Standing in the first-class lounge and waiting for his

majesty to arrive she tried to calm her nerves, and her morning sickness, by gnawing on a saltine and pacing the length of the room. There was plenty of plush, very comfy looking seating, but she was much too nervous, too edgy, to think about sitting down.

How had everything become so complicated? For the past three years she'd done nothing but plan for this. Everything had been geared toward this, toward the pregnancy. She'd saved her paychecks obsessively, driven a junky car, lived in the smallest, cheapest apartment she could find, in the hopes that when she had her child she could buy a house and stay home with him or her for the first few years. She'd quit her high-stress job at a prestigious law firm in order to better prepare her body for pregnancy. She'd even started a college fund for the baby, for heaven's sake!

And one phone call had annihilated all of it. When Melissa had dropped the bomb about her receiving the wrong sperm from a donor with missing medical records, everything had shattered into a million pieces.

She had been so determined to be smart, to ensure that the father of her child wouldn't put the baby's health at risk. She hadn't wanted to give up her anonymity, hadn't wanted to involve the father in any way, and she certainly hadn't wanted the father to be a man who would claim the baby for himself. It was the worst-case scenario as far as she was concerned.

Maximo had been nice enough to her yesterday, but she sensed ruthlessness in him simmering just beneath that aura of power and sophistication. Even when he was being nice his every command was just that: a command. He was a man who did not ask permission.

He was being civil to her now, working with her, and yet she knew he wouldn't hesitate to play on every advantage he had if it came to it. But she would, too. He may hold more cards by virtue of his wealth and position, but she wasn't a doormat. Far from it.

For now, though, civility seemed to be the order of the day, and she was willing to try to work something out with him, even if it was about the last thing she wanted to do. He had a right to his baby, whether or not she liked the idea of sharing custody. He was as much a victim in the circumstances as she was. He was a widower, a man who had already endured loss and heartbreak. As much as she wished she could go back and change her mind about telling him, she wouldn't be a part of hurting him again.

Alison looked out of the heavily tinted windows that gave the lounge a view of the terminal below. She watched as the automatic doors opened and Maximo strode in, security detail and photographers on his tail. Even with the massive entourage of people, every eye was drawn straight to him. He was as big and fit as any of the men on his security team, his chest broad and muscular, the outline of his pecs visible through the casual white button-down shirt he wore. The sleeves were scrunched up past his elbows, revealing muscular forearms and deliciously tanned skin.

He disappeared from view and a few moments later the door to the lounge opened and he strode in, minus the photographers and security detail.

She couldn't stop herself from taking a visual tour of his well-built body. His slacks hugged his thighs just enough so she could tell they were as solid as the rest of him. And, heaven help her, she was powerless to resist the temptation to sneak a peek at the slight bulge showing at the apex of those thighs.

She lowered her eyes, embarrassed by her uncharacteristic behavior. She honestly couldn't remember ever looking at a man there before. Not on purpose, anyway. She tried to tell herself it was nerves making her heart pound and her pulse flutter. She couldn't quite convince herself.

Maximo approached her and took his sunglasses off, tucking them in the neck of his shirt. Again, totally without permission, her eyes followed the motion and she was transfixed by the slight dusting of dark hair she could see on the tanned slice of chest that was revealed by the open collar of his shirt.

"Glad to see you made it," he said. He seemed totally unruffled by the fact that he'd just had a team of photographers taking his picture. He was maddeningly self-assured. If she'd had camera lenses stuck in her face she would have been worried that she might have had a poppy seed in her teeth from the muffin she'd eaten earlier.

"I said I would be here," she returned frostily. "I keep my word."

"I'm relieved to hear that. You're feeling all right?" He took her arm, the gesture totally sexless, more proprietary than anything else, and yet it made her heart jump into her throat. He was so much bigger than she was, so much stronger. Something about that masculine strength was so very appealing. It was easy to want to sink against him, to let him shoulder some of the stress, to bear some of her weight.

And the moment she did that she could almost guarantee he would abandon her, leaving her half crippled and unable to support herself any longer.

She ignored the little flutters in her stomach and tried to focus on the nausea. Anything was preferable to this strange sort of attraction that seemed to be taking over the portion of her brain that housed her common sense.

"Actually I feel horrible, but thank you for asking."

A slight grin tilted his lips. "You can bypass airport security," he said. "My plane is waiting on the tarmac. One of my security agents will escort you out and I will join you in a few moments. We aren't looking to create a photo-op."

She shook her head. The image of herself, pale as a corpse, plastered over a supermarket tabloid was enough to make her shudder.

One of the bodyguards came in and Maximo gestured for her to follow him out. She bowed her head as she crossed the wet tarmac and headed toward the private plane. She thought she might have seen the flash of a camera from the corner of her eye, but she kept her head down, determined not to seem interesting in any way.

She followed the guard up the boarding platform and into the lavishly furnished private jet. It was massive, its plush carpet and luxurious furnishings making it look like a trendy urban penthouse rather than a mode of transportation. But she'd been to Maximo's house and she'd seen the kind of lifestyle he was accustomed to. She really shouldn't be surprised that he didn't do anything by halves. He was the prince of one of the world's most celebrated island destinations, a country that rivaled Monte Carlo for high-class luxury and enter-tainment. Maximo was simply adhering to his national standard.

The bodyguard left without so much as a nod to her and she stood awkwardly just inside the door, not really feeling as if it was okay to sit down and make herself comfortable.

Ten minutes later Maximo boarded, his expression

grim. "There was one photographer hanging out on the tarmac. But since we didn't board together it's likely you might be mistaken for a member of my staff."

She nodded, not quite able to fathom how dodging the press had suddenly become a part of her life. "Are we the only ones flying on the plane today?" she asked, looking around the space.

"Well, you and me and the pilot. And the copilot. And the flight crew."

"That's awfully wasteful, don't you think?"

His dark eyebrows winged upward and she experienced a momentary rush of satisfaction over having taken him off guard. *"Scusami?"*

"Conducting an overseas flight for two people, who could easily have flown commercial, and employing an entire staff to serve them. Not to mention the greenhouse gas emissions."

He offered her a lazy grin that showed off straight, white teeth. It transformed his face, softening the hard angles and making him seem almost approachable. Almost. "When the U.S. President ditches Air Force One, I'll rethink my mode of transport. Until then, I think it's acceptable for world leaders to fly in private aircrafts."

"Well, I imagine it's hard to get through the security lines at the airport with all that gold jingling in your pocket."

"Are you a snob, Alison?" he asked, amusement lacing his voice.

"Am I a snob?"

"An inverse one."

"Not at all. I was simply making a statement." To keep him at arm's length and annoyed with her if she could help it. There was something about Maximo, something that made her stomach tighten and her hands get damp. It wasn't fear, but it was terrifying.

She had never wanted a relationship, had never wanted to depend on someone, to love someone, open herself up to them only to have them abandon her. She had been through it too many times in her life to willingly put herself through it ever again. First with the loss of her beautiful sister. She knew she couldn't blame Kimberly for dying, but the grief had been stark and painful; the loss felt like a betrayal, in a way. And then her father had gone, abandoning his grieving wife and daughter. As for Alison's mother, she might not have left physically, but the person she'd been before Kimberly's death, before her husband had walked out, had disappeared completely.

Through all of that she'd learned how to be completely self-sufficient. And she had never wanted to take the chance on going back to a place where she might need someone else, where she might be dependent in any way.

But she did want to be a mother. And she'd set out to make that happen on her own. Now somehow Maximo had been thrown into her perfectly ordered plans. Everything had been so carefully laid out. It hadn't seemed as if there was a possibility anything could go wrong. And now those idyllic visions she'd had for her future were slipping through her fingers.

Her baby had a father, not just some anonymous donor of genetic material. Her baby's father was a prince. A prince whose arrogance couldn't be rivaled, and whose dark good looks affected her in ways she didn't want to analyze. So much for the best-laid plans.

"You seem to have a statement for everything," he

said, settling into the plush love seat that was positioned in the middle of the cabin.

Alison took her seat on the opposite side of the cabin, settling primly on the edge of a cream lounge chair. "I'm a lawyer. Making statements is an important part of my job."

Max couldn't help but laugh at her acerbic wit. She wasn't like the women he was used to. She didn't cling or simper or defer to him in any way. Some men might be bothered by a woman like her, threatened by her strength and intelligence. He enjoyed the challenge. And it helped that he was certain he held the upper hand in the situation. Now that he had coaxed her into coming to Turan with him the power balance would be shifted completely in his favor.

It wasn't his plan to force Alison's hand in any way; on the contrary he planned to make her an offer that was too good to pass up, once he figured out exactly what he wanted to do. He could tell that Alison would defend their child to the death if she had to, could see that she would lay everything aside for the sake of her baby. But he would do the same. There was no way he was taking the chance that she might disappear with their baby.

It was a strange thing to him that a woman would be so resistant to the idea of having his baby. He wasn't a conceited man, but he was pragmatic in his view on things. First and foremost, he was royal and extremely wealthy. He was to be the next king of his country and along with that would receive an inheritance worth billions, coupled with the personal fortune he'd amassed with his hugely successful corporation. His chain of luxury hotels and casinos were popular with the rich and famous, both on the island of Turan, and in almost every other major tourist spot in the world.

In the eyes of most women he would be the golden chalice. A ticket to status and riches beyond most people's imaginations. And yet Ms. Alison Whitman had acted as though carrying his baby was equivalent to being sentenced to the royal dungeon—which they did *not* have at the Turani palace, regardless of what she thought.

"And your job is very important to you?" he asked, still unable to understand where a child was supposed to fit into this cool businesswoman's schedule.

"Yes. My job is important. I'm a court-appointed advocate for children. My law firm does the work pro bono with funding from the government. The pay isn't what it could be, but I put in some time at a more high-profile law firm and quickly found that handling the divorces of the rich and petulant isn't very rewarding."

"You're an advocate for children?" That didn't mesh with the picture he'd been developing of her in his mind. He'd imagined her to be a toothy shark of a lawyer. With her sharp wit and obviously keen intellect, combined with her cool beauty, he had a hard time imagining her as anything else.

"It's what I've been doing for the past year. I wanted to make a difference, and I knew that if I was going to get ready to have a baby I couldn't be pushing myself the way we were expected to at Chapman and Stone. Corporate cutthroat doesn't really suit me anyway."

"Then why did you get into law in the first place?"

"It pays well," she said simply. "I'm good at it... It just doesn't suit me. But I worked in the industry as long as I could stand, and then I moved into an area of law that was a much better fit. Children shouldn't have to stand in court and face those who made victims of them. I speak for them. I won't allow those who defend abusers and pedophiles to revictimize a child so that they can line their pockets with a little more cash." She offered him a rueful smile. "I am a lawyer, but sometimes there isn't anyone I hate on the planet more than another lawyer."

Alison's cheeks were flushed, the passion that she felt for her job, for her calling, evident in the way she spoke of it. The woman who was carrying his baby made her living advocating for children. Could he have selected better? It was a turnaround from how he'd felt about her before. Instead of seeing a hard-as-nails career woman, he now saw a defender, willing to fight for the right thing, a woman who dedicated herself to the service of others. It only cemented in his mind what he'd already been considering.

Marriage was not a part of the plan for his life. He'd been married. He'd loved his wife. But not even love and respect had made them happy in the end. It hadn't erased their problems. He hadn't been able to fix it, and ultimately, his wife had spent that last months of her life in misery. That was something he would bear for the rest of his life.

But Alison was carrying his child and duty demanded that he do the honorable thing and make her his wife. Perhaps there was a different protocol when a woman had conceived through means other than sex, but it felt the same to him.

A heavy ache pulsed in his groin area, reminding him that it wasn't the same at all. And yet he couldn't have felt more responsible if the baby had been conceived in his bed rather than a lab. He felt responsible for Alison in much the same way, as though they had made their baby the good old-fashioned way.

And the fierce attraction he felt for her was an added bonus. He hadn't intended to remain a monk for the rest of his life, but neither had he felt ready to enter the world of casual dating and one-night stands again. He'd been married for seven years and it had been more than nine years since he'd been with any woman other than his wife. It was safe to say his little black book was outdated. And at thirty-six, he felt far too old to reenter that world anyway.

In that respect, a marriage between Alison and him would be beneficial. The ferocity of his attraction to her was shocking, but that could easily be attributed to the long bout of celibacy. Men simply weren't made to deny their sexual needs for that long and it didn't really come as a surprise to him that now his libido had woken from hibernation it was ravenously hungry.

The beautiful temptress sitting so primly across from him with her milk-pale skin and flawless figure was what he craved. She was different than his wife. Selena had been tall, her curves slight, but the top of Alison's head would rest comfortably beneath his chin. And her curves—they were enough for any man. Her breasts were lush enough to fill his hands to overflowing. Lust tightened his gut and he shifted to relieve the pressure on his growing arousal, and to hide the evidence of his arousal from Alison. He didn't relish the idea of being caught like an adolescent boy who had no control over his body.

"So you like children?" he asked.

She nodded, a shimmering wave of strawberry hair sliding over her shoulder. "I've always wanted to be a mother."

"Not a wife?"

She shrugged, and he couldn't help but notice the gentle rise and fall of her breasts. "Relationships are complicated."

"So is parenthood."

"Yes, but it's different. A child depends on you. They come into the world loving you and it's up to you to honor that, to care for them and love them back. With relationships, with a marriage, you're dependent on someone else."

"And you find that objectionable?"

"It requires a measure of trust in human nature that I just don't have."

He couldn't deny the truth of her words. Selena had depended on him, and in his estimation he had failed her.

"So you elected to become a single mother rather than deal with a relationship?"

She frowned, her full lips turning down into a very tempting pout. "I hadn't thought of it that way. My goal wasn't to become a single mother. It was to be a mother. I wasn't giving too much thought to the exclusion of a relationship. I was just pursuing what I wanted."

"And this complicates things."

"Very much."

"Is it so bad for our child to have both parents?"

She turned her face away from him and fixed her gaze on the view outside the window. "I don't know, Maximo. I don't think I can deal with everything at once. Can't we just get through the testing and talk about the rest later?"

He inclined his head. "If you like. But we still have to discuss our options at some point."

"I know."

"It isn't what you had planned, I understand that. None of this is what I had planned, either."

Alison knew he wasn't just referring to her pregnancy, but to the death of his wife. Finding a woman he had loved enough to marry, and then losing her—she couldn't even imagine the void that must be left in Maximo's life.

She didn't really want to feel anything for Maximo. Already her awareness of him was off the charts, and it scared her. Adding any kind of emotion to that was asking for trouble.

Romantic love had never really appealed to her, and neither had any kind of intimate relationship. She'd seen the aftereffects of romantic love turned sour in her childhood home, watched her parents fall apart and self-destruct. Her mother had simply folded in on herself, leaving Alison to fend for herself.

When her father had left they'd lost their financial stability. People her mother had considered friends had all but abandoned her. Alison never wanted to find herself in that position, never wanted to place so much of her life in someone else's hands that losing them could undo everything. Those experiences had taught her that she had to make her own way, find her own security, her own happiness.

Every inch of her life had been in her complete control since her disastrous childhood. She could control how good her grades were, and in high school she'd been obsessive about keeping her 4.0 so that she could get scholarships. In college she'd been single-minded in the pursuit of her degree, so that she could get a job that would allow her to remain independent. And every step in her life since then had been carefully planned and orchestrated, down to when and how she would become a mother.

All of that seemed laughable now that she was on a plane, headed to a foreign country with a shockingly handsome prince who also happened to be the unintended father of her baby.

CHAPTER THREE

HER first glimpse of Turan stole her breath. The island was a jewel set in the bright Mediterranean Sea. Gleaming white rock faces beset with stucco houses dotted the pale sanded coastline. The beach faded into lush greenery, and set into the tallest visible mountainside was a stone castle with masculine angles that gleamed gold in the late-afternoon light.

"It's lovely." Lovely, and yet untamed. Sort of like its master. For all of Maximo's urbane sophistication, there was something about him that was raw and almost primitive. It appealed to her on a basic level she'd hardly been aware of before she'd seen him descending the stairs of his elegant mansion.

The entire flight had been thick with tension, at least on her end. Maximo seemed totally unaffected by her presence. Which was more than she could say for herself. It wasn't as though she didn't *like* men or that she had never felt any kind of sexual desire—of course she had. She simply hadn't acted on it, hadn't wanted to. The very idea typically made her feel as if she was on the edge of a panic attack. Sexual intimacy, opening herself up to someone like that, exposing herself, and possibly even losing some of her carefully guarded control, was usually about the least appealing thing she could think of. And yet something about Maximo ignited a curiosity that was starting to override her normal sense of self-preservation.

"Thank you," he said, his voice full of total sincerity. "It is my belief that Turan is one of the most beautiful places on Earth."

The plane began to descend, taking them low over grassland where cattle grazed free-range. "I wouldn't have thought you could do much cattle farming on an island."

"Not much, but we try to make the most of every natural resource we have. Vineyards and olive groves do well. And our grass-fed beef is almost world renowned. Of course, being an island, seafood is also a large part of our exports. But we don't export as much as we might. My first priority has always been self-sufficiency."

She made a small sound of approval. "What do your duties encompass? Your father is still the official ruler, right?"

He nodded. "I have been put in charge of managing the economy. In the past five years I've managed to increase tourism by fifty percent. With the new luxury casinos and the renovation of some of the historic fishing villages, Turan has become a popular destination for wealthy people looking for a high-profile vacation spot."

She arched an eyebrow. "So you're more of a businessman than a prince."

He gave a low laugh. "Perhaps. Maybe in another life that's what I would have been. But in this one, I'm happy to fulfill my duty. I do have some business interests on the side, but my main responsibility is still to my country."

"And duty is the most important thing?"

"It means a lot to me. I was raised to believe that it was duty before self."

Duty before self. And did that mean she had a duty to her child to ensure that he knew his father? If her father had wanted her and her mother had never given him a chance, how would she have felt? Pain twisted her. She would have given anything for a father who wanted her. For the protection and safety it would have represented. Did she have any right to refuse her own child this amazing gift? Especially one she would have given just about everything to have herself? She didn't want to face the fact that having Maximo involved in the raising of their child was the right thing to do. What she wanted was for things to turn out according to her plan. But she knew that wasn't possible now.

The plane touched down on the tarmac and her stomach rose into her throat.

When the small aircraft came to a stop, the stairs let down and Maximo took her arm in a very proprietary manner, his posture stiff. He held her as far from his body as was possible, as though too much contact was beneath his royal self. Which was just fine with her. She was still disturbed by the strange effect he seemed to be having on her equilibrium. It was as though her self-control had gone on vacation and now her body was making up for it by craving a whole host of things that had just never seemed important before.

She would much rather have him be aloof than have him touch her again like he'd done at his house. She could easily remember the slow burn against her lip as he drew his thumb over the sensitive skin. She shivered, trying to shake off the little thrill that assaulted her as the scene replayed in her mind.

A crew of five lined the runway, ready to unload his

royal highness's luggage, and her one little carry-on bag. She'd chosen to pack conservatively since she planned to be back in Seattle in just a few days, but seeing all of his belongings next to her one well-used suitcase made the disparity between their social standing widen before her eyes.

He ushered her into the back of the black limousine that was waiting for them, and she complied, mostly because she was in such awe of the wealth that surrounded her.

Money she was used to. For the early part of her childhood her family had enjoyed quite a bit of luxury, and though there were a few years of poverty after her father left, she remembered what it was like to live in the most coveted home in the cul-de-sac. Even now her income was healthier than most, though she chose to save her money rather than spend it on frivolous possessions.

But this…this was like nothing she had ever encountered.

The sleek limo slid through the wrought-iron gates that served to divide the castle and its inhabitants from the serfs who populated the rest of the island. Massive stone statues of men with swords stood watch by the gates, as if to reinforce the exclusivity of the location.

"No moat?" she asked facetiously as she gazed up at one massive turret that rose from the inner walls.

"No, the crocodiles could never discern between the intruders and the residents, so it made for a lousy security system. Now we just have a silent alarm like everyone else."

His unexpected stab at humor brought a giggle to her lips. "No hot oil, then, either?"

"Only in the kitchen." A small smirk teased the

corner of his mouth and she noticed a small dimple that creased his cheek. Why couldn't he stay austere and distant? It was easier to see him as the opposition when he was being an autocrat, much more difficult to do so when he actually seemed *likable*.

They came to a stop in front of the heavy double doors that were flanked, to her amusement, by formally dressed guards who didn't look so different from the stone soldiers that stood at the gates.

He turned to face her, the full impact of his masculinity leaving her close to breathless. "After the doctor comes to perform the test, we will be having dinner with my parents so that I can introduce you to them."

"Why would you need to introduce me?"

"Apart from the fact that you're a guest, you are also the mother of my child, and their grandchild."

Grandparents. He could even give her son or daughter grandparents, while she…well, her own father was heaven-knew-where and her mother was an extremely bitter woman who drank her issues away and forced everyone around her to listen to her vitriolic diatribes about life and men in general. Alison would never subject her child to that. She didn't even subject *herself* to it unless absolutely necessary.

"This just gets more and more complicated." She put her hand over her face and pressed hard on her eyes, trying to stop tears from overflowing. It was overwhelming in so many ways. Being pregnant, actually knowing she was having a baby, had been change enough, but to add all of this seemed impossible.

"They have every right to their grandchild, as I have every right to my child. Just as much right as you have, Alison. I will not allow you to deny my family this chance."

Anger rolled through her, heating her blood, giving her strength. "By royal decree, is that it? Is this where the dungeon comes into play?"

"What is it with you and dungeons? Do you have some kind of weird fetish?"

"Just concerned I might end up on a twenty-four-hour cable news channel. *American held captive by primitive prince*," she snapped. She pressed cool hands to her cheeks in an effort to release some of the heat that had mounted at his mention of fetishes. As if she would ever, *ever*, let a man tie her up so he could have his way with her.

Oddly, instead of the distaste she expected the thought to evoke, when she placed Maximo in the role of her captor, a sensual thrill tightened her stomach. Completely shocked by the direction of her usually sex-less thoughts she turned her burning face away from Maximo and opened her own door, not waiting for any of the overeager staff who had appeared outside the palace, to assist her.

Maximo caught up to her in two easy strides, his long legs eating up the ground much faster than her five foot four inches would allow her to do. "Have I embarrassed you, *tesoro*?"

She ignored him, thrusting her chin up and trying to look unaffected by him, his presence and his innu-endos.

He gripped her hand and stopped her from walking, drawing her close to him. Her heart began to pound so hard she was certain he must be able to hear it. Standing this close to him she could feel the heat emanating from his body, smell the heady, masculine scent that was one hundred percent raw, sexual man. One hundred percent Maximo.

Since when had she noticed how a man smelled? Unless she was at the gym and it was in a negative connotation she didn't think she ever had. So why did Maximo's smell appeal to her like this? Why did it make her pulse race and her breasts feel heavy? He wasn't wearing cologne or any other kind of added scent. It was just him.

"I would have thought that a sophisticated career woman like you wouldn't be so easy to embarrass." He brushed his thumb across her burning cheek. She knew she was flushed, could tell by how hot she felt. "But it seems as though I've made you blush, *cara*."

"Stop with the foreign endearments," she said, her voice sounding breathless rather than snappy as she'd intended. "I don't like them."

"Really?" He dipped his head and her stomach dropped. She had thought, for one breathless moment, that he might be leaning in to kiss her. "Most women find them very sexy."

"I'm not most women."

He frowned, his dark gaze searching. "No, you're not."

She didn't know whether or not she should feel complimented by that, but she did. Not that she would let him know it. His words shouldn't have the power to flatter or hurt her in any way. They shouldn't have any effect on her at all. *He* shouldn't have any effect on her. The only thing they had between them was their baby. Their relationship had nothing to do with personal feelings. If not for the mistake at the clinic they never would have met. They ran in totally different social spheres. He never would have given her a second look if it weren't for the baby.

It was important for her to remember that.

"When are you seeing the doctor?" she asked, hoping to distract him, eager to not be the focus of his undivided attention.

"She will come as soon as I call her."

She nodded, not knowing why she'd thought he might need an appointment. Maximo wasn't the sort of man who made appointments. People made them to meet with him, not the other way around.

"When will you call her?" she asked, pretending that all of the edginess she was feeling was over the test, and that none of it was due to Maximo's proximity and the way it made her feel.

"Right away, if you like."

She nodded, her stomach fluttering. "Yes, please. I'd like that."

The doctor came immediately, and Alison followed Maximo and the beautiful young physician into his office. When he'd mentioned having a personal physician she'd imagined an elderly man, not a blonde in her early thirties who was tall and willowy enough to be a model.

It shouldn't really surprise her. Maximo was a handsome man. A *very* handsome man, she amended herself. He was rich. And powerful. Plus, of course, there was that very basic feminine nurturing instinct that likely made women want to heal all of his wounds. He probably attracted women in droves. It was likely he welcomed the female attention. He was in his prime; a powerful, sexually attractive man who probably took pleasure when it was offered.

She felt hot all over again and she tried hard to quell that physical response that had become so darn instant and predictable. Maximo was entitled to do as he liked, with whom he liked, which included the sexy doctor, and that was fine by her. Because she didn't want to engage in those kinds of relationships. She had no desire to sacrifice her independence and self-sufficiency for a few hours of hedonistic enjoyment in a man's bed. None at all.

Besides, she seriously doubted she would actually find it enjoyable. It was fine with her if other women wanted to have affairs just for the sake of them, but she never had, and her aversion to relationships had prevented her from actually finding out about physical relationships in a practical, hands-on kind of way. But she was twenty-eight and she wasn't born yesterday. She had a full intellectual knowledge of sex, even if she didn't have actual firsthand experience, and she couldn't imagine such an intimate activity holding any appeal to her. She avoided intimate relationships altogether. She was hardly going to pursue something so...so...profound with a man when maintaining a healthy distance between herself and others was an important matter of self-preservation, as far as she was concerned.

So why did it make her stomach clench when the beautiful doctor slid her feminine hands over Maximo's arm? The sexy blonde drew his shirtsleeve up and wiped at the inside of his elbow with a small cleansing pad, her movements seeming slower, more sensual than was strictly necessary.

"We just need a little blood," she said, her attention on Maximo, her eyes never once straying to Alison.

Alison had to turn her face away when the doctor drew a phial of dark blood from Maximo's arm. She was never very good with things like that and being pregnant made her feel all the more fragile about it. And the last thing she wanted to do was something as ridiculously weak as passing out in front of him. As much as she imagined he was used to women falling at his feet, she couldn't afford to show that kind of vulnerability.

"All done." The doctor all but purred as she tugged Maximo's shirtsleeve back into place, covering up his sexy, well-muscled arm. "It will take five days for us to run the complete carrier screening. As soon as I know, I'll be in touch. If you need anything before then let me know. I'm always available." The good doctor offered Maximo a sympathetic arm squeeze and Alison couldn't help but think that she knew exactly what the other woman would be *available* for if Maximo needed her.

After the doctor left she and Maximo simply sat, silence stretching between them. Anxiety gnawed at Alison's stomach. A few more days and she would know if there was a chance their child might be affected.

Their child. It seemed so surreal that this stranger was the father of the baby nestled in her womb. At least if the baby had been the product of a one-night stand they would have known each other on a basic level. As it was, they didn't know anything about each other. They didn't even share the physical attraction that most people expecting a baby together would have shared.

Liar.

Okay, so she was attracted to him. She'd been attracted to men before. Not like this, but she had been, and she hadn't acted on those feelings. She wouldn't have acted on them with Maximo, either.

"Is there a hotel that you can recommend?" she asked, desperate to break the tension that was thickening the air in the room.

The test was weighing heavily on him, too, she could tell. The corded muscles of his arms obviously tense beneath his well-fitted shirt, his jaw locked tight. He really did care about the baby already. Knowing they shared that made her feel linked to him, even if it was only by one tenuous thread. It was comforting in a way, knowing that someone else cared about the baby. That if something was wrong she wouldn't be alone in hurting for her child. For now at least, Maximo didn't feel as much like an adversary.

"Why would you need a hotel?" he asked, flexing the arm that the doctor had taken blood from.

"I don't want to sleep in a field somewhere. I'm not big on camping."

"You do have a very smart mouth," he said, his focus dipping to her lips. She darted her tongue out to moisten them, feeling very self-conscious of the action as she did it. But with him looking at her like that all she could think about was her mouth, and that made it feel dry. And tingly. His dark eyes conveyed an interest that made her stomach tighten. He was attracted to her, too. The realization made her feel light-headed. It had been one thing to experience the errant desire on her own, but to know he might feel even a fraction of it for her…

Just as suddenly as the interest had appeared in his eyes, it was gone, his expression flat and unreadable. She must have manufactured the moment. There was no other explanation. She wasn't ugly by any stretch; she knew that. Men asked her on dates often enough. She wasn't a beauty queen, though. Maximo's first wife had even made Supermodel Doctor look average: her features exquisitely stunning, her sleek dark hair always styled so elegantly, her slim figure the perfect showcase for designer clothing.

She could remember his wife's face clearly. She'd graced the covers of fashion magazines and had been a minor celebrity prior to her marriage to Maximo. An opera singer who had performed in the most prestigious venues around the world, she'd been talented, beautiful and cultured.

So, it wasn't that Alison didn't have her own brand of beauty. She just didn't have that universal appeal, that unquestionable, unrivaled loveliness that Selena Rossi had possessed. There was no way Maximo could want her. She was average, and he was just as perfect as his wife had been. A demigod of masculine perfection.

And now she was dramatizing.

She licked her lips again and silently cursed herself.

"You will be staying here at the palace," Maximo said, his tone so confident she knew that it absolutely didn't occur to him that she might refuse. Or, if it did occur to him he was supremely confident that he could change her mind.

"I don't need you to put me up. I'm perfectly capable of getting my own accommodations."

"No doubt," he said, flashing her a wry smile. "I imagine your extensive education has left you more than capable of booking your own room. But you're pregnant with my child and I don't want you staying at some hotel by yourself."

"Seedy hotels in Turan, are there?"

"Not at all," he said, dismissing her statement with a wave of his hand. "But that doesn't mean I will allow you to—"

She cut him off, anger bubbling in her chest and spilling over. "*Allow* me? You have no authority to allow or disallow me to do anything."

"You are pregnant with my baby. I would say that

gives me some rights over where you go and what you do."

Her mouth dropped open and she was certain she was doing a fair impression of a shocked guppy. He honestly believed that he had some kind of dominion over her, over her body, because he happened to be the accidental father of her baby!

The fine, gossamer strand that she had felt connecting them earlier snapped.

"That is the most primitive thing I have ever heard. You don't have any rights over me!"

"I want to keep you safe. You and the baby. What's primitive about that?"

"Other than the fact that it's controlling beyond belief?"

"Che cavolo! How is it controlling to want to protect you? You are pregnant with my baby and that makes you my woman." He looked completely exasperated, as though she were slow in comprehending something that should be completely obvious.

"Your woman?" She ignored the sensual thrill that shot through her. It wasn't something to be excited about. It was insulting. Ridiculous. "I'm not *anyone's* woman. Even if we had…" She swallowed and tried to fight the involuntary urge to blush as she spoke her next words, "Even if we had made this baby the traditional way I wouldn't be your woman. I am more than capable of running my own life."

"Yes. You certainly are," he said drily. "How is that going, by the way?"

"About as well as your life is going I would imagine."

He ignored her tart statement. "What's the point of fighting me on this, Alison? I want you here for your

safety and the safety of the baby. If the press figure
out who you are and you stay here without my protection they will hound you constantly. And what would
happen if you get chased by the paparazzi? You have no
idea how ruthless and single-minded they can be." His
dark eyes were bleak, black holes of bottomless, intense
emotion that stunned her momentarily. And just like
that, all of the depth was gone, his expression composed
again.

"Is that a…is it a possibility?"

"You saw the press at the airport in Washington. Here
in Turan it can be much worse than that."

"Oh." She hadn't really taken that into consideration.
Hadn't believed that she might be a point of interest to
the media. She'd seen how they'd gravitated to Maximo
at the airport, but he was…well, he was worthy of press.
And they had loved his wife, but she had been gorgeous
and talented. Alison truly hadn't thought that they might
want pictures of her.

"Yes, 'oh.' I will not take that kind of chance with
our baby's safety."

"I won't, either," she said softly, hating that he was
right.

"I'll show you to your room."

He placed his hand on the small of her back and led
her gently from his office out into one of the main cor-
ridors of the palace. The casual touch ignited a flash
fire of sensation that scorched a path from the point of
contact all the way to her toes and up to her fingertips,
hitting all kinds of interesting points in between. A pulse
beat, hard and heavy at the apex of her thighs, and she
squirmed slightly, in an effort to gain some distance
and to quell the insistent ache that was making itself
known.

She tried to focus on something other than his touch. A touch that meant nothing to him, and shouldn't mean anything to her. She looked around, taking in her surroundings and gritting her teeth against the onslaught of sensation that was rioting through her. The wing of the palace they had entered was his own personal quarters, and rather than resembling the interior of a Gothic castle it had a light, modern aesthetic that was similar in appearance to his home in Washington.

The walls had been textured and were painted a bright white that contrasted with bold pieces of artwork and sleek, dark furniture. Whoever Maximo had hired to decorate had excellent taste. Maybe his wife had done it. The thought made her chest tighten.

He led her to a curved staircase, winding his arm around her waist and placing a hand over her stomach as they walked up to the second floor. She found the proprietary nature of the gesture oddly comforting rather than offensive, and that scared her. When they reached the landing she moved away from him, not wanting to draw any kind of comfort from his touch. That was not a road she was willing to go down.

He pulled her to him again, placing his hand back over her flat stomach, slowly pushing the hem of her shirt up, his dark eyes intent on hers. He stroked his fingers slowly over the bare skin of her belly, as though he had every right to. It wasn't a gesture of ownership, but an acknowledgment of the fact that they shared something infinitely special.

Tears stung her eyes. It was his baby that she carried and she couldn't deny the connection that he felt with their unborn child, or the connection it made her feel with him. His touch felt right, so right that the steadily growing anxiety that had been gnawing at her since her phone call about the lab mix-up was momentarily masked by the comfort the simple contact gave her.

She looked down at the place where his hand rested on her, his golden skin contrasting with her pale flesh. It fascinated her, held her attention, made her stomach tighten with a deep kind of longing that went way past the desire for something simply physical. But that was there, too. Part of her wished that he would continue moving his hand upward, palm her breast, squeeze her aching nipple between his thumb and forefinger.

She looked up, trying to break the spell that he had somehow woven around them. His face was inches from hers and she was awestruck by the perfection of his striking features. Even close up she couldn't find a single flaw with his sensual mouth, his strong nose and jaw, his dark, compelling eyes. She found herself moving closer to him, leaning in, drawn by an instinct she couldn't understand or control.

When his mouth brushed hers she held her lips still for a second. Then he moved, pressed his hand to the small of her back, closed the gap between them and brought her up against his hard body. She parted her lips, allowing the tip of his tongue to delve between them, to lightly tease her. It wasn't a demanding kiss. It was a slow seduction of her body, her mind, her senses. She'd never been kissed like this, with this level of skill and sensuality.

She'd kissed men before. Mostly back in college when she'd bothered with the pretense of casual dating. But never had a kiss made her feel so hollow, so desirous for more, as if she was in need of something only this man possessed.

Always, the kiss itself had been the main event for her. Other kisses had either been nice, or not so nice, but never had they made her want to lean in, to press her body more firmly against a man, to rock her hips against his hard length to bring herself at least some small measure of satisfaction.

His tongue slid over hers and she felt it all the way in the core of her body. Muscles she'd never been aware of before clenched in anticipation of something much more intimate.

When Maximo pulled away she swayed slightly, her brain totally scrambled by the drugging power of his lips covering hers.

"Max," she whispered, touching her lips, feeling for herself that they really were swollen and hot from the press of his mouth against them.

His mouth curved into a slow smile. "Max. I like that."

The fog of desire was starting to clear and awareness was creeping into the fuzzy edges of her mind, shame mingling with her slowly ebbing arousal.

He placed his hand over her stomach again, his expression intense. "This is my baby that you carry, Alison. Our baby. I could not feel it more if you had conceived in my bed." His accent was thicker than she'd ever heard it, his voice a husky rasp that made her nipples tighten and her pulse pound. "The attraction between us is very convenient."

"Convenient?" Her tongue felt thick and clumsy, her mind still clouded by passion.

"Of course. How could it not be convenient for me to feel desire for my future wife?"

CHAPTER FOUR

"YOUR future wife?" Her head was still fuzzy from the kiss, her limbs heavy with arousal, and she was certain she must have heard him wrong.

"Yes. I have thought it through and it is the only thing to be done." He said it so pragmatically, as though anyone should be able to see his point.

"I'm not going to marry you," she said, trying to match his tone. If he wanted to try to have an insane discussion as calmly as if they were talking about the weather then she was more than up to the challenge. She certainly wasn't going to give him the satisfaction of rattling her self-control more than once in a five-minute time span.

"Alison, I credit you with a very high level of intelligence, and given your career choice it's obvious to me that you're not only very smart, but very compassionate. With those two qualities I can't imagine that you have not arrived at the same conclusion as me."

"I fail to see how intelligence and compassion would lead me to conclude that you and I should get married." But darn if it didn't make her heart thunder harder in her chest. The thought of being married to a man like Maximo made her stomach turn over, and not in an unpleasant way.

"Logic would tell you that we won't be able to share custody as well as we might if you are living in the U.S. and I'm living here. Also, there would be the added stigma of my child being illegitimate. An illegitimate child will not be eligible to assume the throne, neither will they be able to claim the bulk of their inheritance. Compassion would prevent you from allowing that to happen to our son or daughter."

She shook her head. "That's your version of logic, but that can't possibly be the best thing for our child. We don't even know each other. How could it be good for them to grow up in a home where their mother and father are essentially strangers?"

"But we would not be strangers," he said, supremely confident. "We share some pretty combustible passion. I think we would become acquainted very quickly."

"I don't even know you. You expect that I would just sleep with you?"

He shrugged. "It is not unheard of for strangers to sleep together. And anyway, if we were married it would only be natural."

For him it might be natural to just sleep with a woman because he wanted her. For her there was nothing natural about it. Nothing natural at all about the idea of getting naked with him, of letting him touch her everywhere, see her totally uncovered. Her whole body tensed at the thought.

She tightened her lips and forced her expression to remain neutral. "Sorry, I'm not in the market. If you re-member from previous conversations I'm not interested in snagging myself a husband."

"Yes, that was your original plan. But things have changed."

"Nothing has changed. Not really. My goals haven't changed."

His jaw tensed. "But the reality has changed. Believe me, marriage was not on my 'to do' list, either. I've been married. I don't believe I have the ability to fall in love again. No woman will ever replace my wife."

"Don't break your no-marriage vow on my account."

He cupped her chin and tilted her face up. "I wouldn't be breaking it on your account. This is for our child. I thought you would be able to see that, and that it would matter to you."

"Don't for one moment imply that the baby's happiness doesn't matter to me!"

"Then do not act like it. It's selfishness, Alison, pure and simple, for you to refuse to marry me." His dark eyes glittered with dangerous heat and an answering spark ignited in her belly, anger and desire acting as accelerants.

"And it's plain bullheadedness for you to think that you have the only answer!"

"So passionate," he said, his voice low and husky. He slid his hand up so that he could put his palm on her cheek, the slight roughness of his skin creating delicious friction. "It's a shame you choose to express it this way."

"How would you have me express it?" she snapped.

"In my bed," he said, each word succinct.

"That's about as likely as me taking a trip down the aisle," she returned.

A wicked, dangerous, smile curved his lips. "That, *cara*, sounds very much like a challenge, and I'm the wrong man to issue a challenge to."

"Sounds like you're issuing a challenge of your own,

Maximo. And believe me, you might be bullheaded, but I'm not exactly a shrinking violet."

"I believe it. That is why I find you so intriguing. You are a woman who knows her own mind."

"That's right," she bit out, "and my mind says that marrying you would be a very stupid thing to do."

"It is the only logical thing," he said. "I trust you will come to the same conclusion."

He turned and continued walking down the corridor, acting as though the conversation hadn't happened. She followed, if only because she didn't relish getting lost in the labyrinthine hallways of the palace, especially since she had no soda crackers at her disposal and she was beginning to feel nauseous again. If not for that, she might have taken her chances.

Maximo didn't say another word as he walked and she was more than happy to maintain that status quo. Instead of talking, she played the conversation over in her mind. Was he right? Was marriage the only option?

In the U.S. she hadn't considered being a single mother an issue. But this was a different country, and not only that, her baby was royalty.

A wave of sadness washed over her. It wasn't what she wanted for her child. She had dreams of sitting at a small kitchen table, eating family dinners, coloring, finger painting. Never had she imagined pomp and circumstance and palaces. If she were to marry Maximo their child would be next in line to the throne. And if she didn't, he or she would be off the hook. She honestly wasn't certain which scenario was best. She'd had dreams of a normal childhood for her son or daughter, but what would *they* want? Would they hate her for denying them not only an intact family, but a place in history? It was too much to even take in.

The only thing she was remotely certain of was that she wanted the very best for her baby. If only she could figure out what that was.

"This is your room." Maximo opened one of the doors and gestured for her to go inside.

She looked back down the endless hallway and cursed the fact that she hadn't been counting doors on her way down. She was never going to find her way back.

"Don't worry, I'll escort you back later," he said, amusement lacing his voice.

"Businessman, prince and mind reader?" she asked.

"I promise you I can't read minds. Faces are another matter. And you have a very expressive face."

She put a hand to her cheek. She had always prided herself on control, and that included control over what she let others see. She didn't like that he had the ability to read her.

"Don't worry," he said laconically, "it wouldn't be obvious to everyone. But when you are worried you get a little crease between your eyebrows."

She rubbed at the spot absently, trying to smooth it. "Well, who doesn't?"

"You don't like that I can read your emotions?"

"Would you like it if I could read yours?"

He frowned. "I don't consider myself an emotional man."

"You showed plenty of emotion when you found out about the baby," she said softly.

"Yes. Of course I did. The love a parent feels for a child is above everything else. It's as natural as breathing."

"Not to everyone." She thought of her own father,

unable to love anyone anymore after the loss of his youngest daughter.

"It is to me." He shifted, his jaw clenched tight, the tension evident in his entire body. "Selena and I wanted very much to have children."

For the first time Alison wondered what it must be like for him to be having a baby with a woman who wasn't his wife. She'd had plans, dreams that hadn't included him, and it was the same for Maximo. When he'd pictured having children he had imagined sharing it with his wife, the woman that he loved. As far removed from perfect as this was for her, it must be much more so for him. Her heart squeezed. She didn't want to feel sorry for him, didn't want to understand him, didn't want to see, even for a moment, why he might be right to ask her for marriage. But she did. In that moment, she did.

"Why don't you go in and rest for a while. We'll meet my parents for dinner in a couple of hours. Your things should already have been brought in." Maximo seemed to be done discussing the past, and she wasn't going to press him for more.

She stepped into the room and her eyes widened. It was decked out for a princess. From the plush cream carpets to the lavender walls, the rich purple bedding and the swags of candlelight fabric that were draped over the canopy bed frame. This bedroom was a feminine fantasy. And she couldn't help but wonder who the fantasy had been created for. The prince's mistresses? She could hardly imagine a man like him would be without female company for very long.

Completely without permission her mind began to play a slideshow of what that might look like. She could see it clearly. Maximo's hands gripping a woman's rounded hips, his dark hands covering full breasts, kissing the white column of his lover's throat. And when she saw strawberry blond hair fanned out over the pillow she blinked to try to banish the images. A hot tide of embarrassment assaulted her when she realized she'd cast herself in the part of Maximo's lover. It was laughable. Apart from the fact that she had no desire to sleep with him, there was no way he would want to take a twenty-eight-year-old virgin to bed.

She knew that some men got off on inexperience, on being a woman's first lover, but she had a feeling that at her age it ceased to be sexy and started to look a lot more as if there must be something wrong with her.

"This is nice," she managed to squeak out through her suddenly tight throat.

"Glad it meets with your approval. Is there anything you'd like to have brought up to you?"

A sudden roll of nausea assaulted her. "Yes. Saltine crackers. And a ginger ale if there's one handy."

He drew his eyebrows together, his expression full of concern. "You are not feeling well?"

"I'm never feeling well these days."

"This is normal?"

She shrugged. "Morning sickness. Although mine lasts most of the day. But yes, that's normal for some women."

"Rest," he said, his tone commanding. "I will see that you are cared for."

Suddenly she was so tired her only wish was to comply with his command. "Thank you."

He turned and left the room, closing the door behind him, and she stumbled to the bed and climbed on top of it, relishing how she sank into the soft bedding. She didn't bother to take her shoes off or to get under the covers, and in a matter of seconds she was completely dead to the world.

When Maximo returned to Alison's room half an hour later with her requests she was sound asleep, her arm thrown over her face, her hair spread into a golden-red halo. His eyes were immediately drawn to the gentle rise and fall of her generous breasts. She was an amazingly beautiful woman.

Kissing her had been shockingly exciting. He couldn't remember the last time simply kissing a woman had aroused him so much. Maybe when he'd been a teenage virgin, but certainly not any time in the twenty years since then.

He hadn't intended to kiss her. Not yet. Seduction wasn't the way to win Alison over to his way of thinking. She was cerebral; the way to appeal to her would be through logic and reason, not through sensual persuasion. At least that's what he'd thought. She'd been surprisingly passionate in his arms, a little hesitant, but she'd been all the sweeter for it.

The temptation to join her in the bed, to lift the hem of her shirt again, touch her flat stomach and move higher to the lush swell of her breasts, was so powerful his teeth ached. It wasn't only his teeth that were aching, either. He steeled himself against the hot flood of arousal that was coursing through him, fighting to maintain control over his body.

"Alison, *cara*." He reached out and touched her bare arm and desire raced through him like a shot of pure liquor into his system. She was so beautiful. So different from any other woman he'd been with or even wanted to be with.

Always he'd gravitated to tall, slender women.

Models, actresses, women with style and sophistication. Alison was slender, her waist small, but she had a woman's curves; her hips rounded, her breasts enticingly full.

Unlike the extremely fashionable women he'd preferred in the past, Alison seemed to dress simply to stay warm, or to avoid indecent exposure. There was nothing unflattering about her wardrobe, but there was nothing especially flattering about it, either. It was as though she honestly didn't give it a second thought. She had been wearing some makeup the first day he'd met her, but today she'd gone without it entirely. Most women of his acquaintance would have moaned about how pale they looked without it in an effort to get some sort of compliment. Alison didn't seem to care either way.

She shifted beneath his hand, a sweet moan escaping her lips. Her eyes fluttered open and she fixed her sleepy copper gaze on him, her full lips turning up slightly.

"I know you're half asleep," he said softly, "because that's the only way I could have earned a smile from you."

Just like that her brow creased and she frowned. "Oh," she said softly, putting her hand on her stomach.

Anxiety shot through him. "Is everything all right?"

"Everything's fine. Well, my stomach hurts and my mouth is really dry, but everything's fine with the baby."

"That's why I brought your requested items." He gestured to the tray that was sitting next to her.

The crease between her eyebrows deepened and her lips tugged further down at the corners. "You brought me saltines and ginger ale?"

"Not just any ginger ale." He picked the long-stemmed

glass up from the tray. "My personal chef mixed it especially for you. It has fresh ginger and honey, good for your nausea."

She extended a shaky hand and took the glass from him, lifting it to her lips. Her expression turned to one of relief almost immediately. "The ginger is amazing. It solves all my problems. All my physical problems, anyway."

"Still viewing all of this as a problem?"

She took another sip of her drink and shot him a hard look. "Well, yes, morning sickness *is* kind of a problem. Anyway, you can't tell me you're ecstatic about this."

"I'm not sorry about it."

"How is that possible?"

"I want to be a father. I had given up on that ever happening. There is no way I can regret this."

She lowered her head and pressed the glass to her forehead. "I don't know what to do."

"Marry me. It's the best solution. For the baby. For us."

Her head snapped up. "Why is it the best for us?"

"If we were married we would have our child all the time. No missed Christmases, none of this every-other-weekend business. If we had shared custody there is no way you or I could be there for everything."

"That's true," she said softly.

"And I can't imagine that you intend to spend the rest of your life without a man. You're what, twenty-nine?"

Her copper eyes narrowed. "Eight."

"Either way you're far too young to embrace a life of celibacy. Raising a child and having a personal life is not easy. If we were married, that would be taken care of. You and I share a pretty potent attraction, you can't deny that."

"I'm not exactly concerned about the baby's impact on my sex life," she said drily, pulling a cracker off the tray.

"Perhaps not now, but eventually you will be. I can also offer you financial security. You would be free to do what you liked."

"I could stay at home with the baby?"

"If you like. Or you could continue to work and our child would be provided with the best caregiver available."

"I wouldn't keep working," she said.

"I thought your career was important to you."

"It is. But raising my child, being there for everything, that's more important to me."

Maximo only looked at her, his eyebrows raised as if he were waiting for her to continue. Alison wasn't sure how to explain how she felt to him, or if she even wanted to.

She wanted to be the kind of mom who was there when her child got home from school; she wanted to have cookies baked, and to drive them to soccer practice. She wanted to be there, be interested, be involved. She wanted to be everything neither of her parents had bothered to be.

"If that's what you want then I can't imagine you want to spend a good portion of our child's life shuttling him back and forth between households."

She bit her lip so hard she tasted blood. "Well, it isn't as though we're bitter exes. We could share some of the time together. I could stay here sometimes."

"And you think some kind of pieced-together living arrangement would be better than an intact family?"

"What I think is that we have an extremely unconventional situation and you're playing like we can make it into the perfect, model family, when that just isn't realistic."

"I'm trying to do the best thing. You're the one that's too selfish to do the right thing by our son or daughter."

She took another swallow of ginger ale to prevent herself from gagging. She'd been touched when she'd realized that he'd brought her the crackers and soda, but she was much less impressed now that she realized he was just using it as an opportunity to try to goad her into agreeing to marry him.

"I don't understand why you're the one pushing for marriage," she said when she was certain she wasn't going to be sick all over the floral duvet. "Shouldn't it be the other way around?"

A short, derisive laugh escaped his lips. "Perhaps traditionally, but then this is hardly a traditional situation. In this case, I am the one who has the most realistic concept of what it means to be a royal bastard."

"Don't call him that!" she said, putting a hand on her stomach, anger flaring up, hot and fast. "That's a horrible term. No one even uses it in that way anymore!"

"Maybe not in the U.S., or maybe just not in the circles you're in. But I can guarantee you that here, among the ruling class, legitimacy matters a great deal. Not just in terms of what our child can inherit. Do you want our son or daughter to be the dirty secret of the Rossi family? Do you want him or her to be the subject of sordid gossip for his or her entire life? The circumstances of the conception don't matter. What matters is what people will say. They will create the seediest reality they can possibly think of and that will be the new truth. Whether you like the term or not, if you're intent on refusing to marry me, you had better get used to it."

The picture he painted was dark. She could see it clearly. People would stop talking when their child walked into a room, their expression censorious, their rejections subtle but painful.

"You may not want to be married to me, and frankly, I don't want to be married at all," he said. "But you can't deny that it makes sense."

"I just don't like the idea of it."

"Of marriage without love?" Maximo knew that most women would reject the idea, at least outwardly, even if their motive for marriage was truly money or status and not finer feelings at all. "I can assure you that love within a marriage does not guarantee happiness." He didn't like to talk about his marriage to Selena. Inevitably it brought up not only her shortcomings, but his own failures. And neither were things he revisited happily.

"That isn't it." She drew her knees up to her chest, the action, combined with her messy hair spilling over her shoulder and her pale, makeup-free face, made her look young and extremely innocent. "I never planned on marrying at all. So love isn't really an issue. I just don't want to be married."

"Is this some kind of feminist thing?"

She snorted. "Hardly. It's a personal thing. Marriage is a partnership, one that asks a lot of you. I don't have any desire to give that much of myself to another person. Look how often marriages end in divorce. My own parents' divorce was horrible, and during my two years as a divorce attorney I saw so much unhappiness. Those people grew to depend on each other and for one of them, usually the woman, divorce left them crippled. It was like watching someone trying to function after having a limb chopped off."

"I know what it is to lose a spouse," he said grimly, the brackets around his mouth deepening. "You can survive it. And what you're talking about is love gone sour. That isn't what we have. Our reasons for marriage are much stronger than that, and they will be the same in ten years as they are now. Love fades, lust does, too, but our child will always bond us together."

He was right about that. Whether they married or not, Maximo Rossi was a permanent part of her life, because he would be a permanent part of her son's or daughter's life. A key part. One of the most important parts. He was her child's father. Hadn't her own father, or rather his absence, shaped her life in more ways than she could count?

And that was a whole other aspect of the situation she hadn't considered before. It wasn't just the presence of a parent that had an effect on a child, but the absence of one. What would it do to their child to live in a separate country from his or her father? What would it mean for them to be shuttled back and forth?

That was another tragedy she'd witnessed during her time as a divorce lawyer. The way it hurt the children involved. What it did to their self-esteem. Often, the children she helped in her new job, the ones who were on trial for petty crimes, were from broken homes.

She knew she would never let her child fall through the cracks like those children had, but the issue remained the same. If she could offer her son or daughter a greater amount of security, a better chance at success, shouldn't she do it?

But marriage hadn't factored into her life plans. She

didn't want to be a wife. Didn't want to need Maximo. But no matter whether or not *she* needed Maximo her child would.

Logically, if she'd never intended to get married she wasn't sacrificing anything by marrying Maximo. But… she still didn't want a husband-and-wife-type relationship. It was too much. Too intimate. Too revealing. Even without love.

"I don't want to do this," she choked.

"It isn't about what we want, Alison. It's about what's right. What's best for our child. You've already made so many decisions based on that. I know you love the baby already, that you were already prepared to make major changes in your life in order to offer him the very best you could give. Now the best has changed."

It would be so much easier to refuse him if he were simply being an autocratic tyrant, if he were being demanding and arrogant and commanding and all those things she knew he was capable of being. But he wasn't. He was appealing to her need to reason and plan and choose the best, most sensible way to do something. And he was winning.

He was right. The only reasons for her not to marry him were selfish. All of the reasons to marry him benefited their child. If she could see another way she would grab it.

"Okay," she said slowly, feeling the words stick in her throat, "I'll do it. I'll marry you."

CHAPTER FIVE

A SENSE of triumph, along with a compressing sensation in his throat that felt suspiciously like the tightening of a noose, assaulted Maximo. It was necessary; the only thing that could be done. The only way for him to truly claim his child, make him his heir. And the only way to claim Alison.

A heavy pulse throbbed in his groin at the thought of claiming Alison in the most basic, elemental way. He wanted her with a kind of passionate ferocity that was foreign to him.

He would have wanted her no matter what, would have desired her had he passed her when she was walking down the street. But the intense, bone-deep need to take her, to enter her sweet body and join himself to her…that had to be connected to the pregnancy because it was outside anything in his experience. He'd experienced lust—the basest kind that had nothing to do with emotion—and he'd been in love. This didn't resemble either experience.

He could satisfy his lust for her without marriage, but marriage was necessary for him to have the sort of relationship with his child that he wanted, that he craved. And it was the only way he could give his child everything he or she deserved.

"My acceptance isn't without provisos," she continued, her gorgeous face deathly serious. "I agree that marriage seems to be the best solution, but don't expect that I'm just going to cave into all of your demands."

"Even after knowing you for only a few days, I would never expect that," he said drily.

She swung her legs over the side of the bed, a cracker still in her hand, and stood. She wobbled and he reached out for her, hooking his arm around her waist to steady her. His response was immediate and fierce, his blood rushing south, his body hardening instantly. He could feel her heart pounding hard against his chest. Her copper eyes were wide, her lips parted slightly. How easy it would be to dip his head and taste her again...

She straightened, much too quickly for his taste, and pulled away, adjusting the hem of her casual T-shirt, her mouth now pulled into a tight line.

"Thank you," she said tartly, moving back from him again, creating even more distance between them. "I'm not feeling very well."

"So you said. Is it like this every day?"

"Pretty much. It hit with a vengeance right when I entered my sixth week."

"How far along are you?" He realized then that he'd never asked.

"Seven weeks."

His stomach tightened. She was nearly two months along already. It wouldn't even be nine months until he held his son or daughter in his arms.

She was still slender, her stomach flat. He had to wonder if her breasts had already changed or if this was her normal shape. He could easily imagine her filling out, her belly getting round. Some previously undiscovered, primitive part of him surged with pride at the thought.

Pride…and a hot tide of arousal. He'd never actually thought of pregnant women as sexy before, but he could very easily imagine running his hands over Alison's bare, full stomach, feeling his child move beneath his hands.

"The baby's due in October," she said.

He'd heard of pregnant women glowing, but he'd never seen it before. Until now. Alison's whole face was lit up, a sweet, secret smile curving her lips slightly. The absolute joy he could see shining from her eyes was staggering. And it reminded him again why marrying her, providing his child with both parents, was the absolute best choice. She would be a good mother; he was absolutely certain of that. Were he not, there was no way he would have considered marrying her. If he wasn't sure of that he would have simply sought sole custody of their child, and he would have done it without compunction.

"You are excited about it," he said, tucking a strand of hair behind her ear.

"Of course I am."

Their eyes locked and held, and the tightening in his stomach intensified, radiating outward, desire gnawing at him with an urgency that was impossible to ignore.

"We'll have to have the wedding soon. Before you start to show," he said, his voice harsher than he'd intended.

She chewed her lip, her eyes betraying insecurity, fear, for the first time since he'd met her. Anger he'd seen, sadness, too, but never this bleak hopelessness. It made his chest ache as fiercely as the rest of his body.

"As I said, there are provisos to my agreement."

"You did say. What you didn't say was what those little stipulations were."

"I don't want our child in boarding school or anything like that. I want him or her to have as much of a normal upbringing as possible. No team of nannies, no catering to his every whim. I don't want a spoiled child, either."

"Do I seem like I was a spoiled child?"

"Yes." She replied without missing a beat, and then continued. "I want to continue being active in advocating for children. Maybe organize a charity or something."

"A wonderful idea. We have several organizations in place and having my princess closely involved would probably do wonders for them."

"And I don't... I want my own room."

He inclined his head. "That is a common practice in royal marriages."

"I don't think you understand. I don't want for us to... I don't want to have a sexual relationship with you."

Alison tried to clamp down the wild fluttering in her stomach. She knew Maximo wouldn't be happy. Hadn't he referenced their physical attraction as a reason for marriage? But this was what she needed in order to be able to accept his proposal, such as it was.

His kiss had decimated her control, had made her forget who she was, who *he* was, where she was. Going to bed with him... What would that do to her closely guarded self-control? The thought of surrendering herself like that, of stripping herself bare both physically and emotionally before another human being in that way, terrified her to her bones. Marriage she could deal with, but sexual intimacy was several steps beyond her.

She was attracted to him; unreasonably so. And that only made her more determined to maintain a healthy distance between them. If she didn't want him like this, if being near him didn't make her limbs weak and her pulse pound in her chest, at the apex of her thighs, if she didn't get embarrassingly wet with wanting just from the brush of his mouth over hers, she might be able to simply deal with it. But it was the ease with which he robbed her of her common sense, her ability to think coherently, that had all of her internal alarms going off. He had too much power over her already, and throwing sex in with that big mess of emotions was a recipe for absolute disaster.

"That makes no sense. You can't deny that we are extremely attracted to each other."

"Maybe not. But I don't feel like I can commit to that sort of relationship with you. Things are complicated enough. A marriage in a strictly legal sense I can handle. But I've only known you for twenty-four hours and I can't even begin to consider a sexual relationship with you. And you're a very attractive man. I'm sure there will always be lots of women who want to…"

"If you're concerned about my fidelity, don't be. I was married for seven years and never once did I look at another woman. It was not a hardship for me."

Maybe not, but Maximo had been in love with his wife. They weren't in love. Not that she cared. But if she were to sleep with him, she would need to know that he was being faithful to her. And that was just one more reason not to cross that line with him. Even imagining a hypothetical situation where they were intimately in-volved made her care about who he slept with. It made her feel things like jealousy and insecurity, and other emotions she had no business feeling. If she actually made love with him it would no doubt be multiplied by a hundred, and that was just one of the many things she was trying to avoid.

"I'm not concerned about that. But if we *were* sleeping together then yes, I would want you to be faithful. You would want the same from me. Emotions would become involved."

"Not for me," he said starkly. She knew he spoke the truth. But he probably had lots of sexual experience. Divorcing love from sex was probably second nature to him. For her…she knew instinctively that sex could have a seriously devastating emotional effect on her. She just wouldn't be able to open herself up like that to someone without becoming involved. It was one of the reasons she'd avoided it for the past twenty-eight years.

The last thing she needed was for him to become a necessity to her, and she knew that if she let herself she could easily melt into Maximo, let his strength hold her up when things were hard. She could grow to depend on him, and she'd spent far too long learning to be independent, to be in control, to take that chance.

"Maybe not. But this is what I want."

"And you wouldn't mind if I were having sex with other women?" he asked, his words obviously chosen to elicit a response from her. One they most certainly got, but she wasn't going to let him know that.

"I wouldn't care either way. If we aren't sleeping together then there isn't a relationship to be faithful to."

"You may feel differently once we speak our vows."

"I can't imagine that I will. What we have in common is the desire to do what's right for our child. Nothing more. We didn't even conceive in the way most couples do."

"But we very easily could have."

It wasn't true—she *knew* it wasn't—and yet it was far too easy to visualize the image, a picture of her meeting Maximo in a bar, a restaurant, on the street. Of them talking, smiling, laughing. Having dinner together. Going home together. Making love.

No. It was easy for him to assume that might have happened, because he figured her for a normal woman who dated, had casual relationships, had sex. She didn't do any of those things. And she had never felt lacking in any way because of it. Until now. Now she felt at a disadvantage. How was she supposed to deal with a man like Maximo? A sophisticated, experienced man who probably knew a lot more about women and sex than the average male. And *she* knew far less about men and sex than the average female.

"Those are my terms, Max," she said softly. "I can't marry you if you won't agree to them."

"Then I agree to them. I don't want a martyr in my bed. I've never had to coerce a woman into sex in my life and I don't intend to start doing so with my own wife."

It was the absolute truth. He wasn't about to black-mail or beg to get a woman to have sex with him, not even one he desired as much as he did Alison. He hadn't even begged Selena when she'd moved out of their room. No was no, even from his wife.

He was surprised that Alison was denying them both what they so obviously wanted, but not even a sexless marriage was new to him. He'd been there. He imagined it had been Selena's way of punishing him for not giving her a baby, although the issue had been with her body and not his. It hadn't mattered to him. He had never once seen her as less of a woman. But she had been so frustrated with their timed lovemaking that never, ever produced the result she wanted, that she hadn't even allowed him to touch her in the last six months of their marriage. The last six months of her life.

He knew why Selena had denied him, and he wasn't sure he hadn't deserved it. But he didn't know what Alison's game was. She was twenty-eight, a career woman, not sheltered or shy in any way. And she was very clearly heterosexual and very clearly attracted to him. So it didn't make any sense for her to turn down a physical relationship with him. Especially since she obviously wanted him. Women might be able to fake orgasms, but her response to his kiss was very real. There was no way she could have engineered her body's response to him, and no reason for her to do so.

But if she needed to put up a pretense of morality by insisting she couldn't sleep with a man she didn't know, she was welcome to do it. Although he doubted that she would hold on to that stance. The attraction between them was far too strong for that. It was certainly beyond anything he'd ever known in his experience.

She licked her lips and his body ached with the need to taste her sweet mouth again, to move his tongue over hers. He was instantly hard, his body raging with his need.

If she felt half of what he did, and based on that explosive kiss they'd shared in the corridor he was certain that she did, her play at resistance wasn't going to last for very long. It simply wasn't possible.

"Are you feeling up to dining with my parents?"

She sucked that sweet lower lip into her mouth and chewed on it thoughtfully. When she released it there were little dents left by her teeth, and he wanted to soothe them with his thumb, his tongue.

"I don't suppose it's acceptable to cancel dinner with the king and queen. What would Miss Manners say?"

His lips twitched and she felt an odd sense of gratification over having amused him. "If you're not feeling well we will cancel."

Selena would have canceled. His wife had frequently felt under the weather. She had been very delicate, emotionally and physically, and he had looked on it as his duty to protect her, shield her. It would be his duty to do the same for Alison. She was under his protection now. And he wouldn't fail her.

The look of steely determination that lit Alison's copper gaze surprised him. "I'll be fine. I've been going to work, cooking my own meals, functioning just fine without being coddled. I'm more than able to meet with your parents."

A brief spark of vulnerability shadowed her eyes. "What are they going to think about all of this?"

He shrugged. "I don't know that the nature of our relationship is any of their business."

"You mean you don't want them to know how the baby was conceived."

"They didn't know about Selena's fertility problems."

"I see." She looked at him, her expression searching. "And you don't want them to know."

"It was important to her that no one knew about her infertility. I have honored that." She had seen it as a failure, one she couldn't face sharing with the public, or his parents.

"Then I don't think it's important for them to know how we conceived the baby." Alison didn't really relish having to keep up any kind of facade, but neither did she want to be a part of damaging his late-wife's memory.

It made her heart break a little to know that she was going to have the dream Selena had been denied, having a baby with Maximo. As much as she would have rather been honest about the nature of her relationship, or lack of it, with Max, she felt she owed the other woman some protection.

"I'll leave you to shower and get ready. I'll be back in an hour."

She watched Maximo, her fiancé, turn and leave the room. A feeling of longing, so intense she felt it physically, filled her. Part of her wanted him, impossibly, irresponsibly, almost as much as the sensible part of her craved distance and protection from him. It was like a tug-of-war, each desire pulling at her from opposite sides. And the sensible part of her had to win. It *had* to.

The dining room at the *castillo* was extremely formal. The high ceilings and ornately framed artwork gave the room a museumlike quality. The long banquet-style table could easily have seated thirty or forty people, and added to the wholly impersonal feel of the room. It made stupid, emotional tears prick at her eyes.

A child couldn't sit and color at this table. They certainly couldn't eat milk and cookies and peanut butter and jelly at this table. Finger painting was probably out, too, since it was likely a priceless antique.

Of course, she knew there were other tables in a place this big. Maximo's quarters likely housed its own dining room. But what this room represented was everything she feared. Not for the first time since she'd said yes to Maximo's proposal she wondered if she'd made the right choice. It had seemed like it then. His logic had made so much sense. But now...it seemed impossible standing at the entryway to this formal, forbidding room with two equally formal, forbidding people staring at her and Max, his arm clamped tightly around her waist, looming over her.

"Come in and sit down, son." The king gestured to a place at his right at the head of the table. "We're both very interested in why you've asked to have dinner with us tonight."

The king was obviously a man of advanced years, but there was nothing frail about him. His hair was silver-gray, his skin tanned and healthy-looking, wrinkles almost entirely absent from his face. The queen was beautiful, years younger than her husband, her dark hair drawn back into a tight bun, her face also free of lines. They were both terribly intimidating and neither one of them offered a smile as she and Max moved into the room to sit down at the table.

The only friendly smile on offer came from a young woman who was sitting to the left of Queen Elisabetta. Her full lips stretched into a grin that showed her bright white teeth. With her golden skin, dark hair and shockingly blue eyes, she was one of the most beautiful women Alison had ever seen. A strange feeling settled in the pit of her stomach.

The woman jumped up from her seat when they approached and ran to throw her arms around Maximo. "Max!" she cried. "I'm so happy you've come home early!"

"It's good to see you too, Bella." He dropped a kiss on the younger woman's head. "Alison," he said, tightening his hold on her waist, "this is my younger sister Isabella."

The suspicious knot that had been tightening in her stomach released its hold on her as soon as he announced his relationship to the very beautiful Isabella. She was relieved, she realized, to find out that she was his sister and not…

She cut off that train of thought before it could go any further. It wouldn't have mattered if she were a lover or a former lover. It wasn't her business. And there was no reason for her to care.

"Nice to meet you." Isabella dropped a light kiss on Alison's cheek. "I'm so pleased that Max brought a friend with him." She cast her brother a sly look that seemed to say she had guessed that there was more to the relationship than he'd admitted.

"And these are my parents, King Luciano and Queen Elisabetta." Maximo gestured to his parents who were still sitting, rigid as stone, at the head of the table.

"It's nice to meet you, too," Alison said, grateful at least for Isabella's enthusiastic greeting. "All of you."

Maximo pulled a chair out for her and she sat gingerly, feeling unbearably self-conscious. It was one thing to stand in front of people in a courtroom—that was her domain. She was confident there. She was in control. Here, she was very much the colloquial fish out of water, and she felt as if she was gasping for air.

Isabella offered Maximo an impish smile. "You didn't tell me you had a girlfriend, Max."

Maximo took her hand beneath the table, twining his long fingers with hers and lifting their hands, joined, onto the table. "I was trying to keep it just between Alison and myself until we were certain how serious things were."

Alison nodded—any words she might have spoken jammed in her tightened throat. She hated this. Hated feeling so out of her depth. But, dear heaven, this was as far outside of her experience as anything could have possibly been. She'd never met a man's parents; not in this sense. And these weren't just any parents: they were royalty. And their faces were so stiff she had no doubt they felt she was quite patently beneath them.

"Is it serious?" his mother asked, her eyebrows raised, her lips unsmiling.

"I've asked Alison to marry me," said Maximo simply. It was all the answer anyone needed.

"So soon after Selena's death?" His father's tone and expression were rebuking, and Alison felt a knot of guilt tighten in her stomach.

"It's been two years," Maximo said, his voice firm, "and I have chosen Alison to be my wife."

"It would be best," Elisabetta said slowly, "if you would wait at least a year for the wedding, out of respect to Selena."

"The three-year mourning period is outdated," Maximo said. "I have no intention of waiting another year to make Alison my wife. It is not possible for us to wait so long."

"That's very romantic of you, Max." His younger sister looked positively moonstruck over the perceived romance of the whole situation. If only she knew.

"Romance has very little to do with it," Maximo said, obviously taking no issue with disabusing his sister of her fantasies. "Alison is pregnant. The wedding needs to take place before she starts to show."

Alison wanted to crawl under the table and die of mortification. She was treated to a very shocked look from Isabella and to a couple of very disapproving glares from the king and queen.

"Has there been a paternity test?" The king gave her an assessing glare that made her stomach roll.

"That won't be necessary," Maximo said through

gritted teeth. "I am sure the child is mine, and I never want to hear you suggest otherwise again."

Maximo's rage shocked her. It wasn't as though they were a real couple. He didn't even necessarily like her all that much. It was probably more related to his masculine ego than anything else.

Luciano gave his son a hard glare. "Then there is nothing else to be done," he said. "We will begin planning the wedding immediately."

Queen Elisabetta narrowed her eyes, her mouth pursed. "We know nothing about her, Maximo. Is she suitable? Who are her people?"

Alison shifted in her chair, extremely uncomfortable being discussed as though she wasn't in the room.

Isabella's blue eyes lit with anger. "What does it matter who her people are, Mamma? If Max loves her he should marry her. That's the *only* reason people should *ever* marry."

"This is not about you, Isabella," Luciano said curtly. "But she is right. It is of no consequence who her people are, or where she comes from. She is pregnant with Maximo's heir and that is all that matters."

If King Luciano had stood up from his place at the table and walked over to check her teeth she wouldn't have been surprised. She felt like some sort of royal broodmare. She was acceptable because of the baby she carried. She imagined that if she really had been the woman Maximo loved, if there hadn't been a baby, the king wouldn't be so sanguine about the marriage. He would probably take the stance his wife had. If the damage hadn't already been done she would have been found wanting based solely on her bloodline or her background. She couldn't help but wonder if that were the situation, if they were in love and she were the woman

Maximo had decided he wanted to marry, whose side he would have taken.

She couldn't imagine Maximo being intimidated by anyone. He would never give in to his parents' demands simply because he felt pressured to do so. But he had proven that, above all else, he had the ability to be coldly logical if he needed to be. He didn't want marriage any more than she did, and yet he had immediately accepted that it was the best course of action for the sake of their child. Would he have made the same choice if he felt that marrying the woman he loved conflicted with the best interests for his country?

Oh, what does it matter?

She would never know. She didn't need to know, or want to know. She didn't *love* Maximo. She didn't have any feelings for him at all. She *respected* him. Respected his strength, his drive to do the right and moral thing, his love for their unborn child. But that was all.

He moved his thumb over the tender skin of her wrist and a team of butterflies took flight in her stomach, calling her a liar.

So she was attracted to him? It didn't mean anything. He was an attractive man. And then there were the pregnancy hormones. But that was all it was. And thank God for that.

"I'm glad we can agree on this," Maximo said, his tone containing a hint of warning that Alison assumed was meant for his mother.

"We will not have you marry in some civil ceremony," Luciano said, his tone imperious. It was obvious where Maximo had inherited his arrogance from. "You will marry in church, and we will make a formal engagement announcement. We will not treat it like a dirty secret.

You are giving our country an heir and we will celebrate that."

His mother looked as though she had swallowed a lemon. "I suppose a wedding is preferable to the birth of a royal bastard."

Alison sucked in a sharp breath. It was no less offensive hearing it said now than it had been to hear Maximo say it earlier. And she knew now that he'd been telling the absolute truth about how their child would have been viewed had they not married. And it wouldn't have just been the people or the media, but his own family who would have branded their child with that label.

"I won't tolerate hearing our baby talked about like that!" The words tumbled out of her mouth before she could stop them. "I won't allow anyone to hurt my child. Ever."

Maximo cupped her chin and turned her face to him. "No one will hurt our child, *cara*. I will not allow it." He gave his mother a dark look. "This is your grandchild, Mamma. Think about that before you ever say such a thing again."

He stood, and pulled her gently with him. "Alison and I will have dinner in our room." His mother looked offended at that, but she didn't say anything.

Alison elevated her chin, careful not to look defeated in any way. They were just rich, titled snobs. They had no right to judge her. And anyway, she'd dealt with far worse from her own mother. She was hardly going to let venom spewed by a complete stranger make her crumble now.

As soon as they were out in the empty corridor he released his grip on her hand.

"That went well," she said.

"As well as I expected. My mother loved Selena like a daughter. This is difficult for her."

"Then wouldn't it be better if they knew how I got pregnant instead of assuming that…"

"Selena did not wish for my mother to know. She did not want my parents to see her as a failure."

Maximo began to walk back toward his quarters, and she had to take short, quick steps to keep up with his long strides. "That's ridiculous. Not being able to have children doesn't make you a failure."

"It felt that way to my wife." He paused for a moment. "My mother introduced us. It was her opinion that Selena was perfect for me. Her family was wealthy and well-known, she was talented and cultured. In my mother's estimation she would make a wonderful princess. A wonderful mother. When Selena could not fulfill that part of what she considered to be her requirements, she became very depressed."

"But that wasn't the only thing you loved her for," Alison said softly.

Maximo turned to face her, his mouth pressed into a grim line. "No."

"I understand why you don't want it to become public knowledge. I won't tell anyone." It might make things easier in a way, although Alison imagined the queen would dislike her regardless, but she just didn't want to hurt Maximo by dredging up things from the past. And it would hurt him. His expression was always stoic when he talked about Selena, but she had seen glimpses of devastating pain in his dark eyes. And she cared about that. A lot more than she should.

She shouldn't be able to feel his pain in her chest, shouldn't ache for him, want to take his hurts and heal them. She really shouldn't want that at all. But she did.

Her heart hurt for him, felt linked to his. Was that because she was pregnant with his baby? It was a link between them that was impossible to ignore. He was a part of her, in a way.

On the heels of that revelation came a slug of panic. She didn't want to feel so much for him. Didn't want to feel anything for him beyond a circumspect amount of tolerance.

Once they were back in Maximo's quarters he led her into a small dining room that looked as if it belonged in a more casual home. A very, very upscale home, but the room was definitely intended for family use, unlike the massive dining hall in the main portion of the palace.

He sat at the head of the table and it seemed natural for her to sit at the other end. It was easy for her to picture a child sitting between them, chubby fingers gripping a cookie, a big smile on their baby's face. Would their child be fair like her? Or olive-skinned like Maximo? The thought made her stomach tighten painfully, the image of family, their family, so poignant that it touched her more deeply than she'd imagined possible.

This was a new picture, one that was quickly replacing the original images she'd had of life after her baby was born. Now she couldn't help but see Maximo, his presence there both physically and in the features of their child. The ache that settled in her heart was both sweet and scary at the same time. She shouldn't want this. But part of her did. Very, very much.

"Anything special you want to eat?" Maximo asked.

He was so handsome. She couldn't help but notice. With the overhead lighting from the chandelier above the table throwing the planes and angles of his face into sharp relief, making his cheekbones look more prominent, his jaw even more chiseled, he was almost devastatingly handsome. That was a term she'd never understood before this moment. It had never made sense that a person's looks could devastate. But his could. And did. Because looking at him filled her with so much longing, for things she shouldn't want, that it made her heart squeeze tight.

"Honestly, all food sounds basically disgusting to me so it doesn't really matter."

He nodded. "Then I will have the staff bring what they prepared for my parents."

A few minutes later a woman came in pushing a trolley that was laden with silver domed trays. She set two in front of Alison, along with another glass of homemade ginger ale.

Alison didn't even bother to uncover the trays, but went straight for the ginger ale to calm her perpetually unsettled stomach.

"You need to eat," Maximo said. "You are too thin."

She paused midsip. "I'm not too thin! I've been to see a doctor and he said I, and the pregnancy, were perfectly healthy."

"Well, it doesn't seem like you should allow yourself to get any thinner." Maximo rose from his spot at the end of the table and leaned over to uncover her food. There was pasta with marinara sauce on one and what looked like half of a beautifully roasted chicken on the other. But the sight of poultry turned her stomach.

"I might be able to try the pasta," she said, shoving the bird away from her.

Maximo sat in the chair next to her, putting the chicken in front of himself.

"Was your wife on a special diet?" She regretted saying anything the moment the words left her mouth. Usually she was very selective about what she said, but she'd had her fair share of outbursts in the past forty-eight hours. Maximo seemed to have that effect on her.

He shrugged slightly. "Vitamins. Any kind of herbal remedy she could think of. Hormones for the IVF. Plus any food rumored to benefit fertility."

"She really wanted to be a mother," Alison said softly, guilt and anguish almost stealing her breath. Selena had tried so hard to have Maximo's baby, had wanted it so badly, and here Alison was, pregnant with his child. And it had been an accident. It seemed like a cruel joke for fate to play on all of them.

"Yes. She did. We tried IVF three times. We were unsuccessful. She had just taken the final negative test a few hours before her death."

Alison put her hand over his, the gesture intended to comfort. Heat spiraled through her from the point of contact down to her belly. His skin was warm beneath her hand, the hair on his arm crisp and sexy. She'd never imagined that arm hair could be sexy. His was. It reminded her that he was very much a man, and that she was a woman. A woman who was going to marry him in just a few weeks.

She pulled her hand away and set it in her lap, but she could still feel the burn of his skin on her palm. Her heart pounded hard in her chest and an answering pulse pounded in the core of her body, not letting her deny that what she was feeling was definitely arousal. She looked up at Maximo. His eyes were dark, the heat from them searing her, making the flame that had been smoldering in her belly flare up, the fire threatening to consume her at any moment.

She pushed her chair back and stood, desperate to put distance between them. What was it that he did to her that stole all of her ability to think rationally? Being near him, touching him, it took all of that carefully guarded control of hers and stripped it from her, leaving her bare and unprotected.

"I'm tired," she said. "I need to... I'm going to go to bed."

A knowing smile curved his lips. "You are so intent on fighting this thing between us."

"This isn't what I want, Max," she whispered, closing her eyes, trying to block out his handsome face.

"Did someone hurt you?" he asked, his voice suddenly hard.

She shook her head. "Not in the way you mean. But I can't...don't ask me to do this."

"I would never force myself on you."

She knew that. She had no doubts, none at all, that Maximo was a man of his word. A man of honor. But it wasn't the idea of him forcing himself on her that she feared. It was the fact that force wasn't necessary. All he would have to do was touch her, kiss her, and she would forget all of the reasons it was such a bad idea to become physically involved with him.

And she was afraid that, like her mother, if she allowed herself to become dependent she would forget how to take care of herself, and if he left she would just crumble.

She and Maximo were getting married to give their child a family. They were committed to being in each other's lives for at least the next eighteen years. She was already far too dependent on him due to the nature of the situation, and adding feelings, adding sex, had the potential to make it deadly to her.

"I'm tired," she said again, turning to go.

"Get some rest," he said, his voice rough, and she wondered if it was due to arousal; the kind that was making her blood thick and her throat tight. "Tomorrow we will be announcing our engagement to the world."

CHAPTER SIX

ALISON shifted and winced as the boning in the corset top of her gown took another dig at her side. It was hot. Dear heaven was it hot! And humid. Stray wisps of her hair hung down out of her glamorous updo in lank strands. The air seemed thick, and breathing it in only seemed to increase the nausea that was her constant, reviled companion.

The servant that had helped her get dressed had insisted that this was a formal announcement and would require formal dress. So here she was, made-up, sucked in, pushed up and buffed to a highly glossed sheen, waiting behind a heavy red curtain for her time to step out onto the balcony with Maximo so they could make a horribly clichéd announcement to the television cameras and the citizens who had gathered below.

It wasn't just the people of Turan that were watching, but the world. Maximo was charismatic and popular, both in his home country and abroad, and his wedding would be attended by the rich and famous from every corner of the world. No pressure, though. She almost laughed at that thought.

She took a deep breath and tried to ignore the fact that her breasts seemed to be trying to make an escape from the sweetheart neckline of the gown. She imagined it was supposed to be demure, in its jewel-tone sapphire color, with cute ruffled cap sleeves. And it might have been, if she hadn't been quite so generously endowed up top.

She could hear Maximo out on the balcony, on the other side of the curtain, addressing his people, speaking in Italian. If there was a sexier sound in the world she'd never heard it. His voice did things to her, and not only her. He was an amazing public speaker; she could tell from behind the curtain. He had charisma. She couldn't understand a word he was saying but it sounded good.

He was the sort of leader that inspired. The sort of leader his country needed.

She straightened and nearly cursed out loud when the boning dug into her again. She was making the right decision. Maximo was a good man. He would be a wonderful example for their child, and a wonderful father. No matter how overwhelming all of it seemed to her, this was her son's or daughter's legacy. The people waiting down there were her child's people. There was no way she could have denied them this chance.

Luigi, the man who coordinated most big events for the royal family, signaled for her to make her entrance onto the balcony. He swept the curtain aside for her, careful to keep himself out of view, and she took a tentative step out into the blinding Mediterranean sunlight.

The height, the heat and vibrating sea of people below made her head swim. She tried to paste a smile on her face, as she had been instructed to do, and took her place at Maximo's side.

He put his arm around her waist and drew her close. His father, who was standing with the queen, took the center of the balcony and spoke into the microphone. A cheer erupted from the crowd.

Maximo turned to her and brushed her cheek softly with the back of his hand. The light touch sent a shimmer of something wonderful through her. His eyes were intent on her face, his expression serious, but almost caring.

He leaned in and pressed a light kiss to her lips. She hadn't been expecting a gesture of affection like that and it had her heart pounding so hard she was afraid the microphones would pick it up, and everyone would be able to hear for themselves just what Maximo did to her. He held her tightly against his body, his strong arms cradling her. She shifted and her breasts brushed his hard, masculine chest. Electricity zinged through her.

She couldn't stop staring at him, couldn't tear her eyes away from him. Her future husband. He was so handsome dressed in a traditional mandarin-collared suit with a long dark jacket that accentuated his broad chest, slim waist and spare hips. The plain jacket was adorned with medals pinned to the right breast, over his heart. The Latin words written on the pin spoke of duty to God and country.

An intense feeling swelled in her chest. Pride, she realized. She was proud to stand by his side. Proud that he was the father of her baby. And who wouldn't be? He was a *good* man, a man who understood responsibility, a man who valued honor. Maximo wasn't the kind of man who would walk away from his responsibilities. He was the kind of man who would stand and face challenges when they came. When the results of the test came, the test that would tell them if there was a chance their child might be affected by Cystic Fibrosis, Maximo would face it head-on, of that she had no doubt.

He wouldn't run from a painful situation, wouldn't walk away if things were hard.

Maximo leaned in again, his hot breath touching her neck, making goose bumps break out over her skin, despite the heat.

"Wave at your people," he commanded gently. She turned, still in his arms, and put her hand up in a shy wave. She was greeted by another round of enthusiastic cheering. Many of the people waved back or waved flags.

"*Bene,*" he whispered near her ear and nuzzled her gently with his nose.

Lightning flashed through her from that simple brush of skin on skin, igniting a desire that was hot and insistent, and totally outside of her experience. It was all for show. She *knew* that. It didn't mean anything to him. But her body didn't seem to know, much less care. She felt her knees weaken and she slumped against him, against the solid wall of his body. She realized how easy it would be to just melt into him, to lean against him forever.

The strength of those feelings shocked her, made her knees shake. She wasn't supposed to feel like this. She moved then, turning her body away from him, trying to keep her lips glued into a smile. And then she was being ushered back behind the curtain, leaving the king and queen to continue speaking to the crowd.

"You did very well," Maximo said, releasing her from his hold once they were out of view.

"A smile and a wave," she said breathlessly. "Not too impressive."

"When a woman looks like you, that's about all it takes. They loved you."

She laughed shakily. "It's the dress."

"It's a lovely dress." His eyes traveled over her, over each of her curves.

For once, such a close inspection didn't make her think of what might happen if she let a man get too close to her. It lit a fire that smoldered hot in her belly.

It wasn't virginal nerves that made her draw back from the obvious attraction between them. It was a different kind of fear. Fear of the strength of her response to him, of the almost overwhelming need she felt to melt into him, have him assuage the ache he made settle between her thighs. The intense desire to allow him to make her lose control.

"You are truly beautiful." His eyes, those hard, dark, commanding eyes, softened. He cupped her cheek and let his thumb trace her upper lip.

The curtain was swept aside again and the rush of heat that came from outside broke the bubble they'd been cocooned in.

"It is done," Luciano said firmly. "The wedding will take place in eight weeks, after Sunday Mass." He turned to Maximo and said something in his native language.

A dull red stained Maximo's cheekbones and his eyes hardened, a muscle in his jaw jumping with tension. "*Si*. I am certain."

"It's good to be sure." Luciano patted his son on the back before stopping in front of her. "Make him happy."

Luciano and Elisabetta exited the room, leaving Alison and Maximo alone.

"What did he say?" she asked, knowing it hadn't been flattering to her.

"It isn't important."

She let out an inelegant snort. "For something unimportant it certainly made you angry."

"He asked if I was certain it was my child."

That stung a little bit. But then, the king didn't know her. He had to suspect that she and Maximo hadn't known each other for very long. Really, she couldn't blame him for his concern.

She shrugged. "Well, I suppose we don't know for sure. If they were careless enough to give me your sample they might have been mislabeled. That would let you off the hook." The color in his face darkened and she felt instantly contrite. "I'm sorry. That was a tasteless thing to say."

"It was." He slipped his arm through hers and led her back toward their rooms. "I don't consider myself *on the hook*. I want this child."

"I only meant the marriage," she mumbled.

"The marriage should hardly be noticeable for either of us. Despite the change in location for you."

"Glad to know I won't be too heavy a ball and chain," she snapped.

"Not at all. And make no mistake, I've been married, and I'm not looking for that sort of relationship out of this." He released her arm and made his way up the stairs without her.

He had mentioned that he hadn't been planning on getting married again and up until then she had been certain it was love for his wife that kept him from wanting a new wife. Now she wasn't entirely certain.

And why should she care? He wasn't going to be her husband in any true sense of the word. He would be her partner. They would raise their baby together during the day and at night he would warm the bed of some lithe, six-foot-tall blonde. And she would go to bed alone and enjoy the solitude of her bed. And cold sheets. So why didn't that sound fair, or appealing, at all?

* * *

"This is wonderful!" Isabella hadn't stopped chattering since she and Alison had gotten into the limo. "My *mamma* never allows me to go shopping."

"Your mother never lets you go shopping?" Alison couldn't imagine being controlled to such a degree. The very thought of it made her feel claustrophobic. "And are we supposed to be doing this now?"

Isabella had been very excited about taking a trip to help furnish a new, princess-worthy wardrobe for Alison, but Alison had assumed it had been Max's idea. And she certainly hadn't imagined that her future sister-in-law might be forbidden from going.

A slight blush stained Isabella's high cheekbones. "Not exactly."

Anger, not directed at Isabella, tightened her stomach. "Why aren't you allowed to shop?"

A mutinous expression creased Isabella's forehead. "Shopping is not a skill required of the future wife of a sheikh."

"You're engaged?" The other woman seemed very young to her. Naive, but very sweet.

She shrugged one very lovely shoulder. "More or less. I have an arranged marriage."

"An arranged marriage?"

It felt wrong to Alison, the thought that such a lovely, gentle person was being farmed out to a man she didn't even love. But then, wasn't that essentially what was happening with her? Except it was different for her. Isabella was clearly a romantic, and Alison had never imagined that *she* would marry for love. Anyway, Max was an honorable, handsome, decent man and any woman would be lucky to marry him.

Her own line of thinking shocked her. When had she come to think of him like that? It was ridiculous. She'd only known him for a few days. And she didn't *want* to marry him. She was only doing it because it was the right thing to do. That was all.

Isabella's eyes shone with passion now. "I thought I was entitled to experience a little something before I gave it all up for duty and honor. I just want to live a little bit of life. The life of my choosing." She took a deep breath as though she was trying to regain some composure. "But arranged marriages are normal in our family. It's just how things work. Well, except with you and Max, of course."

"Was Max and Selena's marriage arranged?" She felt a tiny twinge of guilt for digging into Maximo's past. It would have been one thing if she were really the woman he loved, if they had the sort of relationship where they shared confidences. But they didn't.

"Yes. Well, my mother met Selena after one of her shows. She was an opera singer…a very talented one. My parents had been pushing Max to settle down and start having babies. They encouraged him to pursue Selena and he did. I know he loved her, though, after a while. I could tell. So it was an arranged marriage in a way. Not like mine, though." She sighed. "I've never even met my fiancé."

Alison only half heard the rest of the conversation. She was too busy processing the information she'd just received. No wonder Maximo's view on marriage was so pragmatic. He'd made it sound as though his mother had introduced them, but she had assumed that he'd married her for love, not duty. Although Isabella was certain he'd grown to love Selena.

She was also starting to suspect that his marriage hadn't been a perfect one. She could see it in the tension that pulled up around his eyes when he spoke of his late wife. But they had been through so much as a couple, perhaps it was only natural that they would have had some strain put on the relationship.

She couldn't figure out why it all suddenly seemed so important. It just did. The more she got to know Max as a person, the more she wanted to know about him. She just wanted to…to understand him. And that was normal. He was the father of her baby; of course she wanted to understand him.

The limo pulled up to the curb of what looked like a very upscale row of boutiques. The driver opened the door and Isabella slid out. Alison followed. The ocean was only a hundred yards away from the shops, and the chilly salt air did wonders for the eternal churning in Alison's stomach. The shops were all set into small, historic stone buildings, but just at the end of the row of boutiques there was a new, massive casino. It wasn't all lit up like Vegas, rather it was more sedate, in keeping with the theme of the rest of the district. Maximo really was a genius. What he'd done to revamp the economy of his country was brilliant.

Women in expensive clothing milled around on the cobblestone walks sipping coffee that was as designer as their handbags. The men, Alison assumed, were in the casino.

"Princess Isabella!" Both Isabella and Alison turned to the sound of a man shouting. A flash went off, followed by more flashes.

Alison's eyes widened. There was a pack of people, men and women, holding cameras, They were moving toward the limo quickly, microphones and recorders held out.

"Are you Alison Whitman? Prince Maximo Rossi's

fiancée?" A woman shouted just before snapping a picture with her camera.

"Why are you getting married so quickly?"

"Does it bother you that you aren't as glamorous as his first wife?"

"Is he good in bed?"

Questions—lots of questions, inappropriate questions—were flying at her from all directions, and the paparazzi was moving in closer, crowding them up against the side of the limo.

"Back up!" Alison yelled, afraid she was about to get crushed against the side of the car. Afraid for her baby. But no one was paying attention because her statement hadn't included any hint of scandal.

Isabella managed to get the door open, and Alison slid into the car after her, closing the door and locking it behind them. "Drive!" she said, banging on the partition between the front and backseat. The princess drew a shaky hand over her face. "No wonder I'm not allowed to do this."

"That was...overwhelming," Alison said, leaning back against the seat. She hadn't expected that. Hadn't factored it in when she'd imagined being married to Max. She wanted to cry. Nothing was going like it was supposed to. Living like this was so foreign, and such a complete departure from how she'd imagined her life. It was only just now sinking in, how much she was changing her life to give her baby a father.

Isabella's expression turned sad. "It was always like that for Max and Selena. The press couldn't get enough of them."

Alison couldn't imagine how hard it must have been for them. Cameras following them all the time, the constant, insistent crush of bodies every time they went out in public. She wasn't sure she could cope with it.

But it's your life now.

She put her hand on her stomach and tried to calm the wild, fluttery wings of panic that were making her entire body tremble.

Isabella picked up her cell phone and punched numbers rapidly. "Max," she all but shouted into the phone. "We just got ambushed by the paparazzi."

She cast Alison a sideways glance, her expression guilty. "I wanted to go shopping. I didn't think…"

Alison could hear the muffled tirade that Max was subjecting his sister to. Isabella grimaced, but let him talk until he was through yelling. "She's fine. The baby, too, I'm sure. We'll see you in a moment."

Isabella hung up the phone. "I've never heard him sound like that before. He's worried. He must really love you."

Alison's heart squeezed and a restless, burning ache seemed to open up inside of her, one that she was desperate to have filled. But she didn't know what she needed to fill it.

That was a lie. She was starting to think she knew exactly what would fill it. But that was a something she was too scared to face. Everything seemed to be closing in on her at once; the stark reality of what all the changes becoming a princess would entail, and even more terrifying, the reality of the feelings she was starting to have for her future husband.

When they got back to the *castillo* Maximo was pacing in the vast entryway, his expression thunderous. "That was incredibly foolish and immature of you, Isabella," he ground out. "You could have both been hurt."

"I didn't know it would be like that!" Isabella protested. "How would I? I'm never allowed out anywhere!"

The fierceness in his expression diminished slightly and he blew out a hard breath. "Did you see any press badges?" he demanded, the moment they walked into the room. "If you have names I will see that the people responsible for this are thrown in jail."

Isabella shook her head. "I don't think any of them had ID on display."

"They were just doing their jobs, Max," Alison said. "There's no need to throw anyone in jail. We're fine. It was scary but they weren't trying to hurt us or anything."

"I don't tolerate that kind of gutter press in my country," he bit out. "If a reporter wants to take pictures that's fine, but there is no excuse for chasing down a couple of innocent women. Whether they intended to hurt you or not isn't the issue. They *could* have hurt you."

Alison put a hand on his arm, the need to touch him, to offer some kind of balm for his rage, was too strong for her to fight against. "We're fine. The baby is fine."

"We're leaving," he said curtly. "Until the media firestorm is over we're not staying in Turan." He pulled his phone out of his pocket and punched in a number, then barked orders in Italian to whoever was unfortunate enough to be on the other end.

He hung up and turned to face Alison. "Go and pack, *cara mia*. We're going to start our honeymoon early."

CHAPTER SEVEN

THE flight to the island of Maris was short. The small plane touched down in a field of moss-colored grass only ten minutes after takeoff. The island itself was less mountainous than Turan, with white sand beaches that bled into expansive fields and thick olive groves.

There was no car waiting for them when they disembarked from the plane.

Maximo had spent most of the half-hour flight on his phone making arrangements for any work he needed to do to be finished remotely from the island. She'd spent the whole flight feeling shaky and...excited? No. Just shaky about the prospect of being almost alone with him in such a beautiful, isolated, romantic place.

"You were joking about the honeymoon thing, right?" she asked, surveying the vast expanse of green around them.

He turned to face her, the expression in his dark eyes so hot it burned her down to her toes. "I promised I wouldn't force you, Alison, but I didn't say I wouldn't seduce you."

Her stomach flipped, and as her nausea was starting to fade already there was no way she could place the blame on her pregnancy. "Well, that isn't...it's not...you won't be able to."

He leaned in, his lips just a breath away from hers. "What did I tell you about issuing challenges?"

"I…" She couldn't tear her eyes away from his mouth, couldn't stop herself from leaning in just slightly…

He withdrew suddenly and began to walk, as though nothing had just passed between them. As though she wasn't about to melt into a puddle of satisfied longing in the grassy field. "It's just a short walk through the grass. The villa is just through the grove." He pointed to the knot of olive trees that were directly in front of them.

They came through the brush and into a landscaped clearing with stone paths and beautifully kept gardens. A large circular fountain was at the center of the court-yard, and beyond it was the three-story villa with cream stucco walls and Spanish-tile roofing.

"It's gorgeous!" She couldn't help but think that Selena must have loved it here. It was idyllic. There were no roads, no city noises of any kind; just broad expanses of azure sky and acres of virgin land. It was the perfect escape for a couple who were desperately in love and wanted nothing more than to spend all of their time devoted only to each other. Talking, laughing, exploring, making love.

"Selena never came here."

It was as if he could read her mind sometimes, and given the recent tenor of her thoughts, that was a disquieting notion indeed.

She turned her head sharply and he laughed. "You wear your thoughts pretty openly. You looked sad. Although I can never understand why you feel so much for my late wife."

A deep sadness filled her and she felt tears sting her eyes. "It's just that…I have all that she wanted. It feels wrong somehow that I'm here with you. With the baby you both wanted. I'm the wrong woman."

He took her hand and led her to a stone bench. He sat and pulled her down gently, bringing her close to the heat of his body, her thigh touching his. "*Cara*, I don't know what the future would have held for Selena and me if she had lived. None of us can know that. But I don't think of this baby as belonging to Selena. This is *our* baby. Yours and mine."

She gave him a watery smile. "I appreciate that."

"I cannot regret it, Alison. I can't regret that you're carrying my baby, our baby. It is a dream I never thought to see realized, a child of my own. You have given that hope back to me and I can only be grateful for the mix-up at the lab now. Without it, I would not have this chance."

He put his hand over her stomach. He did that a lot now, and she had come to enjoy the gentle pressure of his touch, the tingling warmth that the contact always brought. She couldn't regret it, either. There was no way she could. She cared for Maximo, respected him. She was very glad that her baby would have him for a father.

He turned his focus from her and onto the house. "I started building the villa before her death. She was very unhappy with the location and refused to visit it. I had hoped it would be our family home. But she preferred the city."

"I'm sorry you lost her."

He shielded his eyes from the sun with his hand. "I lost her long before she died."

Again she caught that glimmer of sadness in his otherwise composed expression. And she wanted to fix it with a ferocity that shocked and scared her. "I know you were going through a hard time, but I'm sure she loved you, Max."

"She was unhappy. Being a princess demanded much more of her than she'd anticipated it would."

"But she had you."

"Sometimes. My position has always demanded that I travel a lot. Selena didn't want to be dragged around on business trips. She wanted someone to entertain her. Someone to be with her. Take care of her. She did not suffer from that same independent streak that you do," he said, the ghost of a smile touching his lips. "I can't fault her for that. I can't fault her for being unhappy."

Alison couldn't understand how Selena could have been unhappy with Maximo. There was something about him that just made her want to be with him. She liked his smell, the comforting heat of his body as he sat next to her on the bench. The way he touched her belly, so gently, reverently. Being with him made her feel secure. Happy. Cared for in a way she couldn't remember ever being cared for.

The realization was enough to shock her into standing from the bench. She was starting to need him too much. Even without sex and romance he was burrowing under her skin. Yes, Maximo was a good man, but he was also an arrogant autocrat who expected her to just fall in line and do exactly as he said. When he said marriage was the only option he expected her to see it his way, and when he said they were going on an early honeymoon she'd found herself on a plane within five minutes of his edict.

It was far too easy to forget all of that when he turned on his charm and flashed that sexy smile at her. But she wasn't going to let herself do that anymore. It was too dangerous.

"I'm hot. I want to go inside," she said.

Maximo didn't know what had caused the dramatic shift in Alison's mood. She had been sweet one moment, not resisting his attempts to touch her, and then she had gone stiff and jumped as far away from him as she could manage in one movement.

He wanted her. He had been totally honest about his intention to seduce her, and he did intend to. He was going to make this advanced honeymoon a honeymoon in the most basic sense of the word. He ached for her every night as he lay in his empty bed, images of her fiery hair spread around her head as he laid her back onto his pillows. That gorgeous mouth parted on a sigh as he sank into her willing body...

His need for her was so strong, so intense that his entire body ached with it. Desire on this level was a madness he'd never before experienced. And it was an ideal scenario for it. Alison did not want love, but he knew she felt the same kind of lust for him that he felt for her. Lust he could handle. Love was not on the agenda.

This feeling, this overwhelming passion, was about as far removed from love as anything he could think of. But then, Alison was as far removed from Selena as one woman could possibly be from another. And for that he was grateful. Alison was fiery, independent. When she was angry with him, as she seemed to be, inexplicably, at the moment, she let him know.

Selena had been so delicate. She had needed him, needed his protection, his support. He had failed at that. Failed spectacularly. In the end she'd withdrawn from him completely and he'd had no way to reach her, no way to stanch the flow of grief that had seemed to flow endlessly inside of her.

At least with Alison it would be different. He wouldn't be caught in that same, endless hell his first marriage had been in the end. She wouldn't cling to him, expect him to solve all of her problems then blame him for everything that seemed to go wrong.

Guilt struck him low and fast. Yes, Selena had been difficult at times, but hadn't it been his job to slay her dragons? Even if there had been more dragons in her life than there were in most people's, that was irrelevant. She had been his wife. It had been his job to make her happy. He had failed.

But with Alison at least he could stay out of those murky waters. Alison didn't want a real marriage relationship and neither did he. They had that in common. And, whether she wanted to admit it or not, they also shared an attraction.

He stood and moved to follow her into the villa, banishing all thoughts of his first marriage as he watched the gentle sway of Alison's hips as she walked ahead of him.

Oh, yes, he was going to enjoy the seduction of his fiancée very much.

Maximo was in his private office, giving Alison a chance to sleep off the afternoon's stress. She was tired. She needed to rest. That was the refrain he kept replaying in his mind, when his body was demanding that he find her immediately and commence with his seduction plan.

He'd been trying to concentrate on work, trying not to focus on the woman sleeping down the hall. But it was a useless endeavor. His desire for Alison was slowly taking him over; an almost primitive need that seemed bone deep, as though it was in him, inseparable from him now.

He was almost ready to give up on his attempt at productivity when his mobile phone rang. It was his personal physician calling with the test results.

The call took only a minute, and in that minute his life was changed.

CHAPTER EIGHT

MAXIMO opened the door to Alison's bedroom without knocking. She was asleep and her beauty stole his breath, made him feel weak with desire, like a starving man in desperate need of nourishment. Even with all of the turmoil inside of him, he still wanted her.

"Alison." He sat down on the bed and took her hand in his. "Alison." He moved his other hand over her face, brushed her hair back. She stirred beneath his touch, her body arching, a soft sigh escaping her lips.

His body hardened instantly, his stomach tightening. "Wake up, Alison."

She rubbed her hand over her eyes and rolled to the side, her coppery eyes cloudy with sleep, her hair tousled. And he had never seen a more beautiful woman. She was so beautiful it made him ache.

"Max?" his name on her lips, her voice thick with sleep, was the single most arousing thing he'd ever heard in his life.

"The doctor called."

She sat up quickly, pushing her hair back. "What did she say?" The film of tears in her eyes made his heart feel too large for his chest.

"I'm not a carrier. There isn't a chance our baby will have Cystic Fibrosis."

A short cry escaped her lips and she threw her arms around his neck, sobs shaking her frame. He held her close and let her release all of her emotion, let her do it for both of them. He held her until his neck was wet with her tears.

"I was so afraid," she whispered, her lips brushing his jaw. "I thought... I didn't want to watch our child die, Max."

"You won't have to."

"My sister was so young when it took her. It was horrible. It killed me to see it happen to her, to watch her just get weaker. I couldn't have gone through it with our baby."

His heart burned for her, her pain so real, so much a part of him, that he felt it all the way in his bones. "I didn't know you'd been through that."

"That was why..." She took a gulp of air. "That was why it was so important to me to know. I needed to prepare myself. I couldn't just be blindsided with something like that. I don't know if there would ever have been a way to be really prepared for it...but knowing now. Oh, it's such a relief."

She pulled back and started to wipe the moisture from her tearstained face. Her nose was red, her eyes swollen, and still he wanted her so much it was physically painful to hold himself back. Seeing the intensity of her love for their child only increased his desire for her.

He cupped the back of her head, stroking his thumb over her silky, strawberry locks. "No matter what, we would have made it. There's no way we could love our baby more or less than we do. But I'm very glad that we don't have to worry about that."

"Me, too."

Her arms were still linked around his neck and she very slowly moved her hands so that her fingers were twined through his hair. She moved them slowly, sliding them through, her touch sending shock waves of hot pleasure rippling through him. It was such a simple touch. In general he would have said there wasn't anything erotic about it. Except in this moment, with this woman, it was the single most erotic sensation he could ever remember feeling.

She leaned in slightly, her eyelids lowering, her lashes fanning over her cheeks. Her mouth was so close to his that one slight movement would join them together. But he wanted her to do it. Wanted her to make the move.

"Max, I don't really know what I'm doing here, but I don't know if I can stop myself, either," she whispered, her breath hot and sweet against his lips.

Then she closed the distance between them, settling her lips over his, her kiss tentative, almost shy. It was strange because there was nothing insecure or shy about Alison, and yet she kissed almost as if she was an innocent. Not that he could claim personal experience in that area.

When the tip of her tongue touched his lower lip his control snapped completely. He growled, deepening the kiss, sliding his tongue against hers. She parted her lips for him, granting him access, her feminine moan of pleasure tightening his gut, increasing his arousal.

He slowly pressed her down on the bed. She arched her back, rubbing her breasts against his chest. They had too many clothes on. He needed her naked. He needed to be naked. To be able to slide inside of her, and finally purge himself of the almost surreal level of desire he felt for her.

He moved his hands over her curves, cupped her

breasts, teased the hardened points of her nipples. He could come just touching her, even through her clothes. Never, not even when he'd been a teenage virgin, had a woman ever tested his self-control like this.

"Wait," she said, rolling away from him, her eyes wide. "I don't… I can't…" Her breathing was ragged, her lips swollen. "I can't."

"Why is it that you can't all of a sudden? You want this—I know you do."

"I don't," she said, her breathing ragged. "I'm sorry. We…it would be better if we were just friends. What would happen if this—" she gestured to the air between them "—didn't work out? Then we would be bitter divorcés shuttling our child back and forth and sharing holidays. But if we just keep it platonic then things would be simpler. It's the smartest thing to do."

"I have no trouble keeping my commitments. When I speak my vows to you I will mean them. If you see divorce in our future it will not be me that's instigated it."

Alison forked her shaking fingers in her hair. "Well, I have no intention of divorcing you, but when you introduce sex into a relationship it complicates things."

Maximo stood up from the bed, not bothering to hide the thick length of his erection that was pressing against the front of his slacks. "Things are already complicated by the attraction between us. Sex would only alleviate some of the tension."

He turned and walked out of the room. Alison cursed out loud to the empty room. Why had she done that? Why had she kissed him like a sex-starved maniac?

And why did you stop him? That was the question her body was asking. She was so hot for him, wet for him, needy for him. His kiss had totally stolen every ounce of her control. She'd been ready to let him do anything he wanted with her, to her. She'd craved the loss of control, the descent into blissful oblivion at his hands.

And in the end that was what had jarred her back to reality. The feelings inside of her had gone so far beyond just a simple case of lust. And she couldn't deal with that. She just couldn't.

She didn't want to fall in love. She liked Maximo too much already and if she gave into her desire for him what would keep her from falling all the way? Nothing. She was too dangerously close to love already to take the chance.

In that moment when he'd told her that the test was negative she'd just wanted to cling to him, and it had been so easy to imagine that their relationship was real, and that they were a real couple, drawing support and strength from each other.

But that wasn't the case. They were just two strangers thrown together, making the most out of a crazy situation. He had his life, she had hers, and together they had the baby. But that was all that linked them.

Maximo had said he wouldn't divorce her, and maybe he wouldn't. No matter what he would never abandon her baby.

He'd been faithful to Selena, but he'd loved Selena. Without love what was going to keep him interested in her? When she gained baby weight and got stretch marks, what would make her more interesting, more attractive than other women? And he could certainly have any woman he wanted.

There was no way, no way at all, that she was going to set herself up for that.

And if she had to spend the rest of her days achy and

physically unsatisfied it would be a small price to pay to keep her soul from being irrevocably shattered.

Over the course of the next three weeks Maximo broke his promise to her. Oh, he never once tried to force himself on her, not that she had ever believed he would, but he didn't try to seduce her, either. And some small, confused part of her was disappointed that he seemed to have accepted that she truly didn't want a sexual relationship with him.

Now that he'd come to that conclusion she lay awake every night, her body on fire, her mind replaying snatches of every encounter she'd ever had with him. And then adding some more interesting things.

In her mind they hadn't stopped the day they'd found out the test results. No, in her fantasies she had kept kissing him, had unbuttoned his shirt to reveal the hard muscles and golden skin she knew lay underneath. And he'd done the same to her: unbuttoned her shirt, flicked open the clasp of her bra and then he'd lower his head and take one tightened bud into his mouth...

Alison snapped the laptop she'd been using shut and stood abruptly. It was the computer Max had given her to establish contacts at the Cystic Fibrosis Foundation. She and Max had discussed getting a Turani branch established after they'd found out the test results, and he'd given her the task of getting it mobilized. She didn't really like doing all of the work over the Internet, but it had been better than just sitting around wallowing in her lust for the man she couldn't, wouldn't, let herself have.

Maximo had been nice enough to provide her with a computer, and a staggering budget. He'd also given her the use of an empty bedroom that had been converted into an office. The windows faced the ocean, the bright crystalline water offering her at least a modicum of stress relief, even if it could not take away the hunger that constantly gnawed at her.

It was getting so bad that she was starting to wonder exactly why she was denying herself what she so desperately wanted.

Imminent heartbreak, possible abandonment, the loss of all of your independence and hard-earned self-worth!

Her practical self remembered all of the reasons. It was the wanton little hussy that had control over her erogenous zones that seemed to forget.

Thankfully her morning sickness had abated. If she couldn't have some measure of relief from the constant arousal that kept her in a perpetual state of heightened awareness, then at least she wasn't also spending most of the morning with her head in the toilet.

Even now she felt restless, her body humming just from the knowledge that Maximo was down the hall working in his own office.

He'd been so good to her since they'd come to the island. He'd been kind and attentive and taken care of anything she could possibly need. He was playing the part of doting, but platonic, fiancé just perfectly. It was as if he was doing it on purpose to make her life miserable.

She stretched and tried to shake off the electric feeling of arousal that seemed to have attached itself to her every nerve ending. Her skin felt as if it was too tight for her body, and everything inside of her felt as if it might jump out and escape at any moment.

What she needed was some physical exertion. Badly. She'd been feeling so awful since she'd gotten pregnant that she hadn't worked out at all. Maybe that was why she felt so jittery. She'd had no outlet for her energy; none of the release that a good bout of exercise always gave her.

It was way too easy to imagine ways she and Max might find some physical release together.

Walking out of the office and down the hall to her room, she made the decision to get out of the house and get some air. Maybe breathing in the stale atmosphere of the villa was chipping away at her common sense. Except the villa smelled wonderful and there was nothing stale about it, but hey, a girl needed her excuses.

She rifled through her belongings until she found a swimsuit that Maximo had had sent over to Maris a few days after they'd arrived. It was brief…shockingly so. The black, stretchy fabric didn't have enough yardage to swaddle a newborn, and yet it was intended to cover a grown woman's curves. And hers had only become more ample as her pregnancy progressed.

Her breasts were always a little full for her petite frame, but now they just made everything she wore seem indecent. The swimsuit was an extreme example of that.

She tried to ignore her reflection in the mirror, tried not to focus on her pale flesh spilling over the midnight fabric of the miniscule top. Sighing, she grabbed a towel and wrapped it firmly around herself, hiding her new, extra-lush curves and her burgeoning tummy, before padding down to the large Olympic-size pool.

Thankfully the pool area, like the rest of the villa, and the rest of the island, was extremely private. Large flowering bushes had been planted around the perimeter of the pool, just high enough to guard against curious eyes, but low enough to leave the view of the ocean visible.

Alison slid beneath the surface of the water, sighing as its coolness washed over her heated skin. She began to swim laps, reveling in the chance to burn off some of her restless energy. To let her mind go blank so that she could just forget about Maximo, even just for a moment.

When she reached the edge of the pool she gripped the cement lip, wiping the droplets of water from her face.

"You swim well."

A sensual shiver shot through the length of her body. Would that voice never stop affecting her this way? Would she ever be able to just find Maximo's presence… boring? Every day?

She looked up, her eyes widening as she took in the muscular legs, partially revealed by his board shorts, and, her eyes widened further, the broad expanse of his well-defined chest.

"Thank you," she said tightly, swimming away from that end up the pool and moving to the ladder that hung over the side. "I was on the team in high school." She climbed out of the water and grabbed her towel quickly, trying to cover the acres of bare skin that were on display thanks to her ridiculous swimsuit.

She turned to face him and her eyes were immediately drawn back to his superbly masculine chest. Good Lord, but he was one hot man. All hard muscle with just the right amount of dark chest hair sprinkled over his golden skin. Just enough to remind her how much of a man he was. As if she needed reminding. What she needed was to forget.

"So you swam in high school?"

She nodded, sitting on the lounger chair that was positioned beneath a palm tree shading the patio area. "I did a lot of things in high school. Swimming. The debate team. I worked on the school newspaper. Anything and everything to earn extra credit."

"Let me guess...you had a 4.0 GPA?"

She shrugged. "I was capable of it so anything less would have been a failure. I needed to earn scholarships so that I could go to school."

"Your parents didn't offer to pay for your schooling?" He crossed his arms over his chest, the motion creating a fascinating play of muscle that she was powerless to look away from.

"My mother couldn't have afforded it. When my..." She didn't know why she was telling him anything, and yet it seemed so easy to talk to him. She wanted to talk to him, wanted to keep him there with her. She cleared her throat. "When my father left things became difficult for us financially. My mother didn't have the means, or the drive, to earn a living for us."

He lowered his dark eyebrows and rubbed a hand over his jaw, his skin rasping against the black stubble that was starting to grow. "Your father didn't pay child support?"

"We didn't even know where he was. He walked out the door one day and never came back. I haven't heard from him in fifteen years."

"That must have been hard."

"Yes. It was harder for my mother, though. She just kind of self-destructed after he left. Kimberly was gone, and then Dad was, too, and she just didn't seem to have it in her to keep going. So she sank instead. She nearly took me with her."

He sat in the chair next to hers and leaned close, the

musky scent of him teasing her senses. "Is that why you're so independent?"

"I had to be. People aren't going to take care of you—they're going to take care of themselves. I just learned that at an earlier age than some. But I survived. I made my own way. My own success."

"But there is no shame in accepting help from others."

"That's quite something coming from you. When was the last time you accepted help?"

A slow smile curved his lips. "I can't remember."

"I didn't think so."

"But some people need more help than others," he said, a shadow passing over his face for a moment.

"I don't believe that. Some people wallow rather than moving forward."

"Is that what you think? That your mother should have tried harder?"

She nodded emphatically. "Yes. That's what I think. You can't just self-destruct because somebody leaves you in the lurch. It's never a good idea to depend on someone like that. You become so accustomed to leaning on them that you get weak, and then when they leave, when they fail you, you won't be able to stand on your own anymore because you've lost all of your own strength. And everybody fails at some point."

His eyes darkened. "Yes. And some damage is irreparable."

"Yes," she said softly, thinking of the void left by Kimberly, by her father and then, even though she'd still been there physically, by her mother. "That's why I don't need people."

"Don't you?"

"No. I earn my own living. I've achieved my goals on my own, without help from anyone. I don't do need."

"Neither do I," he said, his voice growing thicker, deeper. "And yet, something about you..." He took her hand and placed it on his bare chest, the heat of his skin singeing her fingers, his heartbeat raging against her palm. "Something about this feels a lot like need."

She sucked in a breath. She couldn't deny it. Her own body was on fire with response to his. Her heart pounding in time with his, her nipples beading, aching, slick moisture dampening her core.

"That's why we can't," she said bleakly, trying to pull her hand away, but he gripped it with his, held it tightly against the hard wall of his chest.

"And you think if we deny it, that it will go away? Has it faded at all in the past three weeks for you? Because I have been spending all of my nights dreaming of you. Of making love to you, touching your soft skin, thrusting into your beautiful body."

Heat coursed through her and she knew her cheeks were bright red, but not from embarrassment. Well, not only from embarrassment, although his frank description of what he wanted to do with her was a little bit beyond her experience level. But the heat was from desire, the fierce pulse of it that pounded through her and made her limbs feel weak, made her feel as if she could be reckless. Like she could grab what she wanted with both hands and forget that such a thing as consequences even existed.

He leaned in, his mouth covering hers, his tongue parting her lips expertly. She didn't hesitate. She opened to him, let her tongue tangle with his, wrapped her arms around his neck so that he could kiss her harder, deeper.

His hands deftly worked at the knots on her bikini top and before she realized what was happening the fabric had slipped away, leaving her breasts bare to him. She arched against his chest, the slight dusting of hair that covered his skin lightly abrading her nipples. The coarse friction sent a wave of sensation washing through her body, making her internal muscles clench in anticipation of his touch. His possession. She squirmed, trying to find some way to alleviate the hollow ache that was slowly taking over her body. She knew it wasn't going to work, that whatever she did, even if it brought her to orgasm, wasn't going to satisfy her. Because she wasn't going to be satisfied until their bodies were joined together, until he was filling that void.

He lowered his dark head and she watched, completely spellbound as he sucked one pink nipple into his mouth, his tongue working the sensitized tip. She let her head fall back, let a loud moan escape her lips. She was past the point of caring about what noises she made, past the point of caring about anything except for this. Maximo. His touch. His wicked mouth doing such wonderful, shocking things to her.

"You're so beautiful," he said thickly before lowering his head and drawing her other nipple into his mouth. He released her, laving her with the flat of his tongue before scattering kisses over her breasts, her collarbone, down to her belly button and back up again.

She was on fire, dying for him, all remnants of control long since thrown out the window. She couldn't think when he was kissing her. Couldn't plan. Couldn't do anything except revel in the things he, and only he, could do to her.

Would it have been like this with any man? If she

had given someone the chance sooner would they have lit her body on fire, too?

No. She knew that instinctively. She didn't need a vast amount of experience to know that this wasn't everyday garden-variety attraction. This was something much hotter, something much more lethal. And she was willingly partaking in it, even knowing how potentially deadly it was.

She felt the hard evidence of his arousal against her thigh and she moved her hand down, pressed her palm against his firm length and squeezed him gently.

A short curse fell from his lips and he captured her mouth again, bucking his hips against her hand, his control obviously as shredded as her own. She squeezed him again and she reveled in the low growl that rumbled in his chest. Always before when she'd imagined being intimate with a man, she'd imagined it meant giving him power over her. But what she hadn't realized was just how much power *she* would have over him.

She moved her hand over the length of him, not quite able to believe just how thick and hard he felt. She hadn't realized that men could be so big. And yet, there was no fear with that revelation, only a sensual thrill that rushed through her, making her feel light-headed, breathless.

Dimly Alison registered the chirpy tones of a cell phone. Despite the interruption, her hands continued to roam over him, to explore him, the everyday sound not quite able to penetrate the fog of desire that was totally clouding her ability for rational thought.

"Che cavolo." Max swore and jumped away from her as though her touch burned him. He moved to the table where he'd placed his mobile phone and answered it in rough Italian, his chest rising and falling harshly with

his breathing, the aggressive jut of his arousal pushing visibly against the thin fabric of his shorts.

Alison's heart was pounding hard in her ears. Very slowly she started to come back to reality. She could feel the heat of the sun, the salt breeze...hear seagulls screaming at each other down on the beach. She had just about made love with a man outside. Correction: she had been in the process of making love with him even if they hadn't been quite to the point of actual intercourse. And any of the household staff members could have come out and seen them, caught them in the act.

She crossed her arms over her breasts, acutely aware of her nudity. Before it had seemed freeing, so nice not to have anything between her and Max. Now it just seemed embarrassing. She didn't feel sexy anymore. She just felt bare, exposed.

She fished her swimsuit top from beneath the chair and turned her back to Maximo, who was still engaged in his phone conversation, tying her top back on with shaking hands, her clumsy fingers taking twice as long to get herself covered again. She picked up the towel and knotted it fiercely at her breasts, craving all the cover she could get. She took advantage of Maximo's distraction and sneaked quietly back into the villa. She was not hanging around for another postmortem on an aborted make-out session.

More importantly, she wasn't going to risk being there if he wanted to pick up where they left off because, despite the healthy dose of humiliation she was suffering from, she wasn't certain she would be able to resist him.

CHAPTER NINE

MAXIMO got off the phone with the casino manager and cursed. Not because the problem at the casino hadn't been easy to solve—that issue had been handled in only a few minutes—but because of the unsatisfied desire that was still raging through him.

He couldn't believe he'd almost had sex with Alison outside by his pool, with all of the speed and finesse of a very horny schoolboy. He had never, ever lost control with a woman like that before. He had always taken time when romancing a woman. Selena had never wanted it any other way. She had always needed candles, a dimly lit room. He had always spent at least an hour arousing her body before he'd even considered taking things to their natural conclusion.

But with Alison there had been no romance, no candles. He'd been ready to plunge into her without a full five minutes of foreplay. And what foreplay there had been was clumsy, driven by an intense need, not any kind of skill or consideration. He didn't know this part of himself; the part that only Alison seemed to be able to bring out in him.

He was a man who prized his control. He always thought things through, always led first with his mind before jumping into action. And yet, Alison, his beautiful, bewitching fiancée, the woman who was pregnant with his child, robbed him of his ability to think coherently.

It was the unknown that was causing his body to respond this way. It had to be. He had desired her from the first moment he'd seen her and every night since then he'd dreamed of her, her smell, the touch of her soft hands, and the wet press of her lips over his body. There was no way the fantasy would live up to the reality, though, because it never did.

He needed to take her, to know once and for all what her desire for him would taste like, know what it felt like to be inside her, know what sounds she would make when he brought her to completion. And once the mystery was solved, the edge would be worn away. It had to be.

He couldn't wait anymore. He wanted her, and he knew for certain that she wanted him with the same ferocity, that she was just as hungry as he was. And he wasn't going to allow her to deny it any longer.

Alison scrubbed the chlorine from her skin and wished she could wash away the imprint from Maximo's touch half as easily. No such luck. Even with the scalding water from the shower coursing over her body, she could still feel the impression of where his hands had touched her, teased her, where his mouth had seared her. She shivered despite the heat and shut the water off.

During her shower she'd decided that she wasn't ashamed of what she'd done with Max. She was entitled to sexual pleasure if she wanted it. And that was a massive admission in and of itself. She *was* embarrassed, though, because she'd totally lost track of time and place, and anyone could have walked right up to them and she would have been much too lost in what they were doing to notice. Maybe Maximo, with his stable of previous lovers, was sophisticated enough to deal with something like that. He could probably turn it into a saucy anecdote and laugh about it with his sophisticated friends. Not her, though. She just didn't have the experience for that, which just went to prove how out of her league Max was.

Ashamed as she was to admit it, she'd looked him up when she'd been on the computer in the office, and she'd seen the kind of women he'd had in his life. Even before his marriage to the supernaturally lovely Selena, he'd had a very high taste level where his girlfriends were concerned. All of them were high-profile models, actresses, socialites, and all of them had been tall, thin and gorgeous. They weren't the kind of women to run and hide from sexual attraction. They were the kind of women who would pounce on it and tame it, take what they wanted and enjoy doing it.

She realized that she was clenching her fists so tightly that her knuckles were white and she slowly released them.

She'd never considered herself a coward. On the contrary, she'd always been prideful about how brave she thought she was. Brave and sensible. Sensible enough to protect herself, keep herself from coming unraveled and completely dependent on someone. Brave because she'd gone out and learned to stand on her own feet, made things happen for herself.

And she'd been the biggest, delusional idiot.

She'd been a coward. She hadn't dealt with anything. She'd completely walled off a portion of herself so she wouldn't have to deal with all of the complications that might result from a relationship.

She'd denied any sort of desire for companionship, totally squashed her sexuality, and all the while she'd been congratulating herself for being so strong. It wasn't strength that had led her to do those things, it was fear. And that was a bitter pill to swallow. She wasn't much better than her mother. It was just that her general wariness was preemptive rather than a response to something that had happened to her. The result, however, was much the same. Oh, she might not subject everyone to lengthy, vitriolic speeches about men and how you couldn't trust them, but she carried that belief inside of her. If she wasn't careful it was going to poison her.

It had to change. She was crippling herself. Ironic, since she'd always been so terrified that losing a lover would do that to her, and she'd done it to herself.

She wasn't ready to rush headlong into falling in love, but maybe…

Maybe she could fulfill her desire for Max. Those women in the magazines, the women who had dated Max before his marriage, knew that sex wasn't love. Knew it and reveled in it. They didn't suppress that part of themselves, not like she had done for so long.

She exited the bathroom and went into her connecting bedroom, sinking onto the bed, holding her towel tightly around her naked body. She was such a hopeless case for Max that even the rough abrasion of the terry cloth over her bare skin was turning her on.

It had always been easy to act aloof around men. She hadn't really wanted any of them. There had been a few times when she'd really liked someone, felt a kind of bitter melancholy over not pursuing anything serious with them. But this, what she felt for Max, was a consuming hunger that was with her all the time. A spark that smoldered in her belly, ready to burst into flame when Max so much as looked at her.

The fact that they were engaged to be married, that they were having a baby together, was the biggest thing holding her back. If she could just indulge in a fling with him, one night of passion maybe, just so she could experience it, so she could exorcise this thing that had flared so strongly between them, then she would more than happily jump into bed with him.

But the fact remained that they were engaged, and they were having a baby. And those were very, very permanent ties.

But her body was still screaming for the release she knew only Maximo would be able to give. She just didn't know if she could fight it anymore. Or if she even wanted to...

She stood from the bed and crossed to the massive closet on the other side of the room. It was packed full of designer clothing, all chosen by a personal shopper without Alison present, since the paparazzi had made shopping an impossibility. Every last article was beautiful, and a lot more revealing than anything she would have chosen for herself.

Sliding her hands over the fabrics she stopped at a midnight-blue silk dress with a low halter neckline and a floaty, knee-skimming hem. It was an extremely sexy dress, one she'd privately vowed never to wear as she'd hung it up in the closet. But now...now it seemed perfect.

She pulled it out quickly before any doubts or fears could invade and talk her out of it. She hadn't known what she was planning until that moment, but, even though she might think she was stupid in the morning, she was committed. She was going to seduce Prince Maximo Rossi.

The glow of the candlelight bathed Alison's skin in golden warmth. And there was a lot of bare skin on display. Her barely-there midnight-blue satin gown clung to her every curve and showed off the swell of her breasts, her lovely shoulders, her perfect legs. And when Maximo had pulled her chair out for her and she'd turned to look before sitting, he'd been unable to tear his gaze away from her perfect, rounded derriere.

Dinner had been an exercise in torture. She had savored every bite that she'd put in her mouth, making sensual, delighted noises and darting her slick pink tongue out to catch any flavor that had lingered on her lips. He wanted her. More than he could remember wanting any other woman in his entire life. And she wanted him, too. Yet something was stopping her from taking the final step.

She certainly didn't kiss like an inexperienced woman; she kissed like a woman with highly developed passions, a woman who knew what she wanted, knew what her lover would want. And yet she seemed to take sex very seriously. Or at least the prospect of heartbreak. But Maximo knew from experience that there were some women who simply couldn't divorce sex from love. Perhaps the idea of sleeping with a man simply because she desired him was something she was having trouble coming to terms with. But then, she was the one who claimed she hadn't been interested in love and relationships, and he couldn't imagine that she'd been planning on living a celibate existence. She was far too sexy, far too sexual, for that.

He nearly groaned out loud when she lifted her dessert spoon to her lips and licked the last remnant of chocolate from the silver surface, her pink tongue so tempting, so provocative that he could have almost found his release just watching her work the spoon in that slow, sensual way. It was way too easy to imagine that tongue on his bare skin.

"What's your stance on love?" she asked, lowering the spoon and setting it on the table.

"I've been in love. I don't believe I'll ever love anyone besides my...Selena. I don't want to love anyone else." Not because he was so attached to her memory, but because nothing about it had been worth the pain he'd endured. He'd lost Selena several times over. In the end, an impenetrable wall had gone up between them, and he hadn't been able to reach her anymore. He hadn't been able to protect her, from her grief, from death. He had no desire to ever go through that kind of hell again.

"So you don't think you're going to meet someone else?" she asked, her copper eyes deadly serious.

"I'm marrying you. You're the only 'someone else' there's going to be."

"But if you *did* want someone else would you tell me?"

"I won't."

"But if you did," she persisted, "would you tell me? I don't want to be played for a fool, Max, and I really don't want to be cheated on."

"I would tell you. You have my word that, if we were to enter into a physical relationship, I would never even entertain the thought of being unfaithful to you."

"I've been thinking a lot about what happened by the pool," she said slowly.

Tension knotted his muscles and the fire in his stomach was starting to rage out of control.

She raised her eyes to meet his and he was struck by how dark they'd gotten. She was aroused. He was definitely familiar with the signs, and his own body was more than ready to take hers up on its blatant offer.

"I want to make love," she said, her voice steady. If he hadn't spotted the slight tremor in her delicate hands he would have never known she was nervous.

"You wanted to make love by the pool. You wanted to make love that day in your room. In fact, you wanted to make love that first day in Turan, but you pulled back every time."

"I know. But I've had a lot of time to think about it." She rose from her chair, moved to stand in front of him, then leaned in and he was transfixed by her beauty, by the clear, pale skin of her flawless face, by the creamy swells of her breasts spilling over the skimpy neckline of her dress. Splaying her hands over his chest she explored him, ran her fingertips over his muscles. He sucked in a sharp breath, his body so close to the edge he was in danger of going right over.

"I want you," she said softly, leaning in and pressing her lips against his. He let her control the kiss, let her explore his mouth slowly, her tongue moving tentatively over the seam of his lips. When they separated she was panting, and he realized he was, too. "I trust you. I'm certain of that now."

"And you needed to trust me?" he asked, running his fingers through her silken, strawberry hair, reveling in her softness, her femininity.

"Yes. The attraction between us is so strong... I've never felt this way before and it scared me. It still scares me. But now I know you aren't going to use it against me."

"I'm not going to fall in love with you, either," he said roughly, hating himself for needing to be honest, especially if it might make her change her mind again.

"I know. I don't want to fall in love with you, either. But I do want your respect. I wanted to make sure you weren't just going to play with me, and no one wants to get cheated on, or abandoned."

He cupped her chin. "I swear to you that I will never leave you. And I will never humiliate you, or disrespect you, by taking another woman into our bed."

"I believe you."

She sank onto his lap and twined her arms around his neck, threading her fingers through his hair. "My whole body aches for you," she said, meeting his eyes.

"Mine, too," he said, taking her hand and placing it over his erection, showing her how much he wanted her. She moved her hand over his length, her expression so full of awe that he couldn't help but take stupid masculine pride in it.

"I think we should take this upstairs."

"The table looks fine to me," he growled, not knowing where this feral, uncivilized desire came from, not knowing what he could do to control it. She revealed something inside of him he hadn't known existed. And he didn't want to tame it; he wanted to unleash it.

"One of the staff could come in," she said breathlessly.

He pressed a kiss to the elegant line of her neck. "Now *that* we don't want. This is definitely a two-person party." He nuzzled the tender spot just beneath her earlobe and reveled in the feminine sigh of pleasure she rewarded him with. She was so eager, so responsive, and he loved it.

Alison slid from his lap, her heart pounding wildly. She'd done it. She'd committed to doing this. And she wasn't sorry for it at all. She wanted him. Needed him in a way that shocked and terrified her. She didn't know this wild, wanton version of herself. She felt as if she could do anything with him, could let him do anything to her. She trusted him with her body, wholly and completely, and the prospect of doing that only excited her.

As he stood from the chair and took her hand, his eyes burning with erotic intent, she wished, for the first time in her life, that she'd had sex with someone at some point, just so she wasn't going into this blind. Maximo had lots of experience—she'd seen the evidence of that thanks to the photos of the parade of women he'd dated in his early twenties, and he'd been married for seven years. She didn't even have a lot of kissing experience to recommend her.

On the other hand, he would make it good for her. He would know what he was doing. At her age, after having received exams from gynecologists and OBs and having the artificial insemination done she doubted there would be much of a barrier for him to deal with, if there was one at all. And that, coupled with all of his experience, would probably lessen any discomfort she might feel. And, with any luck, he might not notice.

She nearly laughed at that thought. Of course he would notice her inexperience. There was no way she was going to be able to fake some kind of blasé sophistication. Not when his touch just about melted her.

But his hand felt so good, so warm encircling hers that it was hard to care too much. He held on to her as he led her up the stairs, took her to his bedroom. There was no turning back now. And she didn't want to.

"Alison." He closed the door behind them and pulled her to him, bringing her up hard against his masculine chest. She spread her hands over his pecs, running them down his flat stomach, feeling the ridges of his ab muscles through his shirt. She'd never explored a man's body like this before, never took the time to appreciate all of the delicious differences between men and women.

He kissed her again, his mouth hard on hers, and she parted her lips willingly, meeting each thrust of his tongue with her own. He slid his hands over the silken material of her dress, over the curve of her buttocks and down her thighs. He gripped the hem of the skirt and began to pull it up slowly, bunching the slippery fabric in his hands until he had it drawn up to her waist. He moved one hand down over her rear end again and he groaned when his hand touched bare skin. His obvious appreciation thrilled her, and combined with his touch sent a shock wave of need rocketing through her.

He released her dress, keeping his hands beneath the fabric. He gripped the sides of her thong panties and dragged them down, kneeling before her on the floor as he removed them. She lifted one foot to step out of her underwear and wobbled slightly, but he steadied her by holding tightly to her hips.

He leaned in, his breath hot against the silk fabric as his mouth hovered over her slightly rounded stomach. "So beautiful." He laid his palm flat against her belly, the expression on his face so reverent, so awed, that it made her throat tighten with emotion. He leaned in and kissed her there, and she felt as if her knees would have buckled if she hadn't been held firmly in his strong grip.

Standing again he kissed her lips, her neck, her collarbone. She wasn't even aware that they'd been moving until the back of her knees came into contact with the edge of the bed. He lowered her slowly to the soft surface, his hard length brushing her hip as he joined her on the mattress.

"You're so beautiful," he said, reaching around and untying the flimsy knot that held the halter top of her dress in place. He pushed the fabric aside and revealed her breasts.

He'd seen her before, out at the pool, and already knowing that he liked the way she looked bolstered her confidence. He cupped her breasts, teased the aroused tips. She tilted her head back onto the pillow and just enjoyed his touch, relished the knot of arousal that was tightening in her pelvis. She could just stay like this forever, with him caressing her, lavishing attention on her body.

She let out a moan of disappointment when he abandoned her breasts, his hands skimming over her curves, still clothed in the thin silk of the dress. He pushed the fabric up again and exposed her naked body to his gaze. She hadn't been embarrassed for him to see her breasts, but having him so close to a part of her only her doctor had ever seen had her blushing hotly.

"Max." She was about to ask him to turn the bedroom light off, but the warm press of his lips on her thigh stalled the words. And when he parted her legs and ran his tongue along her inner thigh she lost her command of the English language entirely.

She fought to regain some control, some kind of command over her senses. Impossible when she felt as if all of the feeling inside her were too big to be contained by her skin, when she was certain she might shatter into a million pieces. A needy moan escaped her lips and her body trembled as he moved closer to the place where she was wet and aching for him. She didn't have control anymore; she felt as if she might fall from the earth and float away, as if there was nothing holding her to the bed.

She gripped the sheets, tried to focus, tried to find some shred of sanity, because this, what he was doing to her, making her feel, was terrifying. She couldn't temper it, couldn't lead it, or plan it. But she felt her hold slipping, felt herself ready to plunge over the edge, and if that happened she was afraid she would go on falling forever.

"Let go, Alison," he growled, pressing a hot kiss just above her feminine mound. "I want to make you lose control."

She shook her head, even though she knew he couldn't see. "No."

"Yes. I want you to stop thinking. I want you to feel." He ran his tongue over her flesh, flicked it over the sensitive bundle of nerves and continued down, dipping inside of her. Her hips came off the bed and he gripped them tight, holding her to him, not letting her escape. "I want you to come for me."

He continued his intimate assault, pleasuring her with his lips, his tongue, as he whispered exciting, erotic words. He pushed one finger into her tight passage and moved it in rhythm with his tongue.

A moan rose in her throat and she couldn't do anything to stop the needy sound from escaping.

"That's right, Alison," he whispered. "Let go. You can let go. I've got you."

Her mind blanked, all thoughts of control, all of her worries, falling away. And she really could only feel.

She felt as if she was reaching for something, something beautiful that shimmered before her, just out of reach. She moved against him, edging toward the nameless need that had taken over her whole being. And finally she touched it.

Her mouth opened on a soundless cry and she arched up as her orgasm washed over her. Her internal muscles pulsed around his finger in waves of endless pleasure that seemed to go on and on.

When it was over she was self-conscious again, where before she'd been so lost in her pleasure that she hadn't really stopped to realize that she should be embarrassed about what he was doing to her.

"Don't," he said, deftly undoing the buttons on his shirt.

"Don't?"

"Don't be embarrassed." He shrugged the shirt off then removed his pants and underwear in one fluid movement.

She could only stare, openmouthed at the vision of masculine perfection he'd unveiled. That muscular chest was bare for her again and she ached to touch him, to taste him. And then her gaze dropped to his erection, thick and fully aroused, and she forgot her embarrassment. How could she be embarrassed when she could see for herself how much he'd enjoyed doing that for her? When she could see how much he wanted her still? Men couldn't fake a reaction like that, and she couldn't help but feel an immense amount of feminine pride over his obvious desire for her.

He stood up from the bed and moved over to the dresser where there were several pillar candles set out. She took the opportunity to admire his tight male butt, her arousal almost unbearable despite the orgasm she'd just had. He grabbed a lighter from the top drawer and picked up one of the candles.

"What are you doing?" she asked, craving his skin against hers, craving his touch, his kiss.

"Setting the mood," he said, the corner of his mouth lifting into a smile.

"There's no time for that," she said, shimmying out of her dress. "I need you. Now."

A feral growl rose up in his throat and he crossed to the bed in three quick strides. Then he was covering her, gently pressing her legs apart with his hair-roughened thigh. She kissed him, moved against him, rubbed her breasts against his chest. She loved being naked with him, skin to skin, their bodies twined together. It was the most amazing feeling in the world. She was completely out of control, and yet she was safe. With him she was safe. No matter what. She knew it instinctively, even if she didn't know why.

He rubbed his shaft against her slick opening. She was so wet, so ready for him after her first mind-numbing orgasm that she didn't feel any pain when he started to ease into her. She opened her eyes and looked at him. His face was tense, the tendons in his neck strained with the concentration it took for him to go slow.

She looped her calf over his and urged him on. In one quick motion he thrust inside of her to the hilt. She felt too full, the stretching sensation uncomfortable, but not painful. She shifted, trying to ease some of the pressure.

He pulled away and then pushed into her again and she felt her body adjusting, felt her muscles expanding to accommodate him. And when he thrust into her for a third time all of the discomfort was gone. She moaned with pleasure, the sweet feeling of impending orgasm beginning to coil in her pelvis again.

"Oh, Max," she breathed, arching against him, meeting each of his thrusts.

He buried his face in her neck, his movements wild, hard. Wonderful. Neither of them were quiet, both of them whispering words of encouragement, letting the other one know how good everything was. And when she felt ready to go over the edge again she jumped willingly.

If her first orgasm was a release, this one was an explosion of feeling. She couldn't stop the hoarse cry that escaped her lips as she lost herself in her own pleasure wholly and completely. He thrust hard into her one last time and pressed a hot kiss to her lips as he came.

He held her until their raging heartbeats calmed, their bodies still joined.

"I didn't know," she said, dazed. "I didn't know that losing control could be so...empowering."

His lips twitched against her neck. "Was it?"

"Yes. I didn't know it could be like that."

"Was it your first orgasm?" he asked, surprise lacing his voice.

She hadn't planned on telling him, but after that she knew there was no place for lying or even sidestepping the truth. "Yes. My first everything."

Max was stunned by that admission. She'd been tight, so tight it had been a battle not to come the moment he'd thrust into her, but he'd been too lost in his own pleasure to question it.

"And why is that, Alison? You're a beautiful woman. A sensual woman. There wouldn't have been anything wrong with you exploring that."

"Control," she said softly. "I never wanted to give

anyone the power to hurt me. So I avoided relationships. Avoided sex."

"What made you change your mind?"

She shifted in his arms and turned to face him, her copper eyes still cloudy with the aftereffects of her orgasm. Something that felt a lot like pride swelled in his chest. "You're the first man that I wanted to be with. Before I… It scared me to think of being with someone like this. Being naked, not just physically, but in every way. But I trust you. I trust that you won't hurt me," she said simply.

He felt as if a steel band was clamping down hard on his heart. She'd been a virgin. She'd trusted him where she hadn't trusted any man before. And what could he offer her but a cold, clinical relationship, void of any kind of sentimental emotion. She deserved more than that. But he just didn't have it in him.

"I can't give you love. I can't give you the promises a woman should expect after her first time."

"I don't need any more promises. And we're already engaged," she said pointedly. "And what we have is better than love. We have honesty. We have a common bond. "

She was right. Love was no guarantee of anything, and they'd both seen that firsthand in life. He only hoped she wouldn't have a change of heart. Virgins tended to take sex very seriously, which was why he'd always avoided them.

She slid her silky smooth thigh over his and her damp core brushed against his penis. He felt himself getting hard all over again. He wanted her. Already. Wanted her so badly his muscles were knotting with tension as he tried to hold himself back. But she'd been a virgin less than a half hour ago and he wasn't going to hurt her by trying to find his own satisfaction again so soon.

She moaned and moved against him, her lips curved into a dreamy smile.

"Alison," he bit out. "Be careful."

"Why?" she asked, a full-blown smile spreading over her face. He found himself smiling back.

"Because you're new at this and I don't want to hurt you."

"You didn't hurt me at all the first time."

"But I can't promise I'll behave myself this time. It's been a very long time for me."

Her eyes widened. "It has?"

"I haven't been with a woman since before Selena died."

The stricken look on her face made his gut tighten. "Was this…? I mean…you don't feel guilty, you don't feel like…?"

"Do I feel like I betrayed my wife?"

She nodded. "Yes."

"No. It wasn't about that. There was no woman that I wanted to be with. I'd dated casually and I had put that behind me. I was married for seven years and I still wanted the stability it offered. Yet I didn't want to get married again, either. That didn't leave me with a lot of options."

"And then you got stuck with me," she said, her smile sad now.

He shifted to his side and propped himself up on his elbow. "I didn't want to get married again because my marriage was such a disaster in the end," he said, finally saying what he'd never before voiced out loud. "Selena and I no longer shared a bed, or much of anything else. There was no way for me to reach her anymore, and I stopped trying. Then she was killed in the car accident while I was away on business. I wasn't even there to hold her hand while she died. It was my job to protect her, and I didn't."

"Oh, Max." She buried her face in his chest as he cupped the back of her head, stroking her hair. "You couldn't have protected her from that."

"I should have been there for her. At the very least I could have done that. I could have tried harder to make her happy."

"If she wouldn't talk to you there was nothing you could do to make her. She chose not to share with you."

"One person cannot bear all the blame when a marriage dissolves. She was fragile, and life forced her to endure things that would have wounded a much stronger person. I had a duty to my wife that I didn't fulfill."

Her expression turned fierce, a golden spark lighting her eyes. She put her hand on his cheek. "We have a duty to each other, Max. To make this work. I promise I'll never close up like that on you. I won't freeze you out. We'll always talk."

He kissed her softly on the corner of her lips, then more firmly as he rolled her underneath him. The feeling that swelled in his chest when she made that promise was far too much, far too intense. It shouldn't matter. His relationship with Alison was about passion, and their baby. Nothing more. Emotions simply didn't enter the equation.

But that simple vow kept pounding through him as he made love to her, fueled his desire for her. And when she cried out his name during her orgasm it pulled feelings from his hardened heart that he'd no longer imagined himself capable of.

CHAPTER TEN

"YOUR belly is starting to show." Maximo put his arms around Alison from behind and caressed her bare midsection. She had been examining herself in the mirror in the master suite, sucking in her expanding stomach.

She swatted at his hand. "Just what every woman wants to hear!"

"It's sexy." He nuzzled her neck and kissed the hollow just beneath her ear. "You must know how sexy I think you are."

She knew. Maximo had spent all night showing her just how sexy he thought she was. It had been a revelation. She'd discovered a whole, huge part of herself she hadn't even known existed. A part of herself she'd spent far too long suppressing. She'd given her control over to Maximo for a while, and it had been freeing in a way she'd never imagined it could be. And now that they were out of bed she had her control back, and her heart was still intact. She could do this. She could maintain her independence and have a relationship with him. She wasn't going to love him, or need him in any way beyond the physical.

"The feeling is definitely mutual." She turned and wound her arms around his neck and traced his squared jaw with her fingertip. A tidal wave of possessiveness crashed over her. He was so very handsome. And he was hers. "I'm going to hold you to that forsaking all others bit in the marriage vows."

"I will keep my vows, Alison. Why take them otherwise?"

"Millions of people make the same vows all the time. It doesn't guarantee the promise will be kept."

"It may surprise you to know that I'm familiar with the issues people face in marriage."

She winced. "Sorry, but I told you I'd talk to you if I had issues. I just wanted to let you know I was feeling possessive."

He offered her a tight smile. "I appreciate that. Maybe if Selena had talked to me we wouldn't have grown so far apart." He moved away from her and walked to the closet, pulling out a T-shirt and shrugging it over his head. "Of course, even saving our marriage wouldn't have changed anything in the end."

"You couldn't have saved her if you were there, Max. It was an accident. It wouldn't have changed anything. You did what you could in your marriage. It isn't your fault that she wouldn't talk to you."

He shook his head. "She depended on me. I should have tried harder. Instead I got frustrated. I worked more. I should warn you that I'm not a very good husband. I'm not good at reading emotions. I travel a lot. I get absorbed with my business."

She put her hand on his arm. "You're a good man, Maximo. You're going to be a good husband, and a wonderful father. In my line of work I've dissolved more marriages than I care to think about, and then, at the Children's Advocacy Center I saw a lot of men who were lousy husbands *and* fathers. You're not like them."

"You say that, Alison, and I think you even mean it,

but you've only known me for three weeks. Selena had seven years to grow disenchanted with me."

"I think all marriages can lose their luster if you let them," she said firmly. "But we're getting married for a reason."

"The baby." He put his hands over her rounded belly and rested her palm over them.

"Yes. That reason is never going to go away. We'll always have our child in common."

"And that's enough for you?"

She gave him a level stare, her eyes never wavering from his. "It has to be, doesn't it?"

He nodded firmly. Decidedly. "Yes."

"Then it is. We're going to make this work for our child. We're going to make a family. That's all that matters. When I make my vows I'll keep them."

Maximo ignored the tightening sensation in his chest. Ignored the voice in his head berating him for allowing this woman to settle for so much less than she deserved. "Then you would be in the minority."

She shrugged one delicate shoulder. "I'm used to that by now. I was a twenty-eight-year-old virgin until last night, remember?" She gave him a sly grin.

"How could I forget?"

"I don't know. Perhaps you need your memory refreshed." And then she was in his arms, stroking his back with her hands and practically purring.

This was enough. Enough for both of them. He would do everything in his power to make it enough.

"Alison?" He cupped her bare hip bone with his hands and did wicked things to the indent that led from there to her femininity.

"Hmm?" she half moaned.

"I want to show you something."

"You already did that—" she snuggled into him "—twice," she added playfully.

"Not that."

She sighed. "I suppose we have to get out of bed at some point."

"It is advised."

They had spent most of the morning in bed and it was late afternoon now. Alison was languid, satisfied in a way, but far from sated. There would never be a time when she wouldn't crave the way Max made her feel. When he kissed her, caressed her, entered her, she felt complete.

"All right, but you have to feed the baby and me first."

"I wouldn't dream of being neglectful."

He made good on his promise and fed her lunch—a creamy pasta dish that made her very happy. Now that her morning sickness had passed she found she was loving food again, more than usual even. After she was finished, Max took her hand and led her out of the villa and into the courtyard.

"Why do I get the feeling I'm being led astray?" she asked, the wicked grin on his face making her stomach flutter.

"I have no idea. I promise you my intentions are entirely pure."

"Somehow, I very much doubt that there's anything pure in your mind except for purely naughty thoughts."

He laughed and the sound made her heart jump in her chest. "No. You'll see."

There was a small whitewashed building that rested on an outcrop of rock that overlooked the beach below.

It seemed as though it was nearly carved into the cliff, a part of nature. It had obviously been built years earlier than the villa, the mature, creeping vines that covered the side attesting to that fact.

"This is lovely," she said.

"It's one of the reasons I picked this location to build the villa. The natural lighting inside the studio is amazing." He took a key out of his jeans pocket and put it into the ancient keyhole.

Alison was surprised by the renovation that had been done to the inside, which was light and airy, modern.

"There's a bedroom and bathroom through there." He pointed through the galley-style kitchenette and to a door that stood closed. There was sparse furniture in the main room, a couch, an easel and paintings lining the walls, all beautifully, photo-realistically done.

"Max...you did these, didn't you?" She could see it in each brushstroke, so controlled, so carefully placed. Maximo captured the essence of what he painted, kept the life that possessed his subject in the real world and translated it to the canvas. It didn't possess the freedom of expression, the broad, abstract work of a modern artist, but it wouldn't have been Max if it had.

"Yes."

"Does anyone know?"

He shook his dark head and came to stand close behind her. "It's something I've dabbled in over the years, but never devoted much time to."

"That's a crime! Max, these are beautiful!" She moved up close to a landscape portrait of the waves crashing on the rocks. It was the view out the window it was placed next to, and it rivaled the real thing. The water was alive and the wind was a living thing, too, moving the grass in a sea of green ripples.

"It isn't what's popular. I invest in art. I wouldn't invest in these. They're the kind of pictures that hang in a doctor's office."

"They're amazing." She reached a hand out, letting it hover over the exquisite work. "Do you only do landscapes?"

"So far. As I said, I haven't had much time to devote to it."

"Selena never saw them?" she asked gently, watching his eyes darken with stormy emotion.

"No." Just no. No explanation. She didn't need one. Selena had not loved the man standing before her. She may have loved the idea of him. The powerful, handsome prince with the gorgeous body and amazing bedroom skills. But she hadn't loved *him*. He was so much more than what he chose to show the world. And she had been blessed with a window into his heart.

"I'm honored that you showed me."

He turned to her. "I want to paint you."

"Me?"

He laughed. "Yes. I have never done a portrait. I haven't been inspired to. But I want to paint you."

This was more intimate for him, she realized, than making love. He was sharing something with her that he had not shared with any other woman, any other person, period. That did something to her. It made the most bittersweet pain twist her heart, made her stomach tighten with longing.

"I would like that."

He put an arm around her and took her chin in his hand, tilting her face up so that their eyes met. "I want to paint all of you."

Realization of what that meant dawned slowly. "I can't do that!" she protested, her cheeks heating at the idea of getting naked in such bright daylight and lying exposed for hours on end.

"I'm realizing that you're the kind of woman who can do anything she decides to do, and heaven help the man who stands in your way. But I wouldn't want you to be uncomfortable."

She bit her lip. Still unsure.

"Have I ever done anything to hurt you? Disrespect you?" he asked gently. She shook her head. "And I never will."

She nodded slowly. And she realized that in this moment he would be as bare as she was. Because this was a part of himself he'd never shared before. And he was exposing it to her, revealing himself. And she wanted to do the same.

"I trust you." She pushed the top button of her blouse through the loop and separated the fabric that concealed her body from him. Then the next one. And the next. And on to every other piece of clothing until she was standing bare in front of him. She fought the urge to cover up. It was different during lovemaking. He was so busy kissing and touching her, he wasn't simply *staring* at her. And she was never fully conscious enough to be embarrassed of her body during sex. But now she was acutely aware of the fact that her stomach was no longer flat and that her breasts had only grown more voluptuous, along with her hips. And he wanted to capture it eternally on canvas.

She felt her whole body flush. "I'm not beautiful like…"

"Don't say you're not beautiful. And don't ever compare yourself to other women. You're *my* woman. And I happen to find you exquisitely beautiful."

She thrilled at the raw, masculine possession that

laced his voice. She should find him arrogant, or at least sexist. She couldn't.

Maximo could barely keep his desire leashed. She was so enchanting, pale and vulnerable, in the midafternoon sunlight that filtered in through the picture window, when she was normally so strong, wearing her independence like armor. The artist in him longed to paint her; the man in him simply wanted to make love to her until neither of them could think or move.

He settled for picking up a sketch pad and a clutch pencil. "Sit on the couch."

She backed away from him and lowered herself onto the chaise-style couch, reclining. She rested her head on the gentle slope of the armrest and put one arm high above her head, raising her plump breasts.

He wanted to capture everything, every curve, every line. The dent in her sweet lips, the pout in her nipples, the perfect V at the juncture of her thighs... Mostly he wanted the molten fire in her golden eyes to translate to the canvas.

Her body, tense at first, began to relax as he began to sketch. His hand moved fluidly, shaping her curves, shading the dips and hollows of her body. He drew the fullness of her breasts and ached to cup them. She arched her back as though she knew what portion of her body he was stroking with the pencil, as though she knew and wanted his touch as badly as he wanted to touch her. His body hardened painfully.

He added her small waist, her soft belly, the small bump where their baby sat. He moved lower and she gasped, her pulse pounding at the base of her neck. She moaned softly as he traced the outline of her sex on the paper. She pressed her legs together and slid her foot up her smooth thigh as he continued his study of her, as he continued to capture her forever.

A throaty growl escaped her throat. "Max." It was a plea, and it was one she didn't need to make twice.

He placed his notebook on the table and joined her on the chaise. Her hands were on him, pulling his shirt over his head, fumbling with the closure of his pants.

"What is it that you do to me?" he growled, moving his hand over her curves, tracing them as he had just done with a pencil. This was much more satisfying; flesh on flesh instead of lead on paper.

He kissed her neck, nibbling the tender flesh of her throat. "I hope it's the same thing that you do to me."

"Without a doubt it is." He shoved his jeans down along with his underwear, and relished the sensation of her hot skin against his. "I think this is going to be fast."

She gripped his buttocks with her hands and looked him in the eye. "Good. I don't think I could handle slow."

He positioned himself and sank into her tight, wet heat. He had to grit his teeth to keep from exploding then and there. It took all of his strength to stay still, to keep it from ending without her reaching satisfaction, too.

He had never felt this, this overwhelming desperation to claim a woman, to make her his, to lose himself inside of her body. Before Alison it had been years since he'd been with a woman. But this was about much more than prolonged, willful abstinence. This was something more…something unfamiliar, something that seemed to have taken on a life of its own.

His self-control snapped. He moved uncontrollably, pounding into her. She pulled her knees back so he could thrust harder, deeper. The only sound was their labored breathing and the slap of flesh meeting flesh. There was nothing gentle about their coming together. It was fire and brimstone, passion and torture. She cried his name out as she came and he followed, pumping into her, releasing everything he had into her body.

She kissed his neck, a smile curving her lips. "You're amazing, do you know that?"

He had no idea what he'd done to earn the trust he heard in her voice, and he wasn't sure he wanted it. Wasn't sure that he could fulfill all of the hopes that he saw shimmering in the depths of her beautiful eyes.

They lay in silence for a long time and he was content to simply move his hands over her curves. A small sigh escaped her lips and he wanted to understand it. And he suddenly realized he wanted to know more than that. He wanted to know everything about her, who she was and why. He couldn't recall ever feeling that need before, not concerning anyone.

"Tell me about your sister," he said, not sure why it suddenly seemed important to know.

"She was my best friend." Alison burrowed against him. "She never let having Cystic Fibrosis affect who she was. She was always smiling, even when she was sick. Kimberly was the glue for our family. When she was gone everything fell apart. My parents fell apart."

"How old were you?"

"I was twelve when she died."

"They didn't have any right to fall apart, not when you needed them," he said.

"No argument from me. But my dad just couldn't stay anymore. I don't think he could walk in the house, or look at us without remembering. And that just left Mom and me."

"And she didn't look after you, either?"

"She had enough trouble dealing with her own issues. She depended on my father. She needed him for everything. Without him, she had no security and she just… It never pays to lean on someone so much because one day they might just be gone. But then, you know all about that."

"I do," he said slowly. "But I didn't depend on Selena. She depended on me. I wasn't there for her, and because of that she had to live the last month of her life completely unhappy."

"That's not fair, Max. If you could have done something to fix Selena then I could have fixed my parents."

He let silence stretch between them. There was no point debating with her. She had been a child, while he had been an adult man, Selena's husband. And she'd been hurting, spiraling into depression, and he hadn't even realized it. Not truly. She'd said she hadn't wanted to talk, and at that point he'd been so tired of trying that he'd simply accepted it.

Alison ran her soft hand over his abs, and his stomach tightened, his whole body aching, ready for her again. If it was only his body that was affected it wouldn't be so dangerous, but his chest felt too full when he looked at her, when he touched her. It was too much. It wasn't what this was supposed to be about.

He thought about what his father had said. About the paternity test. Alison had even commented that if they'd made a mix-up at the lab in the first place, it was possible they had made a mistake and that he wasn't the father.

If that were true she would be free to go back home. They wouldn't even have to get married.

He'd imagined that thought might make him feel

free, that the prospect of escaping marriage might make the tightness in his chest lessen. Instead it sent an intense pain shooting through him, targeting his heart. It shouldn't hurt like that to think of her leaving.

"We should have a paternity test done," he said firmly. "Just in case. Like you said, they made one mistake, they might have made more."

Her sweet little body that had been so soft and pliant against him went rigid in his embrace. "If you think it's necessary."

"It would be responsible."

She paused for a long moment and he could feel her drawing in short, shallow breaths. "Is there a way to do it without risk to the baby?"

"I'll find out."

"Okay." She didn't move away from him, but she wasn't melted into him anymore, either.

"We're going home tomorrow," he said, tightening his hold on her and tracing circles over the bare skin of her arm. "I need to get back and deal with some issues with one of the larger casinos."

"Okay." The note of sadness in her voice hit him like a punch in the gut. He'd upset her. He'd hurt her.

"You're disappointed?"

He felt the shrug of her slight shoulders. "This has been wonderful. But it's kind of like a fantasy. Tomorrow we're going back to reality."

"You prefer the fantasy?"

"Well, it was a wonderful fantasy."

He looked around his studio, the place he'd never shown another living soul. "Yes, it was."

After their return to Turan, Maximo's work schedule kept him away from the *castillo* during the day. He was hands-on with his work, something she greatly respected, but, despite the fact that she was keeping busy by helping to establish a Turani branch of the Cystic Fibrosis Foundation, she missed him horribly while she rattled around the huge castle.

Isabella was a cheerful, fun presence in her life, but she was busy studying her college tele-courses, and in her spare time her parents were practically keeping her under lock and key since their shopping escapade.

But even though Maximo was gone during the day, the nights were theirs. That part of the fantasy, at least, was still intact. Her passion for him hadn't ebbed, and it didn't seem as if his had for her. It was a strange thing, going from giving sex no more than the random, cursory thought, to having it be so much a part of her. Her long-denied sexuality was definitely no longer repressed, and honestly, she was happy about that. She felt more like a whole person, a whole woman, rather than someone who had a host of private hang-ups and issues that were so wound up around her she had to find an alternative way to function.

She spent every night in Max's bed, in his arms. But she kept her own room, kept her clothes hanging in the closet there, kept her makeup case in the bathroom that adjoined it, because she just wasn't ready to have everything in her life melded together with Max's. It would be too much like depending on him, and the very thought of that made her chest feel tight with panic. The wedding was in two weeks and she expected him to want her to move into his room fully after that, but until then she was retaining some sort of independence.

He was already getting under her skin, and if she wasn't careful he was going to get into her heart, too.

She sighed and checked the time on her cell phone.

Max's personal physician, Dr. Sexy, was due any minute to draw her blood for the noninvasive paternity test. And Max wasn't there. Alison clutched her orange juice, her sugar boost and last line of defense against passing out when the doctor drew the blood. She was trying not to be emotional about Max's absence, but she was pregnant and more than a little hormonal so she was finding it difficult to keep tears from welling up.

When Max had asked for the paternity test her heart had felt as if it was splintering. It had become easy to forget that they didn't have a real relationship. That their baby had been conceived in a lab. His demand for the test had been a stark reminder.

The worst thing was that she wasn't certain which result Max was hoping for.

When the beautiful doctor arrived it only took a few minutes to collect her blood sample. "All done. And we have the buccal swab from Prince Rossi already, so there really isn't anything more we need. This is a relatively new way to test paternity," she said. "If there isn't sufficient fetal DNA in your blood stream we won't get a result. But if there is then the results are just as accurate as CVS or amniocentesis."

Alison nodded, feeling the first stab of anxiety over what the test results might be.

The other woman offered her a sly smile. "Well, good luck. I know if it were me I would really be hoping it was the prince's baby. He's incredibly handsome, and of course he's wealthy enough to take care of you."

Alison shook her head. "It…it isn't like that."

She was treated to a raised eyebrow. "I only know of one reason to test for paternity. But then, what do I know? I'm just a doctor."

Alison's hand itched to do something very out of

character and very hormonal and slap the smug smile right off the other woman's face. But just a few moments later she'd collected all of her things, and with a promise to call within the next twenty-four hours she left Alison by herself again.

She collapsed into Max's plush office chair and tried to fight the tears that were seriously threatening to spill over. She'd wanted him here for this, needed him, despite her best efforts not to. Not even keeping her clothes confined to their own closet had been able to save her from it.

Cradling her face in her hands, she rested her elbows on his desk and let herself wallow in her pain. It wouldn't hurt to just give in for a while. A tear slid down her cheek and she wiped it away, annoyed at herself for crying. If she'd never found out about Max she would have done all of her testing alone, so it was just stupid to cry because he'd missed the test. But he was the one who'd wanted it, and then he hadn't even bothered to show up for it.

She lifted her head when the door to the office opened. Her pulse jumped when Maximo walked in. Even when she was mad at him he still had the most powerful effect on her body. On her heart.

"You missed the test," she said, swiping at the remaining moisture on her cheeks.

"What happened?" he asked, his expression tight.

"Nothing. She came and drew my blood. She'll tell us the results within twenty-four hours."

"Then why are you crying?"

She sucked in a deep breath. "I wanted you here."

"Why? We won't have the results until tomorrow? Why did you want me here for the blood draw?"

"I…" The words stuck in her throat. "I needed you."

His eyes darkened. "I thought you didn't do need."

"Well, I don't usually, but I needed you for this."

He set his laptop case hard on his desk, his body radiating tension. "I told you that my work keeps me away. I may be royalty, but contrary to what you might think about royals, I have duties to attend. I don't have less responsibility because I'm a prince…I have more."

"This isn't about general neediness," she said, standing up and planting her hands on her hips. "I wanted some support for a paternity test, which *you* demanded, by the way. I don't think that's very outrageous."

"I don't have time to deal with temper tantrums." His clipped words hung in the silence of the room and she let them, let herself absorb how much they hurt.

She brushed past him and out of the office, her heart feeling as if it was cracking to pieces inside of her. She didn't know how she'd let this happen. But sometime in the past six weeks she'd done what she'd vowed she would never do. She'd started needing someone. And worse than that, she was almost certain that she loved him, too.

CHAPTER ELEVEN

ALISON was more than thankful for having an opportunity to get out of the palace later that day. The meeting with the men and women she was working with to organize the Turani branch of the CF Foundation had gone well. And it had provided some much-needed distraction from the anxiety of waiting for the test results, from the stifling solitude that came from being in a huge building surrounded by people who basically never talked to her. But most of all, she needed a distraction from her earlier revelation.

She didn't want to love Maximo. She was saving her love for her child. She didn't want to have her emotions tangled up in loving him, not when he was only going to hurt her. She didn't want to be like her parents. Didn't want to become a bitter, angry person simply because her strongest emotions had been tied up in someone who neither wanted, nor deserved them.

She hiked her purse up higher on her shoulder, clinging to the leather strap as if it might offer her some kind of support. How had she let Maximo come to mean so much to her? He was infuriating. He always thought he was right and he was ridiculously self-confident. And he was handsome. Smart. Funny. A great conversationalist. And great in bed.

She sighed audibly. She couldn't even list his sins without turning sappy. And lustful. Even now, when she was furious at him, she wanted him. The mental countdown to when she would be able to see him tonight had already begun, and she was more than a little ashamed to admit that.

"Excuse me, miss."

Alison turned her head sharply to follow the sound of the person who'd spoken to her and a flash went off in her face. Putting her head down she walked faster, her face set into the most hostile expression she could manage. She wasn't about to be intimidated by an idiot reporter, and she certainly wasn't going to stop and answer questions.

"Miss Whitman, is it true you recently underwent a paternity test?" A second voice, a woman's, joined the first.

Alison's heart jolted. They knew about the baby. About the test. She doubted it was the doctor who'd told. The position of private physician to royalty probably paid way too much to betray confidences. A lab tech, though, might be tempted. However it happened, the news was out and she'd have to deal with it as best she could.

The jostle of equipment behind her grew louder and more questions, by more people, starting swirling around her.

"Is it the prince's baby?"

"Who's the father?"

"How many men are being tested?"

She bit her lip to contain an onslaught of angry words. She wasn't going to turn around and freak out at all of the people holding cameras. That photo was not going on the front page of a tabloid.

The knot of people caught up to her and suddenly she was in the middle of them, cameras and tape recorders being shoved at her from every direction. One of the men got pushed into her and she wobbled, losing her balance and falling onto the sidewalk.

That didn't seem to bother any of the rabid paparazzi. They continued to snap pictures and shout anything to get a response from her, questions, accusations.

"Alison?"

She recognized Maximo's voice over the din that surrounded her. One of the reporters who'd been leaning over her jerked back sharply, a look of shock on his face. Then she saw Max. He reached down and took her hand, pulling her gently to her feet. The reporters weren't at all deterred by his presence and they continued to crowd in.

One of the men physically grabbed Alison's arm in an attempt to slow her down. A feral growl escaped Maximo's lips and he released his hold on Alison, grabbing the man's camera and smashing it against the side of one of the brick buildings that lined the sidewalk.

"Do not lay a hand on my woman," Max gritted, his voice fierce, his normally subtle accent thick.

The photographer paled and fell back, as did the rest of them, obviously sensing impending violence if they continued their assault.

"Get in the car." Max didn't have any tenderness for her, either. He jerked open the passenger door of the black sports car that was parked against the curb.

She wasn't exactly thrilled at the thought of being in an enclosed space with him in his current mood, but she'd rather take her chances with him than have him leave her with the pseudopress. She got in and buckled up quickly.

Maximo didn't speak the entire drive back to the palace. He sat straight, gripping the steering wheel, his jaw locked tight, tension radiating off him. And she wasn't going to be the one to break that silence, not when she knew any words coming from him were going to be extremely unpleasant.

As soon as they were closed into his bedroom he unleashed his rage. "What were you thinking? You didn't tell me where you were going, you didn't take a bodyguard. I had to find out by calling your driver and he informed me you were at a meeting. Alone. That was incredibly irresponsible of you."

"Irresponsible?" she shot back. "I was trying to keep busy, trying to do something worthwhile. I am not going to sit around the castle by myself until you need me to be your royal accessory!"

"I never said that I expected you to that, but I do expect you to possess some modicum of sense." He grabbed her arm and pulled her to him, bringing her tight against his chest. "Do you have any idea what might have happened to you?"

Maximo took a sharp breath. Anger and panic roared through him, mingling with the fierce pumping of adrenaline in his veins. She affected him far too much. He had been there. He'd tried love and marriage. It had been hell. Losing Selena by increments, and finally to death, had been an exercise in torture. He had no desire to go back to that, to ever feel that way again.

When he'd seen Alison on the ground with that pack of wolves surrounding her…it had taken all of his self-control to stop himself from beating the man who'd touched her until he was unconscious. In that moment, seeing the paparazzi around her…it had been a return to the darkest moments of his life. He'd been able to imagine far too clearly what it would be like to lose her, to lose the baby. It had felt as though his world was caving in. She was starting to matter far too much, this whole tentative future with a wife and child was starting to mean too much. He had let it all go before, had had no choice but to give up on that desire. And now it had become the center of everything again. He had not intended for that to be the case.

It had seemed a simple task to keep her at arm's length. And she'd seemed more than happy to hold herself separate from him. He'd thought he could exorcize the intense passion he felt for her by making love with her, and yet every night his need for her only seemed stronger.

He'd loved Selena, but he had been in control of that love. She'd needed him, had looked to him for her everything, for comfort, for strength. That had been a role he was comfortable with then. He'd liked that she'd depended on him.

But Alison had burrowed beneath his skin. She had made herself important to him, essential in so many ways.

"Nothing was going to happen to me!" she protested.

"They knocked you over and still their only thought was getting the dirt on you, on us, digging up whatever scandal they possibly could. The night Selena was killed, they'd been following her. After the accident they took pictures," he spat. "They wanted to know if she was drunk, or on drugs. They wanted scandal."

Alison's face paled. "I never knew. It was never in the paper…it didn't…"

"I paid them off," he said, his voice low. "There was

no scandal anyway, but I feared they might publish the pictures. I bought them and had them destroyed."

Her eyes filled with tears, for him, for Selena. It rocked him, made his heart seize and his chest ache. She cupped his face and kissed him tenderly, her lips soft against his.

"I'm so sorry," she whispered.

He wanted to pull away, to leave so that he could gather his thoughts, regain control. But he couldn't leave, not with her standing there, looking devastated and vulnerable and so beautiful she made his hands shake with desire for her. He cupped her chin and tilted her face up, kissing the streaks her tears had tracked on her lovely face.

His heart thundering in his chest, he began to release the buttons on her silk blouse, baring her demure lace bra. He swallowed, nearly undone by the fierce desire rocketing through him. But it was more than that, more than just physical need. He had never felt anything like this before, not with Selena, not with any woman. He felt incomplete unless he was touching her, kissing her, stroking her gorgeous body.

His mind rejected that thought even as his heart, his body, ached to be joined with her. He could not allow her to matter so much. He had loved Selena, but she had not touched him in this way, had not wielded this kind of power over his body and his emotions. And still, when he'd lost her it had felt as though his world had crumbled.

Alison meant far more to him. In that moment when he'd thought she might have been hurt he had been able to imagine losing her. It had been like staring into a dark void that was opening up, preparing to swallow him whole, leaving him with nothing but eternal blackness. He could not allow that. But he couldn't stop kissing her.

He growled roughly and tightened his hold on her, kissing her hard, bruising her lips with the force of his passion, his rage. It was a kiss designed to punish her for what she made him feel, designed to reassert his dominance. He plundered her mouth, dipping his tongue deep inside before nipping the fullness of her bottom lip.

When he parted from her, her eyes were huge, her breathing ragged. Her nipples were beaded, pressed against the flimsy bra. She wanted him still, even though she'd been angry with him. And God help him, he wanted her.

He denied the refrain that was playing through his mind, denied the insistent tattoo of her name that was beating through him. It wasn't about her. She wasn't special. She was just a woman. And he was a man. He wanted what a man desired of a woman and nothing more. It wasn't Alison; it was just sex. He had been without it for too long; that was why she affected him so strongly.

He backed her across the room and turned her so that she was facing away from him before bending her gently over the surface of the dresser that was positioned up against the wall.

"Max?" she asked tremulously.

"Trust me," he grated.

He moved his hands up her still-slender waist, around to her stomach and over the little bump that housed their baby. His heart jumped and he curled his hands into fists before opening them again and palming her breasts, releasing the front clasp on her bra and letting it fall open. He covered the creamy mounds, squeezed her sensitized nipples, drawing a low, desperate moan from her lips.

He abandoned her breasts to push her skirt down her hips, taking her tiny pair of panties with it. He pressed his hand against her mound, pushing one finger through her slick folds and finding the bud that housed her most sensitive nerve endings. She shivered, her head falling back to rest against his chest. The sweet scent of her perfume, so uniquely her, assaulted him. He swept her hair to the side and kissed her neck, her bare shoulder.

Unsteadily he reached for the closure on his slacks and freed himself, bringing his naked flesh against the softness of her bottom. She gasped and arched into him, pressing the heart of her, her glorious wetness, up against his aching body.

Keeping one hand centered on her clitoris, stroking her mercilessly; he splayed his other hand across her stomach and tilted her back gently as he thrust into her tight heat.

He lost all sense of control, all sense of time. He had wanted to take her this way to make it impersonal, so he couldn't see her face. But he knew…her scent, the feel of her soft skin beneath his hands, the soft sounds of pleasure that she made…the fact that his body had never responded this way to any other woman. It was Alison, and he could not deny it.

He kissed the side of her neck, gentled his touch on her breasts, let his hands slide over her soft curves. His heart squeezed in his chest. This was Alison. His woman. The mother of his child. There was no denying it, and he didn't want to.

Suddenly he needed to see her, needed to watch her face as he brought her to the peak, needed to cradle her close to his body. He withdrew and swept her into his arms, crossing the room quickly and settling her onto the bed. "Alison," he whispered, brushing her hair back off her forehead.

She raised her hands and cupped his cheek, the emotion in her eyes nearly undoing him completely. "Max."

He entered her slowly, his entire body trembling with the effort to maintain control. She locked her arms around him, moved with him, her soft sighs of pleasure gratifying him in a way that went far beyond the physical. And after she had cried out her climax he rushed to follow her, and it was her name that he whispered hoarsely as he came hard, spilling himself inside her, branding her. Branding himself.

Emotion tightened his chest, squeezed down hard on his heart and refused to release him from its iron fist. The look in her eyes, the one of pure wonderment, affected him too much. He rolled away from her suddenly, pulling away from the feelings roiling inside of him.

She turned to her side, facing him, and his breath caught when the full impact of her beauty hit him. Her face was flushed, her mouth swollen. She had never looked more enticing, more lovely. He gritted his teeth against the rising tide of emotion that was threatening to swamp him.

"I have work to do." He turned away from her and buckled his belt, his breathing ragged, his heart pounding hard. His instinct was to go to her, to hold her. But he wouldn't allow himself that. Wouldn't allow himself to show that level of weakness.

He could hear her behind him, collecting her clothing, and when he turned to face her again he could read the hurt and confusion she clearly felt. He didn't have to say anything for her to know that he was distancing himself from her. That itself was enough for him to want distance. He didn't want her feelings involved any more than he wanted to involve his own.

"I'll be working late tonight. You should sleep in your own room," he said, his voice clipped.

She flinched as though he'd struck her. "Okay."

Her mobile phone rang and she reached down and fished it out of her purse, which had been thrown to the floor at some point in their frantic hurry to come together.

She checked the caller ID. "It's the lab." She answered, but neither her face nor her tone gave away any information. She hung up and focused on him, her lips pressed firmly together. "Congratulations. You're the father. We're ninety-nine-point-nine percent certain now." She didn't sound happy, she didn't look happy.

Alison watched Maximo's face, hoping for some kind of reaction, something she could hold onto to let her know that she hadn't lost him, lost everything they'd built together in the past six weeks. When he'd withdrawn from her physically she'd felt his emotional withdrawal just as keenly, could see his dark eyes flatten as he walled his emotions off from her.

"I have to go," he said, his dark eyes unreadable.

Alison tried to do what he'd done so easily, tried to block out the pain she knew was about to hit. But it was impossible. She loved him too much, and she was losing him already. He might never leave her, but she would never have his heart, either.

She pushed hard against her closed eyes, trying to stop tears from falling. She was going to be strong, for herself, for her baby. She would never let anyone know that her heart was shattered irreparably.

* * *

The fragrant air caressed her skin, the intense warmth of the summer day heating her. But only on the outside. Everything inside of her was cold.

She'd arrived on the island of Maris only twenty minutes ago, hoping she might find some solace for her pain. Instead being in the place where she had been so happy, where she had been awakened to love and making love, was a bittersweet pain. She had never felt more separate from him.

He'd been away on business more often than not over the course of the past week, and when he'd been home he'd been unfailingly polite. Distant. It was worse than his anger—at least that was passionate. He was acting like a stranger. He hadn't made love with her, not since the day she'd been attacked by the paparazzi.

That was when things had changed. When he'd shut her out completely. Her worst fear was that it wasn't related to the incident with the press, but that it had to do with him finding out for certain he was the father of her baby. Maybe he didn't want them anymore. And now, his get-out-of-jail-free card had been taken away from him.

She moved away from the balcony and reentered the room. The one she and Max had shared when they'd stayed here. She shivered. It had been a stupid idea to come to the island. But her heart was breaking, splintering with every beat it took, and she had to try to fix it somehow.

Maybe if there would have been a big blow-up fight it would have been easier. If he'd said ugly things and told her he didn't want her, maybe then her love would have died. But it had just been this sudden, silent break. He had withdrawn from her completely with no explanation, but the separation had been a no less definite or final feeling than if they had experienced some kind of dramatic end to their relationship.

The greatest irony was that their wedding was in two days. In two days they were going to stand before the congregation and make vows to love, honor and cherish each other. It would be difficult since they were barely speaking to each other.

She rested her palm on her burgeoning belly and felt renewed determination. She wasn't destitute. She had her baby, the most precious thing in the world. She loved Max. She loved him so much it actually hurt, but their baby was a piece of them. They may not have created life in the usual, physical way, but the baby was the best of both of them.

She heard footsteps behind her on the travertine floor and turned, expecting to see Rosa Maria, the housekeeper. Instead she saw Max striding toward her. He was as intimidating as ever, a man who oozed control and sophistication. But there was something different. She noticed the fatigue etched in his handsome face. She could definitely relate.

"What are you doing here, Maximo?"

He laughed, the sound hollow, void of any joy or humor. "The same thing as you, I would imagine. Trying to escape."

"What is it you need to escape from?"

He laughed again. "The same thing as you I would imagine."

"Please, Max, I'm not up to playing games with you."

"So it's Max again, is it?" His voice softened and he took a step toward her.

"What do you mean?"

He gave her a half smile. "I was demoted to the more formal Maximo."

"I didn't even realize."

"I did," he said huskily.

Her throat tightened. She couldn't take this. This tease. He didn't want her. He was stuck with her.

"Why are you here?" she asked, anguish lacing her voice.

"This is where I've been for most of the past week," he confessed.

"I thought you were working."

"In a way I was."

Frustration bubbled through her. "I don't want your passion one moment and your silence the next. I can't do hot and cold. I don't know what happened to change things between us. But you won't tell me. If I've done something then say it. If you've found someone else, or you're simply tired of me, *say it*. Don't freeze me out. Don't make me play guessing games."

"I'm not a man of words, Alison. I'm a man of actions. You may have noticed that," he said with dark humor. "I don't always say the right things. But I want the chance to make you understand me. To make you understand how I feel."

She shook her head, her throat tightening with tears. "Don't play with me."

He took her hand, and their first physical contact in a week rocked her to her core. The wanting hadn't gone away. Not even for a moment. She could see from the molten heat in his eyes that he felt the same.

"I've never been playing with you," he said, his voice intense. "Please know that. I've handled things badly, but hurting you was the last thing I wanted."

"But you did hurt me," she said. "We promised we

were going to talk about things, but we didn't. You just shut me out, and I have no idea what happened to cause it."

He raised his eyes and met hers; the stark, raw emotion in them shocked her. "I know," he said roughly. "You cannot know how sorry I am. Please come with me, Alison."

She nodded slowly and let him lead her from the villa. When she realized where they were headed she stopped. "Max. I can't."

"Trust me. Please."

She took a breath and allowed him to take her the rest of the way to the art studio, her heart a leaden weight in her chest. This was the place where she had shed her inhibitions, where she had laid herself bare to him. Where she had lost her heart. Coming here was the worst sort of torture mingled with the sweetest of memories. They had been connected then, and even though she hadn't been able to name the things he'd made her feel, it was where she'd fallen in love with him.

He opened the door and took her into the sun-bathed room. There was no question of what he had wanted her to see. It was there in the middle of the room, lit up by the incandescent natural light. It was her, but it wasn't her. The woman captured on the canvas was beautiful. Her skin glowed with youth and joy. As though she had just been with her lover and he had left her satisfied. The painting was exquisitely detailed. Her hair was a lush mix of reds and golds, her flesh palest peach, her lips and nipples a dusky rose. Her eyes were closed, her full mouth curved, hinting at secrets. Secrets between her lover and herself, because there could be no doubt that this woman was well-loved.

She looked at the painting piece by piece, something

inside of her moved by it. The features were hers, but there was something more, something she didn't see when she looked in the mirror. Something Maximo saw that she didn't see in herself. It was more than a portrait, it was a revelation. A declaration. It spoke of feelings deeper than words; it mirrored what she felt in her heart.

"Max?"

"This is what I've been doing. I wasn't working. I couldn't work. My mind was filled with you, Alison." He cupped her cheek and dropped a light kiss on her mouth. He tasted of desperation, of need, and her body responded; along with her heart.

"Max…"

"No, I have to say this. I was scared, Alison. Scared of how much you had come to mean to me. That day forced me to face what it might feel like if I were to lose you. I don't think I could survive it. I realized how much you'd come to mean to me, how much I counted on seeing you every day, kissing you, making love with you. I realized how much I needed you. I did not want you to have so much power over me. I didn't want to love you." A sad smile touched his lips. "I tried to shut you out. To prove to you, and to myself, that I didn't need you. I was very wrong."

He kissed her fiercely and she parted her lips for him, closing her eyes as she reveled in being held again by the man that she loved.

He tilted his head and rested his forehead against hers. "I have more to say, but I'm afraid I won't say it right. I need to show you first." He kissed her neck, her cheek, her forehead. "Can I show you?" he asked against her lips.

"Yes," she half sobbed, half laughed.

He lifted her shirt up over her head, exposing her sensitive breasts to his inspection. He groaned when he saw that she was bare beneath her shirt. "Oh, my darling, what you do to me." He cupped her aching flesh reverently, his thumbs moving back and forth over her distended nipples. A cry formed on her lips and he kissed it away.

She put her hands on his broad chest, touching him, tasting the salty skin at the base of his throat as though it was the first time. Everything seemed new. Fresh. She pushed his shirt up over his head and tossed it on the ground to join her rumpled blouse.

She undid the snap on his jeans, her eyes utterly transfixed on the line of hair that ran down his taught, flat belly and disappeared into his pants. She knew where it led, and yet the curiosity and excitement she felt made it seem as though she didn't.

"You're so sexy," she breathed.

With a growl he pushed her onto the couch, settling between her willing thighs. "Oh, Alison, my love, you don't know how that makes me feel. It's unlike anything else in this life."

"I think I have an idea." She opened herself to him, bring his shaft against the moist heart of her body.

He kissed her, deeply, all consuming, as though he was trying to devour her. He stripped her pants and underwear off in one fluid movement and then took care of his own, leaving them naked. No barriers. Nothing between them. It was as honest as two people could be with one another. There were no secrets between them, no way to hide anything. Not their insecurities, not the bulge of her tummy that housed their child, not the feeling of pure, sweet love, coursing between them.

She positioned herself over his body and took him

inside of her slowly, relishing the feeling of becoming one with him. She felt herself expand to accommodate him and she sighed with completion and satisfaction when he was buried in her up to the hilt.

She rose and fell, taking him in and pulling away almost completely each time. The rhythm took them over and they were both climbing together, their breathing synchronized, her body tightening, his expanding.

She locked eyes with him, felt tears starting to fall as she looked at the emotion in them. Emotion she was certain was mirrored in her own. They went over the edge together, holding each other, his arms the only thing keeping her from flying apart.

He cradled her in his arms, whispering soft, sweet words, flowing seamlessly from Italian to English.

"Te amo," he said. "I love you."

"Max." Her voice was thick with emotion, her heart so full she thought it might not be able to hold all he was making her feel.

"I love you. I know I could have said it earlier, but I wanted to show you. I wanted to show you my heart, the painting. I wanted to show you my need, my desperation, by making love to you. Words are only words. By my actions I hoped to prove it to you. I have never felt anything like this before. You talked about need making people weak, and I was certainly a believer in that principle. But you were so brave, so enchanting. Your love for our child, your strength, everything about you called to me on such a deep level, and I couldn't control what I felt for you. I wanted you to the point of constant distraction. I needed you. It—" he hesitated "—it frightened me. I didn't want to love a woman so much, with such an all-consuming passion. But you gave me no choice.

I was powerless to stop myself from falling in love with you."

"I thought you didn't want the baby anymore. Or me, for that matter."

"What?"

"It started after the call from the doctor. I thought you were having second thoughts about tying yourself to me, about being a father. You didn't choose this, Max. You didn't choose me and I…"

"No, I didn't choose you. You were chosen for me. I didn't know what was best for me. I can only be thankful for divine intervention."

"Who said you weren't good with words?"

He leaned in and kissed her, his lips teasing hers softly. She sighed when they parted, absolute bliss radiating through her.

"I'm much better at other forms of communication," he said.

"Show me."

"It will be my greatest pleasure for the rest of my life."

EPILOGUE

PRINCIPESSA Eliana Rossi came into the world with her mother's golden hair and her father's set of lungs. At least that's what Alison said.

"She's beautiful. Just like her *mamma*," he said, bending over to kiss both of his women. He had only been a father for a few hours, but they had already been the most spectacular hours of his life. His love for Alison had only deepened in the past few months. Seeing her now, holding Eliana, he felt so full of love he thought he might burst.

"She's hungry," Alison said, lowering the top of her hospital gown and helping her daughter latch to her breast. Maximo had never seen anything more wonderful.

"Let's have lots of children," he declared, utterly fascinated by the miracle in front of him.

She gave him a hard glare. "Wait until I recover before you even mention such a thing."

He grinned at her, sheepishly. "Good idea."

"Someday she's going to be the queen," Alison said softly.

"Yes," he agreed, "but for now she's just our daughter, and we'll do all we can to make sure she stays a little girl as long as possible." He looked down at the tiny pink bundle. "I'm in no hurry for her to grow up."

"You know something, Principe Maximo D'Angelo Rossi?" Her golden eyes shone with love as she looked at him, and he was concerned that his heart really might burst. "I think I love you even more today than I did yesterday."

He bent and kissed her again, savoring the taste of her sweet lips. "I feel the same way. And I think I'll love you even more tomorrow."

HIRED BY
HER HUSBAND
ANNE McALLISTER

Award-winning author **Anne McAllister** was once given a blueprint for happiness that included a nice, literate husband, a ramshackle Victorian house, a horde of mischievous children, a bunch of big, friendly dogs and a life spent writing stories about tall, dark and handsome heroes. 'Where do I sign up?' she asked, and promptly did. Lots of years later, she's happy to report the blueprint was a success. She's always happy to share the latest news with readers at her website, www.annemcallister.com and welcomes their letters there or at PO Box 3904, Bozeman, Montana 59772, USA.

CHAPTER ONE

WHEN THE PHONE RANG that evening, Sophy grabbed it as fast as she could. She didn't need it waking Lily. Not just when her daughter had finally fallen asleep.

Lily's fourth birthday party that afternoon had exhausted them both. Normally an easygoing sunny-natured child, Lily had been wound up for days in anticipation. Five of her friends and their mothers had joined them, first at the beach and then here at the house for a cookout, followed by ice cream and cake.

Lily had been on top of the world, declaring the party, "the bestest ever." Then, in the time-honored fashion of overtired four-year-olds everywhere, she'd crashed.

It had taken a warm bath, a cuddle on Sophy's lap, clutching her new stuffed puppy, Chloe, and half a dozen stories to unwind her.

Now finally she was asleep, sprawled in her bed, but still clinging to Chloe. And, with the house a wreck all around her, Sophy didn't need Lily wide awake again. So at the phone's first shrill ring, Sophy snatched it up.

"Hello?"

"Mrs. Savas?"

The voice was a man's, one she didn't know. But it was the name she heard that gave her a jolt. Of course her cousin and business partner Natalie was now Mrs. Savas—had been ever since her marriage to Christo last year—but Sophy wasn't used to getting calls asking for Natalie at home. For a split second she hesitated, then said firmly, "No. I'm sorry. You've got the wrong number. Call back during business hours and you can speak to Natalie."

"No. I'm not trying to reach Natalie Savas," the man said just as firmly. "I need to reach *Sophia* Savas. Is this—" He paused as if he were consulting something, then read off her telephone number.

Sophy barely heard it. Her mind had stuck on *Sophia Savas*.

That had been her name. Once. For a few months.

Suddenly she couldn't breathe, felt as if she'd been punched. Abruptly she sat down wordlessly, her fingers strangling the telephone.

"Hello? Are you there? Do I have the correct number?"

Sophy took a quick shallow breath. "Yes." She was relieved that she didn't stammer. Her voice even sounded firm to her own ears. Cool. Calm. Collected. "I'm Sophia. Sophia McKinnon," she corrected, then added, "formerly Savas."

But she still wasn't convinced he had the right person.

"George Savas's wife?"

So much for not being convinced. Sophy swallowed. "Y-yes."

No. Maybe? She certainly didn't think she was still George's wife! Her brain was spinning. How could she not know?

George could have divorced her at any time in the past four years. She'd always assumed he had, though she'd never received any paperwork. Mostly she'd put it out of her mind because she'd tried to put George out of her mind.

She shouldn't have married him in the first place. She knew that. *Everybody* knew that. Besides, as far as she was concerned, a divorce was irrelevant to her life. It wasn't as if she were ever marrying again.

But maybe George was.

Sophy's brain abruptly stopped spinning. Her fingers gripped the receiver, and she felt suddenly cold. She was surprised to feel an odd ache somewhere in the vicinity of her heart even as she assured herself she didn't care. It didn't matter to her if George was getting married.

But she couldn't help wondering, had he finally fallen in love?

She had certainly never been the woman of his dreams. Had he met the woman who was? Was that why she was getting this call? Was this official-sounding man his lawyer? Was he calling to put the legal wheels in motion?

Carefully Sophy swallowed and reminded herself again that it didn't matter to her. George didn't matter. It wasn't as if their marriage had been real. She'd only hoped...

And now she told herself that her reaction was only because the phone call had caught her off guard.

She mustered a steadying breath. "Yes, that's right. Sophia Savas."

"This is Dr. Harlowe. I'm sorry to tell you, Mrs. Savas, but there's been an accident."

"Are you sure about this?" Natalie asked. She and her husband, Christo, had come over the minute Sophy had rang them. Now they watched as she threw things in a duffel and tried to think what else she needed to take. "Going all the way to New York? That's clear across the country."

"I know where it is. And yes, I'm sure," Sophy said with far more resolution than she felt. It had nothing to do with how far she was going. It was whom she was going to see when she got there. "He was there for me, wasn't he?"

"Under duress," Natalie reminded her.

"Snap," Sophy said. There was going to be a fair amount of duress involved in this encounter, too. But she had to do it. She added her sneakers to the duffel. One thing she knew from her years in New York was that she'd have to do plenty of walking.

"I thought you were divorced," Natalie said.

"So did I. Well, I never signed any papers. But—" she shrugged "—I guess I thought George would just take care of it." God knew he'd taken care of everything else—including her and Lily. But that was George. It was the way he was.

"Look," she said finally, zipping the duffel shut and raising her gaze to meet Natalie's. "If there was any way not to do this, believe me, I wouldn't. There's not. According to the papers in George's personnel file at Columbia, I'm his next of kin. He's unconscious. They may have to do surgery. They don't know the extent of his injuries. They're in 'wait and see' mode. But if things go wrong—" She stopped, unable to bring herself to voice possibilities the doctor had outlined for her.

"Sophy," Natalie's voice was one of gentle warning.

Sophy swallowed, straightened and squared her shoulders. "I have to do this," she said firmly. "When I was alone—before Lily was born—he was there." It was true and she made herself face that fact as much as she told it to her cousin. He had married her to give Lily a father, to give her child the Savas name. "I owe him. I'm paying my debt."

Natalie looked at her doubtfully, but then nodded. "I guess so," she said slowly. Then her eyes flashed impatiently. "But what kind of grown man gets run over by a truck?"

A physicist too busy thinking about atom smashing to watch where he was going, Sophy thought privately. But she didn't say that. She just told the truth.

"I don't know. I just know I appreciate your dropping everything and coming over to stay with Lily. I'll call you in the morning. We can arrange a time and do a video call, too." She patted her briefcase where she'd already packed her laptop. "That way Lily can see me and it won't be so abrupt. I hate leaving her without saying goodbye."

She had never left Lily in four years—not for more than

a few hours. Now she knew that if she woke Lily she'd end up taking her along. And that was a can of worms she didn't intend to open.

"She'll be fine," Natalie assured her. "Just go. Do what needs to be done. And take care of yourself," she advised.

"Yes. Of course. It will be fine," Sophy assured her, picking up the briefcase as Christo hefted the duffel and headed out to the car.

Sophy allowed herself a quick side trip into Lily's room. She stood there a moment just looking at her sleeping daughter, her dark hair tousled, her lips slightly parted. She looked like George.

No. She looked like a Savas, Sophy corrected herself. Which Lily was. George had nothing to do with it. But even as she told herself that, her gaze was drawn to the photo on the bedside table. It was a picture of baby Lily in George's arms.

Lily might not remember him, but she certainly knew who he was. She'd demanded to know about him ever since she discovered such people as fathers existed.

Where was her father? she'd asked. "My daddy," she said. "Who is my daddy?" Why wasn't he here? When was he coming back?

So many questions.

For which her mother had had such inadequate answers, Sophy thought miserably now.

But how could she explain to a child what had happened? It was hard enough to explain it to herself.

She'd done her best. She'd assured her daughter of George's love. She knew that much was true. And she'd even promised that some day Lily would meet him.

"When?" her daughter had demanded.

"Later." Sophy kept the promise deliberately vague. "When you're older."

Not now. And yet, at the same time Sophy thought the

words again, another thought popped into her head: What if he died?

Impossible! George had always seemed tough, impervious, imminently indestructible.

But what did she really know about the man who had so briefly been her husband? She only thought she'd known...

And what man, even a strong tough one, could fend off a truck?

"Sophy?" Natalie's voice whispered from the door. "Christo's waiting in the car."

"Coming." Quickly Sophy bent and gave her daughter a light kiss, brushed her hand over Lily's silky hair, then sucked in a deep, desperate breath and hurried out of the room.

Natalie was waiting, watching worriedly. Sophy mustered a smile. "I'll be back before you know it."

"Of course you will." Natalie gave her a quick smile in return, then wrapped Sophy in a fierce tight hug intended, Sophy knew, to supply a boatload of encouragement and support. "You don't still love him, do you?" Natalie asked.

Sophy pulled back and shook her head. "No," she vowed. She couldn't. *She wouldn't!* "Absolutely not."

They weren't giving him any painkillers.

Which would be fine, George thought, though the pounding in his head was ferocious and moving his leg and elbow made him wince, if they would just let him sleep.

But they weren't doing that, either. Every time he fell blessedly asleep they loomed over him, poking and prodding, talking in loud kindergarten-teacher voices, shining lights in his eyes, asking him his name, how old he was, who was the president.

How idiotic was that? He could barely remember his age or who the president was when he *hadn't* just got run over by a truck.

If they'd ask him how to determine the speed of light or

what the properties of black holes were, he could have answered in the blink of an eye. He could talk about that for hours—or he could have provided he was able to keep his eyes open long enough.

But no one asked him that.

They went away for a while, but then came back with more needles. They did scans, tutted and muttered, asked more of their endless questions, always looking at him expectantly, then furrowed their brows, worried, when he couldn't remember if he was thirty-four or thirty-five.

Who the hell cared?

Apparently they did.

"What month is it?" he demanded. His birthday was in November.

They looked askance when he asked them questions.

"He doesn't know what month it is," one murmured and made quick urgent notes on her laptop.

"Doesn't matter," George muttered irritably. "Is Jeremy all right?"

That was what mattered right now. That was what he saw whenever his eyes were closed—his little four-year-old dark-haired neighbor darting into the street to chase after his ball. That and—out of the corner of his eye—the truck barreling down on him.

The memory still made his breath catch. "How's Jeremy?' George demanded again.

"He's fine. Barely a scratch," the doctor said, shining a light in George's eyes. "Already gone home. Much better off than you. Hold still and open your eyes, George, damn it."

Ordinarily, George figured, Sam Harlowe probably had more patience with his patients. But he and Sam went back to grade school. Now Sam gripped George's chin in firm fingers and shone his light again in George's eyes again. It sent his head pounding through the roof and made him grit his teeth.

"As long as Jeremy's okay," he said through them. As soon as Sam let go of his jaw, George lay back against the pillows and deliberately shut his eyes.

"Fine. Be an ass," Sam said gruffly. "But you're going to stay right here and you're going to rest. Check on him regularly," Sam commanded the nurse. "Keep me posted on any change. The next twenty-four hours are critical."

George's eyes flicked open again. "I thought you said he was all right."

"*He* is. The jury's still out on you," Sam told him gruffly. "I'll be back."

As that sounded more like a threat than a promise, George wanted to say he wouldn't be here, but by the time he mustered his wits, Sam was long gone.

Annoyed, George glared after him. Then he fixed his gaze on the nurse. "You can leave, too," he told her irritably. He'd had enough questions. Besides, his head hurt less if he shut his eyes. So he did.

He may have even slept because the next thing he knew there was a new nurse pestering him.

"So, how old are you, George?" she asked him.

George squinted at her. "Too old to be playing games. When can I go home?"

"When you've played our games," the nurse said drily.

He cracked a smile at that. "I'm going to be thirty-five. It's October. I had oatmeal for breakfast this morning. Unless it's tomorrow already."

"It is," she told him.

"Then I can go home."

"Not until Dr. Harlowe agrees." She didn't look up while she checked his blood pressure. When she finished she said, "I understand you're a hero."

George squinted at her. "Not likely."

"You didn't save a boy's life?"

"I knocked him across the street."

"So he wouldn't get killed by a truck," the nurse said. "That qualifies as 'saving' in my book. I hear he just got a few scrapes and bruises."

"Which is what I've got," George pointed out, about to nod toward the ones visible on his arm. "So I should be able to go home, too."

"And you will," she said. "But head injuries can be serious."

Finally, blessedly, she—and all her persistent colleagues—left him alone. As the hours wore on eventually the hospital noises quieted. The rattle of carts in the halls diminished. Even the beeps and the clicks seemed to fade. Not the drumming in his head, though. God, it was ceaseless.

Every time he drifted off, he moved. It hurt. He shifted. Found a spot it wasn't quite so bad. Slept. And then they woke him again. When he did sleep it was restlessly. Images, dreams, memories of Jeremy haunted his dreams. So did ones of the truck. So did the grateful, still stricken faces of Jeremy's parents.

"We might have lost him," Jeremy's mother, Grace, had sobbed at his bedside earlier.

And his father, Philip, had just squeezed George's hand in his as he'd said over and over, "You have no idea."

Not true. George had a very good idea. There were other memories and images mingling with those of Jeremy. Memories of a baby, tiny and dark-haired. A first smile. Petal-soft skin. Trusting eyes.

She was Jeremy's age now. Old enough to run into a street the same way Jeremy had... He tried not to think about it. Tried not to think about her. It made his throat ache and his eyes burn. He shut them once more and tried desperately to fall asleep.

He didn't know how much sleep he finally got. His head was still pounding when the first glimmers of dawn filtered in through the window.

He'd heard footsteps come into the room earlier. There had been the sound of a nurse's voice speaking quietly, another low murmured response, then the sound of the feet of a chair being moved.

He hadn't opened his eyes. Had deliberately ignored it all.

All he'd thought was, please God they would go away without poking him or talking to him again. He didn't want to be poked. He didn't want to be civil.

He wanted to go back to sleep—but this time he didn't want the memories to come with it. The nurse left. The conversation stopped. Yet somehow he didn't think he was alone.

Was that Sam who'd come in? Was he standing there now, staring down at him in silence?

It was the sort of juvenile nonsensical thing they'd done as kids to try to psych the other out. Surely Sam had grown out of it by now.

George shifted—and winced as he tried to roll onto his side. His shoulder hurt like hell. Every muscle in his body protested. If Sam thought this was funny…

George flicked open his eyes and his whole being—mind and body—seemed to jerk.

It wasn't Sam in the room. It was a woman.

George sucked in a breath. He didn't think he made a noise. But something alerted her because she had been sitting beside his bed looking out the window, and now as he stared, dry-mouthed and disbelieving, slowly she turned and her gaze met his.

For the first time in nearly four years he and Sophy—his wife—were face-to-face.

Wife? Ha.

They might have stood side by side in a New York City judge's office and repeated after him. They might have a legally binding document declaring them married. But it had never meant anything more than a piece of paper.

Not to her.

Not to either of them, George told himself firmly, though the pain he felt was suddenly different than before. He resisted it. Didn't want to care. Sure as hell didn't want to feel!

The very last thing he needed now was to have to deal with Sophy. His jaw tightened involuntarily, which, damn it, made his head hurt even worse.

"What are you doing here?" he demanded. His voice was rough, hoarse from tubes and dry hospital air. He glared at her accusingly.

"Irritating you, obviously." Sophy's tone was mild, but there was a concern in her gaze that belied her tone. Still, she shrugged lightly. "The hospital called me. You were unconscious. They needed next of kin's permission to do whatever they felt needed doing."

"You?" George stared in disbelief.

"That's pretty much what I said when they called," Sophy admitted candidly, crossing one long leg over the other and leaning back in the chair.

She was wearing black wool trousers and an olive green sweater. Very tasteful. Professional. Businesslike, George would have said. Not at all the Sophy of jeans and sweats and maternity tops he remembered. Only her copper-colored hair was still the same, the dark red strands glinting like new pennies in the early morning sun. He remembered running his fingers through it, burying his face in it. More thoughts he didn't want to deal with.

"Apparently you never got around to divorcing me." She looked at him as if asking a question.

George's jaw tightened. "I imagined you would take care of that," he bit out. Since she had been the one who was so keen on it. Damn, but his head was pounding. He shut his eyes.

When he opened them again it was to see that Sophy's gaze had flickered away. But then it came back to meet his. She shook her head.

"No need," she said easily. "I certainly wasn't getting married again."

And neither was he. He'd been gutted once by marriage. He had no desire to go through it again. But he wasn't talking about that to Sophy. He couldn't believe she was even here. Maybe that whack on the head was causing him to hallucinate.

He tried shutting his eyes again, wishing her gone. No luck. When he opened them again, she was still there.

Getting hit by a truck was small potatoes compared to dealing with Sophy. He needed all his wits and every bit of control and composure he could manage when it came to coping with her. Now he rolled onto his back again and grimaced as he tried to push himself up against the pillows.

"Probably not a good idea," Sophy commented.

No, it wasn't. The closer he got to vertical, the more he felt as if the top of his head was going to come off. On the other hand, he wasn't dealing with Sophy from a position of weakness.

"You should rest," she offered.

"I've been resting all night."

"I doubt you had much," Sophy said frankly. "The nurse said you were restless."

"You try sleeping when they're asking you questions."

"They need to keep checking, you have concussion and a subdural hematoma. Not to mention," she added, assessing him slowly as if he were a distasteful bug pinned to paper, "that you look as if you've been put through a meat grinder."

"Thanks," George muttered. Yes, it hurt, but he kept pushing himself up. He wanted to clutch his head in his hands. Instead he clutched the bedclothes until his knuckles turned white.

"For heaven's sake, stop that! Lie down or I'll call the nurse."

"Be my guest," George said. "Since it's morning and I know

my name and how old I am, maybe they'll finally let me sign myself out of here and go home. I have things to do. Classes. Work."

Sophy rolled her eyes. "You're not going anywhere. You're lucky you're not in surgery."

"Why should I be?" He scowled. "I don't have any broken bones." He was half-sitting now so he stopped pushing himself up and lifted his arm to look at his watch. His arm was bare except for the intravenous tube in the back of his hand. He gritted his teeth. "Damn it. What time is it? I have a class doing an experiment tomorrow. I need to go to work." *I need to get away from this woman—or I need to grab her and hold on to her forever.*

Sophy rolled her eyes. "Like that's going to happen."

For a terrible moment, George thought she was responding to the words that had formed in his concussed brain. Then he realized she was talking about him going to work. He sagged in relief.

"The world doesn't stop just because one person has an accident," he told her irritably.

"Yours almost did."

The baldness of her statement was like a punch to the gut. And so was the sudden change in Sophy's expression as she said the words. There was nothing at all light or flippant about her now. She looked stricken. "You almost died, George!" She even sounded as if she cared.

He steeled himself against believing it, making himself shrug. "But I didn't."

All the same he knew the truth of what she said. The truck was big enough. It had been moving fast enough. If he'd been half a step slower, she would likely be right.

Would they have called Sophy if he'd died? Would she have come and planned his funeral?

He didn't ask. He knew Sophy didn't love him, but she didn't hate him, either.

Once he'd even thought they actually stood a chance of making their marriage work, that she might have really come to love him.

"What happened?" she asked him now. "The nurse said you got hit saving a child."

He was surprised she'd asked. But then he realized she might want to know why they'd tracked her down and dragged her here. It didn't have anything to do with caring about him.

"Jeremy," George confirmed. "He's four. He lives down the street from me. I was walking home from work and he came running down the sidewalk to show me his new soccer ball. He dropped it so he could dribble it, but then as he got closer he kicked it harder—at me. But it—" he dragged in a harsh breath "—went into the street."

Sophy sucked in a breath.

"There was a delivery truck coming…."

Sophy went very white. "Dear God. He's not …?"

George shook his head, then instantly wished he hadn't. "He's okay. Bruised. Scraped up. But—"

"But not dead." Sophy said it aloud. Firmly, as if to make it more believable. She seemed to breathe again, relief evident on her face. "Thank God." And her gaze lifted as if she was in prayer.

"Yes."

Then she lowered her gaze and looked at him. "Thank George."

There was a sudden flatness in her tone, and George heard an unwelcome edge of finality, of inevitability. Almost of bitterness.

His teeth came together. "What? Did you want me to let him run in front of a truck?"

"Of course not!" Sophy's eyes flashed. A deep flush of color rushed into her pale cheeks. "How could you say such a thing? I was just…recognizing what you'd done."

"Sure you were." He gave her a hard look, an expectant look, waiting for her to say the words that hung between them.

She wet her lips. "You saved him."

He almost expected it to be an accusation. She had certainly made it sound that way when she'd flung the words at him the day she'd said she didn't want to be married anymore.

"That's what you were doing when you married me," she'd cried bitterly. "You married me to *save* me!"

He had, of course. But that wasn't the only reason. Not that she would believe it. He hadn't replied then. He didn't reply now. Sophy would think what she wanted.

George stared back at her stonily, dared her to make something of it.

But whatever anger she felt seemed to go out of her. She just looked at him with those wide deep green eyes for a long moment, and then she added quietly, "You are a hero."

George snorted. "Hardly. Jeremy wouldn't have been out there running down the street at all if he hadn't seen me coming."

"What? You're saying it's your fault?" She stared at him in disbelief.

"I'm just saying he was waiting for me." He shrugged. "We kick the ball around together sometimes."

"You know him well, then? He's a friend?" Sophy sounded surprised, as if she considered it unlikely.

"We're friends." Jeremy with his dark hair and bright eyes had made him think about Lily. He didn't say that, though.

Sophy's brows lifted slightly, as if the notion that he knew who his neighbors were surprised her as well. Maybe it should. He hadn't known any of their neighbors during the few months they'd been together.

But he hadn't had time, had he? He'd been too busy finishing up the government project he was working on and trying to figure out how to be a husband and then, only weeks later, a father. The first had been time-consuming, but at least in his comfort zone.

Marriage and fatherhood had been completely virgin territory. He hadn't had a clue.

Now Sophy said, "I was surprised you were back in New York." It wasn't a question, but he assumed that she meant it as one.

"For the past two years."

"Uppsala didn't appeal?"

Ah, right. Uppsala. That was where she thought he'd gone— the job he had supposedly been up for—at the University of Uppsala in Sweden.

He couldn't have told her differently then. He hadn't been permitted to talk about it. And there was no point in talking about it now.

"It was a two-year appointment," he said.

That much was the truth. And though he could have continued to work on government projects, he hadn't wanted to. He'd agreed to the earlier one before he'd ever expected to be marrying anyone. And if things had worked out between him and Sophy, he would have bowed out and never gone to Europe at all.

When their marriage crumbled, he went, grateful not to have to stay in the city, grateful to be able to put an ocean between him and the reason for his pain.

But after two years, he'd come home, back to New York though he'd had several good offers elsewhere. "This one at Columbia is tenure track," he told her.

Not that tenure had been a factor. He'd taken the job because it appealed to him. It was research work he wanted to do, eager graduate students to mentor, a freshman class to inspire and a classload he could handle.

It had nothing to do with the fact that when he took it he'd thought Sophy and Lily were still living in the city. Nothing.

Sophy nodded. "Ah."

"When did you leave?" he asked. At her raised brows, he said, "I did drop by. You were gone."

"I went to California. Not long after you left," she said. "I started a business with my cousin."

"So I heard. My mother said she talked to you at Christo's wedding."

"Yes." Then she added politely, "It was nice to see your parents again."

George, who knew exactly what she thought of his father, said drily, "I'll bet."

He'd been invited to Christo's wedding, too. He hadn't gone because he had had no clue who his cousin Christo was marrying and no interest in flying across the country to find out. To discover later that Christo's bride was a second cousin of Sophy's blew his mind. He wondered what would have happened if he'd gone to the wedding, if they'd run into each other there.

Probably nothing, he thought heavily. There were times and places when things could happen. It had been the wrong time before. And now? Now it was simply too late.

Yet even knowing it, he couldn't help saying, "What about your business? My mother said it's called Rent-a-Bride?"

"Rent-a-*Wife*," Sophy corrected. "We do things for people that they need a second person to cope with. Things wives traditionally do. Pick up dry cleaning, arrange dinner parties, ferry the kids to dental appointments and soccer games, take the dog to the vet."

"And people pay for that?"

"They do. Very well, in fact." She met his gaze defiantly. "I'm doing fine."

Without you.

She didn't have to say the words for him to hear them. "Ah. Well, good for you."

Their gazes locked, hers more of a glare than a gaze. Then

abruptly she looked away, shifted in her chair and tried to stifle a yawn. Watching her, George realized she must have had to fly all night to get here from California.

"Did you sleep?"

She bit off the yawn. "Some." But her gaze flicked away fast enough that he knew it for the lie it was. And he felt guilty for her having been called for no reason.

"Look," he said roughly, "I'm sorry they bothered you. I'm sorry you felt you had to drop everything and fly clear across the country to sign papers. It wasn't necessary."

"The doctor said it was."

"My fault. I should have updated the contact information."

"To whom?" Her question was as quick as it was surprising. And was she actually interested in his answer?

George shrugged. "My folks. My sister, Tallie. She and Elias and the kids live in Brooklyn."

"Oh. Right. Of course." Sophy shifted in the chair, sat up straighter. "I just wondered. I thought—" But she stopped, not telling him whatever it was she'd thought, and George didn't have enough working brain cells to try to guess. "Never mind."

"I'll get it changed as soon as I get out of here," he promised.

"No problem." Sophy's easy acceptance was unexpected. At his blink of astonishment, she shrugged. "You were there for me. It's my turn."

He frowned. "So this is payback?"

She spread her hands. "It's the best I can do."

"You don't need to do anything!"

"Apparently not," she said in a mild nonconfrontational tone that reminded him of a mother humoring a fractious child.

George set his teeth. He didn't want to be humored and he damned well didn't want Sophy patronizing him.

"Fine. It's payback. So consider your debt paid," he said gruffly. He'd had enough. "Now, if you don't mind, I'd like to get some rest. And," he went on for good measure, "as you can see, I'm conscious and I can sign my own papers now. So thank you for coming, but I can take care of things myself. You don't need to hang around taking care of me. You can go."

As the words left his mouth he knew he heard the echo of almost the exact words she had thrown at him nearly four years ago: *I don't need you! I'm not a mess you need to clean up. I can take care of myself. I don't need you doing it for me. So get out of here! Leave me alone. Just go!*

And from the expression on her face, Sophy knew it, too. She looked as if he'd slapped her.

"Of course," she said stiffly and stood up, pulling her jacket off the back of the chair and putting it on.

George watched her every move. He didn't want to. But, as usual, he couldn't look away. From the first moment he'd seen her on his cousin Ari's arm at a family wedding, Sophy had always had the power to draw his gaze.

She didn't seem to notice. Something else that hadn't changed. She zipped up her jacket and picked up her tote from the floor by the chair. Then she stood looking down at him, her expression unreadable.

George made sure his was, too. "Thank you for coming," he said evenly. "I'm sorry you were inconvenienced."

She inclined her head. "I'm glad you're recovering."

All very polite. They looked at each other in silence. For three seconds. Five. George didn't know how long. It wasn't going to be enough. It never would be.

He couldn't help memorizing her even as he told himself it was a stupid thing to do. And not the first, he reminded himself grimly, where Sophy was concerned.

She gave him one last faint smile and turned away.

Her name was out of his mouth before she reached the door. "Sophy."

She stilled, glanced back, one brow lifting quizzically.

He'd thought he could leave it at that. That he could simply let her go. But he had to ask. "How's Lily?"

For a moment he thought she wouldn't answer. But then the smile he hadn't seen yet suddenly appeared on her face like the sun from behind a bank of thunderheads. Her expression softened. And she was no longer supremely self-contained, keeping him determinedly outside the castle walls. "Lily's fine. Amazing. Bright. Funny. So smart. We had her birthday party yesterday. She's—"

"Four." George finished the sentence before she could. He knew exactly how old she was. Remembered every minute of the day she was born. Remembered holding her in his arms. Remembered how the mantle of responsibility felt on his shoulders—unexpected, scary, yet absolutely right.

Sophy blinked. "You remembered?"

"Of course."

She swallowed. "Would you...like to see a picture of her?"

Would he? George nodded almost jerkily. Sophy didn't seem to notice. She was already opening her purse and taking out her wallet. She fished out a photo and came back across the room to hand it to him.

George took one look at the child in the photo and felt his throat close.

God, she was beautiful. He'd seen some snapshots that his mother had given him from the wedding so he had an idea of what Lily was like. But this photo really captured her.

She was sitting on a beach, a bucket of sand on her lap, her face tipped back as she laughed up at whoever had taken the photo. It was like seeing a miniature Sophy, except for the hair. Lily's was dark and wavy and, in this photo, wind-tossed. But her eyes were Sophy's eyes—the same shape, the same color. "British sports car green," he'd once called them. And her mouth wore a little girl's version of the delighted, sparkling grin that, like Sophy's, would make the world a brighter place. Her fingers were clutching the sides of the sand pail, and George remembered how her much tinier fingers had clutched his as she'd stared up at him in cross-eyed solemnity whenever he held her.

He blinked rapidly, his throat aching as he swallowed hard. When he was sure he could do it without sounding rusty, he lifted his gaze and said, "She's very like you."

Sophy nodded. "People say that," she agreed. "Except her hair. She has y—Ari's hair."

Ari's hair. Because Lily was Ari's daughter. Not his.

For all that George had once dared to hope, like her mother Lily had never been his.

They both belonged to Ari—always had—no matter that his cousin had been dead since before Lily's birth. Some things, George found, hurt more than the pounding in his head. He ran his tongue over his lips. "She looks happy."

"She is." Sophy's voice was firm and confident now. "She's a happy well-adjusted little girl. She's actually pretty easygoing most of the time. Once she got over the three-month mark, she stopped having colic and settled down. I managed," she added, as if it needed saying.

He supposed she thought it did. She'd had something to prove when she'd told him to get out. And she'd obviously proved it.

Now he took a breath. "I'm glad to hear it." George took one last look at the picture then held it out to her.

"You can have it," she said. "I can print another one. If you want it," she added a second later, as if he might not.

"Thanks. Yes, I'd like it." He studied it again for a long moment before turning slowly in an attempt to set it on the table next to the bed.

Sophy reached out and took it from him, standing it up

against his water pitcher so he could see it if he turned his head. "There." She stepped back again. "She can…watch over you." As soon as she said the words, she ducked her head, as if she shouldn't have. "You should get some rest."

"We'll see."

"No 'we'll see.' You should," she said firmly.

He didn't reply, and she seemed to realize that was something else she shouldn't have said, that she had no right to tell him what he should or shouldn't do. "Sorry," she said briskly. "None of my business." She turned toward the door again. "Goodbye."

He almost called her back a second time. But it would simply prolong the awkwardness between them. And when you got right down it, there was nothing else.

It had been kind of her to have come—even if it was simply "payback" on her part. Still, it was more than he would have expected.

No, that was unfair.

She might not love him, but she was tenderhearted. Sophy would do the right thing for anyone she perceived to be in need—even the man she resented more than anyone on earth.

He didn't need her, he reminded himself. He'd lived without her for nearly four years. He could live without her for the rest of his life. All he had to do was end things now as he should have done four years ago.

"Sophy!"

This time she was beyond the door and when she turned, she looked back with something akin to impatience in her gaze. "What?"

He made it clear—to both of them. "Don't worry. It will never happen again. As soon as I get out of here, I'll file for divorce."

CHAPTER TWO

OF COURSE GEORGE would get a divorce.

The only surprise as far as Sophy was concerned, was that he hadn't got one already. But even accepting the fact, Sophy felt her knees wobble as she walked away from George's room.

She moved automatically, going to fetch her duffel, which one of the nurses had allowed her to leave in a storage area near the nurses' station. But when she got there, her hands were shaking so much that she nearly brought down a load of paper supplies while trying to pull the duffel's handle out.

"Here. Let me help you." The nurse who had let her put it there in the first place took the duffel's handle, slid it out and pulled it easily out of the storage space. She tipped it toward Sophy, then looked at her closely. "Are you all right?"

"Yes, sure. Fine. Just…tired." Something of an understatement. "It's all right," Sophy murmured. "I'm fine. Truly." She did her best visibly to pull herself together so the nurse could see she was telling the truth. She shoved her hair away from her face and tried to smile. "I just need some sleep."

"Of course you do. It's been a bit traumatic. You go home now and get some sleep. Don't worry." She patted Sophy's arm. "We'll take care of your husband."

Sophy opened her mouth to correct the nurse, but what could she say? And why? Even though she wouldn't let herself think of George that way, it was impossible to lie to herself, impossible to say that walking into his hospital room had left her unaffected.

The very moment she'd laid eyes on him this morning, the years since she'd seen him fell away as if they'd never existed.

And even worse was the realization that, however desperately she might wish it, she wasn't over him at all.

When she'd walked into the hospital room to see George lying there, his head bandaged, his arm in a sling, his whisker-shadowed jaw bruised, his normally tanned face unnaturally pale, she felt gutted—exactly the same way she'd felt seeing her daughter fall off the jungle gym at her preschool.

The sight of Lily slipping and tumbling, then lying motionless on the ground, had shattered Sophy's world. That same sickening breathlessness had hit her again at the sight of George in his hospital bed.

The difference was that Lilly, having landed on wood chips that cushioned her fall, had only had the wind knocked out of her. Seconds later, she'd bounced up again none the worse for wear.

But George hadn't moved.

It was early when she'd arrived, straight from the airport, still stiff and groggy from a sleepless night on the plane. He should have been asleep. But it looked like such an unnatural sleep. And Sophy had stopped dead in the doorway, clutching the doorjamb as she stood watching him never flutter so much as an eyelash. She had been too far away to see the rise and fall of his chest.

She must have looked stricken because the nurse had said, "Watch the monitor." Its squiggly line was moving up and down jerkily. But at least it proved he was breathing because absolutely nothing else did.

"You can wake him if you want," this same nurse had said.

But Sophy had shaken her head. If George wasn't dead yet, the sight of her first thing when he opened his eyes might very well do it for him.

"No. Let him sleep," she said in a voice barely above a whisper. "I'll just wait."

"If he's not awake in an hour, I'll be back. We have to wake him regularly to see how he responds and if he remembers everything."

No doubt about his memory, Sophy thought grimly now.

She turned to the nurse. "He thinks he's going to leave today, to go to work. The doctor wouldn't really let him…."

The nurse smiled. "I don't think you need to worry about that. They'll be watching him today and probably tomorrow. You should go home now and get some rest. Come back this afternoon. Chances are he'll be much brighter by then." She gave Sophy one more encouraging smile, then checked her beeper and hurried down the hall.

Sophy stood there with her overnight bag and her briefcase and realized she didn't have a home to go to.

Home was three thousand miles away.

On the other hand, why shouldn't she go home? What was keeping her here? George had clearly dismissed her. As far as he was concerned, she needn't have bothered to come in the first place.

And she certainly wasn't going to come back this afternoon. She'd done her duty. "Payback," he'd called it.

And he'd rejected it. Consider it paid, he'd said.

That was fine with her. Shooting one last glance toward his room, she turned and wheeled her overnight bag down the hall to the elevator and pressed the button and waited, trying to keep her eyes open and stifle a yawn.

She was in the midst of the latter when the elevator door opened. There were several people in it, but only one, a young, dark-haired, very pregnant woman, swept out, then stopped dead and stared at her.

"Sophy?"

Sophy blinked, startled. "Tallie?"

"Oh, my God, it is you!" And before Sophy could do more than close her gaping mouth, George's sister, Tallie, swept her into a fierce delighted hug. "You've come back!"

"Well, I—" But whatever protest she might have made was muffled by the enthusiastic warmth of Tallie's embrace. And Sophy couldn't do much more than hug her back. It was no hardship in any case. She'd always adored George's sister. Losing the right to count Tallie as her sister-in-law had been one of the real pains of the end of her marriage.

Before she could say anything, a firm thump against her midsection had Sophy jumping back. "Was that the baby?" She looked at Tallie, wide-eyed.

Tallie laughed. "Yes. My girl likes her space." She rubbed her burgeoning belly affectionately. "This one's a girl. But more about her later. It's so good to see you." She gave Sophy another fierce hug, but was careful to move back before the baby kicked again. "George should get run over by trucks more often."

"No." Even for the pleasure of seeing Tallie again, she didn't want that.

"Well, not really." Tallie laughed with a shake of her head. "But if it brings you home—" She beamed at Sophy.

"I'm not 'home,'" Sophy said quickly. "I'm just…here. For the moment. I got a call from the doctor last night. When George was unconscious they needed his next of kin's permission for any medical procedures, and because we're not officially divorced—yet—that was me. And so—" she shrugged "—I came."

"Of course you did," Tallie said with blithe confidence. "Besides, it's about time. How is he?" Her smile faded a bit and she looked concerned. "He wouldn't let me come see him last night."

"He looks like he's been hit by a truck," Sophy said. If

Tallie hadn't seen him yet, Sophy wanted to prepare her. "Seriously. He's pretty battered. But coherent," she added when Tallie's expression turned worried.

"He flat-out refused to let us come last night. Well, there's only Elias and me around. Mom and Dad are in Santorini. And none of the boys—" her other brothers, Theo, Demetrios and Yiannis, she meant "—are here. So he was safe. He probably wouldn't have contacted me at all if he hadn't needed someone to take care of Gunnar."

"Gunnar?"

"His dog."

George had a dog? That was a surprise. "Did he rescue it?" Sophy asked.

Tallie frowned. "I don't think so. I think he got him as a puppy. Why?"

Sophy shook her head. "Never mind. I was just—never mind." She could hardly say, *Because George rescues things.* Tallie wouldn't understand.

George's sister shoved a strand of hair away from her face. "He said to go to his place and feed Gunnar, put him out and absolutely *don't* come to the hospital. He didn't need me hovering." She shook her head.

"George is an idiot," she went on with long-suffering sisterly fondness. "As if I would hover. Well, I will. But at least I waited until this morning. I'll go annoy him for a few minutes, just to let him know he can't push me around. And because the rest of the family will fuss and worry if someone hasn't set eyes on him in the flesh. But now you've come, you take the keys." She dug in the pocket of her maternity pants and thrust a set of keys into Sophy's hand.

"Me?" Immediately Sophy tried to hand them back. "They're not mine," she protested. "I can't take George's keys!"

"Why not? Because you and George are separated? Big deal."

"We're not separated! We're divorcing. I thought we already were," Sophy said. "Divorced," she clarified.

"But you're not? Good. Easier to work things out," Tallie said with the confidence of someone who had done just that and was living happily ever after. "Elias and I—"

"Were not married when you went your own ways," Sophy said firmly. "It is not the same thing. And I can't take George's keys." She tried to hand them back again, but a yawn caught her by surprise and so she ended up covering her mouth instead.

"You're exhausted," Tallie said. "How long have you been here?"

"Not that long. A couple of hours. I got into LaGuardia before dawn."

"You took a red-eye? Did you get any sleep at all?"

"Not really," Sophy admitted. "But I'm hoping I will on the way home."

Tallie looked appalled. "On the way home? What? You're going home now?"

Sophy shrugged. "He doesn't need me here. Or want me here. He made that quite clear."

Tallie snorted dismissively. "What does he know? Besides, it doesn't matter if he needs you or wants you. I do."

"You? What do you mean?"

"You, my dear Sophy, are going to save my life," Tallie told her, taking her by the arm and steering her to a pair of chairs where they could sit.

"Don't you want to see George?" Sophy said hopefully.

"In a minute. First I want to get you on your way." The CEO Tallie had once been came through loud and clear. "I need your help."

"What sort of help?"

"George, bless his heart, thinks that I can simply drop my life and take over the running of his. And admittedly, there might have been a time I could have done it," Tallie said with a grin. "But that time is not now. Not with three little boys, a baby due in three weeks, a homemade bakery business that has orders up the wazoo, orders I need to get taken care of before the arrival of my beautiful baby girl—" Tallie rubbed her belly again "—not to mention a husband who, while tolerant, does not consider sharing me with a dog for more than one night to be the best allocation of my time.

"Besides," she went on before Sophy could say a word, "he has to go to Mystic for a boat launch this afternoon. He took the kids to school, but I need to be home to get Nick and Garrett from kindergarten and Digger from preschool. I was planning to bake today before I had to go get them. And I'd take Gunnar home but he doesn't get along with the rabbit, er, actually vice versa. So—" she took a breath and gave Sophy a bright, hopeful smile "—what do you say? Will you save me? Please?"

Sophy was even more exhausted just thinking about it. She swallowed another yawn.

"And you can sleep while you're there," Tallie said triumphantly.

"George won't like it."

"Who's telling George?" Tallie raised both brows.

Not me, Sophy thought. She should say no. It was the sane, safe, sensible thing to do. The less she had to do with George or any of his family before the divorce was final, the less likely she was to be hurt again.

But life, as she well knew, wasn't about protecting yourself. It was about doing what needed to be done. "Payback" wasn't always what you thought it would be. It didn't mean you had a right not to do it.

"All right," she said resignedly. "I'll do it. But as soon as George can come home, I'm leaving."

"Of course," Tallie said, all grateful smiles. "Absolutely."

* * *

Sophy hadn't let herself think about where George might be living ever since he'd walked out of her life.

If she'd wanted to guess, she'd have picked some sterile but extremely functional apartment where he'd be called upon to do as little interaction with his environment as possible.

She couldn't have been more wrong.

George had a brownstone on the Upper West Side. Not just an efficient studio in a brownstone or even a complete floor-through apartment. George owned the whole five-story building.

And while most of the brownstones in the neighborhood had long since been subdivided into flats, George's had not.

"When he came home he said he wanted a house," Tallie told her. "And he got one."

He had indeed. And what a one it was.

Sophy stopped on the sidewalk in front of the wide stoop and stared openmouthed at the elegant well-maintained facade. It had big bay windows on the two floors above the garden entrance, and two more floors above that with three identical tall narrow arched windows looking south across the tree-lined street at a row of similar brownstones.

It had the warm, tasteful, elegant yet friendly look that the best well-kept brownstones had. And to Sophy, whose earliest memories of home were the days spent in her grandparents' brownstone in Brooklyn, it fairly shouted the word *home*.

It was exactly the sort of family home she'd always dreamed of. She'd babbled on about it to George in the early days of their marriage. He'd been preoccupied with work, of course. Not listening. At least she hadn't thought he was listening…

No, of course he hadn't been. It was coincidence.

All the same it wasn't helpful. Not helpful at all.

At least, she thought as she climbed the steps, the sound of a ferocious dog barking his head off on the other side of the front door belied any homey feelings that threatened to overtake her.

So that was Gunnar.

He sounded as if he wanted to have her for brunch.

"He's lovely," Tallie had said. "Adores George."

But apparently he wasn't keen on rabbits—except perhaps for meals—and the jury was still out on what he thought of her.

Good thing she liked dogs, Sophy thought, fitting the key in the lock and putting on her most upbeat, confident demeanor. She had no idea if it would convince Gunnar. She just hoped she convinced herself long enough to make his acquaintance.

"Hey, Gunnar. Hey, buddy," she said as she cautiously opened the door.

The dog stopped barking and simply looked at her quizzically. He was a good-size dog, all black with medium-length hair and some feathering.

"A flat-coated retriever," Tallie had told her, and when Sophy looked blank, she'd elucidated. "Think of a lean, wiry *black* golden retriever—with Opinions. Capital *O* Opinions." Gunnar's opinion of her was apparently being formed even as she talked to him.

"I hope you like me," Sophy said to him. She'd at least had the wisdom to stop at a pet shop on her way down Broadway, where she'd bought some dog treats. Now she offered one to the dog.

In her experience, most dogs took treats eagerly and without question. Gunnar took his, too. But instead of grabbing it, he accepted it delicately from her fingers, then carried it over to the rug by the fireplace where he lay down and nosed it for a few moments before consuming it.

She dragged her bag in over the threshold and shut the door behind her, then turned to survey Gunnar's—and George's—domain.

It was as impressive inside as it was out. From the mahogany-paneled entry she could see into the dining room where Gunnar was finishing his dog treat, up an equally beautiful mahogany staircase to the second floor and down a hallway to the back where a glimpse of a sofa told her she would find the living room.

But before she could go look, Gunnar came back and poked her with his nose, then looked up hopefully. "Treats are the way to your heart?" she said to him—and was surprised when he replied.

He didn't bark. He didn't growl. He just sort of—talked—made some sort of noise that had her looking at him in astonishment. So he poked her again.

"Right," she said. "Yes. Of course." And she fetched another treat out of the bag she'd bought. He accepted it with the same gravity with which he'd accepted the first one. But he didn't eat it. He simply carried it down the hall.

Sophy followed. She thought he was going to take it into the living room, which indeed was at the end of the hall. But instead Gunnar turned and went down the stairs. He obviously knew better than she did what she was supposed to be doing and was showing her where to go to open the door to the garden.

She let Gunnar out into the back garden with its cedar deck and table and chairs and the bucket of tennis balls that George must toss for Gunnar. Even though it was small and utilitarian, it was still far more appealing than the parking lot behind her apartment in California. She left Gunnar there and went back inside because she was more curious about George's office.

What would have been billed "the garden apartment" in a split-up brownstone, obviously served as George's office. One big room contained a wide oak desk, a sleek state-of-the-art computer with what was probably the biggest computer screen she'd ever seen. There were file cabinets, a worktable and shelf after shelf of scientific books. There were papers in neat stacks on the desk and worktable, and a few spread out that were filled with equations in George's spiky but very legible handwriting. When they'd been together, he had made out shopping lists in the same precise way.

Feeling a bit like a voyeur, though goodness knew she couldn't understand any of whatever he was working on, Sophy deliberately went back out into the garden and threw some tennis balls for Gunnar.

She made a friend for life. He was tireless. She was even more exhausted by the time she said, "Last one," and threw it across the small yard. Gunnar caught it on the rebound from the wall and trotted back to look at her hopefully. "Later," she promised him.

She could have sworn he sighed. But obediently he followed her back into the house, up the stairs and on up the next flight where there was a spacious yet homey family room that looked decidedly lived in—right down to the toys in one corner.

Toys?

Surprised, Sophy looked closer. Yes, there were toys. Blocks, LEGOs, Lincoln Logs and a fleet of scratched and dented Matchbox cars. Boy toys, Sophy thought. But it was clear that Tallie's boys were welcome at Uncle George's. Or did George have a lady friend with children? Not that she cared.

The family room was on the back of the house, just above the living room. Sophy found it cozy and friendly, drawing her in. There were books on the shelves, not only scientific tomes, but also popular mysteries and sailing magazines. She picked them up, noting that they weren't pristine. They had obviously been read.

She scanned the shelves curiously, then spotted a photo album as well. She opened it before she could think twice—and was quite suddenly confronted by memories that seemed almost like a blow to the heart.

The album was full of pictures from the reception after their wedding. Not the more formal portraits, but lots of casual family ones. She and George laughing as they fed each other cake. She and George dancing on the deck of his parents' home. She and George surrounded by his whole family, all of them smiling and happy.

Numbly she turned the pages. After the ones from the reception, there were others of the two of them. On the beach. In a small cozy house before a fire.

Sophy's throat tightened at the sight. At the memories of their honeymoon.

Well, it hadn't been a honeymoon—not really. There hadn't been time to plan one because the wedding had been so hastily arranged and George couldn't take time off work.

All they'd had was a weekend in a tiny groundskeeper's cottage behind one of the Hamptons mansions near his parents' home by the sea.

But for all that it had been impromptu, it had been memorable. They had, she'd thought, forged a bond that weekend. They'd talked. They'd laughed. They'd cooked together, swum together, walked on the beach together. They'd slept together in the same bed—though they hadn't made love.

Her pregnancy was too far along for that.

Still, for all they'd had a less than orthodox beginning, she'd dared to hope, to believe…

Now she shut the album and stuck it back on the shelf. She didn't want to look. Didn't want to remember the pain of dashed hopes, of lost love.

No, she corrected herself. It hadn't ever been love—not really. Not to George.

Deliberately she turned away. "Come on, Gunnar," she said to the dog. "Let's take a look at the guest room."

That's the most she was in George's house, in his life. A guest. She needed to remember that.

"I didn't change the sheets," Tallie had apologized. "I figured I'd either be back there tonight or George would be home. There are other rooms up above. There's a room for the boys up there, but George probably hasn't changed the sheets since the last time they were there. And that's where George's room is, of course."

Sophy felt enough like Goldilocks eavesdropping further in a house where she didn't belong. The last place she wanted to look at was George's bedroom.

George's bed. She didn't want to remember the nights she'd spent sharing a bed with George. Making love with George...

"I'll just take the room where you were," she'd told Tallie. "It will be fine."

It was Spartan—but perfectly adequate. It had a bed, sheets, a blanket and two pillows. What more could she ask?

Sophy kicked off her shoes and pulled off her jacket, already heading for the bed when she remembered that she needed to get on the computer and put through a video call to Natalie and Lily.

She opened her laptop on the bed and was glad she often used the video program to help out and advise the "wives" in the field who worked for her and Natalie. So she was quickly up and running, and felt an instant pang of homesickness when the call went through and she could see Lily at home with Natalie in her living room.

"Mama?" Lily demanded, sticking her face right up against Natalie's laptop. "Are you in the computer?"

Sophy laughed. "No, darling. I'm in New York. I had to come here last night, just for a couple of days. I'll be home soon. Are you being good for Auntie Nat?"

"'Course I am," Lily said. "I'm helping."

"Great." Though whether Natalie would think the help of a four-year-old was such a blessing, Sophy wasn't sure. "What are you going to do today?"

The three-hour time difference meant that Natalie and Lily were just getting started on their day. But clearly Natalie had given some thought to what they would do. Lily rattled off an entire list of things that included "after lunch going to the beach with Uncle Christo," undoubtedly so Natalie could get some real work done.

"Is that a dog?" Lily demanded, abruptly breaking off her recitation.

"Dog?" Sophy was confused, then realized that Lily wasn't just seeing her. Her daughter could see at least a part of the bedroom behind her. And Gunnar was standing by the bed looking equally curiously at the computer screen.

"Um, yes," Sophy said. "That's Gunnar."

"He's big," Lily said solemnly. "An' really, really black. Would he like me?"

"Oh, I think so," Natalie said. Gunnar, for all his ferocious barking while she was on the doorstep, had been an absolute gentleman since she'd crossed the threshold. He actually seemed to be looking at Lily.

"Hi, Gunnar," she said.

He looked quizzical and tentatively wagged his tail.

"He likes me!" Lily crowed.

"Who likes you?" Natalie reappeared and bent down to peer into the screen, eyes widening when she spotted the dog. "Who's that? Where'd he come from? Where are you?" she shot out the questions rapid-fire.

"That's Gunnar. He lives here."

"Here where?" Natalie demanded.

"At George's," Sophy said reluctantly.

"At Daddy's?" Lily demanded, sticking her face close to the screen to peer around the room eagerly. "Are you at Daddy's?"

"Yes, but—"

"Where is he?"

"Yes, where is Daddy?" Natalie demanded, frowning her concern.

Sophy heard the archness in Natalie's tone. "He's in the hospital." She tried to sound calm and matter-of-fact.

"Is Daddy okay?" Lily asked. "He's okay, isn't he, Mommy?"

"He will be," Sophy assured her.

"So what are you doing at his place?" Natalie wanted to know.

"Feeding his dog. And taking a nap. In the guest room," she added in case Natalie had other ideas.

Fortunately whatever ideas Natalie had she wasn't sharing them in front of Lily. She pressed her lips together, then shrugged and said, "Well, get some sleep then."

"I will. I just wanted to see Lily. Love you, kiddo."

"Love you, Mommy," Lily responded. "An' Daddy. An' Gunnar, too." She put her hand on the computer screen, as if she could reach out and pet him. Then she brought Chloe's face up to the screen and pointed out Gunnar to her. "He's your friend, Chloe," she told her stuffed dog. "An' he's mine, too. Oh, Uncle Christo's here. 'Bye, Mommy. 'Bye, Gunnar. See you later." And Lily skipped off, dragging Chloe away by a paw, leaving Sophy staring at the empty chair in the kitchen.

"Sorry about that." Natalie suddenly appeared. "Christo just came in bringing fresh cinnamon rolls from the bakery."

"Ah, well. A girl's got to have her priorities. Give her a hug for me."

"Of course." There was a pause. Then Natalie said, "I didn't realize Lily was quite so gung ho about George. She doesn't know him."

"She's fixated. All families have mommies and daddies. Or they're supposed to. We don't. She wanted to know why. Then she wanted to know everything about him."

"You should have told her about Ari. He's her father."

"No." Sophy didn't accept that. "He sired her. He would never have been there for her. George was."

"Briefly."

"Yes, well—" But Sophy didn't want to get into that. She

had never told Natalie all the reasons for the breakup of their marriage. It was personal. "Anyway, she asked. I told her. She's curious. It's the lure of the unknown."

Natalie looked doubtful. "What about the lure for you?"

"I'm fine," Sophy said firmly. "Besides, it's only one afternoon. I'm only putting the dog out—and grabbing a few hours' shut-eye. George isn't here. His sister asked me. I'm doing *her* a favor."

"If you say so," Natalie said doubtfully.

"I do."

"Right." Natalie shrugged, still looking concerned. "Be careful, Soph'."

"I'm being careful," Sophy replied. "Don't worry. I'll talk to you later, let you know what flight I'll be on."

"So you're coming soon?"

"Tonight. There's nothing to stay for."

Natalie smiled. "Great."

Sophy shut down the computer and put it on the nightstand by the bed. Then she finished undressing down to her underwear, drew back the covers and slid into the bed. It was heaven. And what she'd told Natalie was true: she was being careful. Very careful.

She closed her eyes and didn't let herself think about the photos in the album. She didn't let herself remember those months of hope and joy. She tried not to dwell on the fact that she was in George's house, that she could go up one more flight of stairs and lie in George's bed.

She didn't want the memories of loving him—of making love with him. She didn't want the pain.

The bed dipped suddenly. Her eyes snapped open to see Gunnar had leapt lightly onto the foot of the bed. He stood peering down at her.

She reached up and fondled his velvety soft ears, then scratched lightly behind them. He arched his back, almost like a cat. Then he turned in a circle and lay down next to her, so close that she could feel the press of his body through the covers.

She didn't know if he was supposed to be on the bed or not. She didn't care. The solid warmth of his body was comforting, reassuring. Even if he was George's dog, she liked him. She told him so.

Gunnar twitched his ear.

Sophy smiled, gave him a pat, Then shut her eyes and very carefully and resolutely did not let herself think about George. She slept.

And dreamed about him instead.

George wanted out.

Now. This afternoon.

"You can't keep me here," he told Sam, who was standing beside George's bed saying he needed to do exactly that.

Sam wasn't listening. He knew George. They'd ridden bikes together, climbed trees together and played lacrosse together. They'd even got drunk together and pounded on each other a few times—as friends do. George hadn't decided yet whether it was a stroke of good or bad luck that Sam had been the neurologist on duty when they brought him in last night.

He was leaning toward the latter right now as Sam was standing there with a stethoscope, looking grimly official.

"Well, no. I can't ground you. Or tie you to the bed," Sam agreed drily. "I did think that perhaps I could appeal to your adult common sense, but if that's a problem..."

George bared his teeth. It made his head hurt like hell. But then so did everything else he'd done today, which was pretty much nothing. He'd tried to read and couldn't focus. He'd tried to write and couldn't think. He'd tried to get up and walk around, but when he did, he'd barely made it back to the bed without throwing up. If they'd let him go home, he could at least get some sleep.

"It would be different if you didn't live alone," Sam was

saying. "Having someone who can keep an eye on you would make it more feasible."

"Babysit me, you mean," George grunted.

Sam grinned. "If the shoe fits…"

George glared. Sam just raised his brows, shrugged and looked back implacably.

Scowling, George folded his arms across his chest. "I'll be fine," he insisted. "I promise I'll call if I think it's worse."

"No," Sam said.

"I have work, a dog, a life—"

"A life?" Sam snorted at that. "I don't think so. You teach physics, for heaven's sake!"

It wasn't all he'd ever done, but George didn't go there. He just stared stonily at Sam and waited for him to give in.

"No," Sam said. "Just because I broke your nose in sixth grade doesn't mean I'm going to surrender my obligation as a doctor to give you my honest medical opinion."

"*The hell you did!* I broke *your* nose!"

Sam laughed. "Well, at least your memory's not totally shot." He lifted a hand and rubbed it ruefully across the bump in his nose. "At least I gave you the black eye."

"It wasn't that black."

"Pretty damn," Sam said. "Anyway, we'll talk about it tomorrow. We need to make sure the bleeding has stopped." He nodded toward George's head.

But George didn't notice. His attention had been grabbed by the glimpse of someone just beyond the door. *"Sophy?"*

Was he seeing things? She'd gone, hadn't she? Done her "duty" and hightailed it back to California?

But just as he thought it, she poked her head around the doorjamb. "Sorry. I didn't mean to disturb you. I thought Tallie might have come back."

Tallie? George started to shake his head, then thought better of it. "No. She went to get the boys from school. You talked to Tallie?"

Tallie certainly hadn't mentioned it. His sister had breezed in this morning to see how he was doing. Well, *breeze* might not have been the right word. *Waddle,* maybe. She'd looked as if she was going to have her baby any minute. He hadn't seen her in a month, and she hadn't been nearly that big last time he had. He felt a little guilty calling her last night and asking her to take care of the dog.

That was mostly what they'd talked about when she'd come by this morning.

"Gunnar's all taken care of," she'd assured him. "Don't worry about a thing."

She'd left again, promising to drop by later.

"Don't bother," he'd told her. It was enough that she was taking care of Gunnar. And what the hell did Sophy want with her?

"I talked to her briefly," Sophy was saying. "She came in as I was leaving. She will be back?" she asked now, as if it mattered more than a little.

"I hope not," George said. "Why?"

"I—" Sophy hesitated "—have something to give her."

"Leave it here. I'll take it home when I go. She can get it from me."

"Well, I—"

"But if it's urgent, don't bother," Sam cut in, and George realized that he'd completely forgotten about Sam, who went right on. "He's not going anywhere."

"The hell I'm not!"

Sophy looked from him to Sam and back again, her eyes wide and questioning.

"Ignore him," George said.

"Right, ignore me," Sam agreed. "I'm only his doctor."

"What's wrong with him?" Sophy was looking at Sam.

"Other than being obstinate, bloody-minded and imma-ture?" Sam raised a brow. "Not much. Well, no, that's not true. But the rest is confidential. Patient privacy, you know? He'd have to kill you if I told you." He gave George a sly grin, then turned a far warmer one on Sophy, which was when George remembered that Sam always had had a thing for the ladies.

"Cut it out," George said with enough of an icy edge to his voice that Sam's grin faded.

His friend looked at him, then at Sophy, then back at him. "What?"

George gave him a steely look, but didn't speak.

Sam looked at him curiously, gaze narrowing speculatively. But when George still didn't say anything, he shrugged and made his move. Sticking out his hand he crossed the room toward Sophy. "Hi, pleased to meet you. I'm Sam Harlowe."

She took Sam's hand, smiled warmly back at him. "George's doctor."

"For my sins. And every once in a while—though not necessarily at the moment—his friend. And you are—?" He still had hold of Sophy's hand.

"I'm Sophy," she said. "McKinnon."

"Savas," George said flatly from the bed, loud enough and firmly enough that they both turned toward him. He raised his chin and didn't give a damn if the top of his head blew right off. "George's wife."

CHAPTER THREE

"EX-WIFE," SOPHY corrected instantly, staring at George in astonishment. "You do remember that, don't you?"

George folded his arms across his chest. "I remember no one has filed for divorce yet."

"You said you would. If you don't, I will," she told him fiercely, then flicked a glance at Sam Harlowe. He was, of course, watching this exchange with the fascination of a man with courtside seats at the U.S. Open.

"Well," he said briskly, smiling as he did so, "I'll just leave the two of you to discuss this, shall I? Nice to meet you, Sophy." He squeezed her hand again, then raised a brow and gave her what could only be described as an "interested" look. The smile turned into a grin. "Let me know when you get your marital status figured out."

She didn't blame him for being amused. From the outside it probably was amusing. From where she stood her marriage to George was anything but. But she managed to give Sam a wry smile in return.

"I'll do that," she said, not because she intended to, but because it would obviously annoy George.

"See you tomorrow," Sam said to George with a meaningful arch of his brows.

"Not here," George said.

"No," Sam began.

But George cut him off. "You said I could go home if I had someone to stay with me."

"You don't."

"Sophy will do it."

"I—"

George turned his eyes on her. "Payback," he said softly. "Isn't that what you came for?"

"You said—"

"I didn't know, did I?" He was all silky reasonableness now. "I thought I'd be out of here today. No problem. But Dr. Dan here—" he gave a wry jerk of his head toward Sam "—thinks I need someone to watch over me, hold my hand, wipe my fevered brow—"

"Kick your bony ass," Sam suggested acerbically.

George didn't even glance his way. He sat in the bed, the bedclothes fisted in his fingers, his unshaven jaw dark, his eyes glittering as his gaze bored into hers. "It's what you do, isn't it?"

She'd certainly like to kick his ass right now. Unfortunately she doubted that's what he meant. "What are you talking about?"

"Rent-a-Wife. It's your business," he reminded her, as if she might have forgotten. "I'll 'rent' you."

Sam goggled.

Sophy gaped. She couldn't even find words.

George could. "It's simple. Perfectly straightforward. Like I said, it's what you do. I mean, you did come and offer, but if you're going to renege on your 'payback,' fine. I'll hire you instead."

"Don't be ridiculous."

He gave her a perfectly guileless look. "Nothing ridiculous about it. It's sane, and reasonable. A suitable solution to a problem." George was in professor mode now. She wanted to strangle him.

He looked at Sam. "You did say that, didn't you?"

Sam rubbed the back of his neck. "Well, I—" And Sophy thought he might deny what George had said. But then he shrugged helplessly. "That's what I said. You can go home if you get someone to keep an eye on you. *If* you take it easy. *If* you don't do stupid stuff. No straining. No lifting. No running up and down the stairs. No hot sex," he added firmly.

"Well, damn," George said mildly while Sophy felt her cheeks burn. He gave Sam a quick smile, then turned his gaze back on her. "Dr. Dan says I can go home."

Sophy ground her teeth. He'd boxed her in. Made it impossible to say no. But, why?

It wasn't as if he wanted to be married to her. Clearly he didn't. Just this morning he'd been vowing—promising!—to file for divorce. And now? She pressed her lips together in a tight line.

"How long?" She didn't look at George, only at Sam.

"Depends," Sam said slowly, and she could see him go back into his doctor demeanor as he thought about it. "He needs to remain quiet. Besides the concussion, which he will still be feeling the effects of, he has a subdural hematoma."

He went on at length about the blood spill between the dura and the arachnoid membrane, telling her it was impossible to know how extensive the bleeding could be, that it might organize itself in five to six days, that it could take ten to twenty for the membrane to form. The longer he talked, the more detailed and technical Sam became. Sophy heard the word *seizure* and felt panicky. She heard the word *death* and her sense of desperation grew.

"Then this is no small matter," she summarized when Sam finally closed his mouth.

"No, it's not. So far he's doing so good. But we're not talking about Mr. Sensible here."

They weren't? George had always seemed eminently sensible—sensible to a fault almost—to Sophy. She looked at him, then at Sam.

"I'm giving you worst-case scenarios." Sam assured her.

"Thanks very much," she said drily.

"But it's necessary. It's why I won't let him go if he's going to be alone."

There was silence then. Sam waited for her answer. George didn't say a word, just stared at her with that "is your word good or not?" look on his face. And Sophy wrestled with her conscience, her emotions and her obligations.

"So you're saying it could be days," she said finally.

"Honestly it would be better for him to have someone around for several weeks. Or a month."

"A *month?*" Sophy stared at him, horrified.

Sam spread his palms. "The chances of him needing anything are minimal. They go down every day. As long as he doesn't do something to complicate matters. I'm just saying, if he's alone, how do we know?"

Indeed, how would they?

Oh, hell.

Sophy understood. But she just didn't like it. Not one bit. And she couldn't imagine George liking it, either. Not really. She shot him a glance now to see how he was taking Sam's news. His face was unreadable, his eyes hooded, his expression impassive. His arms were folded across his chest.

"I can't stay a month or two," Sophy said. "I have a life— and work—in California. I can't leave Lily that long."

"Bring her," George said.

"Who's Lily?" Sam asked.

"Our daughter," George answered before Sophy could.

Sam's eyes went round. His jaw dropped. "Odd you never mentioned any of this," he murmured in George's direction.

"Need to know," George said in an even tone.

Sam nodded, but he blinked a few times, still looking a little stunned as his gaze went from George to Sophy and back again.

He wasn't the only one feeling a bit shell-shocked.

All she'd intended to do was drop into the hospital long enough to give Tallie the key to George's house, say thank-you for the few hours sleep and say that Gunnar was fine. She hadn't even expected to have to talk to George again. After the way they'd left things this morning, she couldn't imagine he'd have anything more to say to her.

"There must be 'wives for rent' in New York," she said.

Sam didn't offer an opinion. He tucked his hands in his pockets and retreated into bystander mode.

"I'll rent you a wife," she offered.

"So much for payback," George murmured.

Sophy's fingers knotted into fists. "You'd be able to come home."

George just looked at her. "So you're saying you won't do it." His tone was mild enough, but Sophy didn't have to imagine the challenge in his words.

She clenched her teeth to stop herself saying the first, second and third things that came into her head. She got a grip, reminded herself that he was not himself—even though, frankly, he seemed more like himself than ever. And then she reminded herself as well that she owed him.

Ultimately she might have resented what he'd done by high-handedly proposing marriage and taking over her life.

But she'd let him.

She'd let herself be steamrolled. Had said yes because she knew George was all that Ari wasn't, that Ari—even if he'd lived—would never have been. And she couldn't even put a finger on when she realized she felt about George far differently and far more intensely than she'd ever felt about Ari.

She'd desperately wanted their marriage to work.

Finding out that she was just another obligation, one more of "Ari's messes" that George had had to clean up had hurt her far more than Ari's turning his back on her and fatherhood in the first place.

But that wasn't George's problem. It was hers.

And before she could move forward, she knew she had to do what she'd told him she'd come to do—settle her debts—even if what she was doing reminded her of the old cliché about the frying pan and the fire.

As for why George wanted her to do it when he didn't want to be married to her, well, maybe she'd find an answer to that. Maybe, please God, there would finally be some closure.

She straightened. "Fine. I'll do it."

Sam's eyes widened. George didn't blink.

"But only for a month—or less if possible." She met his gaze steadily. "Then we're even."

He wanted to just walk out then and there.

To get out of bed, dress and stroll out of the hospital as if he'd just spent the night in a not very pleasant hotel.

Of course it wasn't as simple as that. He didn't have any clothes, for one thing. His had been shredded and bloodied in the accident and cut from his body after. Getting out of bed hurt like sin. Strolling, of course, was impossible. He was on crutches and wearing a boot to give his ankle some support.

But at least Sophy couldn't say he'd shanghaied her into staying under spurious pretenses.

What she did say, though, as he asked her to go buy him some clothes, surprised the hell out of him.

"Not necessary," she said. "I'll just go to your place and bring you some clothes back."

"My place?"

She shrugged, dug into the pocket of her pants and held up a key. "Your house. I've got a key. It's what I came to bring back to Tallie."

His jaw dropped. He had to consciously shut his mouth. But he couldn't keep it shut. He demanded, "She gave you a key to my house?"

Another shrug. "I was tired when I ran into her by the elevator. I hadn't slept all night. And she had things to do.

The kids. Baking. Stuff for Elias. She couldn't spend all day with Gunnar. So she asked me to spend the day at your place instead of at a hotel—and get some sleep at the same time. I didn't snoop around," she told him tartly.

He didn't expect she had. Why would she bother? He shrugged awkwardly. "I was just surprised."

"Yes, well, it wasn't my idea. But it was a nice bed," she allowed. "And Gunnar is lovely." She smiled the first really warm genuine smile he'd seen since she'd been here. Better even than the smile she'd given Sam.

"He's a good dog," George allowed gruffly.

Their gazes met, and there was a moment's awkward silence, probably because it was the first thing they'd agreed on since he'd opened his eyes and found her in his hospital room.

Her gaze slid away before his did. She seemed to be staring at the key in her hand.

"So, fine," George said after a moment. "Go back to my place and get me some clothes. I'll be getting signed out of here while you're gone." He told her where things were.

Sophy nodded. "I'll be back." She shook hands with Sam again on her way out. "You'll leave me lots of instructions? Things to watch for?"

"I'll make a list," Sam said. "And you can call me any-time."

Now her smile for him was as warm as the one she'd had when she talked about Gunnar.

"Take your time," George muttered.

Sophy shot him a glare and stalked out, taking her luggage and briefcase with her.

"Well, now. You never told me about Sophy," Sam said with a knowing grin.

"No need."

"Not for you maybe," Sam laughed. "Must be an interesting

history you two have. And a daughter, too? Did I ever really know you, Georgie?"

George just looked at him. "Stuff it."

"A month? You're joking." But it was clear from her voice that Natalie didn't think it was a laughing matter. "You didn't commit yourself to staying a month in New York. Did you?" she demanded.

Sophy sighed, tucking her phone between her jaw and her shoulder as she opened one of George's dresser drawers and took out boxers, a T-shirt and a pair of socks. "Hopefully not a full month. Maybe just a couple of weeks. But yes, I did. I have to, Nat."

"You don't *have* to."

Sophy shut the drawer. "All right, maybe not in the strictest sense of *have to*. But in the world I live in, I owe George."

"For what?"

"For…things. He's a good man," Sophy hedged, moving on to the closet. She didn't want to discuss this with Natalie, but she had no choice. They were business partners. If she was going to be gone three or four weeks, that would require adjustments.

Life, it seemed, was full of adjustments these days. She pulled a button-front shirt off a hanger in George's closet and took a pair of khakis off another hanger. It seemed like too intimate a thing to be doing—prowling through George's clothes—which was why she'd called Natalie while she was doing it. So she'd focus on business and not on being in George's room.

"A 'good man' doesn't explain anything," Natalie said.

So Sophy told Natalie what Sam had told her and ended with, "So he needs someone with him. To keep an eye on him. To make sure he doesn't have more bleeding."

"And you think you're the only one who can do that?"

"No, I don't think I'm the only one who can do it. But right now George does. And—" she sighed "—I need to humor him."

"Did his doctor say that?"

"No. But getting George stressed isn't going to make things better."

"And *you're* not going to get him stressed?"

Sophy gave a short laugh. "Can't promise that, sadly." She had folded the shirt and khakis and now added them to the single shoe she'd stuck into the grocery bag she'd found in the kitchen. No point in bringing the other since he had an orthopedic boot on his left foot. Then, clothes gathered, she started back downstairs. Gunnar followed her down.

"It's not about the head injury," Natalie decided.

"Maybe not," Sophy allowed. "Maybe we just need some closure."

"I thought you were already closed."

"We're not legally divorced. I told you that."

"But you haven't lived together for years, since right after Lily was born. He hasn't been around at all."

"I didn't want him around."

"And now you do?"

Sophy didn't know what she wanted. Her emotions were in turmoil, had been since the emergency room doctor's call last night. Besides, it didn't matter what she wanted. This wasn't about her.

"Of course not. I'm just being a rent-a-wife, Nat," Sophy said with some asperity. "It's what we do."

"Oh, okay," Natalie said after a long moment, and from her tone Sophy could tell her cousin wasn't exactly convinced.

"I need to do this, Nat."

"Do it then," Natalie said more convincingly. There was a pause. Then she said, "I'll bring Lily out on Saturday."

It was far more help and cooperation than Sophy had any right to expect. "You're a gem," she said, relieved beyond measure.

"I'm glad you think so," Natalie replied. "But the truth is, I want a look at the man who's playing fast and loose with your life."

The man who was playing fast and loose with her life looked like death by the time he was dressed in the clothes Sophy had brought and was leaning on a pair of crutches, waiting while she flagged down a taxi.

Fortunately one turned up almost immediately. If it hadn't Sophy would have been sorely tempted to march him right back into the hospital and suggest they rethink things.

He had taken the clothes from her with barely a word when she'd returned with them. She'd gone out to get last-minute instructions from Sam while George got dressed. And while Sam had given her a lengthy commentary complete with all the dire things that could happen, George still hadn't come out of the room when Sam finished.

When he finally had, he was white as the sheets on the bed he'd just left, and Sophy had wanted to push him right back into it.

But George had said, "Let's go," through his teeth, and so they'd gone.

He hadn't spoken again, and he still didn't say a word when the taxi pulled up and Sophy opened the door. He just got in, not without difficulty, and slumped back against the seat, eyes shut, perspiration on his upper lip, when she shut the door again and Sophy gave the driver George's address.

Because he had his eyes closed, she studied him. And the longer she did so, the more concerned she got. His breathing seemed too quick and too shallow. His knuckles were white where he clenched his fists against the tops of his thighs. With his head tipped back, she could see his Adam's apple move as he swallowed. She thought he was swallowing too much.

He didn't open his eyes or his mouth until the driver pulled up outside his place. Sophy eyed him nervously.

"Can you manage?" she asked when she opened the door.

"Yes." The word came from between his teeth.

She didn't know if he could or not, but if he couldn't, she supposed they'd deal with it then. So she got out and paid the driver, then waited as George eased himself slowly out of the car.

Inside the house, Gunnar was barking. She could see him at the bay window, his paws up on the sill as he looked at them on the sidewalk. "He's glad to see you," she said and was pleased to see George's features lighten fractionally as a faint smile touched his mouth.

"I'm glad to see him."

Getting up the stairs was a chore. He wouldn't have had a problem with the crutches if he hadn't also hurt his shoulder in his dive to get Jeremy out of harm's way. As it was, one complicated the other. Finally he thrust the crutches in her direction and said, "Just go on in. I'll get there."

As Gunnar was still barking, she did as George said, opening the door and staying out of sight so he could get up the stairs without an audience. Or at least without her. Gunnar was delighted to see her. He bounced eagerly and nosed her hands. But then he went back to the window to check on George.

Sophy went to the door to hold it open for when he finally got there, which he did at last. He looked like death.

"I know Sam said to get you to bed, but we're not doing any more stairs right now," she told him.

He didn't argue. Wordlessly he headed straight down the hall to the living room, then sank down onto the sofa as soon as he got there. Sophy ran upstairs and got the pillows off her bed and grabbed the comforter folded at the bottom of it, then hurried back down. George hadn't moved. He didn't open his eyes when she returned. The north-facing windows let in some light, but his face was in the shadows. His head rested against the back of the sofa, the skin beneath his stubbled cheeks almost white. He looked completely spent.

Sophy plumped the pillows at one end and said, "How about lying down?"

It was an indication of how bad he must feel that he didn't argue. Slowly, laboriously, wordlessly, eyes still shut, George stretched out on the sofa. She covered him with the comforter.

"Can I get you anything?"

Okay, she knew she was hovering, and he didn't like hovering. But she wanted a response. Yes, he was doing what she suggested. But she needed a word or two. It unnerved her to see him like this. It was so out of character. George took charge. George could do anything, always had.

"No," he said, lips barely moving, his voice low and a little rusty. "I'm fine."

"Of course you are," she said with a smile and tucked the comforter in around him, unable to fight the feeling of fondness—no, not simply fondness…*love,* God help her—that swamped her.

"Oh, George." She swallowed hard and blinked back sudden unexpected tears.

His eyes flicked open. "What?"

But Sophy turned her head away. "Nothing. I'm going to get you some water." She started toward the kitchen.

"I don't need water," she heard him say.

"Well, I need to get it," she replied, not turning around. And she hurried toward the kitchen where, please God, she would get a grip.

She could not survive the coming month if she got teary-eyed at the drop of a hat.

Death didn't seem like such a bad alternative.

George was appalled at how weak he was, how badly his

head hurt—how badly *he* hurt—and how dizzy and dazed and out of control he felt.

There was no way on God's earth he could climb the stairs to his bedroom. Not now. Maybe not even today. All he wanted to do was close his eyes and lie perfectly still.

What he did not want to do was deal with Sophy.

Of course it was his own damn fault Sophy was here.

When he heard her footsteps returning, he forced his eyes open, even though as soon as he did the room began spinning again. "You don't have to stay."

"Of course I don't," Sophy said. But she made no move to leave. She set the glass on a coaster behind his head on the end table. She was so close when she bent to do it that he could smell the scent of her shampoo, enough that he could have reached up a hand and touched her. But God knew what he'd do if he did.

And George, for one, didn't want to find out.

"So go," he said with all the firmness he could manage. "You were right before. At the hospital. There are plenty of home nurses in New York. Call one."

"I don't think so."

"Sophy—"

"I'm going to put Gunnar out. C'mon, buddy," she said as if he hadn't even spoken. She snapped her fingers lightly. And George heard the clink of Gunnar's tags as the dog—*his* dog, damn it!—jumped up from beside the sofa and obediently followed Sophy down the stairs.

He didn't hear them come back.

He must have slept. He didn't know how long. The first thing he was aware of was a mouthwateringly delicious smell. The second thing was that his head didn't hurt quite as much. He moved it slowly, experimentally. The pain was still there, but less explosive now. It hurt, but not enough to make him sick to his stomach.

He cracked his eyes open.

Sophy was sitting in the recliner, her laptop on her out-stretched legs, her head bent, her burnished copper hair, almost brown in the shadows, hiding her face as she looked at the screen. He turned his head to try to see her better.

Her gaze flicked up. "Ah, you're awake. How are you doing?"

The first time he'd met her—with Ari at some cousin's wedding—George had been struck not just by her amazing hair and her pretty animated face, but by her voice. Amid what he thought of as "stage five rapids" of conversational white noise wedding chatter surging all around them, Sophy's clear soft voice had seemed like a cool still welcome pool. It still did.

He shifted his head again experimentally. "Better."

"Can I get you anything?"

He flexed his shoulders and discovered that most of his muscles were still on strike. So he said, "Maybe that water you brought earlier."

Immediately Sophy set aside the laptop and got up to fetch the glass for him. He considered saying he could get it himself, but he wasn't sure he could—not without making a production of it. So he just said, "Thank you," when she handed him the glass.

He wasn't expecting her to kneel down next to him and slide her arm under his shoulders to lift him up enough to drink easily. He let her do that, too, because it did help—and because her hair brushed his cheek and he could breathe in the scent of her just as he used to. Hers was a scent so uniquely Sophy that even if he hadn't known it was her, one breath would have taken him straight back to the night's he'd lain next to her in bed, wanting her.

Now he swallowed too quickly and choked, coughing, making his head pound once more.

Swiftly Sophy set the glass down. Her arm tightened around his shoulders. "Are you all right?"

George coughed again, wincing, then made himself nod even though it hurt. "Yeah. Just…swallowed the wrong way. I'm okay."

She eased him back down and slid her arm from beneath him. Then she sat back on her heels, her gaze intent. "Are you sure about being home, George? I can call Sam. Tell him you've changed your mind. Or he can come over. He said he'd stop by after work."

"No."

"But—"

"No! I'm not going back and Sam is not coming over. No way. Not having him here hitting on you and—"

"What?"

He gave her a derisive look. "You didn't notice Sam was just a little bit interested?"

"Interested in what?"

George stared at her. "In you!"

"Me? Sam? Oh, don't be ridiculous. We just met. We spent five minutes talking about you and—"

"Doesn't take Sam long. He's a fast worker," George muttered. "You don't want to fool around with Sam. He's not dependable."

"I don't even know Sam."

"And now you won't have to. Got you out of there before he could work his wiles on you."

"What?" Sophy's cheeks were nearly as red as her hair. *"You got me out of there?"*

"Don't shout." George put a hand over his eyes.

"I'll shout if I want. And I'm not shouting. I'm enunciating. I don't believe you!"

George heard the sound of her standing abruptly and stalking away. He squinted to look for her, but the room began tilting again. "Just doing you a favor," he said to her back.

Sophy turned and slapped her hands on her hips. "I don't need you—or anyone—doing me favors like that!"

He looked up at her. "Just saying, you don't want to go out with Sam."

"I'll go out with whomever I damn well please!"

"Sam's a womanizer."

"Ari was a womanizer," Sophy said. "I know all about womanizers."

George went suddenly cold. Ari. It always went back to Ari. He dropped his head back on the pillows. "And that's what you want, isn't it?" he said dully. "Go away, Sophy. You're making my head hurt."

Deliberately he shut his eyes.

He refused to eat the chicken soup she made.

She told him if he didn't, she'd call Sam.

He gave her a baleful look, but when she picked up her phone and started to punch in Sam's number, George glared at her, but picked up his spoon and began to eat.

In the end he ate two bowlfuls because once he started he finished the first bowl quickly and Sophy refilled it without even asking him.

She hadn't intended to eat with him, retreating to the kitchen after she'd filled his bowl a second time. But when she didn't come back into the living room, he called after her, "Hiding in the kitchen, Soph?"

"No, I'm not hiding in the kitchen," she retorted irritably. "I'm feeding Gunnar." But then, when Gunnar finished his food and trotted happily back to be with George, she had no recourse but to bring her own bowl and return as well.

He looked a little better now. After another hour's sleep following the Sam incident, he had a bit of color in his cheeks again. He said his headache was better and the room had stopped spinning. So he had sat up on the sofa to eat and he was still sitting up now.

"It's good soup," he told her.

"Thank you," Sophy said stiffly.

"You always were a good cook."

"Thank you again."

He looked up at her. "You could sit down. A guy could get a stiff neck staring up all the time."

She wanted to say he didn't have to look at her. But instead she just sat or, to be more accurate, perched on the edge of the recliner, holding her soup bowl in one hand and her spoon in the other. But she couldn't help giving him an arch look. "Better?"

"Oh, much," George said drily, which had the effect of making her feel as if her irritation was petty and unreasonable at the same time he made her want to laugh.

Damn George could always make her laugh.

It was one of the most surprising things about him—that a man so serious, so responsible and so…so…annoyingly "right" all the time could have a certain subtle wryness that could make her stop taking herself so seriously, could make her smile, could make her laugh.

Could make her fall in love with him again.

No, oh, no. He couldn't.

Abruptly Sophy stood up. "I'm going to take Gunnar for a walk."

She didn't wait to hear what George thought about that. She just grabbed Gunnar's leash and they left. Because it was night, she took the dog over to Amsterdam Avenue and they walked south from there. Tomorrow morning, she promised him, they would go to Central Park where dogs could run off the leash before nine.

"This one isn't for you," she told him. "This walk's for me."

She needed it to give herself some space—a little more breathing room and a little less George Savas and all the feelings he evoked.

She walked briskly—Gunnar was a good pacesetter—trying to regain her equilibrium, to put her mixed-up feelings in a box and lock it up tight. This was a job. It was not a second chance. It was doing what needed to be done so she could walk away knowing that the scales were balanced, that she owed nothing more to the man who had married her.

She lectured herself all the way down to 72nd St. before she felt the adrenaline surge level off. Then they walked more sedately back while she told Gunnar all about Lily and how her daughter loved dogs. Focusing on Lily helped. And when she got back to George's she felt calmer and steadier and as if she was in control again.

The minute she opened the door and unclipped his leash, Gunnar went shooting straight for the living room. Sophy followed at a more sedate, far less enthusiastic pace.

"So," she said as she came down the hallway to enter the living room, "how's the headache now?"

George wasn't there.

CHAPTER FOUR

"GEORGE?" SOPHY BLINKED at the sight of the empty couch, as if once she did so he would suddenly rematerialize there. But no matter how many times she blinked, no George appeared.

"George!" She raised her voice a little and she poked her head in the kitchen, expecting to see him standing there, leaning on his crutches, making a forbidden cup of coffee. When she found the kitchen empty, she checked the first floor bathroom. No George there, either.

She whirled out of the bathroom and back into the living room. "George!" She yelled his name now. "Damn it, where are you?"

His crutches were leaning beside the couch. But he hadn't used them to get up the steps to the house earlier. So he'd probably taken advantage of her not being here to make his way on his own upstairs.

"Idiot," she muttered under her breath.

He could have fallen. He was the one who'd said the world was tilting earlier. She pounded up the stairs two at a time, past her own room, up to the third floor, to George's master bedroom, where she'd come to get his clothes earlier.

Then she had deliberately got in and out as fast as she could, refusing to allow herself time to look around, to imagine George in his surroundings. She'd deliberately rung Natalie so she wouldn't. And she'd barely done more than glance in the direction of his king-size bed.

Now Sophy stalked into the room and flicked on the light, hoping it made his head hurt just a little. She was glad he'd had the sense to go to bed, and at the same time annoyed that he had waited to do it until she was gone.

"Damn it, George! You can't do things like this! You've got to—"

Be careful, she was going to say.

Except there was no one to say it to. The bed was empty.

He wasn't in the adjoining bathroom, either. Nothing had changed from when she'd come up the first time. Now she did feel a shaft of concern. Surely he couldn't have had a relapse and called 911 in the half hour she had been gone, could he?

"George!" Back down the stairs she went, pausing to poke her head worriedly into the room she'd slept in just in case he'd only made it that far. But it was empty, too.

Maybe he had tried to get up, had fallen and was lying somewhere comatose.

"George!" she bellowed again when she reached the main floor, heading back toward the living room to check again.

"For God's sake, stop shouting." The disembodied voice came floating up from the garden floor office.

Sophy's teeth snapped together. She skidded to a halt, grabbed the newel post and spun around it to head down the stairs.

George was sprawled in his desk chair, staring at his over-size computer screen, reading an e-mail. Gunnar, who had obviously found him right away, looked up from where he lay at George's feet and thumped his tail.

George didn't even glance her way.

Sophy stared at him in silent fury, then stalked across the room and peered at the screen over his shoulder. "Is this all you've got open?"

"I don't multitask."

"Is it saved?"

"Of course."

"Good." She stepped around to the side of the desk and pulled the plug out of the wall. Instantly the screen went black.

"What the hell?" At least he spun his chair a half turn to look at her then—even if the action did make him wince and grab his head. "What'd you do that for?"

"I should think that's obvious. I'm saving you from yourself."

"You could have just said, 'turn off the computer.'"

"Oh? And that would have worked, would it? I don't think so." As she spoke she was methodically removing all the plugs from his surge protector, then looking around for some place to put it where he couldn't just hook it up again. Her gaze lit on the file cabinet. She opened the top drawer, dropped in the surge protector, shut the drawer, locked it and pocketed the key.

George stared at her, dumbfounded. "Are you out of your mind? I need to work. That's what I came home for."

"Well, you're not fit to work."

"Says who?"

"Says me," Sophy told him. "And Sam. You hired me to take care of you and that's what I'm doing."

"Then you're sacked."

"Throw me out. Try it," Sophy goaded him. "You can't. And I'm not leaving. I gave my word. And I keep it."

"Do you?" George said quietly.

And all of a sudden, Sophy knew they were talking about something entirely different. She swallowed and wrapped her arms across her chest. For a moment her gaze wavered, but then it steadied. She did keep her word. Always. No matter what he thought. She lifted her chin and met his gaze firmly. "Yes."

He looked as if he might argue with her. But finally he shrugged. "Maybe you do," he said enigmatically.

She didn't know what he meant by that, wasn't sure she wanted to know. She kept her arms folded, her gaze steady.

"I have to get some work done sometime, Sophy."

"Not tonight."

"My head feels better."

"Good. Not tonight."

He looked almost amused now. "Are you going to stand there and say that until tomorrow?"

"If that's what it takes." She didn't move.

George sighed and shook his head. "You're a bully."

And there was the pot calling the kettle black. She remembered so many times when she'd been expecting Lily that he had gently bullied her into taking extra good care of herself. But that was not a memory she wanted to dig into right now. Sophy just shrugged. "It's time to go to bed."

"Is that an invitation?" George's brow lifted. He grinned faintly.

"No, it's an order."

He laughed, then winced at the effect it had on his head. But finally he pushed himself slowly up out of his chair and started to hobble slowly toward the stairs. He had to pass within inches of her to get there.

She wanted to step back, to give him plenty of space, to keep her distance while he passed. Yet she sensed that if she did, he'd see it as a retreat. And Sophy was damned if she was retreating.

She stayed where she was, even looked up to meet his gaze when he reached her and stopped to loom over her, so close that if she'd leaned in an inch or two she could have pressed her lips to his stubbled jaw.

He didn't say anything, just stood there and looked down at her for a long moment. She could see each individual whisker on his jaw, trace the outline of his lips. She flicked her gaze higher to meet his eyes. He didn't speak, but the air seemed to crackle with some weird electricity between them. Sophy didn't blink.

Finally he limped slowly on toward the stairs. "Coming?" he said over his shoulder, with just a hint of sardonic challenge in his voice. "Or are you going to stay down here and set fire to my office?"

Sophy drew a breath and said with far more lightness than she felt, "Of course. I'm right behind you—ready to catch you if you fall."

It was like climbing Everest.

And he couldn't complain because if he did, Sophy would just say, "Told you so," or something equally annoying.

He couldn't even just go lie down on the couch again because when he finally got to the first floor she said, "Might as well go all the way up since you're feeling so much better. I'll get your crutches."

At least the thirty seconds it took her to do that gave him a half a minute's respite before she was standing there, holding them, saying brightly, "After you."

Serve her right if he fell on her.

He didn't. But not for lack of opportunity. Ordinarily he didn't even think about all the times he clattered up and down the flights of stairs in his house. Tonight he counted every single blasted one of them.

There were twenty per floor. It felt like a hell of a lot more. The crutches didn't help, which he already knew from his experience outside. And going down to his office hadn't been a problem. He'd eased his way down by sliding carefully on the bannister. Not that he intended to tell Sophy that!

She stayed behind him the whole way, wordlessly watching while he made the laborious climb. She never said a word, but he could sense her eyes on him.

"Don't feel you have to wait. Go right on up," he said through his teeth.

"No hurry," she replied. "I don't mind."

He did, but he wasn't telling her that, either. So he just kept on going, aware as he did so that sweat was breaking out on the back of his neck and the palms of his hands. He hoped Sophy didn't notice.

He thought she might have, though, because when they got to the second floor, she said, "Would it help if you leaned on me?"

"No, it would not." Then, realizing he'd snapped, he gritted his teeth and added, "Thank you," as lightly as he could.

Not that he wouldn't like to put an arm—hell, both arms!—around Sophy, but not now. Not this way. Not under these circumstances. He used the railing for support as he hobbled down the hall toward the next flight of the twenty thousand steps that would take him to his bedroom.

"Maybe you should just spend the night here." Sophy hovered behind him, sounding worried. "You could have this bed and—"

"You offering to share it with me?"

"No."

"Didn't think so. I'm fine." He wasn't going to admit he couldn't make it because, damn it, he could make it. He took the first step. Only nineteen thousand more to go.

In the end it probably didn't take him as long as he thought it had. All George knew was that his bed had never looked so good.

Sophy had darted around him as he'd reached the door to his room, going in ahead of him and turning down the duvet and plumping the pillows. By the time she'd finished and stepped back, he was able to ease himself down onto the mattress, all the while trying not to make it look as welcome as it was.

"Shirt," Sophy said before he could lie down.

He stared up at her and blinked. She was holding out a hand expectantly.

"You can't sleep in your clothes," she said patiently.

Of course he could. He'd done it often enough after working far into the night. But Sophy was having none of it. She knelt between his legs and unbuttoned his shirt as if he were four years old. Then she stood again and gently eased it off his shoulder, making sure she didn't hurt it any more than he'd already done hauling himself up three flights of stairs.

"Lie down," she directed.

"I thought you said I couldn't sleep in my clothes."

"You won't be." She put a hand against his chest and gave him a soft push so that he lay back against the pillows. Then she lifted his legs onto the bed and took off the orthopedic boot, his single shoe and his sock. Then she started to unbuckle his belt.

He suddenly took a much greater interest in the proceedings.

"Don't," Sophy said briskly, "think this is going anywhere."

With the disinterested efficiency of a hospital nurse, she made quick work of the belt buckle, the button and the zip.

"Lift," she commanded. And he barely had time to react before she was dragging his khakis over his hips and down his legs. She gave the duvet a shake and spread it over him, then stepped back. "There," she said, sounding satisfied. "I'll get you a glass of water. You can take one of those pills Sam sent, then you can get some sleep."

She disappeared briefly into the bathroom and returned with a glass of water and the requisite pill, which she handed to him.

"What's it for?"

"Pain."

"You didn't think to give it to me before I climbed three flights of stairs?"

"You could have asked for it," she told him. "If I'd offered, you'd have said no, wouldn't you?"

He frowned and didn't reply because, damn it, she was probably right.

Sophy grinned at him. "I thought so. You wanted to impress on me how tough you were. Besides, it might have made you dopey and I thought you would probably need all your strength to get up here."

"I could've slept on the couch," he pointed out grumpily.

"But your bed is much more comfortable."

He raised a brow. "You know that, do you?"

Sophy's cheeks reddened. "I'm speaking generically," she told him primly. "Beds are generally thought to be more comfortable than couches."

"Ah." He shifted his shoulders against the pillow. It was true. He shut his eyes and felt like he didn't quite want to open them again.

"Go to sleep," Sophy said, and for once made it sound more like a suggestion than a command. "Good night."

She started toward the door.

"Sophy."

She turned. "What?"

"Don't I get a kiss good-night?"

He was just trying to provoke her. Sophy knew that.

Because she had stood there and watched as he'd battled his way up the stairs, not going away to let him do it alone. Because she'd kept her distance and her equilibrium— barely—while taking his shirt and trousers off. Because she had almost escaped with her sanity intact.

But George wasn't going to let that happen.

"What?" she countered. "And raise your blood pressure? Sam wouldn't approve."

If anything was designed to raise his blood pressure, apparently mention of Sam was it.

The faint teasing grin instantly evaporated. George's bandaged head dropped back against the pillows and he stared at the ceiling.

"And God knows, we wouldn't want to do that," he said bitterly.

She stared at him surprised. Sam wouldn't approve. But she meant Sam in his neurologist suit. That Sam would not want his patient overdoing things. A kiss might not exactly qualify as "hot sex," but after three flights of stairs, who knew what George's blood pressure might be.

George, however, didn't seem to be thinking of Sam the neurologist, but of Sam the hypothetical womanizer.

Now it was Sophy's turn to frown. "What is it with you and Sam?" she demanded.

He turned his head slightly to look at her. "*Me* and Sam? Not a damn thing."

"Then what are you suggesting?"

"Nothing. I'm not suggesting anything."

But clearly he was. And just as clearly he wasn't going to talk about it. Sophy shook her head. "Fine. Be that way."

Then, because she wasn't going to give him the satisfaction of knowing he'd rattled her, she said, "And for what it's worth, here's your good-night kiss."

Crossing the room quickly, before she could have second thoughts, she bent down, dropped a nanosecond-long kiss on George's lips, then stepped back, smiling and, she dared to hope, unscathed.

"Good night, George," she said firmly, turned and flicked out the light.

"Not much of a kiss," he said.

She kept on going, refusing to be baited further as she tried not to notice that her lips were tingling ever so slightly.

"Sweet dreams, Sophy." His voice drifted after her as she headed down the hall to the stairs,

Shut up, George, she thought silently, scrubbing her fingers against her mouth, assuring herself that whatever she was feeling had nothing to do with kissing him.

It was just because...because...

Well, she didn't know. She couldn't think what else might have caused it, and fortunately she didn't have to because just then her mobile phone rang.

It was a local number, but one she didn't recognize. "Hello?"

"Sophy? It's Tallie. I couldn't reach George on his cell phone. So I called the hospital and they said *his wife* had taken him home." His sister sounded surprised to say the least.

"It wasn't my idea," Sophy protested. Then she explained what the doctor had told them. "He wouldn't let George go unless someone came with him. So George hired me."

"*Hired* you?"

"Well, that's what he called it," Sophy said. "Don't worry, I'm not letting him pay me. I owe him, so I'm returning the favor and paying him back."

"I'm sure George doesn't think of it that way."

Sophy was hard-pressed to articulate what George thought. All he did was confuse her—and try to run her life.

"At least you're staying! That's wonderful. We'll have you over. Of course Lily will be coming. When?"

It was a given that she would be staying long enough for her daughter to come as well, Sophy noted.

"On Saturday," she said. "My cousin is bringing her."

"Great. We'll have you over. Elias can grill. Or if George can't do that much yet, we'll bring food and come by your place."

"His place," Sophy corrected. "He's still pretty battered," she felt compelled to say. "He needs calm and quiet right now."

"We'll wait until you say you're ready then," Tallie decided. "This is such good news," she went on eagerly. "Wait till the folks hear."

"No!" Sophy said quickly and more forcefully than she should have. "I mean, they're a long way away. You don't want to tell them about George's accident. They'll worry. And I don't want you telling them I'm here, either," she said firmly.

There was a pause, as if Tallie's thoughts had finally caught up with the eager wheels turning in her brain. "Yes," she agreed, suitably subdued. "You're probably right. Better not say anything until it's settled."

"Tallie!" Sophy protested. "This is not a reconciliation. I'm here for the short-term. I live in California. George lives here. We're getting divorced."

"You could change your mind." Tallie wasn't going to give up.

"Good night, Tallie," Sophy said firmly. "I'm going to bed. It's been a long day."

She took a quick shower, then put on the elongated T-shirt she'd brought to sleep in, brushed her teeth, washed her face and had just turned back the duvet on the bed when her phone rang again.

Again it was a local number, but not the same one. Surely Tallie wouldn't be calling her back to continue the conversation on another phone. No. Tallie was determined, but she would know when to back off.

George?

Sophy felt her heart quicken. But she hadn't given him her number. She probably should have, she realized, so he could call her if he needed her.

She punched the talk button. "This is Sophy."

"Hey, it's Sam." She could actually hear him smiling.

And while she liked him and had felt comfortable with him, she felt herself stiffen. Was he, as George had suspected, calling her up to hit on her?

"Hi," she said cautiously.

"Checking on my patient," Sam said. "Figured I'd get a straighter answer from you than from him."

Sophy breathed again, feeling foolish. "He's alive. Grumpy. Annoying. I took the dog for a walk at one point and while I was gone he went downstairs to his office to work."

"You're going to have to keep an eye on him."

"I will," Sophy said, feeling guilty.

"Tonight. All night."

"What do you mean, all night?"

"If he were at the hospital, he'd be on monitors. And he'd have someone awake and checking on him regularly. You don't need to be awake, but you do need to wake up and check on him regularly. And you need to be right there."

"There?" Sophy said warily.

"Wherever he is."

"In bed."

"Perfect. Wake him every couple of hours. Make him talk to you. Be sure he makes sense. Call me if there are any problems. Do what you have to do."

And just like that, Sam was gone.

Sophy stood there and stared at the phone in her hand, feeling a strange compelling urge to throw it across the room. Then she felt another urge to pretend she hadn't got the call at all, to just crawl into bed and forget it. She could set her travel alarm and go up and check on George every couple of hours like Sam said.

Yes, and what if he needed her?

He wouldn't call her. Not if he needed her. He was too bloody-minded to admit he needed help. But what if he really did?

"Oh, blast," she muttered and, pulling on her lightweight travel robe, then dragging the duvet and her pillow with her, she climbed the stairs to George's room.

It was dark. It was silent. He was probably sound asleep.

She hoped to God he was. She padded over to the near side of the bed and began to make herself a nest on the floor.

"What the hell are you doing?"

So much for him being asleep. She kept right on making her nest. Gunnar came over to see what she was doing. "I'm sleeping here."

"On the floor?" George rolled onto his side and peered down through the darkness at her. "Are you out of your mind?"

"Sam called. He said I'm supposed to stay with you. Keep an eye on you," she corrected herself immediately.

"Did he?" George sounded all of a sudden in far better humor. "Good old Sam."

Sophy snorted. "Right. Good old Sam." She sat down on the duvet. It had felt warm and fluffy on top of her on the bed. It felt flat and thin between her and the floor. At least she'd be awake to wake him up.

"Don't be an idiot. Get up here and share the bed."

"I'm fine." She wrapped the duvet around her and snuggled down with her head on her pillow. Gunnar stuck his nose down and poked her cheek. She reached out a hand and scratched his ear.

"Sophy."

"I'm fine," she said.

"Like I was fine climbing all those damn stairs."

"Exactly." She kept her back turned and snuggled farther down. Damn this floor was hard.

George said a rude word and Sophy heard the bed creak. She ignored it. She ignored him—until she realized he had got up and was dragging the duvet off his bed and throwing it down on the floor beside her.

She rolled over and sat up in the darkness to see his white T-shirt in the moonlight as he eased himself off the bed and down onto the floor beside her!

"What on earth do you think you're doing?"

White shoulders shrugged. "Being as stupid as you are." He stretched out on the crumpled duvet. "Which is pretty damn stupid," he muttered. "God, this floor is hard."

Sophy grunted. "Then get on the bed. You need to be on the bed, George."

"It's up to you," he said.

She glared. She grumbled. She wished she could just say, *Fine, stay there,* and let him be as uncomfortable as she was. But she doubted that was what Sam had had in mind when he'd said to keep an eye on George tonight.

"And here you are again, making me do what you think is best for me," she pointed out.

"And sometimes I'm even right," he said mildly.

Which, damn it, was actually true.

"Fine." She flung back her duvet and scrambled to her feet, flung her duvet onto his bed and plopped down on top of it to glare at him, which might have been more effective if she could really have seen him and not just the shape of him in the darkness.

"Ah, sanity rears its ugly head." George grunted and tried to shove himself up as well. It was harder for him. Served him right, Sophy thought. But then guilt smote her. He was only in this shape because he'd saved a child's life, because he'd put his own life on the line.

"Give me your hand." She offered hers.

Immediately he gripped it, his long hard fingers wrapping around hers as he tried to lever himself up. It was more complicated that she imagined. He didn't have his boot on, so had to be careful of his ankle as well as his shoulder.

"I can't believe you did this." She shifted to get a better grip, had to move in to slide an arm around him to get enough leverage to get him to his feet. "Of all the stupid—"

"Your fault," he reminded her. But as she could hear the words hissing through clenched teeth, she didn't think he was enjoying it.

Neither was she. Having her arm around George's hard body, being so close she could smell the hospital soap, the disinfectant and something male that she remembered as quintessentially George unnerved her more than she wanted to admit. She shoved, hauled, hoisted.

And at last he stumbled to his feet.

"Don't do that again." His arm was over her shoulders and hers, still wrapped around him, allowed her to feel the thundering of his heart.

"I won't if you won't," he said, a catch in his breath.

She didn't answer that. It didn't merit a reply. Wordlessly she edged him over to the bed. He sat. Gunnar put his chin on George's knee. Sophy picked up his duvet and spread it over the bed, then pulled it back so he could lie down.

Then, because she knew he'd just do something stupid again if she didn't get in bed, too, she went around and slid beneath the duvet on the far side. There had to be at least two feet separating them. Plenty as long as they were awake.

But asleep she didn't trust herself.

Like Lily, she had a homing instinct for the nearest warm body. And she didn't want to wake up and find herself in George's arms.

"Told you it was a big bed," George said gruffly.

But not big enough, Sophy thought. "Gunnar," she said. "Here, Gunnar."

It didn't take any urging. In a second she felt the bed move and Gunnar's black form appeared, looming in the moonlight, looking up at them from the foot of the bed.

"For God's sake," George muttered.

"You've never let him on the bed? Oh, right. Tell me another." Sophy patted the space between them, and Gunnar instantly obliged, lying down there and heaving a contented sigh.

George made a disgruntled huffing sound.

"Just be glad you're home," Sophy said. "You could still be in the hospital."

"Promises, promises."

"If you want to go back, I'll call Sam."

"I'll bet Sam wouldn't think much of the dog in my bed."

Sophy smiled. "Sam said to do what I had to do. I'm just following instructions. Good night, George. I'll wake you in a couple of hours. Wake me if you need anything."

She rolled onto her side away from him. Away from Gunnar. It was the best she could do. She wondered if she would get a wink of sleep before it was time to wake him again.

It was a shock the next time she opened her eyes to see that it was morning and worse to discover that the warm body she was snuggled against wasn't covered with black fur.

CHAPTER FIVE

GEORGE KNEW THE MOMENT Sophy woke up.

Her breathing changed tenor. And as she realized where she was, her muscles tensed, her body stiffened. And then her eyes flicked open with something akin to horror.

He steeled himself against giving a damn. "He left," he said, refusing to apologize, refusing to pull back, or make any effort at all to untangle their limbs. Yes, no doubt he would regret it later. But right now he wasn't sorry. And right now he was staying right where he was.

"He?" There was an infinitesimal pause while she computed that, and then realized who he was talking about. "Gunnar." And as she said his name, Sophy was already moving, pulling away, putting space between them.

George didn't hold on to her. He let her go as if it didn't matter to him in the least.

"What time is it?" Sophy demanded. She jerked up to a sitting position and raked her fingers through her long tangled hair, making his fingers itch to do the same thing.

While she'd slept, he'd breathed in the crisp fresh scent of her shampoo, the scent of Sophy herself, and when several long, silken strands of hair had fallen across her face he'd been unable to help himself, and had stroked it slowly back. His hand had lingered, wanting to let his fingers play in her hair, to bury his nose in the silky tresses.

"It's a little before eight." George nodded at the clock on the dresser across the room.

Sophy glared at it as if it had let her down. "I was supposed to wake you up during the night!"

She scrambled out of the bed now and shot another hard accusatory look at Gunnar. He'd been curled up on the area rug. But now, seeing Sophy up and moving, he got up and stretched and wagged his tail at her.

"I can't believe I slept all night."

"You were tired," George said. "You said you hadn't slept much on the plane. You needed your rest. And you must have been comfortable," he suggested.

Now the glare focused on him. She didn't reply, either. She gave her head a little shake, as if she was still trying to make sense of what had happened. Then she shrugged, folding her arms across her chest, denying him the view of her breasts braless beneath the extra-long T-shirt she had slept in.

It still gave him a nice view of her legs halfway up her thighs, though, so he wasn't complaining. He studied them, remembering the sleek smoothness of those legs when they'd tangled with his. Desire had stirred then. It hadn't entirely disappeared now.

Sophy followed his gaze, realized what he was looking at and abruptly bolted out of the room.

"Damn it," George said mildly as she pounded down the stairs. He looked at the dog, who was watching him. "When she comes back she's going to be all proper and bossy," he said.

Gunnar came over to the bed and poked George with his nose. George in turn scratched him behind his ears. It was part of their morning routine. Life hadn't been exactly routine since Sophy had shown up.

"Thanks for leaving last night," George said to the dog. "Appreciate it," he added, as if Gunnar had done it on purpose.

Well, probably he had, because once George was sure Sophy was asleep, he had lain there periodically tapping the dog on the foot.

Gunnar didn't like his feet messed with. He twitched them. He shifted. And, finally, just as George hoped he would, Gunnar got up and jumped down onto the rug beside the bed. Then, unless Sophy's sleep habits had changed, it was just a matter of waiting.

George had waited.

He was used to waiting. With Sophy he felt as if he'd been waiting forever. In fact he was so tired that he fell asleep waiting.

But sometime in the middle of the night he woke up to discover Sophy was curled against him. Her arm lay across his waist, her face was pressed against his shoulder. And if he turned his head, he could touch her hair with his lips.

If?

No "if" about it. He turned to her instinctively. And when she had kept right on sleeping, he'd stroked her hair, had pressed his lips to her jaw, had even allowed himself a lingering kiss on her forehead.

Why not? Self-preservation was highly overrated.

But lying here now thinking about what else he would have liked to have done with Sophy was a bigger exercise in frustration than he wanted to endure. So he dragged himself up, got out of bed and hobbled across the room and got out clean underwear, khakis and a shirt.

It was a struggle to dress. Getting the T-shirt over his head was tricky because his shoulder was painful. Still, when he moved his head, the anvil in it didn't feel as if it were being pounded quite so vigorously. And while his bruises were a Technicolor marvel, they weren't worse. Once he put on a long-sleeve shirt most of them wouldn't be visible.

Nevertheless, by the time he was zipping up his khakis, his head was spinning a bit, and when he hobbled into the bathroom to shave, he ended up gripping the edge of the countertop so he didn't fall over.

He didn't feel like shaving, but the two-plus days of dark stubble on his jaw and cheeks were not a pretty sight. So he ran the hot-water tap and leaned against the countertop while he waited for it to heat up. Gradually the spinning in his head slowed down, the water was hot enough to shave and he began lathering his face.

He had the razor against his jaw when a voice behind him said, "What are you doing?"

In the mirror he could see Sophy, dressed now, looking just as prim and proper as he'd told Gunnar she would be, staring at him. He applied the razor before he answered. "Guess."

She pressed her lips together as if he were doing it to annoy her. He wasn't, and she must have realized it because she said, "Be careful you don't fall over." And she turned away to start straightening up his bed. "You'll be ready to lie down again when you've finished."

Judging from the way the anvil banger was picking up the tempo inside his head, George was pretty sure she was right. Not that it mattered. "I have to teach an eleven o'clock class," he told her through barely moving lips.

She swung around and met his gaze in the mirror again. "Teach? Don't be ridiculous. You need to go back to bed, not teach a class."

He didn't answer, just turned his gaze back to the job at hand. His fingers were none too steady. At the rate he was going he could cut his throat. He slowed the stroke of his razor. His head was starting to spin again. He wanted desperately to finish up and sit down. But he was damned if he was going to hurry, and damned if he would stop and rest while Sophy was hovering. Instead he leaned his weight against the sink.

"The world will stop if you don't teach your class?" Sophy said sarcastically.

"It's my job."

"Ah, yes. Duty. Responsibility." She twitched the duvet, flipping it up and letting it settle over his mattress. Her eyes shot sparks at him.

George tried to remain steady and upright. "You don't believe in them?"

"Of course I believe in them. But I also believe in sanity and common sense. Don't you?"

He started to grit his teeth but it hurt his head. "I'm only standing in front of a class. I'm not herding cattle or climbing ladders or jackhammering up the pavement."

"And you think it's that important that you go?" She met his gaze levelly. Her tone wasn't sarcastic now, but it did have its share of challenge.

"It wouldn't be the end of the world if I didn't, but I can be there, so I should be there. It's a matter of example," he explained. He expected her to scoff, but she didn't.

She pressed her lips together in a thin line. Her mouth worked and he could tell that whatever she was thinking, it wasn't cheerful. Then she sighed. "Fine. If you don't cut your throat shaving before it's time to go, we'll catch a cab."

He paused the razor halfway down his cheek. "We? What do you mean, we?"

Sophy shrugged. "If you're going, I'm going with you. It's my job."

She didn't know the first thing about George's work.

He was a physicist. She knew that. And now he taught physics, according to Tallie, at Columbia University. He had had lots of offers, his sister said, but he'd taken this one two years ago after his appointment in Sweden ended.

"I guess he had reasons to come back to New York," Tallie had said, watching Sophy for a reaction.

But Sophy couldn't think why he would have bothered other than his parents and his sister were nearby. She certainly wasn't. When she left their marriage, she'd left New York. And he hadn't taught physics when she was married to him.

He'd done something with physics. But heaven knew what. Sophy certainly didn't. He hadn't told *her*.

Ari had always said George was brilliant. Sophy knew he had a Ph.D. And the first she'd met Socrates, George's father, when arrangements were being made for their wedding, he had made a point of telling her that George was highly sought after. He had, according to Socrates, a new job offer at a university in Sweden that he was expecting to take a few months after their marriage.

George had brushed off Sophy's questions about it. "It's not important," he'd said at the time.

It had been important to Sophy. If he had been serious about their marriage—about making it real—he would have shared that with her. It had to do with their future, after all.

But in fact he'd brushed off all her questions, not only about his new job offer, but about what he did, period, making Sophy feel out of line asking anything—as if she were intruding where she had no right.

And as far as what he taught, well, he probably had considered her too stupid to understand anyway.

It had not been a good feeling.

Maybe she *was* too stupid. Certainly physics was a far cry from early childhood education, which was what she had majored in. Well, if she was over her head, she'd simply sit there and watch him being brilliant.

Because she was going to class with him, whether he liked it or not.

George didn't argue with her. And that, more than anything, proved to her how very unlike himself he still was. He looked pained at her insistence. But he didn't tell her no. He said, "Whatever," through barely moving lips and went back to shaving.

His sullen acquiescence was all it took to convince her that she was absolutely doing the right thing by going along—provided he didn't see sense and stay home in the meantime.

"I'll make some breakfast," she said. "Gunnar's been out once. Shall I walk him?"

"If you want. I usually take him to the park in the morning," George told her. "Dogs are allowed off-leash in Central Park until nine. But it's okay if he misses a day or two. You can take him this evening…."

At least he didn't entertain the notion that he was going to be able to do that.

"Come on, then," Sophy said to Gunnar. "We'll take a quick run now. Then we'll fix breakfast. Maybe your master will have seen sense by the time we get back." Gunnar began to bounce eagerly, obviously understanding every word she said.

George snorted and went back to shaving.

But Sophy had seen how heavily he was leaning against the sink, and she knew he was bullheaded enough to fall over before he would sit down and rest while she was standing there.

"Men are idiots," she said to Gunnar as they went down the stairs together.

The dog didn't disagree.

They went for a fifteen-minute run. When they got back, she fixed scrambled eggs and toast and put out cereal as well, not sure what George would want, just using what he had in the refrigerator.

She'd been back nearly half an hour and had the table set in the dining room by the time George came downstairs As she worked, she told herself it was just like the early days of Rent-a-Wife when she didn't just do the administration but actually went out into houses and performed wifely duties as required.

Though most of her meal preparation had been dinners, more than a few times she'd been called into a house with a new baby where she'd been in charge of taking care of getting breakfast ready and the older kids off to school.

"It's just like that," she told Gunnar, feeling calm and professional.

But the minute George appeared in the doorway to the dining room things weren't businesslike and impersonal anymore.

And seeing him now, leaning heavily on his crutches, his smooth-shaven jaw nicked here and there with tiny razor cuts, his dark brows drawn down, the normally healthy-looking color in his cheeks now pale and strained, Sophy felt a desperate urge to run to him, to touch him, to fuss over him.

Good thing she would have had to leap the kitchen bar between them to do anything so foolish.

Clutching the edge of the countertop to anchor herself right where she stood, Sophy pasted a smile on her face. "Ah, you made it. Good. Breakfast is ready." She gestured toward the table where she'd set a place for him.

She imagined he usually ate at the bar separating the modern kitchen from the rather more formal dining area. But she didn't want him looming over her from the bar while she was working in the kitchen.

"I don't eat there," he said brusquely.

"You do today."

He shook his head. "No. It's much easier to get up and down from a bar stool than a chair at a table."

Sophy scowled, studied the situation, then sighed, annoyed that he was right. So she moved his place setting to the bar and relaid it all out for him. "All right now?" she said shortly.

"Yes, thanks." And damned if he didn't give her a smile.

George was not normally a smiler. He was far too serious, too intense. His usual expression was grave and made it hard to imagine a lighter-hearted, swoon-worthy George.

So when he did smile, it was very nearly heart-stopping. At least it always had been to Sophy.

She remembered how serious he had been when the nurse had first placed tiny minutes-old Lily in his arms. He'd looked somewhere between wooden and terrified. But then Lily had looked up at him—had tried to focus her eyes on him—and instinctively her tiny fingers had wrapped around one of his. And George had smiled such a smile!

No! Sophy spun away from the memory and jerked open the refrigerator door.

"Do you want juice?" she asked him.

"Yes, thanks."

She poured him orange juice, then started washing the pans.

"Aren't you eating?" George asked.

"I ate." And she didn't want to sit down with him, didn't want more memories to come bubbling back. "And I need to go talk to Natalie. I do have work of my own, you know."

"I know that," George said mildly, making her feel guilty for having flung her responsibilities at him. He hadn't asked her to come after all.

"Sorry, I—" She didn't finish, just shook her head and hurried out of the room, tugging her mobile phone out of her pocket as she went.

George, predictably, didn't change his mind about going to teach. So feeling rather like a Sherpa carrying his briefcase while he maneuvered his crutches, Sophy trailed after him down the steps. She thought she might have to battle him about taking a cab, but all he said when they reached Amsterdam was, "We could take the bus."

"Not today," Sophy said firmly.

He didn't reply. One point for our side, Sophy thought, waving her hand to flag a cab. She wondered if she should have fought harder to keep him home, though, when they got in the cab and he sat wordlessly, his head back against the seat, his eyes closed, all the way up to the university.

"Which building is it?" she asked him when they got close to the university.

He told her. And she told the driver so he could get them as close as possible. It was still something of a walk after they got out of the cab. George looked white. He even stopped once.

Sophy bit her tongue to keep from saying, "All right, enough."

She dogged his steps, and discovered as they got close that she wasn't the only one.

"Dr. Savas? Oh my God!" A bright-eyed blonde coed came rushing up to them as George crutched his way toward the entrance of the building. "What happened?"

She was joined almost at once by a bevy of other students—virtually all of them female—who fussed and fluttered and hovered around George, practically trampling Sophy in the process.

Bemused, she stepped back, curious to see how George would react to this display of concern, how George would react to so many women all determined to take care of him.

"Sophy!" She heard his voice suddenly ring out over the sound of feminine ooohs and awwws, and then the sea of coeds parted as he swung around on one crutch and very nearly sliced several of them off at the knees with the other until his gaze found her. Something that looked remarkably like relief passed over his features when their eyes met. And there was that smile again—maybe not as potent as it had been at breakfast, but definitely remarkable. The coeds were remarking on it, too, Sophy could tell. There was consternation and muttering going on.

Then one of the girls tossed her hair and said, "Who's *she?*" as another one answered quite audibly, "Who cares? She's old."

Sophy wasn't going to bother answering them at all. But George did.

"She's my wife," he said and shut them all up. Then he

tipped his head toward the door. "This way," he said and waited until she joined him before he nodded her ahead of him through the doors.

A trail of disgruntled coeds followed. "I didn't know he was married?" one grumbled.

"Who cares if he's married?" Sophy heard another say.

Three or four of them giggled.

George kept walking straight ahead. He looked hunted, though, by the time they got to his office. She took the key from him and opened the door. "Shut it," he said when they had both gone in. And when Sophy had, he sat down heavily in his desk chair and let his head drop back.

"Wow," Sophy said, dazed. "College has changed since I went. Do they always act like you're a boy band?"

"Not always," George said. "Not recently."

So they had, apparently.

"The ones in my class think I'm tough as nails and the last instructor they ever should have taken."

"But…" Sophy prompted when he didn't finish.

He opened his eyes and shrugged wearily. "They're girls. What can I say?"

"You're implying that all girls are hormone-driven ditzes?" Sophy glared at him.

"Not all," George said, but clearly he didn't think the field of sane sensible females was overly large. "You're not," he said finally, surprising her.

About you, I was. The words were on Sophy's tongue. She didn't say them. But they were true, just as once foolishly, she had been about Ari. But the less said about her feelings in either case, the better.

"No," she said briskly. "I'm not. I can take you or leave you. Now, is there anything I can do to help?"

It was a measure of how much George had already exerted that he simply directed her to the cabinets in his office to assemble the materials he wanted for the day's class. He was demonstrating something with bottles and water and ice. She had to get the ice from a refrigerator in the common room down the hall.

"Anything else?" she asked doubtfully.

"That should do it." George settled his crutches under his arms and led the way to his classroom. And Sophy, with her arms full of bottles and ice and a jug of water, trundled along behind, feeling more Sherpalike than ever.

George in the classroom was a revelation.

There was none of the ivory-tower professor about him— and none of the tough-as-nails teacher he'd assured her he was. Oh, she was quite sure he had high standards and his students had to work hard to meet them. But he engaged them immediately—charmed them at the same time he taught them.

While they were concerned about his injury, he didn't let them dwell on it. "I'm here, aren't I?" he said brusquely. "Let's get to work."

And nine-tenths of the girls might have been infatuated with him, and all of the students might have wanted to impress him, but George was focused on physics—and on making physics come alive for them.

They were a freshman class, Sophy began to understand. Not the crème de la crème of the postgrad population, but the eighteen- and nineteen-year-olds who were getting their first taste. And George was determined to make it a memorable one.

Sophy knew enough about the university system to know that professors of George's status only took freshmen if they wanted to, if they cared. George cared.

When a couple of the girls turned around to give her the once-over, he said, "She's not teaching you, I am. Pay attention to me."

And when one of them said, "What's she doing here?" he gave Sophy one of his heart-stopping grins over the top of his students and said, "She's making sure I don't fall over. Aren't you, sweetheart?"

He'd never called her that before, and she knew he was only saying it for effect. But she couldn't quite ignore the leap in the region of her heart. Still she did her best to tamp it down as she said, "That's exactly right."

And she apparently said it with enough emphasis that the girls in his class began to get the idea that coming on to George was a waste of time.

So they turned around and started paying attention to what he was actually saying as he gave them a minilecture on the topic to set the stage for the experiment to follow.

Sophy suspected that she was the only one who noted that he was hanging on to the podium so fiercely that he really might have fallen over without it. His students seemed to think he was just white-knuckled for emphasis.

After he'd set the stage and turned them loose to prove the theory he'd explained there was much sloshing of water and dropping of ice. Sophy imagined George would go sit down. But he didn't. He moved from group to group, advising, nodding, encouraging.

It was costing him, Sophy could tell. A muscle in his jaw ticked occasionally, and when he was in pain there were brackets of white around his mouth. He watched as they worked, but refrained from directing them too closely.

He shook his head at several questions, saying, "You have to figure things out on your own. It's the only way you'll really understand."

And finally, it seemed, they did.

So did Sophy. She understood about the experiment, but even more she also understood a little bit more about George.

He was everything she'd ever thought he was—strong, determined, hard-working, responsible. He didn't have to be here. He had sick leave. He could have stayed home. But he wouldn't because what he was doing mattered to him—and as long as he could remain upright, he was going to do it.

Just how long he was actually going to remain upright was debatable, Sophy thought, as after the class was over, he propped himself against the classroom wall and continued to give his students every bit of his energy and attention. But even as he spoke and listened she could see a thin film of perspiration on the bridge of his nose, and she noted the deepening grooves at the sides of his mouth.

She considered trying a tactful maneuver to extricate him from the situation, something that wouldn't make her look managing and wouldn't annoy George. But then she saw his jaw lock, the muscle tick again as he tried to focus on whatever one of the students was saying, and she decided there wasn't enough tact in the world.

"Excuse me," she said in the strong but brisk tones of the preschool teacher she'd been before she and Natalie had become Rent-a-Wife, "but time's up."

They turned to look at her, astonished. She gave them her best no-nonsense smile.

"Just doing my job," she told them quite honestly but with a confiding smile, and when they looked blank, she added cheerfully, "making sure Dr. Savas doesn't fall over."

The penny dropped, and they fell all over themselves apologizing as they helped carry the bottles and jugs back to the office while she handed George his crutches and waited until he preceded her out the door.

She expected he would chew her out as soon as the students left and they were alone again in his office. Instead he sank into his chair, bent his head, shut his eyes and said, "Thanks."

She was shocked and not a little alarmed. She wasn't used to seeing George in anything other than command mode. Now she had to resist an impulse to fuss. Instead she simply put the bottles and jugs away and tidied things up while she waited.

And worried and tried to marshal the arguments she would need to get him to see sense and go home rather than head to the lab where his grad students were working on projects.

He'd told her during the cab ride from his place that this introductory course was the only one he taught on campus. The rest of his work, overseeing their research and doing his own, took place at the university's research facility north of the city on the Hudson River. That was where he needed to go after the class, he'd told her.

Now she finished her housekeeping and sat down, knotting her fingers together and waiting for the argument to start.

George still hadn't moved. But at last, when it was obvious that she'd stopped moving around and the only sounds were from outside the building, he raised his head and opened his eyes to look at her.

Sophy, steely-eyed, looked right back, ready for battle.

Slowly a corner of George's mouth tipped up. "Why am I sure that I know what you're going to say?" he murmured.

Sophy opened her mouth, but before she could get a word out, he pushed himself up out of his chair and looked down at her.

"Let's go home," he said.

CHAPTER SIX

SHE GOT HIM HOME, but not up the stairs. He was breathing shallowly and teetering a bit by the time they reached the front door. And once inside, the couch in the living room was as far as he went.

"I'll just hang out here for a few minutes," he said, sinking down onto it with the relief of a camel driver reaching an oasis. He stretched out, sighed and was almost instantly asleep.

Sophy stared at him, taking in his unnaturally pale face and the lines of strain that still persisted around his mouth, and she worried, sure he'd overdone things, but unsure if she ought to call Sam.

"What do you think?" she asked Gunnar.

Gunnar went hopefully to the back door down to the garden, then to the front door and looked at his leash. Sophy supposed she should take him out. Their run this morning had been brief.

"This one will be brief, too," she told the dog, clipping his leash to his collar. She didn't suppose George would wake and need anything, but she didn't want to take chances.

She changed her clothes, left George a note on the coffee table in case he woke, then took Gunnar to Central Park. He looked disgusted that she didn't take off his leash. But when she ran with him along the pathway, he didn't seem to mind too much. They were gone barely half an hour. When they got back it didn't look as if George had moved.

She got her laptop from the bedroom on the second floor and brought it back down to the living room. That way she could work and keep on eye on George at the same time. That was the theory, at least.

In fact she spent far more time watching George. His body had barely moved but, as he slept, his face relaxed. He looked younger now, the bandage on his head gone, his dark hair drifting across his forehead, his cheeks still smooth from the morning shave, his lips no longer pressed tight with pain, softer now and slightly parted.

He looked the way he had when she'd first met him. Not a good thing because it stirred up all those same feelings—feelings that had been as wrong then as they were now. Then she had been "Ari's girl." Now she was George's "rented" wife.

Yes, she was still his wife in name—but only in name. There was no point in pretending anything else. Their marriage had never been real—and there was no point in sitting here staring at him now and wishing for the thousandth time that it was.

She got up deliberately and went to the back door. "Come on," she said to Gunnar.

After their run he'd been lying on the rug next to George. Now he bounded up and looked amazed. Another walk? he seemed to say.

Sophy shook her head. "No, but I need to burn off some steam."

She was losing it, she told herself. She was talking to the dog as if he knew what she was saying. Apparently, though, he did. He went to the basket by the door to the kitchen and picked up one tennis ball, then two, then looked hopefully at her. So she picked up the whole basket of them and took him out in the back garden.

She didn't know how long they were out there. She checked on George several times. He never moved. She threw tennis balls for Gunnar until it got dark.

And when they came back in, she left Gunnar to lie by the sofa while she carried her laptop into the kitchen. She could hear George from there if he needed anything. But she wouldn't have to look at him. Wouldn't have to remember.

She wouldn't let herself wish.

George slept the rest of the day.

When he finally woke briefly it was nearly eight thirty. He was about to simply go back to sleep again when Sophy insisted that he eat some dinner.

She expected he'd argue because that's what mule-headed men did. But George surprised her.

He took a couple of painkillers because his head still hurt, but then he sat up on the sofa and took the tray with the bowl of soup and the piece of fresh sourdough bread she handed him.

"I can come out to the kitchen," he protested mildly.

But when she said no, he didn't argue, just sat there and ate obediently. It made a nice change. And it was a relief to see him sitting up and actually being coherent. He'd been so exhausted and in such pain when they'd got home from his class that she'd been really worried, had given serious thought to calling Sam.

Now she was glad she hadn't. George seemed more alert. He had a good appetite, eating both the soup and the bread with relish. And Sophy lingered to watch.

But then she caught herself looking at him and wishing, and abruptly she excused herself.

"Things to do," she said. "I'll just go finish the dishes." And she hurried back into the kitchen, where she clattered determinedly around making a racket as she tried to distract her weak will and feeble powers of resistance.

She thought she was doing pretty well. Then she heard a noise behind her and turned to find George standing in the doorway holding his bowl in his hand.

"I feel like Oliver Twist," he said wryly, a corner of his mouth turning up, as he loomed over her. He looked very adult, very male and not like a poor starving waif at all. "Any second helpings?" he suggested hopefully.

"Of course." She snatched the bowl out of his hands. "You could have just called me. Why aren't you using your crutches?"

"Can't carry the bowl with them." George shrugged. "Plus, my ankle isn't broken. It's just sprained. The boot helps keep it steady. But I can go without the crutches."

"Well, you're not carrying the soup back with you," Sophy said. She turned her back and began ladling the soup into his bowl. "Go sit down."

But when she turned around, he hadn't moved. He was still standing there, still looming, still watching her, his dark hair tousled, his eyes hooded. "It's good," he said. "The soup."

"Thank you," she replied shortly, then looked expressively toward the living room again, in the hope that he would go sit back on the sofa. Instead he hobbled past her and, wincing, hitched himself up on one of the bar stools in the kitchen.

"That can't be comfortable."

"It's fine. I'll eat here," he said. "Keep you company."

Just what she needed. Sophy shrugged. "Suit yourself."

She turned away again and focused on the last of the dishes. Unfortunately there weren't a lot of them left.

"Thanks for coming along today," George said to her back.

She turned, surprised. "I enjoyed it. I never knew much about what you did."

George's mouth quirked. "I do other stuff, too."

"I'm sure. But that was interesting. I wouldn't have expected you to teach freshmen."

"I like it. They're rewarding. Some of them," he qualified. "When you can wake one or two up to see the world in a new way, you feel like you've accomplished something."

"I can see that. Did you—" she hesitated, then decided to ask "—teach freshmen in Uppsala?"

George hesitated for a moment, too, then shook his head. "No."

She thought he was going to leave it there, expected that he would because he'd always shut her out of that part of his life.

But then he said, "I didn't teach in Uppsala."

She blinked, digesting that, then nodded. "So, you did research?"

He drew a breath. "I wasn't in Uppsala. Not often."

Now she frowned. "You went there to teach. At least I assume you did. You were gone." She shook her head, then shrugged. "How do I know what you did?" she muttered.

"I was working for the government. Several governments, actually. It was a multinational effort. Top secret. Not teaching. Not Uppsala."

She stared at him. *Top secret?* "Not Uppsala," she echoed faintly.

"No." He opened his mouth again, as if he were about to say something else, but then he pressed his lips together briefly and cast his eyes down to focus on his bowl once more.

Sophy stood there, disconcerted, studying him, trying to rethink, to fit this new bit of information into the puzzle that was George. "I had no idea."

He lifted his gaze and met hers. "You weren't supposed to."

She understood that much. "You wouldn't have taken us with you," she said, understanding, too, now why he'd never talked with her about any plans for them to move. There had been no plans.

"I wouldn't have gone."

That made her blink. "What?"

"If we'd stayed together, I'd have told them no." His gaze didn't waver.

Sophy shook her head. "I don't understand at all now," she admitted.

"It was a job that came up before...before Ari died. Before we—" He gave a wave of his hand.

He didn't have to explain. She knew what he meant: before Ari's girlfriend turned up pregnant and alone, in need of a Savas rescue mission.

The memory stiffened her spine. "Another reason you shouldn't have married me," she said flatly.

George gave a quick shake of his head. "No. It was a matter of priorities." He made it sound cut-and-dried—and as if he'd made the obvious choice. "Anyway," he went on, "if we'd stayed together I would never have gone."

"Why not?"

"It wasn't a situation to take a wife and child into. It was potentially dangerous, certainly unstable. No place for dependents. I wouldn't have risked the two of you."

"But you risked yourself!"

He shrugged. "It was my job."

Duty. Always and forever, duty.

And she had just been another one, Sophy thought heavily. She turned away and went briskly back to cleaning up the kitchen, then put the leftover soup in the refrigerator. George finished his bowl and gave it to her when she held out her hand.

"It was good," he said with one of his heart-stopping smiles. "Thanks."

Sophy resisted it. "You're welcome," she said stiffly. "Are you going upstairs now?" she asked as he struggled to his feet.

"I think I will." His mouth twisted a bit ruefully. "Head's

not pounding quite so much, but I'm beat. I may have overdone it a bit today."

His admission made her eyes widen. There was something George couldn't handle? But she didn't say that.

"Can you make it on your own?" she asked. "Or do you want me to stand behind you to catch you if you fall?" She was only half-joking.

"I believe I can make it." One corner of his mouth tipped up. "I'll call if I need you."

So she let him go on his own. It didn't stop her keeping an ear out for any sounds of trouble, though. And she ventured over to peer up the staircase more than once to see how he was doing. It took him a long time, but at last the stairs stopped creaking and she didn't hear him anymore. Sophy didn't know how George felt after his climb, but she breathed a sigh of relief when he was up the stairs.

"Come on," she said to Gunnar, who jumped right up. "Let's go out one last time."

She didn't take him for another walk. They'd get up and go to the park in the morning early, she promised him. He seemed almost to sigh, but he went out back willingly enough. Sophy went out with him. If she stood in the garden and stared up at the windows, she could see the light on up in George's bedroom. There was, every once in a while, a shadow as he moved slowly around the room and passed in front of the lamp.

"He needs to lie down," she said to Gunnar.

Gunnar looked hopefully at his bucket of tennis balls.

"Tomorrow," Sophy promised him. "Let's go in now." When they had, she shut off the lights, picked up her laptop and climbed the stairs, Gunnar bounding on ahead to wait at the top of the stairs.

She put the laptop on the bed in the second-floor room, the one she'd used the day she'd arrived—the one she'd use again tonight because she certainly would be sleeping with George again.

She even flipped it open and turned it on, thinking she'd get some work done because it wasn't all that late yet. She might give Natalie a call and perhaps get a chance to see Lily on a video call before her daughter went to bed.

But before she did that, she should check and make sure George was settled. She didn't know what on earth he was hobbling around for. He needed to go to bed. And if he needed something, she didn't want him calling her while she was on the phone. So she climbed the stairs and went down the hall to George's room.

"Do you need anything?" she began—and stopped dead.

There was George—in all his muscular naked glory—on his way to the shower.

A slow grin spread across his face. "You could wash my back."

Sophy blushed.

George loved it when she blushed.

In four years he had never forgotten the way her eyes snapped with emotion and her cheeks grew redder than her hair. It was rewarding when her normally quick wits seemed—for the merest instant—to desert her. He reveled in it.

She didn't turn and run. No. She stopped in the doorway, her fingers lightly touching each side of the doorframe as she let her gaze rove over him. Then she said slowly, still considering him, "Now there's an idea."

He knew her tone wasn't soft and sultry intentionally. It didn't have to be. It sent a shaft of longing straight through him. And it was certainly no secret which part of him found the words most enticing.

Now it was his turn to feel his face burn. Face, hell. It wasn't his *face* that felt as if it was going up in flames.

George cleared his suddenly parched throat, then casually

turned and limped as nonchalantly as possible into the bathroom where he'd left the shower running.

"Right this way," he suggested over his shoulder. He only hoped his voice didn't sound as rusty as it felt.

He stepped into the shower, shut the door behind him and waited. And waited. Hoped against hope.

But he wasn't really surprised when minutes passed and Sophy didn't come and open the shower door and step in behind him.

He had turned the water on to let it warm up when he'd first come upstairs. He'd decided on the way up that a nice hot shower would soothe his aching body and make him feel better.

Now he thought that cold water—*ice water*—would have been a damn sight smarter.

Still, if he turned the tap to cold right now, while his ardor might fade, his muscles would seize up and his head would start pounding again. Hell of a choice. The proverbial rock and hard place, he thought, and groaned at the appropriateness of the cliché.

Served him right for still wanting her, he thought and tried to will his body into quiescence. His body had other ideas. They wouldn't go away.

Finally, deliberately he leaned forward, braced one palm against the tile beneath the shower head, and put the other on the tap. Then, as the water sluiced down his body, he gradually but inexorably turned it all to cold.

He stayed there until he could stand it no longer. Then he yanked the towel off the top of the door to scrub at his eyes before he stepped out. His teeth were chattering, his head was hammering and his whole body was rigid with cold.

"What on earth is the matter with you? You're blue!"

George jerked the towel away from his face and found himself staring into Sophy's wide eyes. They looked as shocked as he felt.

He clamped his teeth together because he'd have stuttered if he'd tried to speak.

Sophy had no such problem. She put out a hand and touched his arm, then frowned. "You're as cold as ice," she accused him.

Better than the alternative.

"I'm fine," he said. "It's all right."

"Of course it's not all right! I thought you were supposed to be smart! Why on earth would you take a cold shower and—oh!" The bright spots of color were back in her cheeks with a vengeance again, and Sophy was opening and closing her mouth like a fish.

George smiled wryly at her.

"Men!" she fumed.

"Pretty much," George agreed. He snagged another towel off the rack and hitched it around his waist. "You could leave," he suggested. "Unless you want to solve the problem another way."

For a rare and amazing moment, he thought she almost considered it. Then she gave a quick shake of her head and began backing toward the door.

"I'll wait outside," she said. "Don't fall over." She ran her tongue quickly over her lips, Then, as if a three hundred per-cent explanation were required, she added, "That's what I was doing in here. Making sure you didn't."

George grinned. "And here I thought you'd changed your mind and come to scrub my back."

Sophy rolled her eyes. But the color was back in her cheeks and he thought she ran her tongue over her lips as she shut herself firmly on the other side of the door.

For a moment George stood staring at it. Then he shook his head. The woman was a walking mass of contradictions. She came close, she backed away. She told him to get out of her life. She came clear across the country when he was hurt.

She hovered over him as if he mattered to her. Then she went cool and distant in the blink of an eye.

It was no wonder his head hurt, George thought as he dried his body slowly and carefully. And it was irritating as hell that he'd suffered through that damned cold shower because its effect had been instantly nullified by his body's reaction to Sophy's unexpected presence.

Still he wasn't apt to disgrace himself when he finally finished pulling on his boxers and a clean T-shirt, then opened the door to his bedroom.

Gunnar was lying in the middle of the bed. He lifted his head and thumped his tail happily.

Sophy, damn it, was nowhere to be seen.

CHAPTER SEVEN

JUST WHAT SHE NEEDED, Sophy thought, flinging herself onto her back on the bed—an image of a lean, muscular, stark-naked George Savas indelibly emblazoned on the insides of her eyelids!

Eyelids, ha. She had the image burned right into her retinas. Probably branded on her brain.

It wasn't fair!

Even as she thought it, she knew she was whining like a plaintive four-year-old. But it was true.

She was only here trying to make things square between them—to do *her* duty—just as George, by marrying her, had done what he misguidedly perceived to be his. It was a respon-sibility. A job—because George had even "hired" her, though she'd be damned if she would let him pay her a cent. She was doing this to pay him back. She didn't want his money.

Mostly she didn't want to be tempted. She didn't *want* to want George again.

It was bad enough to have lost her heart to him once. Four years ago she had believed that however inauspicious the be-ginning of their relationship had been, they could love each other.

She had already been well on her way to loving him by their wedding day.

Strong and stalwart and dependable, George was the exact

opposite of his cousin. The only things George and Ari had in common were some of their genes and their gorgeous good looks. But while Ari knew how to use his looks to his advantage—and did!—George seemed unaware of his. And while Ari had been there when things were fun and frivolous, George had been there when she'd needed him. Always.

She'd met him while she was dating Ari, had even danced with him at Ari and George's cousin Gregory's wedding. In fact George had been drafted in as an usher because he and Ari were the same size and he could wear Ari's tux when Ari hadn't showed up on time.

"It's not like they weren't going to have the wedding without me." Ari had dismissed the matter when Sophy had fretted about them arriving late.

That had certainly been true enough. In fact, Gregory and his bride were already man and wife by the time she and Ari had arrived.

Ari had shrugged. "Works for me. Anyway, they had George. He'll do." Ari had given his cousin a light punch on the arm. "Good old George."

Later, when she'd danced with George at the reception, she'd apologized for their tardiness even though it hadn't been her fault.

George had just shrugged and said wryly, "That's Ari. Not exactly Mr. Dependable."

At the time Sophy had still been a bit starry-eyed about Ari Savas. He was fun and flirtatious and he had charm to spare. He'd got her into bed, hadn't he? And then he'd left three days later to go skiing out west and she hadn't seen him for a month. She had written to him when she found out she was pregnant, but he'd never replied. And when next she saw him, he seemed surprised that she would have bothered to tell him.

That was the way it was with Ari. He had little interest in anyone else—and none at all in becoming a father.

Sophy got the message. In fact, because he'd bailed on her and their incipient child, she'd been tempted not to go to his funeral three months later. There didn't seem any point.

Eventually she'd decided to go because she thought that someday their child would ask about his or her father.

While Sophy was under no illusions about Ari's fidelity or love by this time, she'd once, however foolishly, cared about him. She knew she would love their child. And she owed it to that child to be able to share what she could of the man who had fathered him or her.

It was a huge funeral for a popular young man who had died before his time. All of Ari's family had been there. Most of them had paid no attention to her. She was just another one of Ari's many girlfriends. The last girlfriend, perhaps, but not a member of the family.

Only George had made a point of coming over to her afterward, taking her hand in his and not just accepting her condolences, but offering his own sympathy to her.

His lean handsome face and tousled dark hair reminded her of Ari, but the resemblance to his cousin stopped there. Ari had always been the life of the party and probably would have been even at a funeral. George was quiet and self-possessed. There was a remoteness about him even though, as they talked, Sophy was aware of his jade-green gaze boring into hers.

They didn't talk long and she never mentioned her pregnancy. It was winter. She was wearing a heavy coat, and at just five months along, she wasn't yet as big as the house she would become before Lily's birth. So George had had no idea. None of his family had. If Sophy had ever imagined that Ari might have proudly proclaimed—or even quietly admitted—he was going to be a father, she knew that day that he'd never said a word.

She'd felt a little bereft as she was leaving, and it must have showed on her face because George had drawn her into his arms and given her a hard, steadying hug. It had felt so good, so supportive, so right that Sophy had wanted to lean into it, to draw strength from it.

From George.

But fortunately common sense had prevailed and she had stepped back, decorum prevailing.

Still he'd held on to her hands. "Take care of yourself." His voice had been like rough velvet. Stronger than Ari's. Deeper.

Sophy had nodded, exquisitely aware of her hands being chafed and squeezed lightly between George's strong fingers.

"Yes," she said, throat tightening. "Yes. You, too."

She'd given him a watery smile, then desperately pulled her hands out of his and fled before sudden tears from God knew what complicated emotions spilled over onto her cheeks.

She'd hung on to that memory of George to get her through the days and weeks that followed. She told herself it was because he reminded her of Ari—but not Ari as he'd been, but rather the man she'd wanted him to be. If this child was a boy, she'd told herself, she hoped he'd be more like George than like Ari.

Not that she had a lot of time to think about either one of them. She had been teaching at a preschool-cum-day-care, a fun but exhausting job, and every day she came home more tired than the last. She loved the children, but as she'd grown bigger and the baby had become more active, simply getting through the day took a lot out of her.

When she went home after school, she had longed for a bit of adult conversation, just someone to be there. But there was none because a few weeks before Ari's funeral, her roommate, Carla, had accepted a job in Florida and moved out.

After Carla had moved, Sophy hadn't looked for another roommate right away. She was nesting and she'd liked having the space to herself. Her cousin Natalie in California, the only relative she was very close to, had suggested Sophy come out there when she'd learned Sophy was expecting.

With her parents dead and no siblings, Sophy was on her own. But while she appreciated Natalie's suggestion, she wasn't ready to take it.

"No. My doctor's here. I'm taking prenatal classes here. My job is here. I want to finish out the school year."

But her West Village apartment was expensive, and while she might have liked to live there alone, she wasn't going to be able to keep it if she didn't make an effort to find a new roommate soon.

So she put an ad up in the faculty room at the preschool and at the gym where she went to her prenatal classes. She got calls. Several of them. Most were not at all what she had in mind. But one seemed possible. A second-grade teacher named Melinda, with a four-year-old boy and a parrot, was looking for a place to live.

Sophy wasn't sure about the four-year-old or the parrot, but she imagined Melinda wasn't sure about a newborn, either, so one afternoon in early May she invited Melinda over to talk and see the apartment.

She'd just put the last of the dishes away and was sweeping the floor, hoping to impress Melinda with her housekeeping skills, when the doorbell rang.

A glance at her watch told Sophy that Melinda was half an hour early. But better early and eager than late or not at all. Besides, if the place wasn't pristine, there was no point in pretending to be something she was not. So she stuck the broom in the closet, pasted on her best welcoming smile and opened the door.

It wasn't Melinda.

It was George.

George? Sophy felt suddenly breathless. Her knees wobbled. She stared at him, words failing her.

George didn't speak at once, either. He just stood there,

lean and rugged and as gorgeous as ever, looking down at her with those smoky green eyes of his. They held her gaze for a moment, then slowly, inexorably slid southward so that she could almost feel them touching her full breasts and her now very noticeably pregnant belly. It wasn't winter any longer, and she wasn't wearing a coat—only a loose smock that did nothing to conceal her shape. Sophy gripped the doorknob so tightly her hand hurt. She didn't move.

She didn't see shock in his gaze so much as curiosity and then something like confirmation. Confirmation?

George's jaw tightened briefly as his gaze lingered on her belly. But then it eased as his gaze traveled back up to meet hers.

"You are pregnant." It even sounded like a confirmation.

Sophy ran her tongue over dry lips. She nodded. "Yes." She was strangling the doorknob now. But she met his gaze steadily. She had nothing to hide. And it was far too late for George to say what Ari had already said: "What are you going to do about it?"

It had to be apparent to him what she intended to "do about it"—she intended to have it, welcome it. In fact the baby's cradle was clearly visible in the living room behind her.

But he didn't question that. He simply asked, "Are you all right?" His eyes were searching hers.

"Yes, of course. I'm fine." Or as fine as a seven-month-pregnant woman with an active kicking person inside her abdomen, a back ache and varicose veins could possibly be.

What did he want? She hesitated, wondering if she should invite him in because at any moment Melinda and her four-year-old and her parrot might be showing up. But she couldn't just say, "Go away." She didn't want him to go away.

"Come in," she said and opened the door wider.

George came in. He didn't sit down. He paced around her small living room even though she gestured toward the couch.

"Won't you sit down? Would you like something to drink?"

He cracked his knuckles and shook his head. "Why didn't you say something?" he demanded, his gaze on her belly again.

Instinctively Sophy put her hands on her abdomen, as if they were a shield. She shrugged. "Say what? 'Oh, by the way, before he died, Ari knocked me up?' Why? What point was there?"

"He's responsible."

"Yes, well, perhaps he was. Now he's not. And he didn't want to be, anyway." She turned her back and fiddled with the blinds, but she heard something that sounded like George's teeth coming together.

"How do you know?" he demanded.

"I talked to him about it. I told him. He said, 'Oh, too bad. What're you going to do about it?'"

George muttered something and rubbed his hand against the back of his neck.

Sophy, watching him, tilted her head. "How did you find out?" she wanted to know.

"Your letter."

"Letter?"

"You wrote him. Told him. It was in his backpack. We found it when they finally shipped his stuff home."

"Oh. That letter." The one she'd sent when she'd first found out. The letter that Ari claimed he'd never got. "It was in his backpack? I see."

So Ari had already known about the baby before she'd tracked him down in person to tell him the news. When she'd never heard from him, she'd been afraid he hadn't received her letter. Obviously he had. He'd simply chosen to ignore the fact.

Somehow Sophy supposed she wasn't surprised. Not anymore. Not about Ari. Hiding his head in the sand and pretending it didn't exist was typical of Ari. Not surprising at all.

But finding George on her doorstep *was* surprising. What did he want?

Her back was hurting, so Sophy sat down.

George didn't. He was still prowling around her small living room, stopping only to stare down at the cradle and the stacks of tiny newborn clothes inside it that several of her coworkers had recently handed down to her. "When's the baby due?" he asked.

"Early October."

He turned his gaze on her. "And how are you going to cope when it comes?"

"What do you mean?"

"Who's going to take care of it? Do you have benefits? Can you afford to stay home with it?"

Sophy pressed her lips together, wondering what business it was of his. "I can manage," she said.

His hooded gaze bored into her. "Can you?"

His eyes were intense, magnetic. She couldn't look away. And at the same time she couldn't lie. "I hope so," she said more truthfully.

He came to stand directly in front of her so that she had to tip her head up to look at him. "We can help. We will help."

Sophy stared up at him. "We? Who's we?"

"The family." He paused. "Not just the family. Me."

"You?" She shook her head. "Financially, you mean? That's very kind. Thank you, but—" She should stand, should face him head-on.

"Financially, yes, of course," George cut in. "Your child will be taken care of." He said that almost impatiently. "Not just your child." He held out his hands to her.

Instinctively, Sophy put hers in them and despite her bulk and imbalance, in George's hands she felt herself pulled easily to her feet.

He didn't step back, so that now they were standing mere inches apart, close enough that Sophy could see that he'd recently shaved, that he had the tiniest chip out of one front tooth, that there were gold flecks in his intense green eyes.

"What then?" she asked.

"Marry me."

Her obstetrician had said, "Don't get up too fast. It can make you dizzy and unbalanced." He'd never said it would affect her hearing. Sophy stared, disbelieving.

"Marry me." George said it again. Urgently. His eyes mesmerized her.

Sophy swallowed hard. There was blood pounding in her ears. "I—I need to sit down," she said faintly—and sank into the chair before she tumbled into it.

"Are you all right?" George demanded. Then, "You're not all right." He crouched down in front of her so she was staring again into his beautiful eyes.

"I'm f-fine. Just—" Dazed? Confused? But he'd said it twice. She couldn't have misheard. Still, even sitting down, she couldn't make sense of it. Her mind reeled. "You don't mean that," she said finally.

"I'm not in the habit of proposing marriage if I don't mean it," George said stiffly.

"No, I didn't mean that. I meant—why?" It was almost a wail. She couldn't help it.

"Why? Because it makes sense. You're alone. You're having a child—my cousin's child. He can't marry you now—"

"He didn't want to marry me anyway."

George gave a dismissive wave of his hand. "I do. I can." So saying, he dropped into a crouch next to her chair and took her hand again, looking at her earnestly, intently. "I can, Sophy," he repeated in a low tone that spoke more to her than all his words combined.

Sophy could see in his eyes that he was serious. She studied his gaze, trying to make sense of what he was suggesting. It was outrageous, ridiculous. And terribly, terribly tempting.

She didn't know George. He didn't love her. He barely even knew her, so he couldn't possibly love her. And she didn't love him.

But she *could*, a tiny voice inside her spoke up. *She could love him.*

And heaven help her, she listened.

Maybe it was that her hormones had gone crazy during her pregnancy. Maybe it was how lonely she had been feeling lately. Maybe it was not wanting to raise her baby alone. Maybe it was how intently George was looking at her, how warm and strong his fingers felt as they wrapped around hers.

There were countless reasons. All sane and sensible and logical—reasons that, as he crouched beside her, George spelled out for her.

But Sophy knew that the tipping point had already happened. It had been his tone of voice when he'd said, "I can, Sophy."

His tone made her believe not just that he could, but that he wanted to.

Call her weak, call her foolish, call her naive. Call her hopelessly hopeful. All of the above.

"I don't know," she faltered.

His fingers squeezed hers. "You do know, Sophy," he said in that same tone. "Say yes."

She said yes. Holding hard to George's strong hard hand, she took a chance—on love. She leapt with eyes closed and heart wide open.

Yes. Take me. Take us. Love us. And let us love you in return.

They had married two weeks later. The ceremony was in the judge's chambers. Obviously not a big wedding. There was a small reception after at his parents' house. Mostly family. Mostly his.

Of hers only Natalie's mother, Laura, had been able to come. It hadn't mattered to Sophy. She was happy to have George's family become her family.

When she said her vows, she meant them. And when she looked up into George's grave handsome face and thought of spending her life with him, it didn't feel wrong. It felt right.

Almost like a dream come true.

Of course it wasn't. And Sophy knew better than to expect that.

But she could try to make it come true. She was going to make him so happy, be the perfect wife. And then maybe... Well, a girl could dream, couldn't she?

After the wedding George had moved into her place because it was near her work. He never said how far it was from his, but the distance didn't seem to bother him. George really never said much about his work at all. And whenever Sophy had asked about it, his replies were vague.

She took the hint and never pressed, not even when, at his parents' late summer party, his father happened to mention the job George would have at the University of Uppsala.

"Uppsala?" Sophy had echoed. She hadn't wanted to say, "Where's that?" So she looked it up when she got home. It turned out Uppsala was in Sweden.

Sweden. Yet he'd never mentioned it to her.

But then they'd only been married a month by that time. And theirs had hardly been a normal courtship and marriage. So if he hadn't mentioned it, maybe he'd just been too busy. And she'd been consumed with the last weeks of her pregnancy. Maybe he was saving it for after the baby was born when they could make plans.

It didn't matter. She didn't mind where they went. She'd always wanted to visit Sweden.

They did talk about a lot of other things—baseball, art, astronomy, food, music, movies, books—and the baby.

Because to her astonishment, in George Sophy finally found someone besides herself who cared about her baby.

At first she didn't talk about her pregnancy or the baby. She didn't think he'd want to know. Besides, she was terribly self-conscious about the way she looked as her body changed and her belly got bigger every day. A major turnoff, she'd have thought.

It wasn't as if he'd ever seen her naked before the baby. They had never been lovers. And the advanced stage of her pregnancy had precluded that happening any time soon.

Still she caught George's gaze studying her frequently, and he didn't seem put off by what he saw. Once when he was looking, the baby had visibly kicked and George's eyes had widened.

"Is the baby kicking?" he asked. "Does it hurt?"

And impulsively, Sophy had taken his hand and placed it on her belly to let him feel the baby's kicks. And watched his eyes widen even further, as if he felt something miraculous.

After that he began to ask questions. Then he began to read all her books on pregnancy and childbirth and asked even more questions—so many that she finally suggested, "Why don't you just come to my appointment with me?"

She'd been kidding, but he'd nodded. "Thanks, I will."

He'd attended the last few in the series of prenatal classes that she'd been attending. Sophy had been doubtful at first about his interest. But he'd never missed a class. He'd helped her with her exercises and practiced breathing with her. He even massaged her back when it ached and her feet when she'd stood on them too long.

And when she finally went into labor, he was right there with her, holding her hand, letting her strangle his, and when the nurse had put Lily in his arms, there had been a look on his face that had allowed Sophy to believe he loved Lily as much as she did, that everything would be all right.

Too good to be true?

In retrospect it felt like that.

Not at first, though. At first it had felt wonderful—or as wonderful as it could feel while Lily was colicky and fretful, Sophy was despairing of ever being able to cope and George, though working long hours, was there when she needed him, made her laugh, gave her the support she needed.

One night she was so exhausted, had no milk left, and Lily didn't want to nurse anyway. Sophy was at her wit's end when George said, "Let me take her. You get some sleep."

She hadn't wanted to be a bother to him, hadn't wanted to make his life difficult, but bursting into tears, which was the other alternative, wouldn't improve matters. She handed colicky Lily to George.

He snugged her against his bare chest, bent his head and kissed the top of hers lightly. "Come on, Lil, ol' girl. Let's go for a walk."

"Oh, but—" Sophy began.

"Just around the apartment," George assured her. "I'm hardly dressed to take her out." He was wearing pajama bottoms, nothing else.

Sophy knew he wasn't going anywhere. She just felt so helpless, and so perilously close to tears as Lily wailed on.

"Go to sleep," George said. "She'll be fine. I'll give her a bottle if I have to."

"But—"

"You've expressed milk. I know how to warm a bottle. Sleep, Soph. Sleep."

He carried Lily out of the room, crooning to her. Sophy watched them go, felt a stray tear slip down her cheek, felt like a failure. Knew she would not sleep.

She listened to Lily's wails disappearing as George carried her out of the room, then sank back into the pillows, miserable.

Turning onto her side, she drew George's pillow against her and buried her face into it to breathe deeply of the scent of him that lingered. And against all odds, she slept.

When she woke up it was to silence. No baby crying. No sound of George's light breathing from the other side of the bed. No George at all.

Lily wasn't in her cradle, either. A glance at the clock told Sophy that she'd slept two hours—a lifetime in the night of a fretful baby. She threw back the light cover and went to look for them.

They hadn't gone far. She found them in the living room. George was sprawled in the recliner, his hair tousled, his lips slightly parted, sound asleep. And Lily, fretful no longer, was lying on his bare chest with both of George's arms wrapped securely around her, fast asleep as well.

Sophy just stood there and stared, awed and in love—deeply in love—with both of them.

They might not have started out the way most families did, but that didn't mean they couldn't have a happy ending. She loved him, after all. And she began to think George loved her, too. But until the night before Lily's baptism, she hadn't really dared to believe it was true.

That night, shortly after Lily's two-month birthday—only a day after the doctor told her they could "resume marital relations"—George and she made love.

She had felt hot and cold and a little panicky at the doctor's assurance that making love would be fine. Physically, of course, she was sure it would be. Emotionally she hadn't been nearly as sanguine. What George thought, she didn't know. He never said. He would talk at length about planets, stars and the immutable laws of nature as well as about baseball and art and Lily, but he didn't talk about feelings at all.

There was no talk, only actions. It started simply enough—with concern and gentleness. A soothing back rub like many he had given her that soon became neither soothing nor confined to her back. His hands ventured further that night. They played in her hair at the nape of her neck. They traced the curve of her ear. They ran down her sides and over the swell of her buttocks.

They made her squirm with longing. She wanted more. She wanted him.

And as she turned and touched him, it was clear he wanted her, too. She knew, of course, after Ari, what a man wanted. But as in every other way, George was unlike Ari in the way he made love. Certainly he wanted what Ari wanted in one respect. But his lovemaking wasn't all about that. He gave as much as he took. And he let Sophy give as well.

It began slowly, but the fire soon burned hot. George's kisses, formerly gentle, now grew hungry and urgent, his touch compelling. His hands moved over her body, learning her secrets, sharing his own with her. When her legs parted and he slid between them, she knew a sense of rightness. And when he braced himself above her and began to move, she met him eagerly, drew him in.

And when they shattered in each other's arms, Sophy knew a sense of completion that she'd never felt before. At that moment she'd understood how two separate beings could become one.

She and George were one. She believed it.

Clutching him to her, then running her hands over his sweat-slick back, she shut her eyes tightly against the tears of joy she felt. But she couldn't quell them and they spilled onto her cheeks. She knew George tasted them when he kissed her.

He didn't speak, just pulled back enough to look down at her.

She opened her eyes and saw the expression on his face. "I'm sorry," she said. "I just—" But how could she explain?

George touched her cheek gently, then rolled off onto his back and lay beside her silently. Finally he said, "It's all right."

He turned toward her and stroked her hair lightly. "It will be all right. Lily will be awake before we know it. Let's get some sleep while we still can." Then he spooned his body around hers and said no more.

It will be all right. It already *was* all right. More than all right, Sophy thought as she had hugged the words to her heart in the same way she had hugged George's arm against her breasts.

But it hadn't been.

The castle of love and happily ever after that she'd dared to believe in that night had crumbled the very next day.

Now nearly four years later, Sophy knew she was in danger again.

All those old feelings were welling up. She had a soft spot for George. He was gorgeous, charming, brilliant and responsible. Everything a woman would desire.

He'd stepped in and helped her when she most needed his help. He'd married her and allowed her to fall in love with him and to believe he might actually love her, too.

It hadn't been true.

She needed to remember that because discovering the truth had hurt too much the last time. And once was definitely enough.

She wasn't about to risk her heart again.

CHAPTER EIGHT

THE NEXT MORNING, she began building a wall.

Not a literal wall, of course. But a professional wall. All nice and neat and absolutely appropriate. He was the client, she was the "rented wife" for the next two weeks or so. And she was determined to make sure they both remembered that.

So she fixed his breakfast before he came downstairs, set a place for him at the bar in the kitchen and placed a folded copy of the morning's *Times* next to the place mat.

When he appeared, she was on the phone, which worked out well. She didn't have to make chitchat with him, didn't have to even acknowledge their encounter last night. She just gave him a wave and pointed to the kitchen and kept on talking.

When she got off the phone, she went into the kitchen to find him staring into the open oven where she'd left his meal to keep warm.

"What's this?" he demanded.

"Your breakfast," she said briskly. "I have a lot of work to do this morning. Fridays I do the billing and fill out all the payroll sheets. I'll be doing some laundry today, too. Changing sheets. Lily's coming tomorrow. She can sleep with me."

He straightened up. "There's a bedroom at the other end

of the hall from mine that Tallie's boys use when they're here."

She'd seen it, but she didn't want Lily up there when she was on the floor below. "She'll be fine with me."

George's jaw set. "Maybe you could let her decide."

Sophy gave him a bright smile. "I'll do that." No problem at all. She was quite confident Lily would rather be with her rather than in a strange room in a house she wasn't familiar with. "Where's the laundry you need washed?"

He gave her a hard look that told her he knew exactly what she was doing, but he told her where the laundry was and then he limped past her to head for the stairs to his office.

"What about your breakfast?" she said.

"Not hungry."

She didn't talk to him the rest of the morning. She vacuumed and dusted and did the breakfast dishes, dumping out the food he didn't eat and muttering under her breath as she did so. The washing machine and dryer were at the other end of the floor on which he had his office, and when she went past, she could see him in there working at the computer.

She didn't stop and ask how he was feeling or make any comments at all because that would have undermined her intent to remain professional. George didn't look her way, either—which suited her fine.

She made his lunch at twelve-thirty and did go downstairs then to tell him it was ready.

He said, "What are we having?"

"You're having a ham sandwich and some coleslaw. I've already eaten." She folded her arms across her chest.

He tipped back in his chair and regarded her from beneath hooded lids. "What did you have?"

She felt a flush rise to her cheeks. "A sandwich."

"Ham?"

She pressed her lips together and made an affirmative sound.

He raised a brow. "And a little coleslaw?"

"I'm going to be busy," she said sharply. "We don't have to share meals!"

"I'm not paying you enough to share meals with me?"

"Damn it, George! Stop twisting things into meaning what they don't."

"Is that what I'm doing?" he said mildly. He shoved himself to his feet and started toward the stairs.

Sophy, who was standing between him and them, stepped quickly back into the doorway of the laundry room to give him room to pass.

He paused when he reached her, so close he nearly touched her. But he didn't. He just looked down at her. "Is it that distasteful, Sophy?"

She shook her head quickly. "No, of course not. I just—"

"You don't have to explain." His voice was curiously flat, and he turned and started up the stairs.

Sophy didn't go after him and when she came upstairs fifteen minutes later with a basket of folded laundry, the plate was empty, the sandwich was gone and so was George.

She felt an unwelcome stab of worry. She checked in the living room, but he wasn't there. Neither was Gunnar. Surely he hadn't taken the dog for a walk? He was moving better, but he still wasn't fit. Annoyed, she checked the back garden. He could have taken Gunnar down the steps from the small TV room behind the living room. He hadn't. She checked out the front door, too, scanning the entire block for any sign of him.

But he'd obviously got enough of a head start that she didn't see him at all. Damn him! How was she supposed to keep an eye on him if he didn't tell her where he was going?

She was still fuming when the phone rang. It was Natalie giving her details about their flight tomorrow, then asking how things were.

"Just peachy," Sophy muttered.

"George acting up?"

"George is gone."

"Gone? I thought he hurt his ankle. I thought he had concussion. I thought you were supposed to be watching him."

"Yes, well—" Sophy hunched her shoulders, feeling guilty "—I was putting laundry in downstairs, and when I got up, he wasn't here."

"You'd better find him then," Natalie said. "Lily is dying to see him."

"Lily doesn't even know him," Sophy protested, though she certainly knew lots about him. "It's Gunnar she'll want to take home with us."

"She's looking forward to seeing Gunnar, too," Natalie said. "And you," she added diplomatically.

"Thanks," Sophy said drily.

Natalie laughed. "That goes without saying. She's missed you tons. It's good she's coming. Now go find George so he's there when we get there."

"I'll be at the airport to meet you."

"Not necessary," Natalie said.

"Yes, it is," Sophy countered firmly. "I need to prepare Lily."

Natalie hesitated, as if she might argue, but then simply replied, "Suit yourself."

When they hung up, George still hadn't returned. Two hours—and more trips to the door to peer out looking for him than Sophy wanted to admit—and he still wasn't there.

She was seriously annoyed now. What did he think he was trying to prove? Just because she'd tried to put them on a business footing, he didn't have to walk out. She was still supposed to be looking after him!

She didn't know what to do. She could hardly call Sam and say she'd lost his patient. And she refused to call Tallie and ask if George had gone to see her. The last thing she wanted to do was upset his sister in the last weeks of her pregnancy.

She remembered how every little molehill had become Mount Everest when she was due to have Lily. She could just imagine what thoughts of a missing brother with a head injury might induce.

She started dinner because the pulled pork she was fixing had to cook several hours. Once it was in the Crock-Pot, she made herself focus on the weekly billing work she had to do for Rent-a-Wife.

Once every bit of billing and electronic filing had been done, she went back into the kitchen, began to shred the pork, and then made Lily's favorite chocolate oatmeal cookies, partly because she knew her daughter would be delighted, but mostly to give herself something to do while she gnashed her teeth and muttered out loud about George.

She washed the kitchen floor, folded the laundry, then, still muttering, hoisted the full laundry basket into her arms and trudged upstairs. She put all her things away, then carried George's laundry up to his room. She could put the clean sheets on his bed while she was here.

Or she could have if George himself hadn't been sprawled facedown, fast asleep on the mattress pad.

Sophy stopped dead in the doorway, staring in disbelief.

He was *here?* He'd been here the whole afternoon?

She sucked in a sharp breath. Gunnar, lying beside George with his head resting on George's back, lifted it to look at her and thump his tail once or twice.

The movement of the dog or the sound of her indrawn breath woke George up. He made a groaning, waking sound and she saw him flex his shoulders, then open his eyes. Catching sight of her in the doorway, he rolled over.

"I'm sorry," she said hastily. "I didn't know you were here. I—I thought you'd gone out."

"Wished?" George asked, his voice still rough with sleep. He didn't get up, but folded his arms under his head and looked up at her.

Sophy shook her head. "No," she said truthfully before she could decide if that was a good idea or not. But she was so relieved to see him she couldn't have dissembled if she'd tried.

"Good." There was just a quiet satisfaction in his tone that touched her somewhere deep within. "Are we eating dinner together?"

"I didn't want to presume," she began.

"We're eating dinner together," he decided firmly. He pulled an arm out from behind his head and rubbed his belly in anticipation as he sighed. "It smells great. I'm starving."

"You had a sandwich—"

"I gave it to Gunnar."

They ate dinner together while Sophy kept the conversation on neutral impersonal topics—the weather, the Yankees' chances to win another pennant, the reviews of a new Broadway play.

George let her. It was enough, he told himself, to share a meal and savor both the food and the conversation.

But of course, it wasn't.

Not even close. He wanted it all.

But he'd jumped the gun four years ago, had manipulated Sophy into a marriage she hadn't really wanted. And he wasn't going to do it again. She deserved better. So did he. He had learned his lesson.

Or, damn it, he was trying to.

But it was difficult. Beyond difficult. Next to impossible to sit there and discuss the Yankees—or worse, a play he had no intention of seeing—when he didn't give a damn about either of them. Only about her.

Patience, he advised himself. At least they were sharing a meal, even if they weren't, at the moment, sharing a bed.

It wasn't just the lack of sharing a bed that bothered him. It was being shut out of her life, being told by her actions as well as her words, that he didn't matter, that she didn't love him.

Because he loved her.

Love. Whatever that was.

He wasn't used to dealing in love. He didn't understand it. He was a scientist, damn it. He dealt in natural laws and forces. Love was not one of those.

And that was why he was grinding his teeth and answering her questions about the Yankees' pitching rotation—because loving her meant letting her make her own decisions. It ought to have been easier. He was a scientist, after all. He was used to setting up experiments and then keeping his hands off, stepping back to observe the results, not provoke them.

But he was a man, too—a man who knew what he wanted and went after it. Which he'd done last time, he reminded himself. And look how that had turned out.

So he resolutely sat through another twenty minutes of talking about the Yankees before he asked, "Do you want to take Lily to a baseball game?"

Sophy blinked, her fork halfway to her mouth. "Lily? To a baseball game? Why would I want to do that?"

George shrugged. "You seem very gung ho," he pointed out. "I thought maybe you'd instilled some of that enthusiasm in Lily, too."

"Not yet," Sophy said. "She's a little young."

"What does she like?"

For a moment George thought she would brush off the question. It was more personal than anything she'd been willing to talk about so far this evening. But then she smiled and got a faraway look in her eyes. "She likes the beach and swimming. She likes books. She loves being read to. She likes going to the park and playing on the swings. She likes dogs," she said, glancing down beside the table where Gunnar lay sleeping. "She'll like Gunnar."

"He'll like her, too," George said. "What time will she be here?"

"I'm going to meet them at the airport about three tomorrow afternoon."

"I'll come with you."

"You don't need to do that."

"I want to," he said before he could stop himself. Ah, well. A man could only stand by and watch and wait for so long. Besides, it was the truth.

Sophy looked mutinous, but he didn't back down. Instead he finished the last of his pulled pork, then stood up and carried his plate to the sink. "Great dinner," he said. "Thanks."

"You're welcome. It's what I'm here for," she said brightly.

George knew that.

But, heaven help him, he was still hoping for a whole lot more.

"Are you sure you wouldn't rather stay home?" Sophy said the next afternoon. She was heading out to get into the hired car for the journey to the airport and, true to his word, George was right behind her. "There's really no sense in your getting worn out."

"It'll be good for me," he said cheerfully.

He wasn't using the crutches today, and he moved much more easily, though he was still wearing the boot. Still, when he'd come downstairs this morning she had seen increased agility in his movements. He didn't act as if every move hurt, either.

She was torn between being glad he was recovering and wishing for something that would keep him home so she could spell out the ground rules to Lily.

"It's really not necessary." She made one last-ditch attempt to dissuade him as he held the door to the car open for her. "You should rest. You've been working all morning."

He had gone down to his office after breakfast—one she'd prepared, like yesterday, after she'd already eaten her own. George had scowled at her when she said she'd already eaten. But at least he'd eaten it this time.

Now he slid in beside her, shut the door and waited until the car service driver pulled away from the curb to say, "I had some stuff to get done so I could come. I did it. And if I need to rest, I can do it right here. Put my head on your shoulder?" he suggested with a smile.

The words and the smile sent a wave of something that might have been desire washing right over her. Her cheeks burned, but she made herself shrug and say, "Of course. But I must warn you, I have very bony shoulders."

The way he looked at them induced an even stronger surge of desire. But he only smiled as if he were considering the option for a moment before he settled back against the seat. So she didn't get his head on her shoulder. But that didn't stop her being intensely aware of him as he lounged easily beside her in the confined space. It was a long drive out to JFK. She found herself wishing Natalie had chosen to fly into LaGuardia.

"Nonstop flight to JFK," Natalie had explained when she'd called. "I figured it was better with Lily."

No doubt it was. But it wasn't better with George.

"You mustn't let Lily bother you," she said to him now. If she couldn't lay down rules for Lily, she'd have to do it with George. "I'll try to keep her out of your way."

"Why?"

"Why?" She stared at him. "Because she's four years old and she's still learning when not to interrupt. Trying to work around her is not easy."

"We'll manage," George said confidently.

Sophy wasn't quite so confident. "Just don't yell at her."

George's eyes widened. "When did I ever yell?"

"Well, you didn't. But she was a baby then. I'm only saying."
Sophy shifted farther away from him, feeling awkward.

George rested his arm along the back of the seat. His fingers were perilously close to her shoulder. "You don't have to worry," he assured her. "I like kids. I know how to deal with them."

Sophy supposed that was true. He had nephews, after all. And it was certainly true that he had a devoted friend in the little boy down the street. Just this morning while George was in the shower, Jeremy had knocked on the front door to see if his friend George was there and ask if he could come out and play.

"Not yet," Sophy had said, biting back a smile. "He's supposed to take it easy awhile longer."

Jeremy's mother, who had come with him, apologized for disturbing them. "I told Jeremy it was too soon, but he wanted to check. We all feel terrible that George got hurt. He saved Jeremy's life. If there's anything we can do for him—"

Sophy shook her head. "He was happy to be there." She knew that, however badly George had been hurt, that was certainly true.

He was, ever and always, responsible. Throwing himself in front of a truck was just another example of his determination to do whatever needed to be done.

And how could you argue with it? How could you say he shouldn't do it?

You couldn't.

All you could do was feel petty and ungrateful when he did it for you—which was exactly how Sophy felt. She turned away and stared out the window, trying to figure out how to explain him to Lily when she would have bare minutes to do so. She still didn't have any good plan by the time they arrived at the airport.

Fortunately their timing was good and as they were approaching the terminal, she had a call on her mobile phone from Natalie saying that they had landed.

"Terrific," Sophy said. "I'll meet you at the baggage claim and George will wait with the driver."

"George?" Sophy could hear the surprise in Natalie's voice.

"Yes," she said and hung up. "It's too long a walk for you," she told him. "You didn't bring your crutches."

She didn't wait to hear any discussion. The minute the driver pulled up to the curb, she was out of the car and striding quickly toward the automatic doors. It took her only a few minutes to find the right luggage area and spy Natalie and Lily waiting for their bags.

"There you are!" she called, and at the sound of her voice, Lily turned, spotted her and came running.

"Mommy!" The little girl launched herself into Sophy's arms and wrapped small arms around her mother's neck in a fierce hug. "It was a long, long plane ride. I was good. Well, pretty good. Mostly good."

Sophy buried her face in her daughter's dark curls and breathed in the scent of fresh shampoo and warm child. Dear God, how she'd missed her baby.

"Mostly good, hmm?" she murmured. She gave Lily a multitude of small kisses, then glanced up inquiringly at Natalie, who grinned in response and gave her a thumbs-up.

"She was mostly super," her cousin confirmed, keeping an eye out for the bags as she answered Sophy's question. "Sometimes a little impatient. But she's just been eager to get here. Ah, good. Here they come."

She grabbed a weekender bag off the luggage carousel. "I didn't need much because I'm going home tomorrow. But Lily, well—" Natalie shrugged and laughed as she wrestled another much larger bag onto the floor "—Lily thought she should come prepared."

Sophy gaped at the huge bag. "Where did you get that?"

"It was Christo's. He used it when he was a kid and flew back and forth between his mother in California and his dad in Brazil. He said he kept his life in this suitcase."

"An' now it's mine. Christo said I could have it," Lily told her eagerly, "so I could bring everything I need. An' I did. I brought my books and my bear and my dolls and my building set and—"

"Good heavens," Sophy murmured, looking askance at Natalie, who gave a helpless shrug.

"I didn't figure George had toys," Natalie offered.

"And some clothes," Lily went on. "An' I brought Chloe 'cause she wants to meet Gunnar." Now she craned her neck and looked around eagerly. "Where is he?"

"He's waiting back at the house. We couldn't bring him to the airport," Sophy told her daughter.

Lily's lower lip jutted. "Why not?"

Before Sophy could answer, a voice came from behind her. "Because she brought me instead."

She spun around.

George was right behind her, his gaze intent—and not directed at her at all. He was looking at Lily.

"I thought you were going to wait in the car."

"No."

"I said you didn't need—" she started to protest, but George cut her off.

"Yes," he said firmly. "I did."

There was an urgency in his tone that made her look at him more closely. His eyes held a glitter of green fire as he added, "I wanted to."

And in his voice she heard it again—the same urgent note, even though he was speaking quietly, his words almost getting lost in the vast noisy room full of people.

"I've waited a long time for this," he said, his gaze meeting hers for a long moment before returning to focus on her daughter. "I wasn't waiting any longer." Then his gaze softened and the corners of his mouth tipped up in a smile. "Hello, Lily."

In the circle of her arms, Sophy felt her daughter stiffen at the sound of her name. Her eyes first narrowed with curiosity, then widened as she regarded him with a certain dawning awareness. "Daddy?"

The look on George's face was all the answer she needed.

Suddenly the little girl began squirming so determinedly that Sophy nearly dropped her. "Lily!"

But Lily wasn't listening. She flung out her arms to George and cried, "Daddy!"

Daddy.

George felt his throat close. And it had nothing—physically, at least—to do with his daughter's stranglehold on his neck. He nearly stumbled as he caught her midleap from Sophy's arms. But he steadied himself and drew her close as Lily's little arms nearly choked him. She gave him a smacking kiss and wriggled closer still in his embrace.

"Ah, Lil." He buried his face in her hair and simply breathed her in. He'd had her in his life such a short time that, after she was gone, he'd told himself he couldn't possibly miss her that much.

It wasn't true. He'd missed them both. He'd felt an emptiness inside him every single day.

"Daddy," Lily was saying, pulling back away enough so that she could look up into his face and pat both his cheeks. She was grinning at him, claiming him.

George was happy to be claimed. He grinned back, his throat still too tight to begin to form words. So he reached up and stroked a hand through her hair, marveling at it. There was so much of it now, a curly glossy thick dark brown that had only been hinted at in the baby-fine hair she'd had the last time he'd held her and kissed the top of her head.

He leaned in and kissed it again now, savored its silky softness against his lips, then found himself blinking rapidly against suddenly watery eyes. He cleared his throat, too, and was relieved to find the constriction had eased, that he could probably talk without his voice breaking like a kid's.

He secured Lily in one arm and held out a hand to Sophy's cousin. "Hi. I'm George. You're Natalie? Thanks for coming." He smiled at her as he gave Lily a squeeze. "Thanks for bringing my girl."

And yes, his voice almost did break on those last two words, but at least he got them out.

Sophy's cousin smiled, too, taking his hand and looking at him with a mixture of avid curiosity and frank assessment. "Yes, I'm Natalie. I'm glad to meet you. At last." There was a wealth of speculation in those added words. He supposed he didn't blame her for them. He didn't know what she knew, what Sophy had told her.

He'd avoided looking at Sophy since Lily had thrown herself into his arms. He'd heard her gasp as Lily's leap had unbalanced the two of them, and her exhalation of relief when he caught Lily and steadied them both. But he didn't want to see whatever raw emotion had been on her face at that moment.

He was too afraid he knew what it would be.

Now he slanted a glance her way. "Do you want to take her while I take her bag?" he offered.

She looked as if she would very much like that, but after a moment's hesitation, she shook her head. "The bag is cumbersome. With your foot, it wouldn't be easy for you. I'll manage it, if you'll take care of Lily."

"You sure?" He was surprised and grateful, guessing how much it cost her. "Really, I can handle it." He nodded again at the bag.

But Sophy shook her head and allowed him a fleeting smile, though her gaze slid away from his almost as soon as it connected. "No. Go ahead. I'm sure."

"Can I ride on your shoulders?" Lily asked him.

Wordlessly, George swung her up onto them, trying not to wince at his muscles' protest.

"Lily, he's been hurt," Sophy admonished her.

"It's all right," George said quickly. Not painful at all compared to what losing her had been like.

But Lily wasn't convinced. She leaned down and tilted her head so she could look him in the eye from about two inches away. "You're hurt?" She sounded worried and she stroked his hair as if she were comforting him.

"I'm fine," George said. "I'm especially fine now," he assured her, leaning nearer to kiss the tip of her nose, "because you're here."

Sophy watched them go.

She didn't even breathe, just stood and stared as George strode off—doing his best not to limp, she noted—with Lily perched on his broad shoulders as comfortably as if she did it every day of the week, her fingers fisted in his hair.

It had to hurt. But George said no.

As Sophy watched, George glanced up at Lily and said something. Sophy saw his teeth flash white in a grin. And Lily gave a little bounce and nodded her head vigorously, then patted George's hair.

"Well, she certainly has him wrapped around her little finger." Natalie came to stand beside her, but her gaze—like Sophy's—was on the two who were almost at the sliding doors.

"Looks like," Sophy agreed, trying not to sound as disconcerted as she was feeling. She hefted Lily's gargantuan bag and began to lug it after them.

"You'll kill yourself doing that," Natalie objected. "You take one handle and I'll take the other." She grabbed one away from Sophy and looped it over her shoulder, then started forward, towing the weekender bag with her other hand. So Sophy did the same with the other handle and kept pace.

"He's nice," Natalie decided after a moment. "I like him."

"You just met him," Sophy said irritably. "Besides, I never said he's not nice."

"You said he broke your heart."

Sophy wished she hadn't. There was such a thing as too much honesty. Now she said, "I was just trying to warn you about Savas men. Warn you off Christo."

"Lot of good that did," Natalie said cheerfully.

Sophy grunted.

"Don't be grumpy," Natalie said. "It worked out all right in the end, didn't it?"

"For you it did. But—"

"Exactly. For us it did," Natalie agreed. "And maybe it will for you, too."

"When did you change your name to Pollyanna?"

Natalie just laughed and shook her head, then nodded toward the two figures on the other side of the glass. They'd reached the car and George had swung her down to the ground. Immediately Lily fastened her arms around his leg and hung on. "She likes him," Natalie pointed out.

"She was supposed to like Gunnar," Sophy said plaintively as they reached the sliding doors which opened for them and they lugged the bag through it.

"She will," Natalie said at once. Then her expression turned to one of commiseration. "I think she might like both of them, Soph."

"Yeah." That's what Sophy was afraid of, too.

If Sophy was a bundle of contradictions, her daughter was an open book.

Lily knew what she liked—and didn't like—and she said so. She liked the beach and the ocean and tall buildings.

"Like that one," she said, pointing up at the one they were passing on their way back to his place. "An' that one." She jabbed her finger in the direction of another. "An' I like to read stories an' I like chocolate ice cream. But I don't like butterscotch." She turned in his lap so she could show him the horrible face she made.

George laughed and made a horrible face right back at her. She giggled and bumped her forehead against his chin.

"Lily, sit still," Sophy said sharply.

George nearly said, "It's all right," because he had a grip on her and she wasn't going to get hurt. But he didn't want Lily to get the idea she could pit one of them against the other. So he said quietly, "Turn around. Look over there. Do you like horses?" he asked as the car came along Central Park South and a line of carriages and horses stood waiting to take tourists for a ride.

Lily turned, following the way he pointed, and bobbed her head eagerly, pointing, too. "Look, Mommy! Horses! Can we go for a ride? Please?"

George didn't know how Sophy would answer that, and he didn't wait to find out. "We can," he said preemptively. "But not today. You've had a big day already today. We'll go one day next week."

"What day?" Lily asked. "Monday? Can we go Monday?" She looked at him avidly.

Out of the corner of his eye, George saw Sophy bite back a smile. In response he felt one creeping onto his own lips, knowing he'd asked for that one.

"Wednesday," he told Lily. "Promise," he added and held his hand out in front of her to make it official, wondering if four-year-old girls even knew how to shake.

This one did. She even gave a firm nod of her head. Then she said, "How many days until Wednesday?"

Sophy smothered a laugh.

Hearing it, George couldn't help grinning, too. "It's Saturday afternoon," he told Lily. "Then Sunday." He ticked it off on his fingers. "Then Monday." Another finger.

"An' Tuesday," she said. "An' Wednesday." She counted up on her fingers, too, then looked at the total in dismay and turned sad eyes on him. "Four days is a long time."

"Not that long," George assured her. "You'll have other things to do as well."

"Like what?" Lily and her mother and even Natalie, who was up front with the driver, all looked at him with interest.

Obviously generalities wouldn't work. He tried to think what little girls liked to do. Trouble was, he had no idea. He'd played with his brothers. He only had nephews so far. And his one sister, Tallie, wasn't any help at all. She had always played cops and robbers like "one of the boys" or fashioned herself as "chairwoman of the board," when playing make believe on her own.

"Well, obviously playing with Gunnar," he said because he knew Lily wanted to do that. "And walking Gunnar. Taking Gunnar to the park. He's really looking forward to meeting you," George added, sure that Gunnar wouldn't mind a little prevarication in the aid of a good cause. "And it won't be long now," he added as their car passed the Natural History Museum heading up Central Park West.

Apparently Gunnar was distraction enough. Lily bounced forward on his knee, looking out the window eagerly. "How much farther is it?" she wanted to know. "How old is he? Do you think he'll like Chloe, too? Can we take him for a walk as soon as we get there?"

The questions spilled out far faster than George could answer them. But he tried. And all the while he could see Sophy next to him, torn between shushing Lily and enjoying the spectacle of his having to deal with a four-year-old.

Let her smile.

She didn't have any idea how glad he was to have to deal

with this particular four-year-old, how much he'd missed her—and her mother—these past four years, or how very badly he wanted them back in his life forever.

CHAPTER NINE

IT WOULDN'T LAST, Sophy assured herself.

Yes, George was being kind now. He was answering Lily's endless questions with remarkable patience, allowing himself to be clambered upon and clung to, and generally tolerating far more childish behavior than any man should have to endure. More than tolerating, he really seemed to enjoy it.

But this was the first day. The first few hours, in fact. And it was a weekend, as well.

It wouldn't last.

George was a busy man, a physicist who was far more at home in the lab than in the playroom. He would soon tire of a four-year-old's chatter and want to get back to meaningful work. He had certainly worked long hours when they'd been together four years ago. She knew from the work she'd seen him doing on the computer that he was working just as hard now.

And though he'd been there to help her in the first months of Lily's life, he hadn't done it because he wanted to.

He'd done it because he'd felt obligated.

Obligated, Sophy forced herself to repeat in her mind now as she looked out the window down to where George was showing Lily how to throw a ball for Gunnar in the back garden. He'd felt obligated.

But there was no need for him to feel obligated any longer. George didn't owe them anything. He never had.

She needed to make sure he remembered that. So that when he lost patience, he didn't need to feel bad. She would just have to make sure he didn't hurt Lily in the process.

"He's a lot more kid-friendly than I imagined," Natalie said, coming to stand beside her and watch George, Lily and Gunnar in the garden. She held a coffee mug to her lips and sipped from it as she watched.

"Early days yet," Sophy replied.

Natalie raised her brows. "You think?"

"Of course."

"Seems to me like they get along fine."

"Yes. But as I said, early days. She's only been here a few hours."

Natalie shrugged. "Maybe you're right."

"I am right," Sophy said in an uncompromising tone.

Natalie laughed. "Famous last words." She glanced at Sophy and added, "But you haven't been here just a few hours."

Sophy felt something like a frisson of danger on the back of her neck. "What do you mean?"

"I've got eyes. And it doesn't look to me like it's business as usual with George. I've seen you working. I know."

Sophy shrugged. "So we have a history. It's over."

Natalie laughed. "Sure it is. That's why you watch him when he's not looking."

"He's been hurt," Sophy said defensively. "I have to make sure he's all right. I have to make sure Lily doesn't inadvertently hurt him more."

"Of course you do." Natalie dismissed that excuse with a wave of her hand. "And that's why he watches you the same way. Hungrily. And that's not in the past, not by a long shot." She paused and then slanted a glance in her cousin's direction. "Wouldn't you like it to work, Soph?"

The question cut far too close to the bone. Instinctively Sophy turned away from it.

"I'm not a dreamer," she said sharply. "I'm a realist. We married for the wrong reasons and maybe he does *want* me, but that's not the same as loving me. Sex is easy for men."

Not for her. She couldn't separate her emotions from the act. It was why she hadn't slept with anyone since…since George, that one night four years ago.

Natalie stared at her, eyes wide, wordless.

And in the face of her cousin's astonishment, Sophy hugged her arms across her breasts and plunged on. "What I would really like," she said fiercely, "is for him not to be quite so charming because when we leave, I do not want Lily to be hurt!"

Natalie's eyes got even wider, but she still didn't say a word.

Of course she didn't, Sophy thought disgustedly. What could you say in the face of a completely unexpected outburst? Damn it. She wanted to crawl into a hole. Why had she shot her mouth off? Why had she acted as if she cared?

Why *did* she care?

The realization that she did pulled her up short. Stopped her dead.

Wouldn't you like it to work?

Casual innocent words. Words that she'd blithely believed would come true once upon a time four years ago.

And when it hadn't, she'd turned her back. She'd had to turn her back. She'd had to make a life for herself and her daughter. She'd had to refuse to hope.

And now hope—a tiny tempting flicker of hope—stirred to life deep inside her.

It made her question her sanity, to tell the truth. Surely she couldn't be contemplating the possibility of life with George again…

Could she?

No. She couldn't!

But…

But she found her gaze once more drawn to the garden where George and Lily were laughing together. It was pure, unaffected laughter between two people totally in tune with each other.

Father and daughter.

No.

Lily was Ari's daughter.

But George was the only father she'd ever known. Not that she remembered him, Sophy reminded herself. But George was the one Lily asked about when she talked about her daddy. George was the one whose picture she kept alongside one of her mother on her dresser. George was the one she had recognized instinctively at the airport, the one she hadn't let go of since they'd arrived.

And he seemed to feel the same way.

Early days, Sophy cautioned herself, distrusting it all, doing her best to kill the flicker of hope.

It didn't make sense. None at all.

Why, given what she knew about why George had married her, was she fool enough to wish?

Of course it was true what Natalie said, on a physical level George probably did want her. Once he had. Once she had wanted him, too. To be honest, she still did.

But so what? She wanted more than that. She wanted love. To love. To *be loved*.

Not to be a duty. Not to be "one of Ari's messes" that George felt obliged to clean up. The very words she'd heard him say the day of Lily's christening. The day when her world collapsed.

George hadn't said it to her. He hadn't said anything much to her. She thought it was his way to do, not say, and she was fine with that.

But at Lily's christening, she'd come to fetch them for the

family pictures and what she'd heard him say to his father had changed everything.

They had been arguing, voices raised. Socrates was a notorious shouter, but she'd never heard George raise his voice until that day. She could still remember the exact words of their conversation as if they were emblazoned on her brain.

It was George's voice she'd heard first as she'd approached the closed door. He was insisting loudly that he didn't want to do something—something that Socrates was just as loudly demanding that he should.

She had been just about to knock, to call them for the family pictures and also to defuse whatever their argument was about, when George said, and she would remember his words forever, "I'm tired of cleaning up Ari's messes, damn it! Give me one good reason why I should?"

Sophy felt as if she'd been punched. She stopped dead outside George's father's office door, unable to breathe, only able to listen.

So she heard Socrates's one good reason. Actually he provided several—all very rational. "Because you're good at it," he'd said. "You don't take things personally. You don't overreact. You do what needs to be done and you never get emotionally involved."

Sophy's mouth went dry. Her heart was hammering so loudly she was surprised they didn't think there was someone knocking at the door.

But they didn't hear her at all. They simply continued, oblivious.

"Well, I don't want to," George said, sounding as quietly rational as his father expected now. "I have other things to do."

He didn't elaborate. Socrates didn't ask.

It struck Sophy that Socrates didn't care. He only cared about cleaning up the loose ends of Ari's life—"Ari's messes." And George was clearly the man he wanted to do it.

"It won't take long. It's hardly a big obligation," Socrates had said. Then he'd continued persuasively, eventually promising that this would be the last time.

"The last time?" George had said doubtfully.

"Well, he's dead, isn't he?" Socrates sounded exasperated. "What more trouble can he make?"

George hadn't answered that. He'd only said grimly, "It damned well better be. Because after this, I'm finished. I've got a life, damn it. Or did you forget that?"

"Of course I didn't," Socrates said indignantly.

"At least you can't expect me to marry this one," George said.

The words were like a knife through her heart.

But as she stood there, Sophy knew them for the truth. He'd married her to satisfy the family's expectations.

It all made a certain horrible sense. That job in Uppsala that George had been supposed to get, the job he hadn't bothered to mention to her—she knew now why he hadn't bothered. It was a part of his life that he'd put on hold because of her. He hadn't mentioned it because he wasn't going to take it— because Ari had died leaving her alone and pregnant.

Needy. *A mess.*

One that marrying her would clean up. For the family, For her. For Lily.

He'd as much as said so when he'd asked her to marry him.

He'd said they would take care of her. They! His family. Not him. She understood then that he had been simply doing what was expected because he was "the unemotional one," the one who didn't take things personally, who came in and did the dirty work when it needed to be done.

He'd never loved her.

She'd only hoped.

She'd believed his actions spoke for him, that by marrying her he was showing how much he did care. And the night before Lily's christening, when they'd made love for the first time, she dared to believe then that he more than cared—that he loved her the way she'd grown to love him.

That night had been magic to her.

But the next afternoon, she discovered how very wrong she'd been. Worse, she had realized that she was standing in the way of George's real life, that he'd married her to "do the right thing," and that she had to do the right thing in turn.

She had to stand on her own two feet, end their marriage and send him away. Set him free. Obligation free.

So she had.

She hadn't done it calmly or rationally or with any of that unemotional detachment that allowed George to do difficult things. No. She'd just turned on him, had told him to get out, that their marriage had been a mistake, that she wanted him gone!

He'd looked at her, astonished, as if he couldn't believe his ears. Then he'd argued a little, had told her she needed "to see reason."

But reason was the last thing Sophy had wanted to see then!

"Go away! We're through." Not that they'd ever really begun. She'd been adamant through her tears.

And in the face of them, George had gone.

He had quietly disappeared from her life as efficiently as he'd appeared in it, leaving her empty, hollow, more shattered even than she'd ever felt in her life.

But she'd pulled herself together and coped. She'd crossed the country and made a new life for herself and her daughter. She was a strong, self-reliant woman who didn't need a man to make her whole.

She and Lily were not obligations, or duties, or, God help her, a mess to be cleaned up.

Did George understand that now?

Did they have a chance this time? Was Natalie right? Was there more to their relationship than even Natalie saw?

Sometimes over the past week, Sophy had thought so. But she'd been afraid to trust. She still was. But was turning her back the coward's way out?

Did she wish their marriage would work?

God, yes. In her heart of hearts, unacknowledged to anyone, even her cousin and best friend, Sophy knew she still wanted it all.

Now, standing next to Natalie, looking down into the garden where George hunkered on the grass with his arm around Lily, their two dark heads bent together as he talked to her, Sophy felt her heart squeeze tight with love.

Yes, she loved him. Still. Yes, she wanted him. Always. Yes, she wanted forever with him.

But did she have the courage to risk gain?

George wasn't sure when he started to hope.

Maybe he'd never stopped. Certainly he'd never got the divorce and he'd never felt the urge to make a commitment to another woman. Hell, he'd never got beyond a few casual dinners.

But he knew exactly when he started to believe they might make it again as a couple—as a family.

It was when they'd seen Natalie off the next morning in a cab to the airport.

They'd stood waving on Central Park West until she was out of sight. And then it was just the three of them.

For a moment it seemed as if there was no sound in all of Manhattan—as if everything stopped. And then Lily had grasped one of his hands and one of Sophy's and then she'd swung between them, beamed up at them and gave a little skip. "Let's go home," she'd said.

And when George's gaze had met Sophy's over Lily's head, she had smiled at him.

Smiled. A real smile. Not a polite one. Not a strained one. Not a defensive one.

It was a little tremulous, perhaps. Even a bit tentative, he admitted, because George believed in accurate assessment of evidence. But it was a smile. It was something to build on.

And George wanted to build.

He met her gaze, held it. Then he offered her a smile, too. "Let's go home."

It was the most amazing thing, but Sophy felt as if she were being courted.

She'd never really been "courted" in her life. She'd had dates with boys and she'd been taken for a ride by Ari and she'd been married in a rush and cared for by George.

But until now she'd never really been courted.

She told herself it was silly to feel that way. But something about George's attentiveness awoke the feeling and she couldn't quite shake it.

Not that she wanted to.

She liked to cook and she would have happily made dinner that night listening to the sounds of Lily and George talking in the living room. But it was so much more enjoyable to have them appear in the doorway as she was peeling the potatoes and hear George say, "What can we do to help?"

She tried to tell them she was fine on her own. But they didn't leave. George showed Lily how to peel carrots, and then he chopped them into pieces for Sophy to add to the potatoes and meat in the stew she was making.

They prepared the food together and then, while it was cooking, George suggested they take Gunnar for a walk in Central Park.

Lily was already running to the door. But Sophy had to say, "Are you sure? You've been on your ankle a lot today. And what about your head?"

"My head doesn't hurt at the moment and the ankle isn't

bad. I won't overdo it.
was half-hopeful, half-co
pealing. "Come on, Sophy. D
do we get such a perfect day?"

And so she went. She wouldn't b
right about the perfect day.

It was a bright sunny crisp autumn afte
were turning gorgeous shades of red and g
to seasonal changes, was thrilled with the "pa
She loved scuffing her feet through the piles on th
then picking up armfuls of them, twirling around and
them over her head.

"You should choose a few good ones," George told her
"and you can make stained glass window pictures."

"With leaves? Window pictures? How?" But Lily stopped
spinning and began hunting leaves with George.

"We want whole ones," he told her. "As perfect as you can
find them. And the brightest colors. My mother used to do
this with me and my brothers and sister every year. Don't you
want to help?" he said to Sophy when she stood back watching
them, not wanting to intrude.

And so she began looking, too. They ended up crawling
around on the ground, sorting through the leaves, picking and
choosing, saving the best of the best.

"This can't be good for your ankle," Sophy protested
once.

But George just shook his head. "Some things are more
important than my ankle." His gaze left hers, found Lily, and
then after a moment of just watching his daughter crouched
down in silent consideration of which was the better of two
leaves, it came back to Sophy again as if to say, "See?"

"You're right," she said. "They are."

Eventually they had collected a dozen brilliantly colored
leaves, which Sophy was pressed into transporting as carefully

Promise." He flashed her a grin that ...spiratorial and altogether too ap-...Don't be a spoilsport. How often

...e a spoilsport. And he was
...noon and the leaves
...d. Lily, unused
...nted leaves."
...e ground,
...ossing

...d carried
...ain.
...ly how to
by laying
...ading one
...h a warm

wax from
de. Here."
he iron on

...ful, to say
...d. But then
...ng careful.
...me making

When at last Lily had pressed them to George's satisfaction, he took the iron and set it over on the counter where she couldn't accidentally touch it. Then he removed the T-shirt and held the rectangle of waxed paper up against the window.

The late afternoon sun shone through it, lighting up the leaves, making them gleam like stained glass against the windowpane.

Lily clapped her heads. "'S beautiful," she said. "Look at the red. An' the gold. Let's do another."

They had leaves enough left to do several more. So she did another. Then George started one. But after he'd put down two leaves, he looked over at Sophy. "Don't just stand there," he said. "Help me. I have no artistic skill whatsoever."

It was patently not true. He knew what he was doing, but she appreciated the invitation. She stepped up to the ironing board to help. George handed her the leaves. Their fingers brushed.

It meant nothing.

Nothing! Sophy assured herself. Yet hers seemed to tingle

after the barest touch. Surreptitiously she rubbed the tips on the side of her jeans, as if that would mask the feeling. It did nothing except make her fumble one of the leaves and tear it as she tried to lay it on the paper.

"Oh! I'm making a mess of this."

"No, you're not. It's only torn. Nothing's missing. Besides, it's easily mended." He took the leaf and laid it flat. Then with careful capable fingers, he pressed the tear together and laid the second piece of waxed paper on top of it, then flattened it down. Sophy took the T-shirt and spread it over them. Then, because he made no move toward the iron, she reached over and picked it up.

With the iron she pressed firmly down on the shirt, moving it slowly, rubbing it back and forth as George had done, then finally lifting it away. "Enough?"

Wordlessly George picked up the shirt and lifted the waxed papered leaves, holding them up to the light so the sun shone through them. "Beautiful," he echoed Lily. Then he pointed to the leaf that had been torn.

"See? It's fine. All better," he said as Lily examined it closely. "Good as new."

It was, Sophy thought, looking at it, too. You couldn't even see the tear. Torn and then mended.

Like her heart?

She didn't know, but it felt that way as the days passed and they grew together as a family...

On Monday George had to go up to the lab. He had grad students to work with and a project of his own he was working on. "Come with me?" he suggested that morning.

"Is your head bothering you?" Sophy asked immediately.

He hadn't complained at all over the weekend. But he'd gone to bed early Sunday night—actually at the same time Lily did, which pleased the little girl no end. And it was much easier to get her to go to bed with the assurance that Daddy was going to bed, too, and would be sleeping right down the hall.

He'd assured Sophy he was just tired, which she had readily believed. But now she wondered if he just hadn't said.

"It's not bad. Kind of a dull ache. Nothing like before. But," he added with a grin, "if it will get you to come, I'll bang it on something and make it hurt worse."

Sophy couldn't help laughing. "Don't you dare."

So she and Lily rode the metro train up the Hudson with George, and while he was working in the lab, they wandered around the streets of the local village, played a bit in a small local park and met George for lunch at a diner overlooking the river.

"Bored?" he asked. "If you want to take an earlier train back to the city, you can certainly do it. I didn't think I'd be tied up this long."

"We're fine," Sophy assured him. "We've had a good time exploring. We went in some antiques shops and a toy store and there's a small local museum."

"Give me another hour then?" George said. "And I'll be ready. Come and get me at the lab."

He finished his lunch quickly and strode away toward the lab. Sophy and Lily dawdled, watching a sailboat on the river and telling stories about where it might have been.

"I like sailboats." Lily said. "Daddy says Uncle Theo has a boat. D'you think I can go on it? Can you an' me an' Daddy go sailing sometimes?"

"I—well…maybe," Sophy said. Could they? Would they? A week ago she would have said it was impossible. Now, like the marines said, perhaps the impossible might happen. It only took a little longer.

When the hour was up, they walked up the hill to where the lab—which was really in a large house on a sprawling Hudson River acreage—was. George was sitting on the steps waiting for them. He had his briefcase beside him. But in his hands he had something else bright blue and red and yellow and green which he finished putting together as they approached.

He stood up, grinning, the breeze tousling his hair, as he held it out toward Lily

Her eyes widened. "It's a kite!"

It was indeed. And George told Sophy he had bought it at the toy store they'd visited earlier. He'd stopped in on his way back to the lab after lunch.

"I thought since you've been so patient, we might give it a whirl," he said to Lily. "Have you ever flown a kite?"

She shook her head slowly, eyes still wide. "But I seed 'em. At the beach. And I wanted to."

"Now's your chance," he said. "Just wait a minute while I put your mother's together."

"Mine?" Sophy blinked.

"More fun with two," George said. "We can share. Okay?"

"Yes," Sophy said, more delighted than she wanted to admit.

George put the kite together quickly, then tied tails on each of them and attached the balls of string. "Here's the rub," he said ruefully to Sophy. "After I had this great idea and bought the kites, I realized I can't run worth a damn. In fact I can't run at all. So—" he held out the ball of string "—if I hold it here, can you move out a ways and give it a pull? Run a bit if necessary?" His grin was abashed, but his eyes were twinkling.

And Sophy wondered how she was supposed to resist a man who made a kite for her?

She took the ball of string and backed away across the grass, playing the line out and keeping up the tension at the same time. Then he tossed the kite as she gave a jerk on the line and—

"There it goes!" cried Lily. "Lookit! Oh, lookit!" She pointed as the kite rose and dipped and then jerked on the line in her mother's hands. Sophy discovered she had to hang on tight or she would lose it.

"Are you sure about two of them?" she asked George, walking back toward him, trying to keep her eyes on the kite but finding them straying more often to the man.

"Let her hold that one," George said. "And we'll get this one up."

"It's pretty strong," Sophy said cautiously.

"She's a pretty strong girl, aren't you, Lil?" George asked his daughter.

Lily held out her hands and bobbed her head. "I can do it, Mommy," she said. "Please?"

So Sophy passed over the ball and George looped it around Lily's wrist so she wouldn't lose it, then placed it in her hands, showing her how to play out the string or pull it back if she needed to.

"How will I know?" Lily asked, her expression serious. Her tongue caught between her teeth.

"You just try," George told her. "You do the best you can. You feel the way the wind pulls it and you trust your instincts."

Sophy hoped that was good advice—to trust her instincts. Not just about kites but about life, because heaven help her, she was trusting hers.

Lily loved the kite flying. They all did. It was a fabulous day. And Lily protested when Sophy called a halt to it because she saw lines of strain around George's mouth.

"It's all right," he said.

"It was," she agreed, even as she brought her own kite down. "It was lovely. But we're not going to overdo it."

She thought he was going to argue with her.

"We can do it again another day," she said quickly.

The mutinous look in his eyes faded instantly and he gave her a brilliant smile. "You're right."

She could tell his head was hurting by the time they got

back home. So she left Lily to take care of him while she took Gunnar out for a quick walk and picked up a pizza to bring home for supper.

When she got back it was nearly dusk and George was lying on the sofa with his eyes shut. Lily sat beside him stroking his hair. She looked up when Sophy appeared. "I'm the nurse," she told her mother. "Daddy says this makes him feel better."

"That's very kind of you," Sophy said gravely. "Now wash your hands and come and eat. Do you want any pizza, George?"

Wincing he sat up. "Yeah. Sure." He got to his feet and started toward the kitchen. The pain in his face was obvious.

"Bed, I think," Sophy said firmly.

"I'm all right. I can eat—"

"If you want pizza, I'll bring it to you. Go up and go to bed. You overdid it. You need to lie down."

"But I told Lily—"

"Lily wants to take care of you. She'll understand that taking care of can mean letting someone sleep to get well. Now go." She pointed toward the stairs.

It was evidence of exactly how much his head must really have been hurting that George didn't object further.

He went.

He slept like the dead all night. Sophy knew because she got up to check on him several times and, in fact, spent the night in the room where Lily was sleeping right down the hall so she could be nearby if he needed anything.

He didn't. And in the morning, while he was a little wan looking, he seemed none the worse for wear. He even took Lily and Gunnar to the park while Sophy got breakfast.

"Are you sure about this? You were pretty exhausted last night," she reminded him.

"We'll be fine," he said. "Besides, I have Lily to take care of me."

The little girl beamed.

Tallie called the next afternoon to see how George was. She was delighted to learn that Lily was there.

"The boys will want her to come over," she said. "They want to meet their cousin. Can she come over Thursday afternoon and stay for dinner? I'd invite you and George, too," Tallie went on frankly, "but I thought you two might like some time on your own, yes?"

Sophy swallowed, feeling slightly light-headed at the thought. She understood the wealth of meaning in Tallie's invitation and in the suggestion that she and George spend time together. She knew, too, that with each step she was getting in deeper. But knowing, while it made her breathless, didn't make her able to resist.

She didn't even want to resist.

She wetted her lips. "That sounds like fun," she said. "Lily would love that."

Lily was, as expected, thrilled at the notion. She had made friends with Jeremy already. And having her very own friend right down the street to play with while George was at work and Sophy needed to get things done online and on the phone, was wonderful.

But the idea of cousins was even better. She'd never met a cousin before—except Natalie who was a grown-up and didn't count. She could hardly wait until Thursday afternoon when she and Sophy would take the subway to Brooklyn and she could meet them.

And when Sophy's phone rang midmorning, she said to Sophy, "Maybe that's them, telling us to come early!"

"I doubt it," Sophy said with an indulgent smile, then answering the ring.

"It's Tallie," her sister-in-law began. "I have a favor to ask."

"Sure, name it." Sophy prepared herself to console Lily when Tallie explained that it wouldn't work out today.

"Could you and Lily come now? And stay? Take care of the boys, I mean," she said apologetically. "I know it isn't what we planned, but I'm afraid I'm having the baby!"

CHAPTER TEN

"YOU CAN BE MY Rent-a-Mom," Tallie told Sophy cheerfully as she kissed her boys and gave them last-minute instructions while Elias tried to chivy her out the door.

"You don't have to rent me," Sophy replied "I'm glad to do it. Just go now—and have a safe quick delivery and a healthy baby girl."

"I will," Tallie promised, giving each boy another hug. And then she gave Lily a hug as well. "I hope she's just as beautiful as this little one."

"Come on. Come on," Elias muttered, Tallie's overnight case in one hand and his wife's arm in the other. "You don't want to have this kid in the entry hall."

Tallie just laughed as Elias steered her out the door toward the waiting cab. "He's always like this," she said. "A basket case."

"Damn right," Elias said, "and I have reason. Digger was almost born in the cab. I'll call you," he told Sophy. "Mind," he said sternly to his sons.

The three of them bobbed their heads solemnly. "We will."

And surprisingly, they did. The twins took Lily off to show her their toys and she went happily. The little boy, a three-year-old named Jonathan, but called Digger, stayed with Sophy and looked worried.

"Everything will be fine," she assured him. "Would you like to read a story?"

He nodded soberly and went to find not one but twenty books, which he brought to her.

"Are all these your favorites?" she asked as she settled him on her lap and opened the first of the books.

He gave another nod. Sophy began to read. By the fifth or sixth book, Digger began to tell her about the pictures and which characters were the best. By the tenth, he was telling the story along with her. And by the last one, he was taking her by the hand and saying, "Wanna see my trucks?"

She accompanied him out to the small back garden where he showed her his trucks in the large sand box where deep holes and tunnels provided evidence as to how he got his nickname. "Did you do all this?" Sophy asked him.

Digger nodded happily, and there was a real light in his eyes. "Me 'n' Uncle George."

"George—I mean, Uncle George dug this with you?"

"Uncle George likes to dig. Sometimes we go to the beach an' dig. We make plans. Wanna see our plans?"

"I'd love to." Sophy followed him back into the house and into the family room, where he tugged out the bottom drawer of a large map cabinet.

"Here." He pulled out papers that held simplified diagrams and elevations of a series of tunnels and pits.

Sophy stared at them, amazed and captivated. The drawings were neat and meticulous—exactly the sort of work George did when he was designing an experiment—but on a basic elementary level.

"You don't just dig a tunnel," she murmured, tracing one of the passages with her finger.

"You can," Digger told her. "Sometimes we do. But sometimes they fall in. So we plan. It works better. When's my mommy coming home?"

Ah. For all that Digger was happy to show her his things, his mother was never far from his mind. "Probably the day after tomorrow," Sophy told him. "She has to have the baby and then have a day or so to rest. It's a lot of work having a baby," she told him.

"Daddy says I was in a hurry," he told her. "Maybe the baby will be in a hurry, too, an' she can come home sooner."

Sophy brushed a hand over his glossy dark hair. "Maybe she will."

But they had no word the rest of the afternoon, so apparently the new baby wasn't in as big a hurry as Digger had been. By the time George got there at five, Elias still hadn't called.

"He hasn't?" George scowled, looking worried.

Sophy stepped between him and the boys so they couldn't see the expression on his face. "Not yet. But I'm sure he will before long. Babies come in their own good time," she said cheerfully to the boys.

"Ours didn't," George muttered under his breath.

Sophy remembered Lily's birth all too well. Her labor had been long and painful and twice had seemed almost to stop before a sudden rapid delivery that had made her strangle George's hands.

"That was my first," she said quietly just to him and then more loudly so the boys could hear. "I'm sure Tallie is an old hand."

"Can we call her?" Nick asked.

"Or Dad?" Garrett suggested.

"I think they're pretty busy right now," Sophy said. "Your dad will call as soon as something happens."

"Come on," George said briskly. "Let's go over to the park and play ball."

Sophy went along and played, too, determined to make

sure that George didn't overdo things. But she needn't have worried. Lily took care of that.

"My daddy gets a headache when he plays too long," she told the boys. "So we can only play for a little while."

"How come you get a headache, Uncle George?" Garrett wanted to know.

So George explained about the incident with Jeremy and the truck. The boys were all wide-eyed with awe and appreciation. And Lily clearly basked in his reflected glory.

"Daddy's a hero," she told them solemnly.

George shook his head. "A guy's gotta do what a guy's gotta do." Then, "Come on, let's play ball."

They played. And Sophy, watching, thought that however good a father George was with Lily, she could easily imagine him with sons as well. Lily brought out his protective instincts as well as his playfulness. But with the boys there was a different sort of rapport and a rugged role model that they could emulate.

She stood there, smiling, as the sun went down, turning the red and yellow leaves to copper and gold. When her phone rang, she plucked it out of her pocket.

It was Elias. "It's a girl. She and Tallie are fine." His voice quavered a little. And Sophy heard him take a deep breath. "It was an emergency C-section in the end. The cord was around her head."

"Oh, Elias!"

"She was cutting off her own oxygen. And Tallie was a wreck. I was, too," he admitted. "But—" another breath "—she's okay now. Everyone's okay."

"Wonderful," Sophy breathed a sigh of relief, too. "I'm so happy for you. Here. You can tell the boys."

She called them over and let them each talk to their father while she told George and Lily the news.

"We can go see 'em after we eat dinner," Nick reported, beaming. "Dad says so."

And Digger's eyes shone when he handed the phone back to Sophy. "Let's go eat dinner."

Alethea Helena Antonides was a lot smaller than her name. But with big eyes, round cheeks, rosebud mouth and a thick cap of fine dark hair, she was absolutely beautiful.

When they got to the hospital, she was snug in Tallie's arms, having just nursed. Her brothers all peered at her, wide-eyed, then looked at their mother as if they were still not sure what had happened or what was going to happen next. Tallie looked exhausted but radiant. Elias just looked beat.

"She's gorgeous," Sophy breathed.

And George, holding Lily up so she could get a better look at her newest cousin, nodded and swallowed as he studied his niece. "Very nice."

"Just nice?" Tallie looked indignant.

"*Very* nice, I said," George corrected her. Then he swallowed again, looking at his sister. "She's beautiful, kid. I'm glad you're both okay."

Tallie reached out a hand to him and he gave hers a squeeze.

"Me, too," Lily said and wiggled her hand in between theirs. "I like your baby," she told Tallie. Then she looked around at her own mother. "Can we have one, too?"

Sophy felt her cheeks suddenly begin to burn. She didn't dare look in George's direction. "Here, Digger," she said, hoisting the little boy in her arms. "I bet you'd like to come sit up here by your mommy and Thea."

Digger liked that very much. Then all the boys crowded on the bed with their mother and sister and father, and George took their picture. Lily wanted to be in it, too.

"No, honey. That's *their* family," Sophy said as George snapped a couple more.

"Then Uncle Elias can take one of *our* family," Lily insisted. "Me an' you and Daddy."

Sophy looked at George. George looked at her. Lily looked at both of them, then took matters into her own hands. "Here." She grasped them each by the hand and pulled them to the chair. "Daddy, sit here."

Obediently George sat. Then without waiting for further direction, he hoisted Lily up on the arm of the chair, then tugged Sophy down onto his lap.

"George!" she protested as she bounced onto his thighs. But he simply wrapped a strong arm around her and tugged her back hard against him. And Sophy had no will or desire to protest. She could feel his breath against the back of her neck. It made her knees weak.

"Smile," Elias commanded and snapped the picture. He studied the image. "Not bad." He took another and another. "Yeah," he smiled at the last one. "That'll do."

Each of the boys then got to have their picture taken with their new sister. And Elias took one of Lily holding Thea, too, because he said, "You girls have to stick together."

Picture taking done, it was time to take the children home.

"Could you guys stay the night?" Elias asked as they were leaving. Under his elation he looked ragged and strained, his cheeks stubbled, his hair uncombed, his shirttails hanging loose. "I hate to ask you. I know you've been there all day. But—" he shook his head wearily "—I want to stay here. I *need* to stay here tonight." He glanced back across the room at Tallie, who was holding Thea again. And there was such tender longing in his gaze that Sophy touched his arm.

She understood his words. Understood his need. Thea's birth had been difficult and scary. No one said so, but all the adults knew it could have had a very different outcome. "Of course," she said. "I'll stay. George will have to see to Gunnar, but—"

"I'll go home and put him out, then I'll be back," George said. "You stay with Tallie."

Elias gave them a grateful smile. "Thanks. I'll be home to take Nick and Garrett to school. And I'll bring Digger back here with me."

"Take as long as you need," Sophy told him. "We'll be fine."

She took the kids home in a taxi while George caught the subway back to the Upper West Side. She oversaw baths and snacks and was letting the twins read in their beds while she read to Lily and Digger when George returned bringing a backpack with a change of clothes for her and Lily. His were in his briefcase, he told her. And he had to leave early to go home and put Gunnar out again before he headed up to the lab for a meeting with some high-powered grant people early the next morning.

"I'm afraid I'm sticking you with a lot," he said. "I'd change it if I could. But it's a meeting we've had on the books for weeks."

"Not a problem," Sophy assured him. "Why don't you read to the kids while I clean up the kitchen?" It was in the same state they'd left it when they'd gone to the hospital right after they'd eaten.

"I could clean up the kitchen if you'd rather," George offered.

Sophy shook her head. "You read. Lily likes it when you read to her. You do the best growly voices," she quoted their daughter with a smile.

George smiled, too, a slow and, to Sophy's eyes, sexy smile that curled her toes. "A man's gotta use his talents," he said in his best growly voice. Then he winked and headed upstairs.

Sophy rinsed the dishes and put them in the dishwasher, then turned it on and wiped off the table and countertops. She didn't get to hear the growly voices because George was up in their bedrooms. When she finished, she climbed the stairs, but it was quiet.

One peek in the back bedroom showed her that Digger and Lily were already fast asleep. Nick, too, was sprawled fast asleep in the top bunk of the room he and Garrett shared. Garrett still had his nose in a book. She didn't see George.

Then she heard a noise and turned to see him coming out of the bedroom at the front of the house, carrying a pile of laundry in his arms.

"I changed the sheets in Tallie and Elias's room," he said.

And that was when Sophy realized there was only one bed.

The look on her face must have betrayed her realization. George's expression didn't really change so much as his eyes seemed to shutter for an instant before he said, "You don't have to share it, Sophy. Not if you don't want to."

But even as he said the words, Sophy knew she did.

"I do," she said, meeting his hooded gaze and feeling rather as if she were making a vow. "If you do."

A muscle in George's jaw ticked and a corner of his mouth lifted. "Oh, yeah."

She gave him a tremulous smile and reached out to take the sheets from him. Their fingers brushed. "I'll just take these downstairs and turn off the lights."

George was waiting when she got back. He had turned down the bed and left on only the single small reading lamp by the bed. "Do you want a shower?" he asked.

She nodded, then made a face. "I feel like I'm covered with peanut butter and jelly and mac and cheese."

He grinned. "A little boy's delight." But the look he gave her, though hungry, was far from boyish. He raised his brows. "Want me to wash your back?"

Sophy wet her lips nervously. "That would be...lovely."

Their eyes met and Sophy felt the awareness tingle all the way to her toes.

And it was. He took his time undressing her, peeling her sweater over her head, then stopping to kiss her neck before proceeding. She fumbled with the buttons of his shirt and felt like an idiot when he did them for her.

"Sorry," she mumbled.

"I'm just impatient," he said, a rough tremor in his voice. "It's been a long time."

Never, in fact. They had never taken a shower together. He had never washed her back. And by the time they were undressed, it wasn't clear that they were going to take one together this time, either—or if their desire would lead them straight to bed.

But just then George, kissing her cheek, murmured, "Mmm, grape, I think," and Sophy laughed.

"Yes, shower time for sure," she decided, and stepped in. Fortunately George had already turned it on, so the water was warm. So was the slick wet body of the man who stepped in behind her, who reached around to cup her breasts and nibble his way along her shoulders.

"I thought you were going to wash my back," Sophy said, shivering with delight at the feel of his lips on her skin and at the press of his erection against her bottom. She leaned back into him, moved.

George groaned. "Getting there," he muttered and went right back to nibbling. But one hand did leave her breasts long enough to snag the soap. He skated it over her belly, then slowly and sensuously worked up a lather, which he spread over her breasts, along her ribs and around to her back.

But washing her back meant stepping away, leaving space between them. And just as she was about to object to that, George turned her in his arms and wrapped them around her, rubbing soapy hands over her back while his chest and her breasts got better acquainted. Then his hands dipped lower, slid between her legs.

Sophy's knees trembled. Her breath caught. She ran her hands up his abdomen, then caressed his chest, his flat belly, his sex.

A breath hissed out from between George's teeth. "Soph," he warned.

But Sophy was beyond warning. She was learning his body all over again. She touched her tongue to his nipples. She scraped her fingernails along his ribs. She smiled at the low growl of need and pleasure when she stroked him.

At that touch his whole body went rigid.

"George?"

"Just…getting a grip," he said through his teeth. His eyes were dark as midnight, glazed with desire.

"I could…get a grip," she murmured.

He gave a strangled half laugh. "Don't."

"No?"

He shook his head. "It will be better…this way." And he rinsed his hands, then grasped her ribs and lifted her.

Instinctively Sophy wrapped her legs around him and felt him fill her. Her breath caught.

"All right?" George held her, didn't move.

Sophy nodded, putting her arms around him, giving a little wiggle that made him bite his lip.

"Ah," he breathed. And then he began to move.

Sophy's nails bit into his shoulders. Her heels pressed against the backs of his thighs. And as they moved she felt the tension grow, the power surge between them, felt her body tighten and then shatter around George even as he came within her.

He sagged back against the shower wall, still holding her, wrapping her tight. And Sophy clung to him as she tried to find words to express what this meant to her. But the words were lost in the emotion. Her heart was too full. And when she tried, when she lifted her face to look at him, and saw him looking down at her, his gaze dark and intent, no words would come.

He stroked her face with the tips of his fingers, then touched his lips to hers. "Beautiful," he said.

Yes, just one word. She could live with that.

They washed all the soap off. They dried each other slowly and carefully. And then George took her to bed and they made love all over again.

Sophy said it now as she curled into George's side and rested her cheek against his chest. He was already asleep. But it didn't matter. She could tell him tomorrow. She could tell him every day for the rest of their lives.

She would, too.

George would have preferred to stay in bed with his wife.

His wife. The words made him smile.

When his watch alarm went off at five-thirty, he briefly debated calling up his colleagues and grad students and the grant from Washington and telling them so, then grinned as he imagined the dropped jaws and the sputtering that would greet any such announcement.

He turned his smile on Sophy, who slept curled against his side, her cheek resting on her hand. There had been no tears last night. No Ari, hovering like a specter, over their lovemaking. This time she was his—wholly and completely.

George bent his head and pressed a light but possessive kiss to her cheek. Then, because there was never any doubt about what he had to do, he levered himself quietly out of bed and headed to the bathroom.

He took a quick shower, trying not to let his mind linger on the memories of what had happened in this shower just scant hours before when he'd last stood under this spray—with Sophy in his arms.

But it wasn't easy, especially when the merest recollection

had him ready to go back to the bedroom, slide back into bed next to her and take things up all over again.

Deliberately he turned the water to cool, then cold. It helped, but not much.

He shaved, dressed and combed his hair, then went into the bedroom to put on his shoes. It was still quite dark and his eyes, unaccustomed to the dimness, didn't notice that Sophy was awake until she said sleepily, "Good morning."

He could hear the smile in her voice. George smiled, too, then finished tying his shoe and crossed the room to bend over the bed and kiss her. "Good morning yourself."

She shoved herself up on one elbow and looped her other arm around his neck, deepening the kiss, making him ache.

God, he wanted her. He glanced at his watch. It was still too dark to make out the time, But he knew he didn't have enough without even looking. Regretfully he pulled back from her embrace. "I have to go, Soph."

She sighed. "I know." She settled back against the pillow and he could feel her gaze on him as he tried to knot his tie in the dark. "Do you always do what you have to do, George?"

"What?" He threaded the end through the loop, then frowned. "Pretty much. Doesn't everyone?"

"Ari didn't."

Ari! Damn it to hell! Was it still Ari? Was it *always* going to be Ari?

"I'm *not* Ari," George said through his teeth.

"I know that."

"I'm not ever going to be Ari," he went on, jerking his tie tight, practically strangling himself.

"You married me because of Ari," she said quietly.

He sucked in a breath, wanting to deny it entirely but knowing that he owed her the truth. "Yeah, I did." He scrubbed a hand over his face. "And I'm sorry I did," he added harshly because God knew that was the truth, too. "I shouldn't have done it."

Sophy sucked in a sharp breath, but she didn't speak. She didn't move. She didn't say a word.

George ground his teeth, then glanced at his watch and could finally see the hands well enough to know there was absolutely no time to discuss and explain anything as important as this right now. He raked a hand through his hair, undoing everything the comb had accomplished minutes before.

Then he sighed and shook his head. "I'm sorry," he said again. "But we can make this work, Soph. But right now I have to get to this meeting…."

Sophy lifted a hand and gave it an almost dismissive wave. "Go," she said quietly. "By all means, just go."

CHAPTER ELEVEN

SOPHY DIDN'T TELL Elias they were leaving New York when she and Lily left the house that morning.

She just said goodbye to George's brother-in-law and told him what a wonderful family he had and how lucky he was to have them. And if she teared up a little saying it, well, the adults in the house were all a little emotional that morning.

Elias was still a bit rattled from his daughter's birth. He still looked tired, and he was clearly distracted, busily chivying the twins into the car to go to school and then putting Digger in his car seat so they could go from school directly back to the hospital to see Tallie and Thea. He didn't notice the quaver in her voice at all. He was simply very grateful she had stayed the night.

"We'll have you guys over when we're home and organized," he promised. "Tallie will want to say thanks. And the boys will want Lily to come over."

"Thank you," Sophy replied because it was all she needed to say. She and Lily saw them off, Sophy did up the breakfast dishes and then they took the subway back to George's.

"Where's Daddy?" Lily wanted to know. "Where did he go?"

"To the lab," Sophy said. "He had an early meeting."

"So we couldn't go with him," Lily said. "Maybe we could

go now?" she suggested brightly after a thoughtful moment's consideration. "We could take the kites."

"No," Sophy said. She had almost said, "Not today." But that wouldn't have been fair. That would have been misleading. "No," she repeated. "We have to go—" she almost said home, too, and stopped herself before she did "—back to the house and let out Gunnar." Then she took a deep breath and added, "And then we have to go home."

"Gunnar is home," Lily said, misunderstanding.

Which just made it that much harder. "No, to our home. With Natalie and Christo. In California."

Lily shook her head. "This is our home," she said. "With Daddy."

Sophy didn't argue. She tried another angle. "It's Daddy's home. And you can come stay sometimes—" because that was obviously necessary now "—but it's not my home. And I need to go home, Lily."

"But—" Lily might only be four, but she had mastered the art of argument.

Sophy tuned it out. She stared straight ahead and didn't listen, though doubtless everyone else in the subway car was. It was a blessed relief to get to their 86th St. stop and get off.

Gunnar was delighted to see them. Lily took him out in back and threw tennis balls for him, pointedly ignoring her mother since Sophy had ignored her arguments. It wasn't ideal, but it was better than the alternative, which was Lily kicking and screaming her way back to California.

Sophy stood in the living room, waiting for an airline ticket agent to take her call, simultaneously looking through the window down at Lily and Gunnar, and remembered the day George had been there with them. She remembered his arm around Lily, their two heads close together as he'd talked to her about the dog. It was then that she'd begun to let her defenses crack. She should have known better.

Well, now she did. She wiped a tear away just as the agent came on the line.

"I need two tickets to Los Angeles," Sophy said. "Yes, for today."

George was not distractable.

His single-mindedness was legendary, his preparation exemplary. He always focused on the object at hand. And he never ever, as his father was fond of saying, got emotionally involved. He was perennially practical and perpetually unperturbed.

Except today.

Today he had to fight to keep his concentration focused on the meeting taking place. He was thinking about Sophy. He had to struggle to remember the details that usually sprung from his lips at the slightest question. He was remembering their night together and the way she closed up on him this morning.

He said, "Sorry?" And "What?" and once he even said, "Huh?" which had his colleagues confused and his grad students befuddled and made the grantors scratch their heads and say they thought they'd like to come back and discuss the project another day.

"Good idea," George said briskly, grabbing at the possibility of an early departure. "Let's do that."

"Here's your hat, what's your hurry?" Karl VanOstrander, the senior physicist on the committee murmured.

"What?" George was already stuffing papers in his briefcase.

Karl just shook his head and clapped George on the shoulder. "Nice to see you're human," he said.

George didn't realize there had ever been any doubt. But he just nodded absently and headed off to the station at a brisk pace.

He tried calling Sophy's phone as soon as he was on the

train, wanting to know whether he should come back to Elias and Tallie's or go to his own place. He supposed he should stop at his place even if Sophy was still at Tallie's. Gunnar would need letting out.

She didn't answer, so he called Tallie and Elias's. No one answered there, either, which didn't precisely help him know where she was. She might even be at the hospital seeing Tallie and the baby.

He cracked his knuckles and punched in Sophy's number again.

In the end he decided to go back to his place. Gunnar would need out. And if Sophy wasn't there, he could always grab clean clothes for all of them and head back over to Brooklyn.

He bought a bouquet of daisy mums at the corner market on his way. It had never occurred to him, but these flowers reminded him of Sophy—they were fresh and bright, and just looking at them reminded him of the joy Sophy brought into his life.

Clutching them, he pounded up the steps to the brownstone. Gunnar was in the entry hall. Sophy and Lily weren't there.

Well, fine. He'd go over to Elias and Tallie's. If Tallie were home, she'd laugh at the sight of him with flowers. She might even think they were for her—and the baby. He'd buy her some if it made her happy, but these were for Sophy.

"Go on out," he told the dog, opening the door to the back garden. Then, while Gunnar was outside, he went up to get Sophy and Lily clean clothes.

The closets were bare.

George stared at them. Shook his head. Felt it begin to pound at the same time that his stomach turned over.

Get hit by a truck? It was nothing compared to getting hit by this.

She'd left him. Turned away from him. Again.

She couldn't do that, damn it! He'd let her do it once because he'd pushed her too fast, had wanted too much.

Now?

He kneaded the back of his neck, tried to ease the pain in his head. Nothing at all would ease the pain in his heart.

Only Sophy's love could do that.

In her university days, Sophy had had one of those old posters on her wall that proclaimed splashily, *Today is the first day of the rest of your life.*

When she was in college that sort of thing had been inspiring. It had urged her to look forward, to see endless possibilities, to forget about the past, the failures, the shortcomings.

Nice work if you can get it.

And Sophy had been able to when she was at university because her past had been short, her failures relatively inconsequential and her shortcomings no big deal.

Now it was different. *She* was different.

Her past was long enough to include Ari and George and consequent disasters. Her failures in these relationships bordered on magnificent. Her shortcomings were obviously substantial.

All that she saw in the future was misery and all that she felt was pain.

And a stiff neck which came from spending much of the night in Lily's bed with her daughter and Chloe to keep Lily from crying on and off the whole night long.

It was what she'd done all day.

Sophy didn't blame her. The fault was hers. If it had been necessary to bring Lily out to New York, she should have made sure her daughter knew it was only temporary. Saying so after the fact didn't have the same effect.

Lily just glared at her or said, "We didn't have to leave without saying goodbye."

And Sophy could only shrug and say, "Yes, we did. I needed

to get back," when what she really meant was "*I* needed to leave." It was as simple as that.

And as selfish, she admitted. So she promised Lily that she could go back and spend time with her father soon. She didn't doubt that George really cared for the little girl. It would be good for both of them.

Lily didn't think that was much consolation. "I want Daddy," she'd sobbed when she went to bed last night. "I want Gunnar."

"You have Chloe, darling," Sophy assured her.

Lily had flung Chloe across the room, then bounded out of bed, grabbed her, then threw herself on the bed, clutching Chloe and sobbing harder.

"She'll get over it," Natalie had said earlier in the evening. "Kids are resilient."

She hadn't asked what happened. She'd just picked Sophy and Lily up at the airport and given them both hugs. Sophy had been grateful for the understanding and the lack of questions. All night long, listening to Lily's periodic sniffles, Sophy had hoped that Natalie was right.

Now she eased herself out of bed so as not to wake Lily, then flexed her shoulders and moved her neck. It hurt. Her eyes felt as if someone had thrown a pailful of sand into them.

"Today is the first day of the rest of my life," she said to herself as she padded into the bathroom.

It did not sound promising.

She took a long hot shower and refused to think about the shower with George. She washed her hair, then put on a clean summer-weight T-shirt and a pair of shorts. It might be fall in New York, but it was nearly always summer in California.

She put on the coffee and then booted up her computer. Work was solace. Or it should have been. But thinking about renting wives was too close to home. She shut off her computer and stared into space—not a good place to be.

The knock on the door was a welcome jolt out of her self-pitying misery. It was barely seven-thirty. Hardly time for visitors. But maybe Natalie had come to see how she was doing on the way to the office. Natalie, after all, had come back from Brazil in a similar state some months ago.

She raked her fingers through still-damp hair and hoped that Natalie wouldn't notice—or at least wouldn't comment on the dark circles under her bloodshot eyes. Then, pasting on her best "I'm doing fine" smile she opened the door.

"What the hell did you think you were doing?" George strode past her into the room and wheeled on her, eyes flashing.

Sophy, stunned, stared at him. This was the first day of the rest of her life, damn it. George was not supposed to be here!

But he was—and he looked as bad as she felt. His hair was tousled, his jaw was stubbled. His eyes were bloodshot, too. He looked strained and pained and angry as hell.

She'd never seen George angry. She didn't want to now.

"Go away," she said, still holding the door open, making a sweeping gesture toward it, hoping he would do just that.

He ignored her, walked in and flung himself on her sofa. "I'm not going anywhere." He looked up at her defiantly, then raised one dark brow. "Want to try to make me, Sophy?"

She ground her teeth, and shut the door, then set her hands on her hips. "I shouldn't have to," she told him. "I don't know what you're doing here. Well, I do know, but there's no reason."

He stared at her, then frown lines creased his forehead. "You know, but you don't think there's a reason?"

"No, I don't." She folded her arms across her chest and met his gaze with a steely one of her own.

For a minute he didn't say a word. She dared hope he would get up and walk out before she begged him to stay.

But then he said, "Why am I here?" in that quiet, measured

very George-like tone. That was the tone she recognized, the one completely at odds with the one he'd used when he'd burst in here.

She could deal with that one. So she made herself shrug negligently. "Because you always do what you're supposed to do. We talked about this yesterday."

"We did not talk about it yesterday!" Calm, measured George vanished in an instant. He jumped up and began to pace around. "You brought it up as I was going out the door to a meeting," he said. "I didn't get to talk about it at all!"

"You said you married me because of Ari." She wished he'd sit back down again. He made her already small room seem even smaller.

"Yes," he said tightly. "I did."

She nodded, justified. "I knew it."

"Partly," he added firmly.

She frowned. "What do you mean, partly?"

"I mean, you don't know everything." He hesitated, rolled his shoulders as if they were stiffening. His gaze flickered away, but then he brought it back to meet hers. "I married you because Ari left you...."

"Yes."

"But mostly I married you because I wanted to. I wanted you." He paused, looked straight at her unblinkingly. "I loved you."

Sophy simply stared at him.

She wondered briefly if her stiff neck had affected her hearing. If it had brought on the sudden wobbliness of her knees. She reached out and grasped the back of the chair she was closest to. It was barely enough to keep her upright. She shook her head, ran her tongue over her lips.

"No," she said. "I don't—" she began and trailed off, afraid.

"Believe it?" George finished for her bitterly. "No, I suppose you don't. I couldn't tell you then."

"When?" she said stupidly.

"When we got married. You still loved Ari and—"

"I did not!"

Now it was his turn to stare. "You loved Ari," he insisted. "You had his child. My child," he corrected firmly.

"Your child," she agreed with that much of what he said. "Ari's genes. That's all. But I didn't love him. Not when I married you!"

"But—" George said a single word of protest, then stopped.

"I did think I loved him in the beginning," she admitted. "He was a charmer."

"He was that," George agreed grimly. "No bigger one on earth."

"And no less dependable man on earth, either," Sophy said. She sighed. "I began to figure it out when he kept running off all the time. He was fun to be with when he was with me. But he never stayed. How could I love a man who didn't care about me or our child?"

George just shook his head, dazed.

"I almost didn't even go to his funeral," Sophy confided. "But then I thought I should go—for Lily. She might want to know about it when she got older." Sophy spread her hands. "I didn't love Ari," she said earnestly. "Truly. I might have thought I did once—but not later. And definitely not when we got married."

George shook his head, still coming to terms. "But you cried."

Sophy frowned. "Cried? About Ari?"

"I thought so. That first night…when we…made love."

Oh, God. Yes, she remembered those tears. "I wasn't crying for Ari. I wasn't even thinking about Ari—except maybe briefly when I thought how unlike making love with Ari was. Making love with you was…beautiful." Just like the last time they'd made love—at Tallie and Elias's. She hesitated, and then thought she had nothing left to lose and gave him the words she had been afraid to say at the time. "And I loved you."

George didn't speak. His Adam's apple moved convulsively in his throat. His fingers flexed, made fists, then opened again. He took a breath and let it out. "Then why were you so angry the next day? Why did you tell me to go?"

"I didn't believe you loved me. I thought I was a duty—one of Ari's messes you always had to clean up."

George grimaced and said a rude word. "No! I never—"

"I heard you say so, George. You told your father you'd always cleaned up Ari's messes and you were sick of doing it and that whatever it was he wanted you to do was the last one. I heard you, George, with my own ears."

"When?"

"At the christening. Upstairs. You and your father were arguing. About a woman. One of Ari's women." She forced herself to be frank. "You said you wouldn't clean up any more of his messes. And that at least he—your father—couldn't expect you to marry this one!"

"Because I was married to you!"

"Because I was one of Ari's messes!"

"No! You got it all wrong. I didn't mean you—for God's sake, how could you think it?"

"What else was I to think?"

"Not you! Not ever you! There was other stuff. Lots of other stuff. Most of my life I was cleaning up after Ari. He got in a car accident in college. His fault. He didn't have insurance. His dad had died the year before. We paid the bills, compensation, that stuff. I took care of it. My father was busy. Theo was gone. And—" he shrugged "—so I did it. Ari was the closest to me in age. We grew up together. People sometimes thought we were the ones who were brothers because we looked the most alike. There were other things, too."

"This woman?"

He shook his head. "She was claiming Ari owed her money. No, but before...there were other things..."

He was silent for so long that Sophy wondered if he would continue, but finally he did.

"He borrowed money from me when I was in grad school. He had a project that he was working on, he said. I believed him. I lent him the money. He was a smart guy, no reason why it couldn't have been a good thing..."

"It wasn't?" Sophy guessed.

George shook his head. "He'd got some girl pregnant." His voice was low, hard to hear. He swallowed. "Paid for her to have an abortion." He looked at her, his expression grim, his gaze grim. "When I found out you were pregnant, I was glad he was dead."

Sophy hugged her arms across her body. "I would never—"

"I know. I knew then. But I didn't want you to have the baby alone. I wanted to be there. Hell, from the first time I met you, I felt a connection, but how could I act on it? You were...his!"

Sophy came then and stood in front of him, looked up at him and met his gaze, stopped being afraid, stopped running. "I wasn't ever his the way I'm yours."

For a moment they just stared into each other's eyes. Then hers brimmed with tears and spilled over as he wrapped his arms around her and buried his face in her hair. She felt a tremor run through him, knew her own body trembled. Held him tight. Felt his arms crush her.

"I love you," she whispered. "I've loved you since the beginning. Our beginning. I didn't say yes so you'd take care of me. I said it because I wanted you, thought I could build a life with you, a good one, with you and me and Lily. And when I thought that family duty was the only reason you were doing it, I knew I had to let you go so you could live the life you wanted."

He drew her down onto the sofa with him and wrapped his arms around her again, kissed her cheek, shook his head. "Family duty has nothing to do with us. Never did. The life I wanted—the life I still want—is with you. Understand?"

But Sophy needed all the loose ends tied up. "What about… Uppsala? You didn't even mention it."

He shook his head. "Top secret multigovernment project. Once we got married there was no way I was going to do that. I told you that last week."

"You didn't tell me what it was," she protested.

He grinned. "Because if I did I'd have to kill you."

She grinned, too, but then her grin faded. "Are you still…?"

"No. Everything I'm doing now would bore the socks off you. But it's what I want to do—if you'll come home with me." Deep green eyes bored into hers. "Will you?"

For just a moment Sophy paused to savor the moment, to breathe in the calm and the peace and the love she'd never hoped to win. It was hers. It always had been. She regretted for an instant the time they had lost, but then thought about all the time they had left that they might never have got if these past three weeks hadn't happened.

Today was the first day of the rest of her life—and it was looking better and better.

She smiled and framed his face in her hands. "I will. Oh, George, yes, please. I will!"

They were kissing when the door opened and small footsteps came padding down the hall. "Daddy!" Lily's joy echoed around the room.

She flung herself on them and they gathered her in.

And then George pulled back. "Hang on," he said and got to his feet. Lily clung to him as he started for the door. "No," he told her. "You wait here. I'll be right back."

Lily looked disgruntled, but reluctantly went back to Sophy and crawled into her arms. Her eyes were bloodshot, too, from all of last night's crying. But her smile was real and brilliant. "I knew Daddy would come," she said.

"You're a smart girl," Sophy told her. "You believed."

Lily nodded. "You gotta."

Then the door opened again and a large exuberant black dog bounded in and leapt onto the couch with them.

"Gunnar!" Lily shrieked and threw her arms around him.

"You brought Gunnar?" Sophy stared at George, amazed. "On the plane?"

"He's part of the family," George said simply. Then he grinned and picked Lily up to find room on the sofa for all of them. "And I figured if you wouldn't listen to me, Lily and Gunnar together couldn't help but convince you." He threaded his fingers in her damp, tousled hair, making her aware of what a wreck she must look.

She said so.

George shook his head. "You are beautiful—inside and out. And I am the luckiest man in the world."

Sophy's tears spilled again. "And I am the luckiest woman."

"We are the luckiest family," Lily said. "Aren't we, Gunnar?"

Gunnar made his agreement noise and bumped Lily with his nose. She wrapped her arms around him and giggled. "Gunnar's a good brother," she said. "But I wouldn't mind one like Digger. Could I please have a brother like Digger?" she asked her parents.

Sophy looked at George. George looked at Sophy. They put their arms around each other—and around Lily and Gunnar.

Then George kissed his wife and said, "You know, Lil, that's a really good idea." He smiled into Sophy's eyes. "I think your mother and I will see what we can do about that."

CAPTURED AND CROWNED

JANETTE KENNY

For as long as **Janette Kenny** can remember, plots and characters have taken up residence in her head. Her parents, both voracious readers, read her the classics when she was a child. That gave birth to a deep love for literature and allowed her to travel to exotic locales—those found between the covers of books. Janette's artist mother encouraged her yen to write. As an adolescent she began creating cartoons featuring her dad as the hero, with plots that focused on the misadventures on their family farm, and she stuffed them in the nightly newspaper for him to find. To her frustration, her sketches paled in comparison with her captions.

Though she dabbled with articles, she didn't fully embrace her dream to write novels until years later, when she was a busy cosmetologist making a name for herself in her own salon. That was when she decided to write the type of stories she'd been reading—romances.

Once the writing bug bit, an incurable passion consumed her to create stories and people them. Still, it was seven more years and that many novels before she saw her first historical romance published. Now that she's also writing contemporary romances for Mills & Boon she finally knows that a full-time career in writing is closer to reality.

Janette shares her home and free time with a chow/shepherd mix pup she rescued from the pound, who aspires to be a lap dog. She invites you to visit her website at www.jankenny.com. She loves to hear from readers—e-mail her at janette@jankenny.com.

PROLOGUE

"I don't want to marry the Crown Prince, Papa."

It had taken Demetria Andreou two days to work up the courage to say that to her father. She'd waited until Sandros Andreou was relaxing by the pool by the palace guesthouse, with plates of *meze* and a bottle of ouzo before him. She'd waited until she was sure there was no hope that the relationship would miraculously change between her and her fiancé.

Now, as she watched the olive tinge of her father's skin take on an ugly ruddy hue, she knew his anger was about to explode. And her insides seized up—for his rage was a terrible thing to witness.

"I care little about what you want," her father said. "The King of Angyra selected you to be the Crown Prince's wife when you were twelve years old. It's an honor! A duty to your family and your country!"

It was also a boon to Sandros Andreou, for being the father of the Queen would elevate his status.

"But I don't love him, and he certainly doesn't hold me in any affection."

"Love!" Her father spat the word out as if it were a curse. "Foolish girl! By the time you are twenty-three years old you'll be the Queen of your own kingdom. Young, rich beyond measure, and never having to want for anything."

Anything but love. Anything but the freedom to do what she wished to do with her life. Like her dream to design clothes. But her father wouldn't understand that.

Neither had Crown Prince Gregor, when she'd broached the subject to him last night over their annual night on the town, which was meant to show him and his young fiancée having fun. A façade—a pretense of what a normal affianced couple in love would do.

He had merely shrugged and said she was free to pursue it now, but after they were married such a career would be frowned upon. However, he would consider her request to embark on it as a hobby when the time came for such decisions.

She'd known then that arguing the finer points would be useless. She knew that her life as Queen would be lonely. Cold. Miserable.

Surely she wasn't the only woman who'd be suitable as the Queen of Angyra! Surely the Crown Prince could find favor with another woman.

"Perhaps if you spoke with the King this evening he'd reconsider…"

"No! That is out of the question," her father said, the underlying threat in his voice chilling her to the bone. "You will marry Crown Prince Gregor Stanrakis one year from today, as your King demands. Is that clear?"

"Yes, Father."

But moments later her heart ached for what would be her very brief career as she took the well-tended path from the palace guesthouse to the equally private beach.

The austere King and her domineering papa had planned her future for her. At least she had a year to make a name for herself in the design world, to follow her dream if only briefly.

For ten years Sandros Andreou had brought his family to

the island kingdom of Angyra as guests of the Royal House of Stanrakis. It was an enchanted place, where the sea sparkled like blue topaz against white sand beaches.

Frangipani and bougainvillea bloomed in profusion, perfuming the air with their sweet spice. Lush stands of olive and cypress covered the rugged mountains that rose majestically against a cloudless sky.

This was old world. Life moved at a slower pace here. The people openly adored their King and Queen. Already they regarded Demetria with open affection.

Her future had loomed as a fairy tale to her when she was young, with the paparazzi snapping photos of her and the handsome Crown Prince on their yearly "date." But now she knew better.

Crown Prince Gregor had only given her a sad smile when she'd brought her worries up to him. "Royalty must marry for duty, not love. That is the way it has always been. I'll be kind to you. All I demand in return is your fidelity until you have given me heirs."

The fact that he still treated her like a child hurt, but not nearly as badly as the cold fate that awaited her. She was to be the virgin bride to a man who didn't even desire her.

Lost in that troubled thought, she left the pristine private beach for the wild lands bordering the royal palace. She walked until the sounds coming from the bustling seaport faded into obscurity. She walked until the palace was no more than a speck in the distance, until the only sound was the wild crash of waves against the rocky shore.

On a slim, deserted stretch of beach littered with driftwood and seaweed she crawled onto a jutting slab of rock and stared out to sea. Life was not fair!

She'd known the Crown Prince for a decade but he was still a stranger to her. After this last visit she held little hope that she'd ever become close with her future husband.

Gregor, ten years older than she, was stoic in the extreme. She'd yet to enjoy her time alone with him. They had nothing in common, which made for very stilted conversations. He'd never even given her more than a perfunctory kiss, and she was sure he'd done that just for show!

There was no romance between them. No passion.

No love.

"What are you doing here?" a man asked, startling her with his closeness.

She shielded her eyes and stared down at the stranger, hoping he wouldn't recognize her. He in turn stared back at her as if he'd never seen her before.

Either a local or a tourist. She decided on the latter, since he was unaware of her identity.

She took a breath and gave the man a closer study. He wore low-slung shorts and sandals, and a knowing smile that took her breath away.

Without a doubt he was the most handsome man she'd ever had the pleasure of meeting. The wind had tousled his wealth of black hair and the sun had turned his tall, muscular body a rich bronze.

And his dark eyes... They glowed with a mesmerizing combination of amusement and desire. All directed at her!

"Well?" he asked when she continued to gape.

"I'm enjoying the view as well as the peace and quiet," she said, and hoped that the turmoil of emotions churning within her weren't written on her face, that he couldn't tell her heart was racing and her insides were tied in knots. "What about you? Why are you here?"

He pointed at the beach, where his footprints remained in the sand. "I've been inspecting the nesting grounds of chelonia mydas. Green sea turtles."

"You're a conservationist?" she asked.

This time his devilish smile was brief. "This beach is closed to locals and tourists. You should leave."

Yes, she should—but not for the reason he cited. This handsome man who embodied the sand and the surf and all things wild was a danger to her senses, for already he was making her feel things she'd only read about. Dreamt of one day having with her husband. And this dark-haired stranger hadn't even touched her, yet alone kissed her!

Kissed her? Heat flooded her face at the wicked thought.

Yes, she should leave. Put as much distance as possible between her and this charismatic man.

Instead she heard herself say, "Tell me more about your work here."

"It is—"

He broke off at the odd sound of thrashing in the water. His gaze jerked toward the sea and he muttered an oath.

Before she could register what had changed his mood, he'd vaulted onto the slab of rock beside her, sitting so close she felt the heat of his powerful length brand her, so close each breath she managed to drag in brought his unique scent of the wild sea deep into her lungs.

"No," she said when he wrapped an arm around her waist and yanked her against him. "Let me go!"

But the last words almost never left her, because he'd clamped his hand over her mouth. Her pulse raced like the wind, for she was no match for the steely strength she felt in him.

Helpless in a man's hold again.

Before full-blown panic overtook her, he whispered in her ear, "Don't make a sound or you'll startle them."

She tore her gaze from his intense one and looked to the sea. Emerging from the surf were lumbering sea turtles, all moving in a mass up the beach as if they were certain of their destination.

They were simply magnificent to watch. The tension gripping her eased and she relaxed against his warm, muscular chest, awed to see this slice of nature up close. Hands that had pushed against him slipped around his torso now, holding him tight as he held her.

And that was how they stayed for an hour or more, arms entwined and bodies pressed together. Two people lucky enough to witness an amazing tableau.

When the last turtle had laid her eggs and returned to the sea, she looked up at the man she clung to and smiled. "That was the most fascinating thing I've ever seen."

He flashed his devilish smile and stroked his fingers along her cheek, the feather-like touch sending ripples of sensual awareness crashing through her. "I've never enjoyed it more than at this moment, *agapi mou*. You made this special."

The endearment melted her heart, but the passion kindled from his nearness left her trembling for more. This was new. Powerful. Addictive.

A part of her brain registered that what she was feeling and wanting was wrong, that being here in this handsome stranger's arms could only lead to heartache.

But she couldn't find the strength to pull away.

Her body naturally bowed into his, her face lifting in silent entreaty. "I hate for it to end."

"It doesn't have to."

If she'd had a protest it was silenced when his mouth swooped down onto hers, commanding, and brimming with all the desire her lonely heart ached for. She clung to him as he pushed her back onto the rock, soon lost in drinking from his kisses like one delirious with thirst.

The rock was hard and hot beneath her, but so was the earthy man stretched out beside her. Without breaking the kiss, she was barely aware of his hand sliding under her T-shirt, of the electrifying sensations of his bare skin brushing hers.

His big hand cupping her bared breast thrilled and shocked her. A sliver of sanity prevailed. "No—"

"Yes," he said, thumbing one nipple into such a hard peak that she squirmed and moaned.

Resistance was laughable when all she wanted was more of his touch, his kiss. And he granted her that wish by shoving her shirt out of the way and capturing her breast in his mouth.

He suckled hard. New sensations exploded within her and her back arched off the rock. Her fingers tangled in his hair, holding him close, as she reveled in her very first taste of passion.

She couldn't imagine voicing a protest when his hand slipped inside her shorts to fondle that very private part of her. No man had ever touched her so, and though she'd read of it the reality was far more erotic.

And when he slipped his fingers inside her thoughts simply ceased as a new and powerful need consumed her. She closed her eyes and clutched at him as she was carried up toward the sun on a tight spiral.

A rainbow of lights exploded behind her eyes. Bells sang out, just as she'd always imagined it would be at this moment.

Bells?

No! Those weren't the bells of passion she heard but the tolling of the village church bells. Five times. In one hour she had to present herself at the royal palace for dinner with the royal family.

She should be fussing over what to wear instead of frolicking on the beach with a stranger. Instead of granting him this intimacy that should be reserved for her husband. How could she have let this happen?

She shoved away from her pagan god from the sea, shaken by the desire still swirling within her like a whirlpool, threatening to drag her back into the languid depths of passion once more if she let it.

"Stop it," she said, and frantically righted her clothes with fingers that felt awkward.

"As the lady wishes," he said, the beautifully chiseled lips that had adorned her body now pulled into a wry smile.

She shook her head, ashamed at what she'd done. Shamed that her body still yearned for more of the same.

Without another word she scrambled off the rock and ran. But even when she was back in the guesthouse, in her room, she realized that she'd never forget this stolen moment with a stranger.

Prince Kristo Stanrakis strode into his father's royal office, wishing he were anywhere but here. Though he loved his homeland, his passions rested elsewhere.

Then too he didn't look forward to being present for this dinner tonight, with the Andreou family. After that first one ten years ago, where the King had announced that Gregor was to marry Andreou's daughter, with the too-big eyes and rail-like form, he'd managed to miss every visit. Until now.

This was a royal decree and nobody, not even a grown prince, could ignore it. Not without incurring the King's wrath.

He strode straight to the King and went down on a knee. "You look well, Your Majesty."

His father snorted. "How good of you to tear yourself away from the gaming tables."

"My duties as ambassador can be taxing," he said—a joke, for if that was all he did with his time he'd be bored out of his mind.

As usual, his father scowled at the offhand remark. For years the King had found disfavor with Kristo for his errant ways, expecting him to spend more time on Angyra. Anything that took time away from official duties was inconsequential to the King, so Kristo had ceased bringing the subject up anymore.

"Rest assured I will be present when the State Council convenes next week," Kristo said, and earned a wave of dismissal from the King.

They both knew he'd leave Angyra as soon as that duty was satisfied. Or perhaps not this time, he thought as he crossed to his brothers.

After the interesting diversion he'd had this afternoon on the beach, staying could prove interesting. He'd never met a woman who was as entranced by the wilds of nature as he. He'd never shared that kind of moment with anyone before.

That fact had made the explosive passion all the more sweet. Even now his body stirred at the memory of holding such perfection in his arms.

If the church bells hadn't tolled, there was no telling how far she would have let him go.

"About time you showed up," Gregor said.

Kristo took the glass of *tsipouro* the server handed him and took a sip before answering the Crown Prince. "The sea turtles were nesting, so I couldn't leave until they did. Where is your fiancée?"

"She just arrived," Gregor said, and yet no sign of elation or pleasure showed on his features. "If you'll excuse me?"

Kristo smiled at his other brother. "He is just like Father— far too intense."

"He'll be a good king," his younger brother Mikhael said. "The question is will he be a good husband to his young Queen?"

Kristo imagined that Gregor would follow in their father's footsteps there as well. His marriage hadn't been a love match, and he doubted the Crown Prince's was either.

"Your Majesty," Gregor said, his voice ringing with

authority. "I present my betrothed—Demetria, the future Queen of Angyra."

Kristo turned, and the welcoming smile on his face froze. No! It couldn't be her!

But it was.

The beautiful woman his brother was escorting toward them was the same one he'd kissed to distraction an hour ago!

No, not just kissed.

The delicate stem of his wineglass popped in his tight grip, and his blood roared angrily through his veins.

Just an hour ago he'd tasted Demetria's full, sensual lips. He'd held the weight of her lush breasts in his hands, known the silken texture of the skin, the tight budding of her nipples.

Gregor, unaware of the fury building within Kristo, escorted his fiancée toward him. Her polite smile vanished the moment their gazes locked. Her soft lips parted. Her face drained of color.

"Demetria, this is my brother, Prince Kristo," Gregor said. "I doubt you remember him, since it's been some time since you've seen him."

An hour ago, Kristo thought morosely. One damned hour ago, when he'd brought her to a shuddering climax.

Yet how could he tell his brother that the woman he was to marry was unfaithful? He was just as much to blame for not recognizing her.

"Your Highness," she said, and dipped into a deep curtsy that felt like a mockery in the face of what had transpired between them.

"My pleasure, Demetria," he said, hating the coil he was caught in with her.

She forced a smile and mumbled an appropriate greeting.

In that moment he knew she'd not confess her sin either. And why should she?

Wealth and position awaited her.

Damn her for her perfidy! He hated her more than he did anyone on earth.

After today, he vowed to avoid the royal palace *and* his brother's unfaithful fiancée.

CHAPTER ONE

PRINCE KRISTO STANRAKIS had never thrown a royal fit of anger in his life, but he was moments away from doing so just now. He flung his tuxedo jacket on a red brocade Louis XV chaise and ripped open his stark white shirt, sending a row of diamond studs flying. One pinged off an inlaid table before falling to the gold Kirman carpet, while another chinked as it hit a window.

This urgent meeting with the future King, his lawyers and the highest officials was over. Angyra would face change yet again.

His life had just been turned on its heel and there wasn't a damned thing he could do to evade his fate.

No! His *duty*!

He paced the impressive length of his apartment. *Duty!* How he hated that word. How he hated *her*!

Just one month ago they'd buried their father, the beloved King of Angyra. *She'd* come to the funeral and sat with her father and sister, looking solemn and royal and aloof. Looking sexy as hell in a black sheath that had hugged her luscious curves.

He hadn't seen her in almost a year, yet the moment their eyes had met he'd been slammed him back to that day on the beach. A roiling mix of guilt, rage and desire had boiled in him.

He wanted nothing to do with her. Yet he still wanted her more than he'd ever wanted a woman.

Being near her needled him with guilt for betraying his brother and he did not like that feeling one bit. But he'd been prepared to suffer through her return in less than two weeks to marry King Gregor. Except that would not happen now!

The rap at his door was preceded by its opening. He whirled to find Mikhael striding into his suite, with a bottle of ouzo under his arm and two glasses clutched in one hand.

"I thought you could use this," Mikhael said, and promptly poured two drinks.

He took the offered liquor and tossed it back, relishing the bite to his senses. "Did you have any idea that Gregor was ill?"

Mikhael shook his head. "He's seemed tired of late, and complained of headaches, but I attributed it to the stress of assuming Father's duties."

The same thought had crossed Kristo's mind. He'd never dreamed that Gregor had secretly seen a doctor just before the King's death, only to discover two days ago that he had inoperable cancer.

The prognosis was grim. With death imminent, Crown Prince Gregor had chosen to abdicate before the State Council proclaimed him King of Angyra tomorrow.

That official announcement had been made just one hour ago.

By order of birth, the crown now passed to Kristo. He was now Crown Prince, which had thrown the council into emergency session. Unless they deemed him truly unfit to rule—which was possible, considering his reputation—the accession ceremony would take place tomorrow promptly at eleven in the morning.

As if that weren't jarring enough, he was now forced to assume his brother's betrothal agreement as well! He had to marry Demetria Andreou—in less than two weeks, if he kept to the schedule that had been set in place.

Damn the fates!

Desirable, unfaithful Demetria would be *his* wife. His Queen.

"I don't look forward to tomorrow."

"For what it's worth, I think you'll be a good King," Mikhael said.

Kristo wasn't so sure. Though he'd done his duty to the State Council, and sat in on required meetings, he'd paid little heed for he'd been in reality no more than a figurehead.

However, he'd taken his role as ambassador much more seriously, as that had allowed him to wine and dine dignitaries around the world. Gambling and carousing, as his father had called it.

At times that had been true. But the setting had allowed him to do what came naturally. In turn, being away from Angyra had allowed him the freedom to do what he really wanted.

But that would soon be in the past.

"Has he contacted Andreou yet?" Kristo asked.

"He was speaking with him by phone when I left."

How would Demetria take the change of plans?

Kristo stopped before the palatial window and looked out on the terraced garden that stepped down to the cerulean sea. He splayed his hands on the casing so hard that he felt the heavy moldings imprint on his flesh.

Dammit, he didn't *want* to be King! And by hell's thunder he certainly didn't want to marry Demetria!

But the only way to surmount his fate was by death or abandonment of his country. Though he'd joked that he could walk away from Angyra and never miss it, the truth of the matter was that he couldn't shirk his duty.

"Gregor felt certain that Andreou wouldn't balk at the

change of plans," Mikhael said. "He suspects that the lady might feel differently."

"How she feels doesn't matter. She has a duty to uphold."

"True, but you are a stranger to her."

In some ways, but in others they were intimately acquainted. But that was his guilty secret to bear.

"As Gregor pointed out today, the betrothal contract simply states that Demetria is to marry the Crown Prince," Kristo said, chafing over the fact that he was now that man. "Surely she is aware of that fact."

"You are being callous about this, brother."

"I'm simply being pragmatic," Kristo said. "Demetria and I are bound by the same laws. There is nothing left to discuss."

The Royal House of Stanrakis had one ancient and non-breakable rule. All future rulers must be of noble Greek blood. As the Stanrakis family continued to produce males, their Crown Princes had only to find a noble bride of Greek blood.

Easier said than done. But then, they weren't marrying for love. Even if such a thing existed, it wasn't ordained for a Stanrakis prince.

It certainly wouldn't be for him!

Demetria had been handpicked by the King. She had been groomed to be the next Queen of Angyra.

She possessed the right lineage. Her maternal grandfather was Greek—one of the old noblemen like Kristo's father. And her mother had married a Greek, even though Sandros Andreou's blood wasn't as pure.

That man had pricked his temper more times than naught over business dealings. As for Demetria—she fired his lust as well as his anger.

"I still think it would be wise for the sake of your marriage if you would take Demetria aside tomorrow and talk to her," Mikhael said. "It would go a long way in allaying her fears."

Kristo stared into his glass, his smile slow to come. "Yes, you're right."

He'd talk to her, all right. He'd let her know that he'd not tolerate her flirtations. That he'd have her watched carefully since he knew she was not to be trusted.

But the following day at the accession ceremony Demetria was embarrassingly absent.

"Please forgive her, Your Majesty," Sandros Andreou implored as he bent in as deep a bow as a man with such a considerable girth could manage. "Demetria went on a shopping jaunt for her wedding trousseau hours before Crown Prince Gregor abdicated. I haven't been able to reach her on her mobile phone to tell her of the news."

"She is alone?"

The old Greek shrugged. "I'm not sure."

"Don't you know where she went?" Kristo asked, furious that the man hadn't kept a closer eye on his daughter. "Couldn't you send a messenger to find her?"

Sandros Andreou's face turned an ugly purple. "I wasn't sure where to send him, Your Majesty. Her sister thought she went to Istanbul, but the maid thought she went to Italy."

"This is intolerable," Kristo growled. She could be anywhere, with anyone. She could even be entertaining some man!

"Rest assured that when she returns I will have her contact—"

Kristo silenced the man with one wave of his hand that looked surprisingly like the dismissing gesture his father had employed. The wave he'd hated.

"I will see to it myself. Considering the turn of events, it would be wise if your daughter stayed here at the palace until the wedding."

"For twelve days?" Then, as if remembering who he was addressing, Sandros quickly demurred. "Of course, Your Majesty."

"You and your family are welcome to avail yourselves of the guesthouse the day before the wedding."

"The day before?" Andreou repeated.

"Yes. That is all."

The old Greek attempted another bow before taking his leave.

Kristo pushed from his chair and stalked to the window, more restless than he recalled being in years. His gaze fixed on the ridge of mountains in the distance.

Graceful cypresses and thickets of olives blanketed the rugged terrain and helped to conceal Angyra's most treasured commodity. Rhoda gold—a pure metal kissed with a rosy blush and prized all over the world.

The ore taken from the Chrysos Mine had made the Stanrakis family rich beyond measure. It had turned this island kingdom into a mecca that now brought tourists here in droves to buy a trinket made of Rhoda gold.

But an equally rare treasure was the sea turtles. Protecting their nesting ground was his personal challenge, and that had evolved into his secretly backing similar programs worldwide. But who would pick up that challenge now?

"What are you going to do?" Mikhael asked.

The answer was simple. At least to him. "Find Demetria and bring her here."

"But the wedding is less than two weeks away. Women have much to do before such an event."

"She can attend to anything that needs be done here." And he could keep a close watch on her that way.

She would not take a stroll along the beach and entertain a stranger the day before *their* wedding!

"What if the lady refuses?"

He cut his brother a knowing look. "I am not giving her a choice."

Mikhael's eyes went wide. "You can't mean to kidnap her?"

"I most certainly do."

In a small shop in Istanbul, Demetria Andreou unwrapped a yard of Egyptian cotton from the bolt, blissfully unaware of the drama taking place on Angyra. She tested the way the soft fabric shot with silver, copper and gold flowed over her arm like a molten waterfall. Her heart raced with excitement, for when cloth seemed this much alive she knew a garment made of it would positively explode with motion.

"How many bolts of this do you have?" she asked.

"Just this one," the Turkish supplier said. "You like?"

She loved the fabric. It fell naturally into folds when bunched, and it felt gloriously sensuous gliding against bare skin.

It was a wonderful find. To know he only had one bolt almost ensured that no other designer would come out with a garment using the exact same cloth.

Originality was further aided by the fact that she preferred buying fabric from lesser-known markets. Fabric defined style. The best designer in the world was nothing without the appropriate cloth. A design didn't pop until the right fabric was paired with the right fashion.

That was when magic happened. That was when she knew she had created something that could eventually compete side by side with the top fashion houses.

"This is perfect," she told the draper, and earned a smile as she handed him the bolt. "I'll take this one."

He laid it atop the others she'd chosen, and scampered off to select another of his high-end specialty fabrics. She ran a finger over the rich fabric, elated with her finds and yet feeling bittersweet that she wouldn't be able to oversee the making of her designs.

How quickly life had changed for her since the King's death.

In two weeks she'd marry Gregor and become Queen. She'd never get the opportunity to stand in the wings while willowy models sashayed down the catwalks in one of her designs.

But she could still select the fabric for her designs. The fashion show in Athens was two weeks away, and her partner would have precious little time to prepare for what was to be their debut into the fashion world.

While Yannis was living their dream in the design world, she'd be marrying King Gregor Stanrakis.

Chills danced over her skin at the thought, and with it came the flood of shame that she'd have to face Kristo again. How could she possibly marry his brother when it was Kristo she lusted for? How could she sit across a table from her husband's brother and not be tormented by memories of him kissing and fondling her on that beach?

The answers continued to elude her as the draper bustled from the back room, bearing more bolts of fabric. She pushed her worries to the back of her mind and focused on the selections before her.

The first two bolts were easy choices, as they were exactly what she'd envisioned for several of the garments she and Yannis intended to make for their debut line. But her heart raced with delight as light played over the cloth on the last bolt. Was it blue? Green? A combination of both, plus it was shot with magenta.

A midnight carnival of color that constantly moved and changed. The warmth of reds and golds twined with blues and silvers to create a marriage of color that commanded attention.

The cloth was beyond rich. It was regal. Royal.

"I am sorry to have picked this one up," the draper said, and made to take it from her. "This has been damaged in transit and is to be destroyed."

Toss out such beauty?

She refused to relinquish the fabric. This would be the perfect cloth for her signature creation. A loose dress. Flowing. Flirty. A dress that would force her husband to notice her.

The fact there was very little of it left undamaged on the bolt only increased its value.

This was her personal find. The perfect dress for her to wear in her new role as Queen. A garment designed by her for her personal use.

"I will take what you have of it."

"But there is only seven meters. Maybe less."

"It's enough—and please wrap it separately." She'd take this one with her for it was her find. Her treasure.

With the last bout of shopping over, she paid her bill with a degree of sadness. When she married, jaunts like this would be unheard-of. She'd have guards around her. She'd have obligations. She'd in essence be a prisoner of her duty.

After securing delivery of the material to Yannis, who was at her flat in Athens, Demetria left the draper's shop with a sense of dread. Freedom as she knew it was quickly ending for her. The next twelve days would certainly fly by too quickly.

Since she'd forgone lunch, and eaten only a piece of fruit for breakfast, she decided to sate her hunger with takeaway food. But even that she'd have to hurry. She dared not miss the ferry back to Greece or her papa would fly into a fury again.

She'd started up the lane when a sleek limo whipped around

her and stopped. Before she could register that it had blocked her way, the doors flew open and two men jumped out.

Both were huge. Both wore menacing frowns. Both came at her.

Her instincts screamed *run*. But before she could force her legs to move a third man emerged from the limo.

Demetria froze as her gaze locked with the one man who'd haunted her dreams.

Prince Kristo of Angyra. His aristocratic features and impressive physique seemed inconsequential under the chill of his cold dark eyes.

"*Kaló apóyevma*, Demetria," he said, but there was no welcoming smile to match the polite form of address. No softening of his chiseled features.

She swallowed hard, unnerved at coming face-to-face with Kristo Stanrakis again. "What is the meaning of this?"

"I am here to escort you to Angyra," he said. "Your marriage to the King will take place in twelve days."

"I'm well aware of when I must marry Gregor, but there is no reason for me to arrive that soon before the wedding."

"Ah, you have not heard the news." His eyes glittered with a startling mix of anger and passion. "Gregor stepped down yesterday."

Had she heard him right? "What?"

"Please—in the car. I do not wish to discuss this further on the street."

As if she had a choice, she thought, as the two large men flanked her. With her stomach now in knots, she moved toward the man she'd kissed to distraction one year ago.

He clasped her elbow, and she jolted as if shocked, for the energy from that touch set her aflame inside. Set her to quivering with a need she'd tried to forget.

She steeled herself against the magnetic pull of him and focused on the startling fact that Gregor was not King. It was too impossible to believe, for surely he'd just taken the crown.

Yet if what Kristo said was true, then why had he said she was to marry the King in less than two weeks?

Just what was going on here?

Knowing she wouldn't get any answers unless she complied, Demetria slid onto the rear seat and scooted to the far side. Kristo climbed in beside her, and despite the roomy interior he simply filled the space with his commanding presence.

"What is this about Gregor stepping down?" she asked.

"Shortly before the King died Gregor discovered that he had a brain tumor," he said, his voice matter-of-fact. "As he didn't wish for Angyra to suffer two Kings dying so close together, or leave a young widow behind, he decided to step down now."

She pressed a hand to her mouth, genuinely stunned to hear he'd fallen victim to such a fate. Her heart ached for Gregor, for though there was no affection between them it pained her to think that his life would be cut short.

"That poor man. I'm deeply grieved to hear this."

"Spare me your false sympathy. We both know you care nothing for my brother. If you did, you never would have offered yourself so freely to a stranger."

She reeled back, as if slapped by the accusation. Denial was pointless, for she *had* succumbed to Kristo. Yet she wouldn't sit here and take his verbal abuse either.

"Yes, I committed a grave error of judgment, and I have regretted my lapse of morals every day since," she said, refusing to cower when his dark brows snapped together over his patrician nose. "But I was powerless to stop the fierce attraction I felt for you."

There. She'd said it at last. But her confession only seemed to anger him more.

Where was the carefree beach bum she'd met that day?

Who was this hard, cold stranger who stared at her with open disgust?

"Are you victim to these fierce attractions often, Demetria?"

"Never before or since."

He snorted and stared out the window. "Of course you'd say that."

As the car smoothly drove on, she stilled the urge to scream in frustration, and asked as calmly as she could manage, "Since you clearly find it so disagreeable to be in my company, why did you come for me?"

"I told you why. I'm escorting you to Angyra."

"This makes no sense," she said. "If Gregor has abdicated, why would I still be required to marry him?"

The beautifully sculpted mouth that had ravished her before pulled into a mockery of a smile. "You won't. The moment my brother rescinded his duty, birth order demanded that I assume the crown and his contractual obligations. I am the King of Angyra. You will marry *me*."

Never! But she bit back that retort. "You can't force me to marry you."

"Ah, but I can, Demetria. I can."

CHAPTER TWO

"THAT's barbaric," she said.

"It's business. Your betrothal contract states you will marry the Crown Prince of Angyra, or her King if he has already ascended the throne."

She frowned, her face leeching of color, her eyes mirroring her disbelief. Or perhaps it was shock. Perhaps she was as unaware of the exact terms as he'd been.

Not that it mattered. Duty trapped them in this together.

"It's not more specific than that?" she asked, her voice strained now.

He shook his head. "No name is mentioned. You are marrying the title, not the man."

"My God, how cold."

"As I said—it is business."

Though in truth his baser needs were just as demanding as any legality. Just as vexing right now.

It had been a year since Kristo had seen Demetria, and his memory didn't do the lady justice. She was beautiful in a classic sense that called to something deep inside him—something that he refused to acknowledge.

But more troubling was the intense desire that gripped him. Even after a year he could clearly remember the weight of her breasts in his hands, the taste of her skin on his tongue, the sense of triumph that had flooded him when he'd brought her to climax.

And if he allowed himself to admit it there had been a moment of shared tranquility when they'd watched the turtles nesting. He'd never revealed that side of himself to a woman before. He'd never experienced that sense of rightness that had come over him as he'd held her close.

To think he'd done so with a woman who was betraying his brother!

He hated her with the same intensity he desired her, and the combination was wreaking havoc on his senses. How could he marry this woman? How could he ever trust her?

Kristo didn't know, and his fierce attraction only complicated things. He was disgusted with himself for dreaming of the moment when he could claim those full lips again, when he could caress her skin that felt like silk.

Just like the day he'd met her on the beach, her black hair fell loose to her waist in thick curls, free and wild as her soul. Her skin was the palest olive, and looked as if it had never been kissed by the sun.

But it was her eyes that took his breath away. They were dark, yet held a patina that rivaled the finest nuggets of Rhoda gold. And they were wary and assessing him with cool regard.

She hadn't burst into tears when he'd told her of her fate. She hadn't begged him to forgive her or let her go.

No, she'd countered with a strong defiance of her own. And that only made him want her more, for he found her inner strength as attractive as her beauty.

Yet what good did their desire do them? He despised her for betraying his brother, and she hated him for forcing her to honor her betrothal contract. As if he had a choice!

"If the wedding is over a week away, then why must I return to Angyra now?" she asked.

Because he wanted her close by. He wanted to watch her. Touch her. Capture her lips with his and silence her protests for once and for all.

He just caught himself from tossing out that paternal wave that was coming far too naturally. "There is much unrest with the people over the King's death and now Gregor's abdication. They need to see that we are a united front. That they will soon have a King and Queen leading their country again. That Angyra will be stable."

And, as his advisors had suggested, his own status among the people was tarnished from his loose lifestyle. They saw him as the wastrel son. The playboy who chose to party over duty.

As for Demetria—they loved her. She was the fairy princess they'd watched grow up. They'd waited for the day she would become their beautiful young Queen.

They didn't know the truth about her—that she was a beguiling tease. A flirt. Thank God it had been him she'd met on the beach that day!

Just thinking of her doing the same with another man filled him with rage. Had she made a practice of this?

"I assume you've discussed this with my father?" she said at last, sounding resigned. Defeated.

"Yes. He is aware I am bringing you to Angyra," he said.

"He'll join me there, then?"

"No. Your father is invited to the palace the day before the wedding," he said.

Her eyes rounded. "I'll be there alone with you?"

"Come, now. We've already shared an intimacy."

"To my shame," she whispered.

"Was it, Demetria?"

Her lips parted the slightest bit, just as full and inviting as they'd been that day. He wanted her still. In truth his desire for her had not ebbed in the least.

"Now, tell me why I found you in a draper's shop when your father told me you were off shopping for your trousseau."

Her cheeks turned a charming pink—proof he'd caught her in a lie. "If you must know, I was buying cloth for my design partner. The Athens fashion show is in two weeks, and it was to be my debut in the design world."

He stared at her, unsure what to say to that surprising news. "Your father allowed you to hold a job?"

"It's a career. And, yes, my partner and I have designed clothes for the past year and a half."

"Was Gregor aware of this?"

"He was, and he advised me a year ago that it must end when I became Queen."

"But of course. The very idea is ludicrous. The Queen of Angyra would never hold a *job*."

"Career," she countered, in the breath of a whisper. And yet he heard the defiance in that singular word.

That explained why she was in Istanbul shopping for fabric. She was bent on living her life as a designer up until the eleventh hour, when she'd be forced to marry.

"If there is any way we can put the wedding off until after the Athens show—" she said.

"Absolutely not. The marriage must proceed as planned."

The pleasure he'd thought to gain from besting her eluded him. Not that feelings had any place in duty. He was honor-bound to take up the reins his brother had relinquished.

"Your role is to be *my* faithful wife and mother to *my* heirs," he said, putting emphasis on the importance of fidelity while fighting the overwhelming urge to take her in his arms and remind her that they had been very good together one stolen afternoon.

The contradictions she dredged up in him made no sense. He hated this off-balance feeling that gripped him when he was with her, for he didn't know what to do that would make him feel steady again.

At least he wasn't the only one afflicted with uncertainty. He saw her throat work. Saw worry and fear flicker in her eyes.

"You don't love me," she said, shocking the hell out of him with that statement. "You don't even like me."

No, but he desired her more than he'd ever desired a woman. "Our bond is about duty, Demetria. Duty to your family and my country."

"I know that," she said, in a voice heavy with resignation.

She fidgeted with the package she'd bought and bit her lower lip, and he was reminded again of doing the same to her on that sun-kissed slab of rock.

"Would you at least allow me to design my wedding gown? I intended to broach the subject to Gregor at our next visit, but the King's death has set things in motion far too quickly."

"Your gown has already been commissioned," he said. "Gregor obviously saw to it right after the King's demise.

Though Kristo wouldn't have known it if the lavish gown hadn't arrived just before he'd left the palace to fetch her. He'd had it placed in the suite he'd reserved for her. The suite adjoining his own.

It made sense that she get accustomed to her apartments now. To his as well?

The thought had crossed his mind more often than he cared to admit since he'd made the decision to bring her to the palace nearly two weeks before the wedding.

"But I wasn't consulted at all," she said, her voice rising in clear annoyance at his brother's actions.

He was not surprised, for he knew that while women adored lavish gifts of jewels, they could be extremely prickly about choosing their own clothes for special occasions. And nothing could possibly be more special than a royal wedding!

In this regard Gregor was exactly like their father—both experts at orchestrating their lives as well as those around them. Hadn't his brother done much the same with Kristo? Waiting until he'd deemed the time was right to step down from the throne without consulting him? Without alerting him of his duty to claim the crown and the woman?

"Please," she said, and the imploring quaver in her voice drew his gaze back to her. The longing in her beguiling eyes moved him more than he would ever admit, for to do so was weakness on his part. "Allow me this one concession."

Of course one request would lead to another, and another…

He shook his head, thinking it was incomprehensible for the future Queen to make her own clothes, let alone design them. What manner of woman was Demetria? What other secrets was she hiding from him?

"I'll think about it," he said as they reached the airport.

In moments they'd climbed into the tram that would deliver them to his private plane. Again she hesitated before choosing a seat, but his guards decided it for her by placing her between them.

A logical choice to hem her in—so why did he resent being denied her company? He should be glad he was being spared further requests that might pop into her head.

He slammed onto the forward seat beside his chief bodyguard Vasos, vexed with himself for softening toward her. When he was in her company it was far too easy to forget that she'd been unfaithful to Gregor. That given the chance she'd likely betray him as well.

That was what he must bear in mind all the time. She was not to be trusted. Not to be pampered one bit.

He certainly needed to know more about this partner of hers. Needed to know what she'd been doing the past year.

As for bringing Demetria to Angyra? He was asserting his power over her because he could. Because he'd thought of her too much in the past year. Because he wanted her where he could watch her, touch her, kiss her if he so desired.

She was his now. Nothing could stop him from taking her.

Despite her reluctance to return here, Demi thought the island was still breathtaking. A true emerald set amid an azure sea.

But the arrogant man sitting too close beside her was a torment she could live without—especially now, when she struggled to control her emotions around him.

Drawing a decent breath had become a battle, for she pulled his scent deep into her lungs, into her senses. Her skin tingled and an unwanted ache pulsed low in her belly.

As the limo whipped along the serpentine road up the mountain to the palace, she hoped that this time alone together would give them the opportunity to get to know one another on more than an intimate level. Perhaps they'd somehow find a common ground on which to build their future.

Thus far her future revolved around duty to the crown. Marriage. Producing the royal heir as well as other children.

If there was any affection to be had, her life wouldn't loom so grimly. But Kristo didn't even like her. In fact he resented her for surrendering to him one year ago.

There was nothing she could do to change that fact. Nothing.

The drive to the palace was thankfully short. In a frantic effort to put him from her thoughts, she took in the pastoral beauty of the grounds as the car sped up the curved drive. But instead of stopping at the guesthouse, where her family had always stayed during their annual visits, the car continued on toward the house.

"Won't I be given my usual room?" she asked, heart racing more the closer they drew to the massive palace perched on the bluff.

"I've had a suite prepared for you in the palace."

"Why?"

"There is no reason for you to move twice. Besides, it is a matter of security."

Security? No, it was a matter of keeping her under lock and key. Of bending her to his will even before they married.

In the guesthouse she'd have been able to sit by the pool. Enjoy the sauna. Or lounge on the terrace and watch the ships ride the azure sea. She could have taken a walk to the beach and lost herself in thought.

But protesting would get her nowhere. In fact, if she was biddable on this count he might relent on what she really wanted to do. Make her own gown.

So she planted a serene smile on her face as the car stopped on the private terrace at the side of the palace.

Kristo untangled his long legs and got out first, and Demi drew her first decent breath of air. But her reprieve was short-lived.

Though the chauffeur opened the door with a smile, it was Kristo who extended his hand to her. *He* wasn't smiling!

In fact he looked as if he could eat her whole and spit her bones into the sea. Well, in this they agreed. But there was nothing they could do about it.

She swung her legs out the door and laid her hand in his. His fingers closed over hers, sending a rush of nervous energy charging through her. But it was the naked hunger in his eyes as he stared at her bared legs that struck fire to the sensual tinder banked within her.

"Beautiful," he said, his voice a rich rumble of sound as he helped her from the car.

Her body warmed to his. Swayed toward him. She felt the power of the man charge through her, tearing down her resistance just as he had before, on that beach.

And that memory was just what she needed to jerk her hand from his and break the spell. "Thank you," she said, her tone too breathy.

He wanted her because she'd been groomed for this. Because her father had made this arrangement long ago. Because her bloodline was that of the old Greeks who had fought and died for their country.

The palace was as she remembered it from those stiff formal dinners she and her family had endured with the King and Gregor. Jasmine and bougainvillea covered the open-air corridor leading to the door, their mixed scent designed to soothe the senses.

But she was too stressed to appreciate the beauty that greeted her.

She walked down the vast hall paneled in exquisite white marble veined with purple. The cypress floors soon gave way to the thickest Kirman carpet. Chandeliers of glittering crystal hung suspended from twenty-foot-high domes.

Gold ornaments, embellishments and wall escutcheons gleamed a rich rosy hue. But for all its grandeur there was no warmth here.

She remembered that about the palace right away, and wondered if the young princes had ever played here. Had their laughter echoed through the vast chambers? Had they even laughed as children?

Looking at the tall, solemn man walking beside her, she couldn't imagine it. The only time that she recalled any levity here was on the one occasion when she'd met the youngest son, Prince Mikhael.

There certainly hadn't been any humor on her last journey here, when she'd met Kristo. No, only raging passion followed by towering anger when she came to dinner that night and realized the stranger's identity.

At that pregnant moment she'd been sure that he would tell Gregor and her father what they'd done on that beach. She'd almost hoped that he would, for that would surely have broken the betrothal agreement.

She would have been free of this obligation she'd never wanted. But Kristo had never said a word. Neither had she, for she had feared what her father would do to her and her sister if she messed up the opportunity that would surely enrich his life.

Then too she didn't want to follow in her mother's footsteps and be the daughter of scandal. That had only made her last trip more fraught with anxiety.

She'd expected Kristo would tell his brother in private. So why hadn't he? Why had he held their tryst in secret?

Those questions needled her now as he escorted her for what seemed like miles through the palace. Finally Kristo threw open double doors and motioned her inside a room. She stepped into a large suite that was thankfully modern—with the exception of its high ceilings and grand size.

The moment he closed the door and secured their privacy she was very much aware of him as a man. If only he'd smile. If only he'd show more than a glimpse of the man she'd met that day.

Her gaze flicked from his tense expression to the room. The sumptuous sofa and overstuffed chairs lost her interest as she focused on the wedding gown that had clearly been commissioned for her. It was glaringly white, and traditional in the extreme, laden with flounces and heavy beading.

She hated it on first sight. "You can't expect me to wear that hideous gown."

He said nothing for the longest time, but his brow furrowed the longer he stared at it. "It doesn't look that bad to me."

"Then perhaps *you* should wear it."

His lips twitched in the barest of smiles. "I'll stick with a tuxedo."

"I'd prefer that over this," she said.

"Don't think you can sway me with this petulant display."

She heaved a sigh, fists bunched at her sides. "Please, let me sketch the gown I have in mind. You can judge for yourself which one I should wear."

He tipped his head back and stared at her. "You're that sure of your ability to convince me?"

"I'm positive that what I design will be far superior to this stark white monstrosity."

Kristo strode to the gown and fingered the stiff overskirt. "Very well. Make a list of what you need and I will see it is delivered today. But understand that the final decision on what you wear rests with me."

Arrogantly put, and surely not a surprise. The Stanrakis men were noted for their draconian ways.

She walked straight away to the desk, and found paper and a pen. In moments she'd listed the equipment needed: sewing machine, serger, various dressmaker supplies and a dress form.

"I'll need to choose the fabric myself," she said, handing him the list and being careful not to touch him this time.

He eyed her as he might a rare bug on the wall. "You expect me to allow you to go on a shopping jaunt?"

"Yes." She'd been hopeful that her name would have started to be well-known in the world of haute couture before she was forced to take up her duty and marry Gregor. "When I was at the draper's in Istanbul yesterday, I happened on a wonderful silk."

"If it was so wonderful, why didn't you purchase it then?"

"Because I was busy getting ready for the show." She stopped and shook her head, for since the King had died her life had been a whirlwind of change.

He stared at the gown for a long solemn moment, the beautifully chiseled lines of his face revealing no emotion. She fidgeted with her hands, uncertain what else she could say to convince that this froth of satin, lace and beads was all wrong for her.

"How long will it take you to make this design of yours?" he asked, neither agreeing with her request or denying it.

"A week at the most."

"Do you always work that fast?"

"Most of the time." And often late into the night, losing time as she became engrossed in a project. "One more thing. All of my clothes and personal belongings are at my flat in Athens. I need to have my partner send them here."

He stroked the arrogant line of his jaw and stared at her so long she felt sweat dot her forehead and dampen the undersides of her breasts. "Very well. Phone your partner and have your things readied," he said. "A courier will pick them up this afternoon and deliver them here by tonight."

She smiled and retrieved her phone from her bag, too excited over being allowed to make her gown to feel annoyance that he listened to her every word.

With her call ended, she slid her phone on the table and jotted down the address to her flat. She handed that to him with a grateful smile. "Thank you. You won't regret it."

"Come now—you can do better than that," he said.

She felt the sudden change in him as he strode toward her with predatory intent, as if she'd just issued a challenge he couldn't refuse.

"What do you mean?" She backed up, suddenly desperate

to keep him at arm's reach when her body ached to do the opposite.

"I've just granted you your wish. This concession certainly deserves more than a mere thank-you."

Her backside hit the wall and slammed a startled squeak from her. But he didn't stop advancing until he was inches from her, so close her body burned from the heat radiating off his.

Any coherent thought she might have had vanished. All she could think of was how much she wanted him to kiss her. Hold her. Love her?

The intensity in his gaze changed, sparking a new emotion in his eyes. Before she could read its meaning he reached out and sifted his fingers through her hair, from the scalp to the ends that reached nearly to her waist.

"Your hair is like dark rich coffee, and holds highlights of the deepest sea and midnight sun, yet against the white it simply looks black."

She froze in place, the gentle pull on her scalp tugging at emotions she kept carefully hidden. Yet she couldn't deny the thread of energy that passed from him to her, tightening to draw her closer.

She tried to push him away, both palms on his chest, refusing to allow that to happen. But touching him was the wrong thing to do too.

For now she felt the beat of his heart, strong and sure, beneath her hand. The solid wall of his chest was as unyielding as the man, yet so hot that her own skin began to heat.

Sensual fire blazed in his dark eyes and her lungs felt scorched, too tight to draw breath. She burned in other places too, and a silent gathering of moisture between her thighs and the tightening of her core muscles proved her body responded on its own to his potent virility.

She hated him for waking her needs with just a look, for making her want him. Crave his touch.

Before she could think of a pithy retort to end this madness, he smiled at her. Any hint of cruelty was gone, replaced by something that took her breath away, something that reminded her of the carefree man she'd first met.

It was really nothing more than a slight curling of his sensuous lips, a knowing smirk like the gods had bestowed upon women. A telling look that told her he was well aware of just how much he affected her, that let her know he was in control, that he could tempt her to do more if he wished.

The puppeteer pulling the strings on the marionette.

Yet she couldn't find the energy or the anger to do more than drop her hands from his chest.

It was enough for her to make a stand, to lift her chin in silent defiance. But her body defied her again, for her breasts felt heavier, straining toward him, the nipples unbearably tight and aching.

"So soft," he said, grazing her lower lip with his thumb until it was full and tingling. His fingers skimmed down the curve of her jaw, stirring the fire of desire in her. "The sun has kissed your skin just enough to make it glow."

Was that a compliment? Even if it was praising her in a good way, she didn't care.

He splayed one hand on the wall by her head, while his thumb continued its meandering path down her neck to rest on the upper swells of her breasts. A pulse pounded in her throat and between her thighs, leaving her tingling with want. With a need so great she could barely draw a breath.

"You are lovely beyond words," he said, his voice dropping to a crushed-velvet baritone that strummed her taut nerves in an erotic melody.

Demi managed a smile, and knew anything more would be a struggle. It had been a year since he'd held her prisoner by a smoldering look. She hadn't been able to break free then. She didn't think she could now. She didn't know if she even wanted to try.

But she couldn't stand here either, and let him stroke her neck and her arm and the heaving upper swells of her bosom. She couldn't let him make love to her with his eyes when he held her in such contempt in his heart.

She grasped his thick wrists and tried to tug his hands from her. "Please. Don't do this."

"Why, when it is something we both take pleasure in?" His palms cupped her breasts with a familiarity that shocked her, that brought to aching life all the feelings she'd held deep in the night.

Her hands slid up his muscular arms to find purchase in the hard muscles as he weighed each one, before his hands bracketed her torso, flinging her back to that day on the beach when she'd granted a stranger far too much liberty because she'd been powerless to stop herself. Because she'd been so hungry for love.

But where she'd lacked the strength of will then, pride gave her a modicum of strength now.

"Stop it," she said, trying to push his hands from her and failing, humiliated he could make her want him so badly that she'd let him have his way with her.

Kristo ignored her protests and continued his exploration. "You have lost weight."

It angered her that he could tell the differences in her from before. Infuriated her that her body ached to sway into his.

His hands slid to her waist and her fingers closed over his, trying to stop him, trying not to feel anything but hatred and anger that he was putting her through this torment.

"I've worked long hard hours of late, in preparation for the Athens show." Time and energy wasted now, for she wouldn't be allowed to participate in it. "Something a royal would know nothing of."

His palms cupped her bottom and pulled her flush against his length. "Are you insinuating that I live a life of leisure? Because I can assure you that I too put in long hard hours working."

Her breath caught, for the hard length of his desire was pressed against her belly. His arousal should disgust her, but her body melted and bowed into him, wanting him.

"Yes, I've seen pictures of you in the tabloids, hard at work for Angyra," she said, her chin lifted in defiance.

Each time she'd seen him linked with a new woman she'd been bitten with unwanted jealousy. On its heels had always come anger for allowing herself to be seduced by him in the first place.

The sensual mouth that had curled into a mesmerizing smile now pulled into a hard line. She knew she'd struck a nerve, and clearly one that was raw.

He pushed away from her so quickly that she stumbled to catch her balance, but he didn't notice. He was already halfway to the door.

"As I said, the wedding takes place in twelve days," he said.

"I'll have the gown finished in one week."

He paused at the door and glanced back at her. "I will approve the design before you begin, understand?"

She bobbed her head. "Of course."

He gave her another exacting perusal that had her skin tingling with awareness again. "I will send a servant up to assist you."

"I'd prefer my own assistants."

Again that slash of white teeth against dark skin, the cocky smile of a shark who had his quarry cornered. Or so he thought.

"I am sure that you would," he said. "But you will have to make do with what I provide for you."

Without waiting to see if she'd argue or concede, he swept from the room and closed the door in his wake. Such arrogance!

How would she ever cope with this man? Being with him rattled her senses so much she'd forgotten to tell Yannis everything that she'd need.

She reached for her phone—but it wasn't there. How odd. She'd finished talking to Yannis and laid it there. She hadn't touched it again the entire time Kristo had been in her room.

Kristo! He must have taken it.

She ran to the door he'd just left by, intending to go after him. The unmistakable click of the lock froze her in place. He'd locked her in. And that drove home the fact that she wasn't simply the bride-to-be. She was a prisoner—not just in the palace but in this room.

Kristo was firmly in control of her. He was smug in his belief that she could do nothing but blindly follow his orders, that she'd melt at his touch.

And to her shame she *had*—every time. She'd never lost control around any man but him. Though she'd believed it had been a fluke, that she'd resist him if ever they met again, she now knew that wasn't true.

Her face flamed with anger and embarrassment. How could one man make her toss aside her convictions? How could he make her want him when she hated the very air he breathed?

"Damn you!" she screamed, venting the anger inside her.

But it wasn't enough.

So, because she could, because he'd left her no other recourse after treating her like a dockside trollop being passed from one brother to the next, she crossed to the lavish gown that had been made for her.

Gregor had never sought her opinion. Neither had Kristo. Neither would ever have done so.

She suffered one moment of indecision, for the gown had certainly cost a fortune. That was her. Always thinking of the other person's feelings—in this case a designer she didn't even know.

She had always done what was required of her, from her papa to the King. And look where it had gotten her!

Locked in a room in a palace and forced to marry a man who despised her.

Quite simply, she looked at the stark white gown and saw red.

With anger pounding through her veins in thick molten waves, she ripped the heavy overskirt off the gown. The mile-long train came next, followed by the grossly puffed sleeves.

She yanked and ripped and reduced most of the gown to rags.

It was petulant. Wasteful. Destructive. But it proved one thing.

She, too, could only be pushed so far.

He shouldn't have touched her. Touched?

Ha! Kristo paced the length of his private salon and battled the lust that throbbed through him, begging for release. He'd done far more than touch Demetria Andreou. His hands had molded over the lush swell of her breasts in a blatant caress, lingering until her nipples budded against his palm, until his sex grew to an unrelenting ache.

For that brief moment time had stood still. He'd been back on the beach with her. Both wet from the surf. Both hot with desire.

Just like then he'd easily gotten lost, stroking the gentle curves of her torso and waist, relearning her shape even though every delicious inch was branded on his memory. The shivers that had danced over her silken skin and into him in an erotic rhythm had pounded in his soul.

He'd pushed resentment and anger from his mind. He'd forgotten who she was. Forgotten they were bound by duty.

He had simply been a man caressing a very desirable woman. A woman who responded to him as no other ever had.

And that was the problem. All he had to do was touch her and he went up like dry kindling, the fires of desire roaring through him so hotly that they burned out all reason.

He could barely think beyond the driving need to sate the hunger that gnawed within him. And now that she was here in the palace—now that they were alone...

This time Kristo had to finish what he'd started with her a year ago. Maybe then he could be near her without being consumed by this primitive lust.

He wanted her. He'd have her. But he'd be a fool to trust her.

The door to his suite opened and Vasos slipped inside, deceptively quiet for such a giant of a man. That was why he was the best bodyguard a man could want.

He could move soundlessly. He could blend in. And Kristo trusted him with his life. Now he trusted him with Demetria's as well.

"Your Majesty," Vasos said, and bowed. He rarely let emotion show on his rugged face. But right now that visage was drawn in deep lines of worry.

"What's wrong?" he asked.

"Demetria has destroyed the royal wedding gown."

"How?"

His mouth turned down. "She ripped it apart with her bare hands."

He'd have never thought her capable of such rage. Such volatile passion.

Anger curdled in Kristo, but he couldn't help but allow a grim smile as well. She would need a strong hand. A man who could match her in bed and out!

"The lady is removing the options," he said.

Vasos lifted one thick black eyebrow, the action far more noticeable due to his cleanly shaven head. "I don't understand."

"She is a clothing designer." A very angry one, because she hadn't been consulted about her wedding gown.

She didn't trust him to abide by his promise either. So she had removed his choice. She played to win.

"I was not aware of her vocation," Vasos said.

He likely never would have been either if Gregor hadn't fallen ill and passed the crown and the lady over into his care. Damn, what a coil!

"Alert the guards to pay close watch on the palace. Keeping her under lock and key will only breed more resentment." She certainly resented him enough already! "I don't wish for Demetria to leave it as yet."

"As you wish, Your Majesty." Vasos bowed and then left the room.

Kristo stared at the closed door for the longest time. In the span of a few days his life had turned into a complication. Duty. Business. Desire.

He'd gone from second son to Crown Prince to King in just one day's time. Now he'd soon add husband to that list.

Kristo crossed to the window that afforded a magnificent view of the mountains. But the peace he usually derived from admiring this vista was lost on him today.

Destiny had brought him and Demetria together again.

Only the gods knew if it would be a marriage made in heaven or hell.

His door opened and closed, and he cast a brief glance at his younger brother.

"She's gorgeous," Mikhael said, shunning greetings to get to the heart of the matter, as always.

"She's the same woman who visited here one year ago," he said, and realized that though that might be true he hadn't truly known her then. He wasn't certain he knew her now.

"Perhaps." Mikhael strode to the wet bar and splashed whiskey in a glass. "Did she balk at the prospect of marrying you?"

He heard the underlying humor in his brother's voice and smiled. "She had no choice."

"A leech then, eager to latch on to to the next in line so she can have a plush life?"

Exactly what he'd thought. But then he pictured what Vasos had told him and burst into laughter. "More like a barracuda caught in our nets. She reduced her wedding gown to ribbons because she hated it."

"A feisty one, then," Mikhael said. "At least your marriage should be somewhat entertaining."

"It will surely be the most talked about wedding in decades." Kristo's thoughts turned to his ill brother. "Have you heard from Gregor?"

"He's checked into a hospital in Athens. I dislike him being alone, so I intend to go there after I conclude my business in London."

"A business or pleasure trip?"

"A bit of both." Mikhael finished his drink and set the heavy glass on the marble counter. "Call if you need me."

"That goes both ways." For if Gregor's health took a sudden turn for the worse he wanted to know. He wanted to be by his brother's side.

He waited until Mikhael had left the room before crossing to the bar. He poured a generous portion of ouzo in a glass and took a sip, savoring the taste of anise on his tongue.

Demetria was not at all what he'd expected. He'd thought her to be a shameless flirt, yet she dreamed of pursuing a career as a designer. She had goals and wants beyond duty.

In that they were the same. But as the King his days would be crowded with state functions and problems, as well as the mundane duties that came with so heavy an obligation.

His life would no longer be his own. What little peace he found would be here in this house with his family.

"A man should love his wife," his mother had told him. And he allowed that was true.

He'd never wanted a union like his parents had had, which was why he was still very much single. Why he'd thought to remain that way until he was at least forty. Until he'd found the one woman who would share his dreams and desires.

But he'd already bored of the nightlife that Mikhael still favored. Having a different beauty on his arm and in his bed had grown as tiresome as the dearth of conversation he'd had with those socialites.

He wanted a woman who was real, who cared about this country and him. Dammit, he wanted Demetria Andreou.

CHAPTER THREE

WITH her rare display of temper ended, and the reality of her situation resting heavily on her, Demi dug into her bag for her sketchpad and pencil.

In less than two weeks she'd be Queen of Angyra. She'd come to accept that fate, which put an end to her career before it had truly even begun. But her entire being was tossed into turmoil when she realized that she'd be Kristo's wife.

A chill ribboned through her, more troubling than ever before. For while she'd seen herself as a convenient wife to Gregor, she knew there would be nothing well suited about an alliance between her and Kristo.

Unless she counted passion.

And that was the last thing she wished to dwell on now!

Angry with herself for her lapse of good judgment where Kristo was concerned, she grabbed her sketchpad and pencil and moved to the chaise positioned by the bank of tall windows. With any luck she'd lose herself in her work.

She certainly needed a mental escape now! But while she'd done hundreds of sketches, perhaps more if she counted the doodles made without forethought, she hadn't designed a wedding gown since her days at university.

Those fanciful sketches born from a girl on the cusp of womanhood had eventually been transformed into a woman's fondest dream. Quick sketches of how she'd wanted her own royal wedding to be, right down to the handsome prince by her side.

Except when that time had drawn near her prince had selected her gown for her.

Everything had been planned without consulting her.

She'd known there would have been no love in her marriage to Gregor. No happily ever after looming in her future. But she'd expected respect.

Now she knew that wouldn't have happened either.

Kristo was little better.

Yes, he desired her. But for how long? When would he tire of his Queen and seek comfort elsewhere?

That thought unsettled her more than she wished to admit. She'd never seen a picture of him in a tabloid without an accompanying beauty on his arm.

The playboy prince had frequented every hot resort in the world. His contemporaries were the filthy rich——those who made a living playing.

Yet she'd met him on a deserted beach, where he'd been working to protect sea turtles.

The two images of the man were at odds. A contradiction that defied explanation.

He'd shown a different side of himself then that she hadn't seen since. It was almost as if she'd dreamed him up. A mysterious Titan from the sea who passionately guarded his world and the creatures in it. Her as well?

She shook off that disturbing thought and put pencil to paper, letting desire guide her strokes as she sketched the design she'd envisioned all of her life. If she had any hope of convincing him of her talent then her gown had to be unique. Totally her.

The lines and details must showcase her figure and what she believed would fire the desires of an arrogantly handsome King. If she could achieve both, her gown would be talked about for years. She would forever be listed as an innovative designer who'd given up her career for royal life.

A sad smile played over her mouth when she realized how she'd just romanticized her fate. If only she had been given choices. If only the Crown Prince had courted her, tried to win her heart.

Minutes slipped into hours.

She'd just put the finishing touches to the sketch of her dream gown when a key jingling in the lock broke her concentration. She looked up just as a young woman slipped inside the room, with garments draped over her arm. Vasos was right behind her, carrying a wicker basket teeming with bottles and delicate vials, his rugged face drawn in stoic lines.

The maid scampered off into a room that Demetria had yet to explore. She'd assumed it was likely a bedroom or a dressing chamber. As she had no desire to sleep and no clothes to change into, she had remained in this room.

A room that was twice the size of her flat! But of all the seating areas in this room she preferred staying in what had been provided as a work area.

"The King requests your presence for dinner at eight." Vasos set the basket of sundries down. "He has selected these fragrances and potions for your pleasure."

"How good of him to release me from my prison," she said, but curiosity goaded her to sort through the array of bottles to see what Kristo thought would suit her. "Is this to be a private dinner or will there be guests?"

"Private," he said. "You will be dining on the terrace."

"An informal meal, then?"

The guard inclined his bald head in agreement.

Good. Her nerves were too jangled to be presented to guests as yet. And yet the thought of dining alone with Kristo did nothing to ease her mind either.

"Either a servant or I will come for you at a quarter of eight," Vasos said.

"Thank you."

Vasos left. The click of the lock in the door signaled she'd be left in peace again.

Peace? She wondered if she'd ever be at peace again.

She'd been willing to do her duty, but she'd also thought she'd have time to live the life she'd dreamed off as well. Now she was reduced to haggling for the opportunity to create her own wedding gown!

Demi bit her lower lip, admitting only to herself that her anxiety went beyond her duty to marry. She'd never set out to betray Gregor. Her attraction to Kristo was simply too powerful for her to resist.

Afterward she'd walked on pins and needles, certain that at any moment the King would demand an audience with her. That Kristo would tell all of his encounter with her on the beach. That she'd be deemed unfaithful. Unworthy of the title of Queen.

That she'd be banned from the kingdom.

That she'd be free to embark on her career as a designer.

But it hadn't happened that way then, or after she'd returned to the university to finish her studies.

Kristo had held their secret. Why?

She knew the reason for her own secrecy. Though she'd wanted nothing more than to be free of her obligation to the crown, she'd known that jilting the Crown Prince would carry severe repercussions.

She'd have been fodder for the gossip mills. That alone had stopped her, for she refused to follow in her mother's footsteps. She wouldn't mirror her shame.

Demi wouldn't live up to the name whispered behind her back when she was only six—*scandal's daughter*.

She'd rather live silently with the guilt of her actions.

Ah, easier said than done.

Demi retrieved her sketchpad and returned to the chaise, desperate to push her troubles from her mind if only for an hour. She couldn't change what had been done.

But perhaps she could have a hand in shaping her own future.

The design she'd just sketched was beautiful, the lines clean and crisp. Yet this design had been done through the eyes of the naïve woman she'd once been. A romantic gown that would showcase her love.

Except there was no love in her upcoming marriage.

But then she wasn't that naïve girl anymore either.

She'd ceased being her the day she'd met Kristo Stanrakis.

It was time she was completely true to the crown. To her future husband. And finally to herself.

With that in mind, she quickly set to work on a new design. There wasn't time to complete it, but she could at least make a few rough drawings. Surely one of them would suit the bride of duty?

Kristo jammed both hands in his trouser pockets and paced the length of the terrace. He was not used to waiting for a woman and he disliked doing so now.

In fact this was the first time he'd been made to wait, for the ladies of his acquaintance were eager to please him—to gain his favor. Not so Demetria.

Duty bound them together. But would it and this sizzling desire be enough to keep them together?

It must. He refused to fail in his marriage. Refused to fail his family and his kingdom.

His body tensed, sensing her near even before he caught a whiff of her perfume. Before he heard the rapid click of high heels on the cypress wood floors.

He turned just as she stepped onto the terrace. Seeing her backlit in a wash of light simply took his breath away.

She wore a slinky strapless dress the color of pomegranates that hugged her luscious curves. No jewelry other than a slim gold wristwatch.

Her hair hung straight and long, a silken waterfall of dark strands that caught and reflected the light. His fingers itched to run through it. If she wore make-up at all, it was just the barest hint of eyeshadow and a kiss of tanned glimmer on the sensuous bow of her lips.

There was no artifice about her. Nothing intently provocative. Yet she oozed sex appeal. His body answered with the throb of awakening desire that pounded through him.

"You look lovely," he said.

A smile briefly trembled on her lips, proof that a case of nerves gripped her as well. But where he could hide his behind a stern mask, the emotions on her face were as exposed as the creamy slope of her neck and shoulders that pebbled under his scrutiny.

"Thank you," she said, managing to compose herself quickly and assume a regal mien.

She clearly had the advantage, for she'd been groomed to be Queen. She was aware of her role, even if she was uncertain of the man she was to marry.

But this life he'd been thrust into was all uncharted waters to him. He'd been as reluctant to accept his fate as the people were to trust him.

On Angyra gossip moved as hot and quickly as a Sirocco, and left tempers just as strained. He was well aware of the whispers that his past exploits would hinder the crown.

There was much speculation among the people as to whether he was capable of leading. He had his own doubts and fears, for he was ill-prepared for this role. He was the second son. The spare who'd grown up in the Crown Prince's shadow.

The man who'd served his country with reckless fervor, gaining allies abroad and censure within Angyra.

Now the weight of the kingdom rested heavily on his shoulders. He'd replaced the favored son. Now he'd claim Gregor's bride as well!

As far as his libido went, that couldn't come soon enough. And why should he wait?

He took a step toward her without conscious thought. "I trust you approve of the garments provided?"

"It was really too much," she said, taking a step back.

"Feel free to send back anything you dislike."

Her eyes widened and her lips parted ever so slightly, as if she hadn't expected him to be that generous. "I'm used to wearing my own designs."

"That isn't necessary any longer."

"But I prefer to. Surely there is no harm in that?"

He was tempted to applaud the manner in which she smoothly kept the conversation on the subject most dear to her heart—the career she was giving up for the crown. She would likely gain much sympathy if that tidbit was released to the press.

It would certainly elevate the people's love for her even more. Though he wanted her to hold favor with them, he didn't wish to do so at the expense of his own shaky reputation.

That was badly tainted already, for the majority still saw him as the playboy prince. He was the spoilt son who'd whiled his time and fortune away at gaming tables across the world.

He'd lived in the fast lane, enjoying a decadent life, while his brother had remained at the palace seeing to the needs of the people. Or at least that was how it appeared.

Only a handful of people were aware that he'd been responsible for the elevated working conditions at the Chrysos Mine. That he'd worked secretly for the good of his country. And that was how he wished it to remain. He didn't want praise for what had needed to be done.

With his own funds he'd bought deserted beaches. He'd ensured that they'd remain a national preserve for the benefit of the endangered sea turtles as well as other wildlife.

On one of those beaches he and Demetria had surrendered to passion. It was hard to believe the poised woman now garbed in the latest fashion was the same woman he'd held in his arms.

He longed to rip away the pretense. To strip them of lies and duty and just revel in the desire that raged between them.

"Why do you insist on working when your duties will command the majority of your time?"

"Surely being the Queen will not take up every waking minute."

"Have you forgotten your role as my wife?"

Without waiting for her to answer, he lifted her hand and placed a kiss on the satin skin. The jolt that tore through her mirrored his own reaction to being near her.

"How could I?" She pulled her hand back as if she'd been burned.

"I'm glad you finally understand that designers will clamor for *your* attention."

She hiked her chin up, cheeks flushed and lips thinned. "Then I'll make certain I'm seen wearing my partner's creations."

He bit back a grim smile. No doubt her own ideas would find their way into those garments as well. Fine! If that appeased her, then so be it.

But it was clear her choice went beyond simple likes and dislikes. Her favoritism would certainly boost her partner's career.

Again, there was nothing wrong in that.

Her loyalty to her partner was admirable. Pity she hadn't held been that faithful to the Crown Prince!

He strode to the liquor cart. "Would you like a drink?"

"Chablis would be nice," she said. "Where are your servants and bodyguards?"

"The servants will deliver the food in due time. As for guards—there is no need for them to dog my steps inside the palace."

He poured a glass of wine for her, and chose *tsipouro* over ice for himself. This was the first time he'd been totally alone with her since that day on the beach.

Unlike then, there was nothing welcoming in the cool gaze she fixed on him. There was no wonder at watching nature unfold reflected in her eyes that were the color of mocha, at finding pleasure in each other's arms.

No, there was only a keen sense of wariness that bubbled between them.

He didn't trust her. She clearly didn't like him.

It was not the way to start a marriage.

But then theirs wasn't a union based on emotion or attraction. Duty forced them together. Forced him to be bound to his brother's betrothed—a woman who hadn't hesitated to betray Gregor.

No, all they had in common was smoldering desire. To his annoyance that had only grown stronger. But would it abate once they finally sated this driving need?

Would they then become like his own parents? Two people who had rarely spoken to each other, who for the most part had lived separate lives?

"I didn't realize we'd be alone," she said, her soft voice holding a quaver of uncertainty now.

He pressed the glass into her hand, noting the increased pulse in her slender neck. "Does being with me sans guests make you nervous?"

"Of course not!"

"You are not a good liar."

She set her glass aside without touching a drop of the vintage wine. "Very well. I'm uncomfortable being around someone who thinks so ill of me."

"How can you expect me to do anything but? You were unfaithful to my brother! You broke your betrothal vows."

"With you!"

A cynical snort ripped from him. "Ah, so now *I* am to blame for your lapse of morals?"

She crossed her arms over her chest, looking hurt and proud at the same time. "I refuse to discuss this, for you've already made up your narrow mind to paint me as a floozy when you were the one who seduced me."

He paused, for in truth he had done just that. He'd seen a beautiful woman and gone after her.

She'd seen him as a man—not a prince, not a rich man who could better her life. She'd seemed fascinated by the work he was doing, and that was the most potent turn-on he'd ever experienced.

"You could have said no," he said, but guilt had served to strip his tone of its caustic bite.

She shook her head, looking shamed. Miserable. Guilty. "I tried, but simply couldn't."

At least she was honest about the powerful magnetic pull of desire that had yet to lose its strength for either of them. "What is done is done. There is no sense rehashing it."

She walked to the railing, her back straight and her shoulders held tight. "There's just one thing I must know. Why didn't you tell Gregor about us?"

Such a simple question, and yet so damned hard to answer. "I was certain Gregor and the King would believe that I was as much at fault as you."

"So you held your tongue for selfish reasons. My God, you

only think of your own needs. You don't respect my wishes. My desires."

"Respect? You've done nothing to earn my respect." He tossed back his liquor and slammed the glass down, but the memory of that moment with her in his arms refused to dim.

"Nor have you done anything to earn mine!"

He stalked toward her, backing her up against the railing. Moving close to her until there was barely a breath of air between them. Until he breathed in her floral scent tinged with anger.

He caught her chin under a bent finger and nudged her face up to him, thinking a man could drown in her turbulent eyes. "Why do you persist in placing the blame on me?"

"Because during the ten years I was betrothed to Gregor we should have known each other." She batted his hand away and slipped from him, her narrowed gaze glittering with censure. "Of course for that to have happened you would have to have been in attendance more than the first time I visited Angyra."

Of course she'd shift the blame back to him again! Did she really think he'd believe she'd kept her head in the sand all these years? That she'd been out of touch with the events of the world in the months preceding her last visit to Angyra?

"The fact remains I had not seen you since you were twelve years old," he said, and let his gaze run admiringly over her curvaceous form once more. "You have changed considerably."

"As have you," she shot back.

"Yet I can't believe you never saw my name or my picture in countless gossip magazines," he said.

Everywhere he'd turned over the years, especially in that tense time frame, he'd seen himself and a woman he'd had a brief affair with emblazoned on every cover. The fickle woman who'd failed to tell him that she was married. Who was responsible for him vowing to avoid marriage until he was at least forty—for he'd been sure it would take that long before he'd ever trust a woman again.

And then he'd met Demetria.

The object of his desire and anger wrinkled her pert nose, as if even the thought of being aware of such celebrity news was distasteful. "I never read them—even when I see them clustered on the news racks."

He had trouble believing that. His father had never read those magazines either, and yet he'd been well aware of the vicious gossip that had ensnared Kristo and the married woman. Hell, everyone on Angyra knew of his dalliance!

The King had been so enraged by his conduct that he'd threatened to remove him from his duties to the crown. But while he wouldn't have minded having someone else take over the role of ambassador, Kristo had refused to relinquish his position safeguarding Angyra's natural treasures, which included the Chrysos Mine.

He'd had to talk long and hard to convince the King to give him another chance. And that was why he'd kept his mouth shut about him and Demetria.

Yes, she was right. His reasons were selfish—but not entirely the ones she believed.

"It was in Angyra's best interests to let the matter of our tryst remain secret," he said.

"Angyra's interests or your own?"

He swirled the liquor in his glass, the chink of ice loud in the ensuing silence. She persisted in thinking the worst of him while seeing herself as the one put upon.

Yet in this they were alike. They were both passionate about their personal interests. Both at fault.

"What of you, Demetria? It is obvious you place your career

above your duty," he said, and had the satisfaction of seeing her body stiffen in silent admission.

Ah, that was her sore spot. Her career. Wasn't it said that the artistic crowd were a sensitive lot when it came to their craft?

She certainly was defensive of her desire to be a designer. Yet if that were true, why hadn't she taken the easy way out when she'd had the chance?

"If you had confessed what you'd done, the King would have been eager to release you from your betrothal contract," he said, watching her closely now that he'd put her on the spot. "Gregor certainly wouldn't have wished to have anything to do with you."

"Or with you?" she countered.

"You are a fine one to talk when you are consumed with this notion of designing clothes," he said. "Why did *you* keep what we'd done secret?"

She refused to look at him, which only convinced him that she wouldn't be forthcoming with the truth. "My father would have been enraged."

No doubt that was true, yet with her career unfolding she could have managed well without him. "There must be more to it than that."

"There wasn't."

Yes, she was still lying to him. But why? What was she hiding?

"Enough talk about the career you failed to grasp when you had the chance," he said. "First and foremost you are groomed to be Queen. Nothing more."

Her features looked as smooth and cold as porcelain. "I am well aware of my duty, Your Majesty. I only ask to be allowed to design my wedding gown. Are you denying me that now as well?"

He stared at her, sorely tempted to pull her flush against

him and prove that she would respond freely to his touch. That this tension that sizzled between them was as much born from pent-up desire as from anger and a good dose of frustration.

"Go ahead and create your wedding gown," he said. "Let it be your one shining moment in the design world."

"I will." Affecting a dismissal that would have done his mother proud, she whirled and strode to the door.

"Where are you going?"

"To my room." She flung it open, and then paused to look back at him. "I've lost my appetite. Do forgive me."

She strode out without waiting for his permission.

Kristo fumed silently, torn between going after her and letting the matter drop for tonight. Enough had been said already.

Duty bound them together, just as it had generations of kings and queens of Angyra.

Like any delicate business endeavor, he must handle Demetria diplomatically. Twelve days seemed an eternity before he could claim her as he longed to do.

He was not one who sat around waiting for events to unfold. He struck first. He *made* things happen, for then he was in control.

This was no different.

He wanted her, and he wasn't above seducing her into his arms. Next time she wouldn't walk away from him.

CHAPTER FOUR

THE sun was just peeking above the verdant mountains that lay black and sleeping by the time Demi finished sketching the design for her wedding gown. It had taken her two attempts before she'd finally envisioned a gown that suited her.

At least she had something to be proud of for her night's work. Something that she could present to the King of Arrogance today.

Just thinking of him set her insides quivering anew, just as they'd been when she'd returned to her room last night. She'd been so furious with his high-handedness that she could have screamed.

Yet that anger had been tempered when she'd returned to find that her personal effects had been delivered in her absence. And that wasn't the only surprise.

A sewing machine, serger and a variety of sundries she'd requested had also been set up, creating a studio that outshone the one she had in Athens. A studio that was a designer's dream.

For a long moment she'd just stood there, stunned that Kristo had kept his promise. That everything she'd need was right at her disposal.

In that exhilarating spate of time she'd been on the verge of rushing back to the terrace to thank Kristo.

But sanity had prevailed—for she'd known in her heart if

she did that she'd not return to her room that night. She'd end up in his arms. In his bed.

She'd not find the willpower to break free of him a second time. Already she was weary of fighting the inevitable.

But she was determined to gain the upper hand over this raging desire. She had to. She would not let her passions control her, weaken her, as they had surely ruled her mother!

In less than two weeks she'd be the Queen of this country. She'd be Kristo's wife. But though she was giving up her career, she refused to lose the essence of who she was.

She studied her new sketch with a critical eye. It was a blend of modern and traditional lines purely from her imagination. New. A bit daring.

This reflected the woman she was now, not the fanciful girl she'd been.

The dream gown of a woman.

A design nobody had ever seen. A style that people would remember forever for the romantic vein it captured while still looking sophisticated.

It was a very simple classical design, with a delicate golden-embroidered edging on the bell skirt. A nearly sheer lace cream shawl shot with gold softened a simple strapless bodice and lent a seductively mysterious air.

The ivory color would complement her light olive complexion. The addition of gold would set it apart from the majority of gowns.

And that touch of gold would lessen its appeal to the masses who wanted virginal white or palest cream. It would set the bride too far from tradition.

Her shoulders slumped as that fact hit home.

For that reason alone she feared the King would dismiss it straight away. He'd likely want a more opulent style, encrusted with pearls. A style that screamed wealth and old world and was totally unlike her. Something in the order of the lavish gown Gregor had commissioned.

She rubbed her forehead, unable to think clearly anymore. She crossed to the sofa on legs that feel wooden.

She desperately needed sleep, and if she was lucky she would be too exhausted to dream of one tall, arrogant King.

Kristo let himself into Demetria's room midmorning, with the intention of asking her to join him for a walk. He wanted to get her away from the palace for a while. He wanted to start over fresh with her before they embarked on this arranged marriage.

But his impatience to put the strained past behind them froze when he caught sight of her curled on the sofa, fast asleep. She looked like an angel, with her dark hair spilling to the floor and her long lashes sweeping her sun-kissed cheeks.

He frowned, noting the darker smudges beneath her eyes. Had she stayed up all night?

He noticed the sketchpad lying on the table, as well as the pages ripped out and lying helter-skelter. Some were of completed gowns. Others were clearly half-formed ideas that she'd discarded for one reason or another.

The one finished design on the sketchpad caught his attention. The detailing was minute, with neatly printed notes explaining the finer points.

He could picture her wearing it and knew she'd turn all heads her way. She'd surely capture *his* attention with her creamy shoulders covered with only the sheerest strip of cloth kissed with threads of gold.

Kristo's gaze lifted to Demetria, lost in sleep. He wasn't a stranger to working all night and grabbing a nap when he could. But he hadn't thought she would work this hard to create a design for her wedding gown. He hadn't thought she was this dedicated.

Again, she wasn't behaving like the conniving woman he'd envisioned. What other surprises would he discover about her?

He paused at the sofa and reached down to slide his hand beneath the dark hair falling over the pillow. His fingers slipped through the mass as if it were spun silk—another memory that had tormented him.

He'd toyed with a woman's hair before, but he'd never felt this deep erotic pull. Never been so distracted by a woman. Never had his pulse quicken and his breath catch just watching her sleep.

He knew her hair and body held the scent of exotic flowers and the sea. He'd been tormented by the brief memory of those long strands brushing against his naked body. But he wanted more. He wanted to bury his hands in her hair when they were in the throes of passion. When he finally made her his.

How much he'd thrill to have her glorious hair blanket them both after they'd sated their need, to sink into her again.

His mouth thinned. She'd lost a night's sleep with her sketches, but his inability to get her out of his thoughts had deprived him of the same for nearly a year.

At this moment he was in the same uncomfortable place he'd been before he'd sought sleep—wanting her with a ravenous hunger. Surely that overwhelming need would be sated once they'd made love. Once she was his and his alone.

She wouldn't invade his thoughts during the day. She wouldn't weave in and out of his dreams at night.

Eleven days before the royal wedding. It seemed a lifetime away.

Kristo let her dark hair fall from his fingers to the pillow, impatient to get her alone. To claim her as his own.

He crossed to the sketches again, no longer taking care to be quiet. Her talent was remarkable. She surely would have made a name for herself among the top designers.

Her soft gasp ribboned toward him on a sense of earthy awareness. "How long have you been here?"

"Only a few minutes." He canted the sketchpad her way. "Is this the design you favor?"

She huddled in the corner of the sofa, a fringed throw drawn around her, cheeks tinged a dusty coral that emphasized the dark half-moon smudges beneath her luminous eyes. Eyes that were surely red-rimmed, proving she hadn't been asleep long.

"Yes. What do you think?"

That her talent was unparalleled. That while Angyra gained a Queen, the world of fashion would lose a budding star.

"It's nice," he said instead. "If your ability to sew is as good as your talent for design, you will certainly be the most gorgeous bride that Angyra has ever had."

A deeper flush stole over her cheeks, giving him the impression she was unused to such compliments. "I'm relieved you approve. With your permission, I'll return to the draper in Istanbul and select the cloth."

He shrugged and dropped the sketchpad on the table, where it landed with a muffled thud.

"It's out of the question for you to travel alone."

Her brow pulled into a deep frown. "Are you always this controlling?"

"I am always this cautious."

"What a convenient answer."

"You are the bride-to-be of the King of Angyra," he said. "From now on you don't leave the palace without a bodyguard."

She slumped back against the sofa and hugged her arms against her pert breasts like a petulant child might do, but the pensive glance she cast out the window confirmed she hadn't considered the need for high security.

"I've always been free to come and go." She shook her head and lifted her gaze to his, a storm of annoyance brewing in her eyes. "How do you adjust to the loss of privacy?"

He gave an impatient shrug. "You are asking me something I have never known—not as you have."

Her lips firmed in a tight line and a chill glinted in her eyes. "Of course—what was I thinking? A man of privilege would have no idea how the other half lives."

He muttered a curse, for she'd hit on a hot button of his own. It was the main reason he'd fought for his role as ambassador. It had carried him away from Angyra and the stiff formality that ruled in the palace.

In Cannes or Vegas or Rio he had been able to mingle with people to a degree. He had lived a somewhat normal life even though he'd had a bodyguard shadowing him.

But that role was history, for his duty now was as King of this kingdom. He had to be more careful. He could no longer take a night on the town without a horde of reporters or, worse, political adversaries of Angyra following him.

His wife would be obliged to be just as circumspect.

"The palace isn't a prison, Demetria," he said, and swore again, for his father had said much the same to him years ago.

"But our marriage will be a life sentence unless—"

"Do not say it!" His gaze shot to hers, and he didn't try to hide the anger burning in his soul for it masked a greater fear. "There has never been a divorce in the Royal House of Stanrakis, and I won't break that tradition with you."

"I wasn't suggesting that!"

He threaded his fingers through his hair. This topic was scraping his nerves raw. Nothing could be gained from bemoaning their fate. Nothing.

"You are not the only one who isn't pleased with this arranged marriage, but this country has seen enough unrest with my father's sudden death followed by Gregor's illness and relinquishing of his title. All of Angyra needs to see us married and united. Is that clear?"

"Quite," she said, her chin snapping up again. "Duty above all else. A public show of support when our marriage is based on the pretense that we are happy."

He inclined his head in a sharp decisive nod. "Angyra needs you, Demetria. *I* need you as well."

"Do you really?"

Dammit, he'd said too much. Let his emotions be bared for a heartbeat. "I need a Queen at my side. The people know you. Like you." Whereas they barely tolerated him.

She was his buffer. The means by which he hoped to gain favor with the people. He hated her because she was favored and he was not. But he wouldn't tell her that. He wouldn't give her that much power over him.

"How good that someone finds favor with me," she said, her tone peevish. "But I still insist on selecting the fabric for my gown, and I need it done as quickly as possible."

"Tell me what you want and I'll have it delivered to you."

She rolled her eyes, as if she found his suggestion foolish. "I need to select the fabric myself. Even the most fabulous design is nothing if not paired with the right cloth."

"I thought the gown was to be made of silk," he said.

"There are thousands of bolts of various types of silk. I can't tell which will be the perfect one until I touch it."

She strode into her bedroom and returned a moment later, with two garments on hangers and a length of cloth draped over her arm. A black blouse held a rich sheen, and a coral dress looked warm and alluring against her skin.

"These are made from silks I bought in Istanbul," she said,

holding each up. "They are ideal for the selected garment, but would be all wrong for the other."

"I will take your word for it," he said.

She huffed out a frustrated breath. "Perhaps this will convince you. Look at this fabric I bought." She held it up and gave the length a shake, causing a dark rainbow of colors to dance across the cloth. "Don't you see? When it moves, it looks alive."

What he saw was an independent woman who would delight in butting heads with him. A passionate woman who fired his blood. A woman who knew what she was talking about in regards to fabric and designs.

Kristo silently admired both traits, for he didn't want a meek wife, nor one who lacked passion. He wanted Demetria.

He wanted to see the desire she felt for her designs directed at him. He longed to nip at the lush fullness of her lips, tease the corners of her mouth before he trailed kisses down the slender column of her neck. Wanted her to moan and writhe against him in a silent plea to do more. Until she begged him to take her now.

But beyond sex he wanted this strong woman to embark on this royal journey by his side. Dammit, he wanted to trust this strong, passionate woman to be his partner in all things.

Yet how could he think of such a thing when she'd been unfaithful to his brother? When she would likely betray him, given the chance? When she was still keeping a secret from him?

Their gazes collided, and he grimaced as her silent entreaty arrowed straight into him. She proved her point well.

It was her design. It was her wedding gown. She should choose the fabric, not someone else.

"Very well. I'll have the plane made ready and inform Vasos we will be leaving the palace," he said. "We'll leave for Istanbul in the hour."

Her face lit up. "Thank you. It will only take me a moment to change."

She dropped the shimmering cloth on the sofa and hurried into the bedroom. In moments he heard the spray of water in the en suite bathroom.

It would be so easy to strip to his skin. To slip into the shower beside her. To take her.

He flexed his fingers. Drew in a deep breath, then another. Now wasn't the time to go to her, no matter now much he wanted her.

His gaze fell on the shimmering fabric. He fingered it and felt something clutch low in his gut. She was right. When it moved it looked alive.

If she wore a gown made from it no man would be able to tear his gaze from her. They would do anything to please her, to earn a rare brilliant smile.

Wasn't that what he'd just done?

With a muffled curse he swept from the room and stalked to his own. No woman had ever dared to stand up to him like that before. None had challenged him.

They fawned and demurred to his will—in bed and out of it. Their simpering disgusted him, for they were all shallow and selfish.

"Find a woman who is your equal, Kristo," his mother had told him.

Perhaps he had.

She was strong. Beautiful. Desirable.

And not to be trusted.

Above all else he must bear that in mind.

The flight to Istanbul seemed far shorter than the one that had brought Demetria to Angyra. On that trip fear had ridden her shoulders and throbbed in her belly. This time she brimmed with an odd mix of excitement and confusion.

She'd been resigned to her arranged marriage to Gregor, but this upcoming wedding to Kristo was too new. Too emotionally charged with anger and lust and hurt.

You could get out of it.

And she could.

She could refuse him at the altar.

Or, better yet, she could escape him today and get lost in the crowds. She could return to Athens and the career she'd dreamed of having.

But to do so would alienate herself from her family. It would create a scandal that would be far worse than the one her mother had caused so long ago.

That was not the reputation she wanted.

"Why the long face, *agapi mou*?" he asked, startling her from her troubled thoughts.

She waved a hand, as if trying to grab an answer out of thin air. She certainly couldn't divulge what had just gone through her mind!

Her gaze fixed on Vasos, who was busy speaking with one of the other guards, likely going over details once they landed.

"Do they always travel with you when you leave the palace?" she asked, her mind ticking off every moment she'd spent alone with Kristo. The times she'd *thought* they were alone. "Everywhere?"

He dipped his chin. "Vasos has been with me for years. Why do you ask?"

Heat rushed to her cheeks, for she knew now that even if the guard wasn't seen he was still nearby. Watching.

Vasos had shadowed Kristo around the globe. From the crush of casinos to the most celebrated ski lodges to those moments he'd needed to get away from it all. Like the beach?

"Why?" A near hysterical bark of laughter burst from her. "My God! That day on the beach. He was there, wasn't he? He

watched it all from some secluded vantage point and *you*—" she spat the word, sputtering with anger "—you let him!"

He was out of his chair and bending over her before she could blink. His dark eyes narrowed into dangerous slits, the irises flaring a warning glint that she'd gone too far.

"Get a grip on yourself," he said.

"How can I when he…? When you…?" She shook her head, too humiliated and angry to finish the troubling thought.

"You must think very little of me if you believe for one moment that I would let any man see you naked," he all but hissed. "I'd never make love with a woman in front of him. Never!"

"But you said he went everywhere with you."

"Within reason." He pushed away, looking down on her with open disgust. "Don't believe everything you've read about me."

Demi caught a note of hurt in his eyes before he slammed shut the door on his emotions. Just like that he shut her out, this time making her feel like a fool in the process.

And this time she deserved it!

She pressed her hot face in her hands, mortified that she'd overreacted so. It wasn't like her to behave so irrationally.

How cruel of her to insult him so when he'd granted her this concession regarding the creation of her wedding gown. When he'd gone to the trouble to take her to Istanbul as she'd asked.

"I'm sorry," she said, her voice as low as her spirits.

They'd done very little but argue and snip at one another. It was time to let the animosity go. Time to try and forge a new future together.

Unless she'd just ruined that one chance.

His heavy sigh echoed between them. "You are quite good at disparaging my name, even though you claim to know nothing about my tainted reputation."

"Then enlighten me," she said. "Talk to me about your wants. Your dreams. Your foibles and your triumphs. Let me get to know you."

His gaze bored into hers, then sliced quickly away. The break as clean and cold as the slash of a blade.

She blinked, hurt that he now stared at the window.

That his silence told her he was ignoring her.

She hated him for his ability to shut her out. To block off all emotion.

And yet for a moment, when their gazes met, she'd glimpsed a keen longing in him. A need that reached out to her. That touched her as nothing else ever had. Almost like a little boy lost.

That was surely a trick of the eye.

Clearly there was nothing soft or needy about Kristo Stanrakis. She'd thought him reminiscent of a pagan god from the sea that day at the beach and that hadn't changed. Nor had the urge to get close to him ebbed. But nothing hinted there was a caring man buried deep inside him.

Had the laughing, passionate man she'd frolicked with been nothing more than a chimera? Had she seen what she'd desperately wanted to see in him instead of the truth?

The answers eluded her, even after they'd landed and the two of them had embarked on this expedition to buy cloth for her wedding gown. Or rather the five of them, if she counted Vasos and the other two brawny guards.

"Do you know the address of this shop?" Kristo asked as he escorted her off the plane, his hand at her elbow firm and sending jolts of sensual awareness coursing through her.

"Yes."

She managed to give the address without stammering, though it was an effort. If he kissed her like he had that day, if he caressed her as she'd dreamed of him doing for a year, if he made love to her with the same intensity that blazed in his dark eyes then she'd be lost.

How could she be drawn to this man who clearly had no tender feelings for her? She didn't know. But keeping her distance from him was her only defense. And even that was a weak one.

She chafed her arms against the sudden chill of loneliness. Would she ever understand Kristo?

It seemed doubtful right now. Instead of growing closer, as she'd hoped, they seemed to be drifting further apart.

Until they reached the car. Then she was all too aware of him as a potent male, as their driver negotiated the congested streets with Vasos up front and the other two guards following in a separate car.

Every curve tossed her against Kristo's broad shoulder. Every breath she took pulled his essence deep into her soul.

Each brush of his thigh against hers served to remind her of them sprawled on a sun-warmed slab of stone with arms and legs tangled.

It seemed an eternity passed before they arrived at the draper's shop. She breathed a relieved sigh and put distance between her and Kristo, but that was short-lived as he kept a hand at her back when they entered the shop.

The congested room seemed more cramped with Kristo towering beside her.

"Ah, you have returned," the Turkish draper said. "What do you wish to have?"

"I'm looking for an ivory silk," she said.

He bobbed his shaggy head. "For dresses? Blouses, perhaps?"

"A wedding gown."

"Ah." The little man flicked a glance at Kristo and smiled. "I have two bolts that you might like."

He rushed into his back room, leaving her alone with Kristo. Of course he was still standing far too close.

She moved to the other side of the tiny shop on legs that trembled and examined the reels of lace on display. But it took several moments of steadying her breath before she could focus on the trims and nets instead of the man. Before she could even begin to imagine which ones she'd need for the gown.

"Do you come here often?" Kristo asked, coming no closer, and yet his rich voice wove around her just the same.

"I've been here a few times," she admitted as she selected a bolt of cream tissue veiling that matched a reel of fine silk lace.

The draper returned with two bolts of silk and her thoughts immediately focused on the fabric. They were spectacular. But only one swirled from the bolt like thick cream. Only one had that rare tactile blend of ethereal and sensual to the touch, making it perfect for her wedding gown.

"You like this one?" Kristo said, reaching across her to feel the fabulous ivory silk.

She nodded, reveling in that special thrill that always rippled through her when she found the right cloth. "It is the perfect texture and color. And see?" she said, running a finger down the weave end. "Nothing has been taken off this bolt yet."

"Then we will take all of it," Kristo said. "You do not want someone to duplicate your gown with the same fabric."

No, she didn't, and she'd been prepared to explain that to him. But he knew. Somehow he'd realized the importance of this fabric being exclusive to her gown, though there would surely be duplications made.

And again she felt that odd bond between them. Here and gone, but he did understand what this meant to her. He was ensuring that this at least remained special to her.

"Thank you." She turned to the draper and smiled. "This bolt and these trims, please."

The little man bobbed his head. "I will send to Athens?"

"No. I'll take this package with me today," she said.

"Vasos will see it's delivered to the plane." Kristo faced the draper. "The price?"

The Turkish supplier rattled off a staggering sum that she was prepared to haggle over. But Kristo tossed euros on the counter and took her arm.

She caught a glimpse of Vasos stepping out of the shadows to see to the cloth before Kristo escorted her out into the street. The market teemed with locals and tourists, and the air was redolent with spicy odors from the vendors.

"There is a restaurant two blocks over that is superb," Kristo said. "We can wait for Vasos and the car, which would be his preference, or walk the distance now."

So he did chafe at the constraints he had to live with. "Let's walk. It's a beautiful day." And on the street she would be spared being closeted with him a bit longer.

He bent to speak with their driver, then took her hand and started down the street. She wanted to resent his hold on her, to pull away from the long strong fingers entwining with hers.

She wanted to find revulsion in his touch instead of pleasure. Her insides quivered in anticipation of a closer intimacy even as her mind tried to rebel against such thoughts.

But the rightness that swept over her at just being with this man left her struggling to make sense of her own emotions. She didn't want to hate him. She wanted to know him. Love him.

But that would be foolish. Dangerous.

He didn't want her love. He wanted her body. She had to remember that. She had to look at this pragmatically.

Duty bound them together. The passion they shared made it bearable. No, more than that. Addictive.

It wasn't love. It never would be. But she had to think it was better than what she would have had with Gregor, for he clearly didn't even lust after her.

With Gregor, she'd forget what he looked like one year to the next. Not so with Kristo.

It had shamed her to admit she'd secretly desired him for a year. She'd grieved over how she could possibly marry one brother while she lusted for another.

But that didn't stop the wanting. She remembered every moment of them together on the beach.

His wind-tousled hair and the curl that stubbornly fell onto his strong brow. The feel of his muscles bunching beneath her hand. The heat of his body covering hers.

And his hands. God, how she would dream of those hands on her body, and some nights shamefully touch herself as he had and wish he was there.

"Be careful what you wish for," her father had told her.

Now that wish was true.

Now she would have Kristo. Or at least the small part of himself that he was willing to give her.

It wasn't enough, even though the sensations rocketing through her now were beyond anything she'd ever felt before. Stronger. More intense.

Surrendering to those feelings would only hurt her in the end. He'd take her. Make her his wife, his lover. But he'd never give her his heart. He'd never fully trust her.

She'd expected him to choose an elegant restaurant, but he led her to a small café with an excellent view of the sea and an old-world charm that embodied the glory of the Ottoman Empire. The owner greeted him as if he were a pasha, and quickly provided a secluded table for their dining pleasure apart from the crowd.

"The *mezzes* are delicious," he said.

She hadn't thought she was hungry, but the spicy smells wafting in the air awakened a hunger in her. She grasped it, for that was preferable to the hunger she felt for Kristo. This was one she could sate without feeling guilty.

"What would you like?" he asked.

"You decide," she said, and was rewarded with one of his rare smiles.

"*Mezzes* to start," he told the waiter. "Then the aubergine stuffed with grilled quail, with a bottle of your best Yeni Raki."

Her resolve began to melt. Was he trying to seduce her? Wine and dine her? Was that the reason for his sudden attention?

In moments the waiter returned with a bottle of wine. Before she could decline any, a glass was poured and set before her.

"A toast to finding the perfect fabric for your gown," Kristo said, raising his glass, his mesmerizing gaze daring her to refuse.

"To the most perfect silk in all of Istanbul." She clinked her glass against his and took a sip, just as a waitress bustled over with a tray laden with cheeses and stuffed vine leaves.

He selected one and lifted it to her mouth, his charming smile simply taking her breath away. No man had ever looked at her with such blatant passion. None had ever flirted with her so openly.

She didn't want his attention, for it held no meaning besides carnal pleasure for him. Yet she was powerless to refuse the offering either.

The café shrank to just the two of them, the air pulsing with hot spices and hotter desire. She opened her mouth, intending to take no more than a bite, but he expertly slipped the morsel past her lips, his fingertips brushing the fullness of her lower one in a move that made her insides clutch.

She trembled at the power in that slight caress. Sighed as the combination of the sour cherry-filled leaves exploded in her mouth, the delicacy more enticing because of his nearness.

"I will take great pleasure in seeing you stand beside me and exchange vows, *agapi mou*."

"Will you?" she asked, feeling suddenly breathless under the intensity of his gaze.

"Of course. Perhaps I should ask you that question."

Her pleasure faded, for that was the last thing she wanted. The truth would surely break this magical spell. Yet she couldn't ignore him either, so she settled on a truth that spared her personal feelings.

"Without a doubt you will be the most handsome groom Angyra has ever had," she said. "I'll be honored to stand beside you."

And she'd be the happiest woman on earth if he would come to care for her. If he'd one day trust her.

If only she hadn't succumbed to him that day on the beach they'd be starting this journey without this sense of betrayal between them. But, as he'd said before, what was done was done. They had to learn to live with their mistakes.

"Have you heard from Gregor?" she asked, aware that mentioning his name would raise that invisible barrier between them.

And it did.

His shoulders racked tight. His gaze grew remote. His features hardened with worry and something she couldn't name.

"No. I can only assume nothing has changed." He popped a sliced feta into his mouth and chewed, but she felt the distancing in him immediately. "Mikhael is with him and will call if—" His brows pulled into a troubled frown and a bleakness chilled his eyes. "If he takes a turn for the worse."

She reached across the table and rested her hand on his. To her surprise he turned his hand over and clasped hands with her.

The bond felt strong. Sure. Yet she knew it was a tenuous thing.

"This has been such a tragic time for your family," she said. "Your father had lived his life, but Gregor is still a young man."

He rocked back in his chair and studied her, breaking the physical connection but not the internal one that pulled at her heartstrings. "Tell me. What did you and my brother talk about when you were alone?"

"My duty as Queen. Gregor was quite honest with me. He promised that he'd treat me kindly, but said that I wasn't to expect a close relationship with him." She gave a wry laugh. "As for his own expectations—all he asked was that I honor my vows until I'd gifted him with heirs."

"A promise you broke before the wedding," Kristo said, but this time the accusation lacked that caustic bite.

Still she refused to look at him, to see the censure and hate that would surely blaze in his eyes. "To my shame."

"To mine as well," he said, surprising her. "You showed interest in the sea turtles, in what I was doing to protect them."

That brought her gaze up to his. "I thought it was a noble thing to do. I still do."

A smile tugged briefly at his mouth. "Then you are in the minority. My conservation work has not always met with approval from the people. Neither have all the safety measures and regulations I have implemented at the Chrysos Mine."

"I didn't know that you were involved in the mine," she said.

"Few people do—which is how I want it," he said. "My

duty to the crown was to serve as ambassador as well as guard our homeland's natural treasures. That includes the rare Rhoda gold that is only found on Angyra."

She stared at him, stunned to see this serious side of the man that he'd kept hidden. "Who has taken over those duties now that you are King?"

A sigh rumbled from him, and a shadow of concern passed over his features. "Mikhael will serve as ambassador, as well as become overseer at the mine. But I've yet to find someone who'll take an interest in conserving the sea turtles' nesting grounds."

"Can't you appoint a committee?"

"The thought has crossed my mind, but I'd prefer having an advocate in place."

"I could do it," she said. "You'd have to teach me—"

He held up a hand to silence her, looking far too regal and commanding for her peace of mind. "Out of the question."

"Why?"

"For one, the job requires intense coordination with the sea turtle conservation network. You could be gone days, weeks at a time." He took a drink of wine, his gaze intent on hers. "There can also be great danger involved. So even if such a position were possible for you, I'd not place you in harm's way."

"But—"

"There will be no more debate on this, Demetria."

They glared at each other across the table, both stubbornly refusing to bend. But Demi knew when she was fighting a losing battle, and really she didn't want to place herself in danger either.

She was in enough of that being with Kristo! So giving up this battle was easy to do.

There was enough animosity between her and Kristo already. She didn't need to go looking for more things that would drive them further apart. Still, she capitulated with a sharp lift of her chin to show she hadn't conceded easily.

"Surely you can convince someone in Angyra of the importance of safeguarding your natural treasures?" she said.

He shrugged, but she caught the pensive shadows in his eyes again and knew that this issue deeply troubled him. "I will not give up hope that someone will take over the task with the same energy as I have exhibited all these years."

And that was the crux of the matter. He was passionate about this, and a control freak as well. She almost pitied the person who'd take over the position, for Kristo would still find a way to oversee it.

How lucky the sea turtles were to have such a champion. What she wouldn't give if he'd devote that same attention to *her*!

An uneasy silence quivered between them. Kristo ate while she toyed with her food, her appetite waning again. As for her wine, she didn't remember drinking it all, but the slight buzz she felt told her she'd done so—and too quickly.

He refilled her glass and his own. "What of you and your half-sister? Are you close to each other?"

"We used to be when we were children," she said, glad for the change in topic, though she felt sad when she thought of her childhood. "After her mother became ill she leaned on me more. She needed my help, and protection from Father."

"Protection?" he repeated.

"Father has a horrid temper, and she tended to strain his patience," she said.

Something shifted in his features—not a softening, but a sharp change nonetheless. "Who was *your* protector, *agapi mou*?"

"I—I could take care of myself."

He bit out a curse. "You were a child."

She couldn't argue with that, but she had learned to do for

herself when she was very young for her stepmother had been too busy with a fussy baby and a husband who demanded all of her time. In fact she had very much been her stepmother's helper until that fateful day when the King of Angyra had paid them a visit.

"I was a child when the King of Angyra chose me to be the Crown Prince's bride," she said. The event was clear to her, for it was the catalyst that had changed everything at their house. "From then on I received special attention by way of a tutor."

She frowned, recalling too that her sister's demeanor had taken a decidedly petulant turn soon after. At the time she'd blamed the change on her stepmother's worsening health, and her death a year later. But had there been another reason?

Jealousy? It pained her to admit that her sister had inherited that trait from their father. That she was very much like him, which was why they constantly clashed.

"What aren't you telling me?" he asked, reaching across the small table again to stroke his fingers along her jaw. "What troubles you so?"

To her surprise, a swell of emotion lodged in her throat and brought sudden tears to her eyes. "I'm fine, really."

"No, you're not. Why the sad face, *agapi mou*? Are you pouting because I refuse to let you take over the task of conservationist?"

"Of course not," she said.

"Then what is it? What do you want?"

She knew better than confess what was in her heart. But as she stared into his dark eyes she felt a commiserating pang shoot from him to her.

He was the second son. The one passed over. Ignored. He must understand. He must feel this connection too.

"I want a husband who loves me," she whispered.

His sensuous mouth thinned, his hand dropping from her face. "That, I am afraid, is impossible."

A knife to the heart wouldn't have hurt as much.

CHAPTER FIVE

THE last thing Kristo wanted to deal with when he returned to Angyra late that afternoon was unrest at the Chrysos Mine. But the death of the King followed by the abdication of the Crown Prince had tended to leave the people feeling adrift. Abandoned. Wary of how effective a King he'd be.

The last was a worry that plagued him as well. The magnitude of his burden rested uneasily on his shoulders.

"Do not expect me to join you for dinner tonight," he told Demetria. "I have no idea when I'll return."

"That's all right. I'm still stuffed from our lunch in Istanbul."

He doubted that, for she'd eaten like a small bird, barely picking at her meal. But if she did grow hungry she had the palace kitchen at her disposal.

He turned to leave, but her words stopped him. "Thank you for today."

"It was my pleasure." And for the most part that was true. "Goodnight."

"Be careful," she said.

He only smiled, for nobody had ever charged him with that before. If he didn't know better he'd swear she cared about his welfare.

The uproar at the mine regarded the miners' concerns over who would be their new managerial overseer. All of them believed, as he and Gregor had intended from the start, that Gregor had been watching over their interests.

A select few knew he was the man responsible for seeing to their needs, and they kept silent as he'd hoped. But even if the truth had gotten out it was too late for anyone to believe he'd held this secretive role at the mine.

So he spent the evening listening to personal complaints and general worries. He took his time listening to each man. He didn't judge any matter as trivial.

By the time midnight rolled around he had the satisfaction of knowing the miners appreciated all he'd done for them. They also seemed relieved to know that Mikhael, who was a much-loved prince, would take over in his brother's stead.

Yet the greatest surprise was their reaction to Demetria. By and large the people loved her. And why wouldn't they?

She was young. Beautiful. Her effervescent smile lit up a room.

Most importantly, it was obvious that during her annual visits to Angyra she'd mingled with the people. She'd spoken with the Angyrans on their level. She'd gained their trust.

They saw her as one of them, soon to be elevated to the exalted role of Queen. Because of her impending marriage to him, they accepted Kristo as King. For now.

All in all it was enough to boost Kristo's much lagging ego as he made the trip back to the palace. Now if *he* could come to terms with his bride-to-be as easily...

He desired her. There was no denying that. But he would never trust her.

As for the love she sought...

It was unbelievable that she thought he could ever lose his heart to her—that she'd even want his affection.

Even if he had been prone to fall victim to such tender

emotions—which he most certainly was not!—he'd never fall in love with the woman who'd betrayed his brother.

His one concession—or was it in actuality a weakening toward her?—was allowing Demetria to design her wedding gown. That could have been a mistake. Not that she wasn't more than capable of designing a gown that would be much celebrated, that would rival any designer in the world, and would surely make him proud to have her on his arm!

No, the problem rested in that he feared she would continue to ask for more. If he wasn't watchful, she'd eat away at his defenses to gain more and more freedoms. Like her eagerness to take over the task of conservationist.

The very idea of her doing that boggled his mind. He suspected she'd put the same passion into that as she did everything else.

It would be like her to turn even that into a national holiday. He would not put it past her to create T-shirts for the school-children to wear. Perhaps host a parade to celebrate the sea turtles returning to nest.

And she'd be away from the palace more than she was there.

If he were not watchful she'd likely usurp his role as King. Already she had the people's favor!

She tested his patience at every turn. Yet he wanted to make love with her so badly he physically ached.

In fact when he reached the palace it took effort to find his own apartment instead of hers. Even then, as he collapsed onto his bed in exhaustion, his last coherent thought was the pleasure he'd feel if she was lying in his arms.

Despite his short night, Kristo was up at six, savoring his coffee while he carefully checked the stock market online. It was a ritual he'd established long ago, when he'd been in the process of tripling his fortune. As it stood now, he was wealthier than any of his relatives—though he suspected Mikhael would rival him in that regard soon.

His concentration was broken when Vasos marched into his apartment, and by the look on the bodyguard's face he dreaded the news. "We have a problem."

"What now?" he asked, curious as to why Vasos had marched directly to the television and turned it on.

A leading celebrity gossip TV show out of Athens filled the screen. "Your upcoming marriage is this morning's top story."

"We've not hidden the fact that we are to marry in a little more than a week," Kristo said, having no interest in listening to the show's fanfare.

"Wait," Vasos said when he made to turn it off. "There is far more to the story than that."

Before Kristo could question his bodyguard, a picture of Demetria filled the screen. In the background was another image, one of an older man he didn't recognize.

"Our sources have discovered that there is much speculation regarding Demetria Andreou's birth," the immaculately garbed reporter said. "Less than a year before Demetria was born, her mother had a torrid affair with a noted Italian vintner."

Kristo stared in stunned silence as the reporter gave the highlights regarding Demetria's mother's story. Like Demetria, she'd been affianced to a wealthy Greek. And, like her daughter, she'd been unfaithful to her betrothal vows.

With a married man!

"The scandal has risen and ebbed over the years, though the last time it was briefly in the news was when Demetria Andreou was six years old," the reporter said. "That's when she was nicknamed 'scandal's daughter.' A cruel insult then, but now we've learned that the daughter has followed in her mother's footsteps. Only this time with royalty!"

No! This could not be happening.

"How could they know?" Kristo bit out, infuriated to hear a sensationalized version of his tryst on the beach with Demetria, of them betraying his brother. How they'd conspired to gain the crown together. "All lies! Who is responsible for this?"

Vasos pressed his thick lips together. "I've yet to discover the source."

"Keep at it. I want a name."

And he hoped to hell that name was Demetria Andreou!

He burst from his apartment and stormed down the hall to her suite, pushing open the door without bothering to knock. "Turn on your—"

The barked order withered on his tongue, for the TV was already on and the same reporter he'd listened to was wrapping up her shocking story. "We are sure there will be more breaking news out of Angyra soon. Stay tuned!"

"This is a nightmare," Demetria said, her complexion gray and her eyes wide with shock.

"It is far worse than that," he said, dreading what the repercussions would be on Angyra. "Who the hell did you tell about us?"

She clutched her head with both hands and sank onto the sofa, her face growing ghostly pale. "My sister. When I returned to the guesthouse that day she saw me and knew I'd been with a man. I tried to put off her questions, but she thought I'd been forced. She threatened to raise the guard. So I had to tell her the partial truth or she'd have caused an uproar."

And the truth would have come out then. In hindsight, that would have been preferable.

Kristo drove his fingers through his hair and swore. He'd

suspected someone close to Demetria had leaked this incident to the press, but he'd never guessed it would be her sister.

"Which she's done anyway, one year later." He planted his feet wide and glared at her. "Why would she do such a thing? Doesn't she realize the trouble this will cause you?"

"I suspect she's lashing out in anger because she won't be able to spend time at the show with me," she said, a dark flush staining her cheekbones. "Six months or more before the King died, I promised her that she could act as one of my models."

When she'd thought she'd have time before she would have to become Queen. But his father's death had slammed the door on those plans.

"She was upset when I told her I'd asked if you'd allow me this one show, but you'd refused."

He had. The very idea was preposterous.

"Your sister should realize that it was not your decision to make," he said. "Why bring this humiliation and shame down on you now? What did she hope to gain?"

"I doubt she thought that through," she said. "She's angry to have lost the chance to model and so she's sought to make me suffer as well."

"Suffer is putting it mildly." He paced before the cold hearth, outraged that her sister had brought this shame down on them, furious that Demetria had yet to show her own anger at her sibling. "Your sister has insulted the future Queen of Angyra. She's insulted the King!"

She flinched and turned a frightful shade of white. "As I said before, I am sure she never considered the repercussions."

He was not so sure. This act had taken malice and forethought. The revelation came when he desperately needed his kingdom to see him and Demetria as responsible leaders. Not two oversexed young people who'd betrayed the favored Crown Prince.

He muttered a dark curse. "I can't begin to imagine the trouble this will heap on us."

Her head bent and her slender shoulders bowed. "I'm so sorry. I vowed not to follow in my mother's footsteps," she said. "Yet I failed."

Seeing her looking defeated tore at his resolve to remain unmoved. He hated that she was getting to him again. But he hated it more that she was ready to shoulder this all alone.

"No! Your sister failed you." He dropped on the sofa beside her and drew her close, cursing silently when he felt a tremor shoot through her. "The scandal surrounding your mother—I need to know the whole story."

A weary sighed escaped her, and she collapsed a bit more against him. "Bear in mind that I only know what Father told me, for my mother died giving birth to me."

"I didn't know that."

Hell, he knew very little about this woman he was to marry other than her father was a greedy man. He hadn't even been aware that her sister was a half-sibling. Hadn't known that she had sought a career. Hadn't been aware she'd been her sister's protector—the mother figure that her sister had now clearly abused.

One year ago he hadn't even known what Demetria looked like now that she was an adult. He hadn't been curious about her.

Which made this particular drama today all the more vexing, for if he'd known about Demetria none of this would have happened.

But all he'd known was that she was the daughter of Sandros Andreou, a man he disliked for his shady business practices, and his first wife, a Greek nobleman's daughter who'd gotten embroiled in a scandal with a married man. Learning that she was their daughter had made it easier to think the worst of her.

Yet right now he was finding it impossible to blast her with the anger that boiled and seethed inside him. Dammit, he wanted to comfort her—for it was obvious that she was suffering over her sister's duplicity far more than he.

"Please. Go on with your story," he said, when the silence became too much to bear.

Again a sigh. A hesitation that told him she wasn't comfortable disclosing all. "According to my father, Mother fell madly in love with a suave Italian she met one summer. They had an affair, and my mother was certain marriage would follow."

"If the reporter was right, the man was already married with a family," Kristo said. "And your mother was unfaithful as well, for she was affianced to another man."

The irony of her daughter repeating history staggered him. But the fact that her sister had blabbed about his tryst with Demetria to the world infuriated him. It was an infraction he couldn't let go of.

"She was crushed when she learned the truth, and went into hiding at her father's house," she said. "But instead of her shame and humiliation fading into history, the story turned into a scandal when her lover's wife reported the story in retaliation. My mother's fiancé called off the wedding, and my maternal grandfather quickly arranged my mother's marriage to my father."

He imagined the old Greek had been well paid to take the scandalous daughter off his hands. Andreou would do anything for money.

"So now you have, in a manner of speaking, repeated history?"

"Yes." She stared at her clasped hands, still seeming only sorrowful instead of angry as was her due. "I was told the story faded until my mother died, nine months after that, and it was briefly in the news again when I was six."

"Why then?" he asked.

She shook her head. "I don't know, but it was a horrible time for me. That's when I was nicknamed 'scandal's daughter' at school. I didn't want to go, but Father made me. He said it would make me stronger, though I certainly didn't feel strong at the time!" She flushed and looked away. "But of course you must have known all of this."

"No, none of it." But hearing it now touched him deeply.

It had taken courage for her to deal with the scandal at such a tender age. Her mother's jaded past was her Achilles' heel.

His as well now. She was his woman. Would be his Queen.

And now they would have to deal with a scandal that could rock Angyra. It wouldn't have been such an issue for Gregor for he was the favored son. Not so for Kristo.

"What does this mean for us?" she asked.

"It is difficult to tell at this point, but it will likely not be good."

He pushed to his feet and crossed to the open French doors. The breeze washed over him but failed to cool his temper.

Below, the town was coming fully awake. The news of this would spread through every house like a summer storm. The question remained what damage it would leave in its wake.

"Your sister will regret causing this uproar," he said.

"You can't mean to seek vengeance against her." She stepped to the rail and stood just out of arm's reach, but he felt her gaze bore into him, felt her silently imploring him.

He refused to look at her. But the very ends of her long dark hair lifted and moved with the wind, as if alive and dancing down her slender back, as if trying to get his attention. Her exotic jasmine scent ribboned around him like ethereal scarves and beckoned him closer.

Not that he needed any urging.

It was his own personal challenge to resist her—holding himself back, not giving her the benefit of knowing he was wildly attracted to her even though her sister's interference could cause him untold grief. Even though he was furious with her sibling.

"Kristo?" she said, laying a tentative hand on his arm. "*Please*. You can't mean to seek revenge on my sister."

He jolted as if hit with lightning, when it was only that damned bolt of lust that he'd yet to overcome. But he would find a way to tamp it down. To control it instead of it controlling him.

"That is exactly what I intend to do," he said, his voice as dark as his mood.

"I can't let you hurt my sister," she said.

"I don't intend to hurt her," he said. "It is your father's responsibility to see that she atones for this fiasco she's brought upon us. I assure you that when Sandros Andreou realizes that his benefits as the father of my Queen could be jeopardized he will seek retribution himself."

Her hand slipped from his arm, and a cool distance yawned between them. Good! He couldn't think straight when she was hanging on him. Never mind that she'd barely pressed a hand to his. It had felt as if she was clinging.

"Please," she implored again, stubbornly defending her sister. "Don't you see? She's young and troubled. She does these things just to gain attention."

He whirled on her then, and grabbed her upper arms, dragging her so close he could see the flicker of uncertainty dance in her eyes. "I am not sure if you suffer from blind devotion to your family, or if you are so used to catering to her whims that you automatically rush to her defense even when it isn't warranted."

"I was the only one she could turn to when she was little," she said.

"But she's no longer a child. She has chosen a malicious way to strike back at you."

She looked up at him with pleading eyes. "Please. Just wait a bit before you contact my father. Let me talk to her."

He ground his teeth, furious with her. Demetria *was* blind to her sister's machinations. Her loyalty rested with someone who didn't deserve her concern. A woman she still saw as a child she needed to protect.

It was clear to him that her sister had exploited that nurturing trait in Demetria. That her sibling was as conniving as Andreou—a man who fed on greed.

But how the hell could he make Demetria see her sister for what she was? What did he have to do to make her open her eyes to the truth?

"Enough talk. I will handle this my way."

He strode to the door. He would not tolerate this slur on Demetria, for any insult to her was to him as well. And to Angyra!

But he'd barely made it halfway across the room before she launched herself after him.

"No," she said, slamming her back against the closed door. "Kristo, give this more thought."

Was she mad? "There is nothing more to think about. Now, move," he said, in no mood to haggle with her any longer.

"No! I am not letting you walk out of here when you are in this black mood."

Did she actually think that she could stop him? "You have no idea just how dark my mood could become if we continue to stand here arguing about your sister's interference in our lives when the answer is perfectly clear to me."

But instead of being sane and getting out of his way she raised her chin in defiance. "I can't let you do this."

That was not the thing to say to him. "You can't stop me."

He yanked her flush against his chest in a move that was

meant to intimidate. To put her in her place. To put an end to this ridiculous standoff.

Except the moment they touched, a different fury exploded within him, with all the raw force of a summer storm. He certainly wasn't a stranger to the pull of desire, but he hadn't experienced anything this powerful since that day with her on the beach.

And that was another sore spot, for since then he had yet to meet another woman who moved him so, who was gripped with the same passions as he. She popped into his thoughts at the oddest times, and haunted his dreams.

She was never to be trusted, yet the thought of her in his brother's arms had enraged him. Except now she was in his arms. Now she was his.

There was no reason to keep her at arm's length any longer. He wanted her. He'd have her.

He ripped out a rough growl and tightened his hold on her. The throb of her own desire pulsed through him.

"No," she breathed, eyes huge, shadowed with a clear understanding of just what erotically dangerous emotion she'd awakened by baiting him.

"Yes," he rasped, on fire for her.

A heartbeat later his mouth claimed hers in a kiss that was long and lusty and sizzling with all the emotions he'd held in check.

Always he held back with women.

Except with her.

She drew the best and worst out in him. God help them, for they would surely drown together in a maelstrom of passion.

He pulled back once to drag air into his starving lungs. For a charged moment the haze of passion cleared and sanity flickered before him.

Her fists pressed against the wall of his chest but her

resistance had ebbed. The wide eyes that had pleaded with him were now clouded with a mixture of passion and confusion.

He should leave now, while he could. He shouldn't take her when his emotions were this wild and troubled.

And perhaps he would have left if that tiny sound of need hadn't escaped her parted lips. If her fingers hadn't uncurled from those tight fists and splayed on his chest.

One strap had slid down her arm, baring skin that was as smooth as cream. At that moment she looked like a Grecian goddess come to life. Diana, perhaps. Or Persephone.

Or Venus?

Reason went up in flames.

He hissed out a breath of raw need. He'd sooner stop breathing than leave her now, when all he could think about was running his fingers down the slender slope of her neck, down to the heaving rise of her bosom, across the nipples that had pebbled against the delicate cloth of her dress.

Dammit, he needed her. He'd have her now!

He wanted his mouth to adore her body again. To kiss every inch of her smooth skin. To savor her taste and texture until she screamed his name. Until she begged him to take her.

He dipped his head and captured her mouth, unleashing a side of him that he'd kept reined in. The moment his lips molded to hers the heat of her passion sent his last coherent thought up in flames.

A shiver ripped through her. Her fingers dug into his shoulders, clinging almost desperately.

Her lips moved against his with the same desperate hunger, on and on, until they were both lightheaded and gasping for breath.

They broke apart slightly to draw in air, foreheads pressed together and breaths sawing hard and fast. Her fingers wadded his shirt, the nails grazing his skin to stoke the fire deep in him, her breath hot on his neck.

If he'd set out to put her in her place, to show her who was the ruler in this, he'd surely failed—for it was clear to him at this moment that her place was right here in his arms. He didn't want to dominate her now. Just to make love with her.

"This would be the ideal time to stop, before this goes too far," he said, surprised his voice remained steady, with his blood roaring in his ears and his skin so tight and hot he thought he'd split in two.

"It would," she said, nipping his lower lip. "But why should we?"

CHAPTER SIX

HE RAN the pad of his thumb over her lips and a sensual energy uncurled within her, leaving her trembling and leaning into his touch. She stared into his dark eyes and felt as if she were drowning in passion so intense that it sapped the strength from her limbs.

Since the day they'd met on the beach he'd invaded her thoughts as surely as his ancestors had invaded this island and claimed it for themselves.

There was certainly nothing to gain by saving themselves for their wedding night. In fact it would be wiser to sate their passions now, for then she wouldn't have that expectation later. She wouldn't be tempted to think how that special night *should* be between newlyweds.

His scent, his kiss, was already branded on her memory— the yardstick by which she'd unconsciously judged other men. Men who should have counted, who should have captured her heart—instead of this dark prince she'd fallen madly, passionately in love with.

Not his brother, the man she'd been destined to marry. But Kristo. Always Kristo invaded her dreams.

It was time to face her future. Face the truth she'd ignored for a year.

Kristo Stanrakis was an addiction she couldn't shake. He

had captured her interest long ago. Now he held her fate in his oh-so-strong hands.

All she was to him was an arranged wife with the correct lineage. The means to an end.

Yet that still didn't stop the yearning that plagued her. It didn't lessen the desire that coursed through her—desire he set ablaze with one heated look.

"You are mine," he said, sliding his palms down her sides and setting off a seismic tremor inside her.

His arrogance should disgust her. Instead she heard herself saying, "That goes both ways, Kristo!"

"Vixen," he said, before his lips captured hers.

Her resistance popped like a soap bubble as the flames of desire licked over her. She clung to him, desperate to know what it felt like to dance this close to the sun again.

She wanted to see if the reality of finally making love with this man came close to the teasing memory of hot kisses and intimate caresses that had haunted her for a year. She wanted to fill this awful emptiness inside her.

Their lips met in a collision of scorching need. The flames of desire danced around her and her skin pebbled, burning for him.

His hands were all over her, pushing up her shirt. He was tearing himself from her while he whipped it over her head. He pulled her up against him a breath later, and the crush of bared breasts to hot muscular chest surely set off sparks in the room. Her nipples budded and burned, and heat arrowed straight to her heart to explode in a burst of color.

No, this was far more intense than that day on the beach. This was cataclysmic. Primitive. Greedy.

His mouth fused on hers in a deep hot lick of desire that made her toes curl and her heart thrum with need. She dragged her nails down his sides to find the fastenings on his trousers.

She'd never been bold with a man, but he brought that out in her as well. Slowly she undid his trousers, her knuckles riding along the hot length of his sex.

A low growling sound came from him, the vibration singing along her nerves. She felt power flow into her limbs, felt the rightness of being with him pulse in her veins.

Still it wasn't enough. She glided her hands down his hot muscular body, her open mouth following the lazy path, tasting salt and spice and finding it a powerful aphrodisiac.

He muttered a torrent of Greek, his voice no more than a rumble of sound. The heat and length of his sex branded her belly when she longed to have him in her.

She heard the button at her waistband pop. Shivered as the pad of his thumb rode the zipper down her side. Then her skirt and her panties were gone.

It went wild after that. As primitive as that day on the beach. Only this time nothing was holding them back. Nothing stopped them from taking this to the limit and beyond.

Their hands were all over each other, tossing embers on a fire that was already burning out of control. They strained against each other in a fluid rhythm that was timeless, mouths feasting on each other in wild abandon, tongues dueling in hot promise of what was to come.

She was dimly aware of him sweeping her up in his arms, of feeling a tremor streak through him. Of feeling the evidence of his desire against her hip.

She gasped as the sharp thrum of carnal need throbbed through her, breathing in his spicy scent and feeling drugged by his power. Feeling free to love him.

Then he was pressing her down on the bed, covering her with his length, and her thoughts blurred. She hooked a hand behind his neck to bring his face down to hers, to hold on to him like a lifeline, for she was spiraling out of control and needed him to ground her.

He obliged with a soft curse, his mouth fixing on hers as he drove into her in one long shuddering thrust. Finally, she thought. And it was beyond what she'd imagined.

Her back bowed on one long trembling gasp as she felt him tremble over her. In her. The connection was electric. Perfect.

"No..." he breathed, going still as death as his glazed eyes bored into hers. "You can't be a virgin."

His arrogantly handsome face looked so stricken, so stunned by that realization, that she slipped her arms around his broad shoulders in a gesture of comfort. He'd believed the worst of her, and in truth she had warranted a good deal of his anger.

She could only hope that he realized now that the incident on the beach with him had been her only indiscretion. That she'd been helpless to refuse him then. Or now.

"I'm not anymore," she said, her fingernails grazing the strong column of his neck.

Some emotion she couldn't imagine flickered in his eyes. Something she didn't understand. That touched her heart as nothing else had.

"A virgin," he said, sounding surprised it was so. That he was the only man she'd known this way. "Mine," he repeated, before his mouth fused on hers in a deep languid kiss that simply drove all other thoughts from her mind.

Then he moved in her. Fast. Hard.

Their lovemaking wasn't refined, but that was the last thing she wanted.

Each hard deep thrust lifted her higher, toward the promise of an explosive climax. The world narrowed to just them. Just sex with the one man she'd never been able to deny.

Yet it was more than that too. It was as if she'd waited a lifetime for this moment. This man.

Don't think like that. But the thought stuck. The fairy-tale wish. A dream to hang on to when she knew—*knew!*—that this wasn't love.

Just when she thought she'd die with need, he pushed her into that blindingly sensual place she'd heard about. This was beyond compare, beyond words.

She dug her fingers into his hot sweaty shoulders and hung on, flying into the mists of an explosive climax and wondering if she would simply get lost in this ethereal wonder of sensations. If she'd ever come back to earth. To him.

As if he knew she was drifting from him, he banded his arms around her as he thrust into her once more, holding her tight, binding her to him. She felt his entire body jerk and quake a heartbeat before she was lost to passion yet again. She could no longer think, just surrender to the sensations tearing through her in hot rippling waves.

Afterward she lay in the cocoon of his embrace, his big body covering hers, his face pressed beside her own. She drank in the moment with short frantic breaths, her heart still beating too fast.

She'd never experienced anything remotely close to this before. Never dreamed anything this powerful could touch her.

"Why didn't you tell me you were an innocent?" he rasped, clutching her close to him, staring at her with an intensity that robbed her of breath.

"Would you have believed me if I had?"

The beautifully sculpted bow of his lips thinned. "No. Probably not at the time. Only when we did make love, when I realized how incredibly tight you were, would I have allowed such a thing was possible."

He still wouldn't have believed her word for it. He'd needed proof.

Well, now he had it—though he didn't seem pleased at the discovery. What a contradictory man!

"It hardly matters now," she said, hoping to put an end to this conversation.

He stared at her, his classically smooth Greek brow furrowing deeply. "How can you say that?"

She wasn't at all surprised that he was agonizing over this. He didn't like to be wrong, and she'd just shattered his perception of her. "Because it's true. We are betrothed."

"We weren't that day on the beach!"

Their arguments always came back to this. As usual, she couldn't say anything but the truth in her defense. She'd never given a man such liberties before. She simply hadn't been able to resist him.

Brittle silence crackled and sizzled between them.

He rolled to his feet, clearly not the least bit shy about prowling the room gloriously naked. And it certainly was much more enjoyable to admire his beautiful body than meet that handsome face when he was angry.

"Do you realize the disaster it would have caused if I'd taken your virginity then?" he asked.

"Yes! I couldn't have lived with myself," she admitted, pulling the sheet over her body, for unlike him she was not comfortable flaunting her nudity, especially when they were in the throes of an argument. "As it was I agonized over how I could possibly attend any family function with you present. How I could be in the same room with you and not be tormented with memories of lying in your arms."

The last seemed to have gotten through to him, for he stopped pacing and just stared at her. Finally he gave a crisp nod. "I was plagued with much the same thoughts in coping with my betrayal as well."

And that, she realized with a sense of sadness, would never change. Neither of them had fought that initial attraction that had surged between them with the force of a tsunami. They'd surrendered to passion.

If the church bells hadn't tolled and broken through that drugging haze of desire she would have given him her virginity that day.

"So what now? Do we keep arguing the same point?" she asked. "Do we let it shroud what we've shared?"

She saw the struggle going on inside him—the deep pulling of his brow, the narrowing of his eyes, the tense bunching of incredibly beautiful male muscles. And her heart ached for this proud, loyal man.

"No," he bit out at last. "But I can't forget the past either."

"Of course not. Please… Let's go forward, because what we just shared was—" Near perfect? A moment she'd cherish all her life?

He returned to the bed and gathered her in his arms, the intensity of his expression shifting from anger to passion. "Go on. Say it. What was it to you, Demetria?"

She stroked the strong line of his jaw and smiled. "Wondrous. I didn't know such pleasure was possible."

"That was just the beginning, *agapi mou*."

His mouth captured hers in a long lingering kiss that had her blood humming with pleasure. In moments she was lost in his arms, his passion.

And for now it was enough.

It was inconceivable that she had been a virgin!

After making love again—this time slowly, tenderly—Demetria had curled against his side and surrendered to sleep. Her right hand rested on his chest, over his heart. Her breath was warm on the skin.

For the first time in his life he didn't wish to leave a woman's bed. He didn't want to be the one to break this connection that he simply had no words for.

Beyond the guilt that plagued him was the pleasure he'd

gained from knowing that Demetria was his and his alone. He was the first man she'd made love with. He'd be her last!

But, as much as he'd enjoyed this interlude with her, and as much as he dreaded to leave their bed, duty called him.

The Royal House of Stanrakis had been struck with scandal before, but never had brother been pitted against brother. Never had a woman come between them—a woman who'd be their Queen.

This latest slur on their names had to be dealt with swiftly. He grabbed his mobile off the bedside table and rang Sandros Andreou.

Kristo made his displeasure clear to the old Greek in a minimum of words. In turn Andreou assured him that he'd deal with his daughter.

With that matter settled, Kristo focused on the larger issues. The probable loss of loyalty among the people of Angyra was another matter entirely, and one that the State Council and the royal lawyers needed to review.

One mistake could cost him the support of those in powerful positions. His popularity among the people was already tenuous. But the high esteem the people held for Demetria would surely dim as well, so he couldn't rely on her to make him more favorable.

The only thing in their favor was that he was certain her sister had no proof of what had happened between him and Demetria on the beach. It was just speculation. Gossip.

He and Demetria simply had to convince the people that this was a vicious attack on the crown. That their day on the beach had been spent observing the sea turtles instead of almost making love.

That he hadn't been the irresponsible playboy prince who cared nothing for his country. That Demetria shared his passion of protecting Angyra's resources.

Passion. They certainly were well suited in that regard.

He toyed with a strand of her dark hair and allowed a grim smile. They'd set a pattern of anger melding into passion that knew no bounds. But this time when they came together it had been a firestorm of desire.

She possessed the ability to storm past his defenses as well as fuel his anger.

And he *was* angry.

At her. At himself for losing sight of his objective and taking her like a rutting young buck.

But it was an experience he'd cherish as well. He'd felt the burn clear to his soul and he wanted more. He knew if he kissed her, stroked her, she'd come alive in his arms again.

His mouth went dry, for though the bedsheet covered her, the image of her womanly curves was branded on his memory. His goddess in the flesh.

Before he could stretch out beside her and fully explore that possibility his mobile rang. He muttered a curse as he grabbed the object of intrusion off the bedside table.

The call he'd been expecting was right to the point. The council and the lawyers would meet with him in one hour in the Royal Statehouse.

He rolled from the bed and threw on his clothes, painfully aware of how delicate this situation was. He wanted it taken care of now, for the sooner they quelled this vicious gossip the better Gregor would be able to cope with it when it reached him—if it hadn't already!

"What's wrong?" she asked.

"The council is convening in an hour."

She rolled off the other side of the bed and gathered the sheet in her wake. The sight of her took his breath away, for she was the image of a Grecian goddess. Pure. Untouchable. The object of all men's desires.

He glanced at his Cartier watch and grimaced. "I must leave now."

"Fine. I'll deal with my sister—"

"I have taken care of that problem."

Her mouth dropped open. "What? How?"

"She is your father's responsibility," he said, and she stiffened as if he'd slapped her. "Finish your gown, *glyka mou*. Stay in the palace—for the people could raise an uproar when the scandal breaks."

"How touching that you are concerned about me," she said.

He set his teeth. She continued to bait him on this. "It is my duty to safeguard you and the heir that you may be carrying."

The color drained from her face. It was clear she hadn't considered that possibility.

But he certainly had after he'd made love with her spontaneously without protection. After he'd realized he was her first lover. When he'd made love to her again and again with the hope of planting his seed in her.

She was his—now and forever.

Hopefully the State Council and the lawyers would reach a swift decision today. He looked forward to returning to her. To making love with her.

He rounded the bed and strode toward her. To his surprise she held her ground. "When I return from this meeting we will face the people together, *agapi mou*."

"Will you stop calling me that?" she said, her voice breaking on a quiver. "I'm not your darling."

He stroked a finger along her jaw, smiling when a telltale moan escaped her softly parted lips. "Perhaps you are."

She stared at him, her breath coming too fast. Once again he was reminded that she wasn't experienced, as he'd assumed.

In that he'd judged her wrongly, but then when they'd first met she'd behaved shamelessly. Her passion had been open. Free. Just as it had been this morning.

"As I told you before, we can make ourselves miserable in this marriage or comfortable. But, no matter what, in public we will always appear happy. Understood?"

She gave a stiff nod. "As you wish, *Your Majesty*."

He dropped his hand from the smooth curve of her jaw, his own hardening. She held such resentment over the simplest rules and orders. Perhaps when she was with child she'd mellow. Perhaps then she'd realize the magnitude of her duty.

"Rest while you can, Demetria."

For when they'd found a way to extinguish the heat of this scandal he intended to light a fire in her. They'd burn in the throes of passion together.

Demetria watched Kristo cross to the bedroom door, his stride assured and fluid. But through his thin shirt she saw the slabs of muscles in his back bunch and ripple with tension.

He wasn't as confident as he pretended to be.

Though he'd taken it upon himself to place demands on her father, this meeting with the council was an entirely different thing. She knew it, and she was worried about how it would turn out, how he would cope with whatever decision was agreed upon.

He was such a conflicted man!

When they'd made love, he had still been the same Kristo she'd met on the beach. Tall, strong and wildly protective of his domain.

Few people understood the significance of his work. Fewer still understood him.

She'd found his inner passion, and though she'd thought it would be trivial his quest touched her deeply.

Yet that didn't solve the greater issue that would always keep them apart. Her betrayal of his brother. His dying brother.

She wished that fate hadn't so cruelly brought them together like this. That they could have begun as friends instead of adversaries. That they were just two people without duty or a sordid past to tie them together.

"Please let me know what is happening," she said. "Don't keep me in the dark."

He stopped, back straight, one hand gripping the door. "Very well."

And then he was gone, his footsteps fading as he crossed the apartment. The door opened and closed with a decisive click.

She stood draped in a bedsheet and felt the ache of loneliness. Of rejection. Of confusion.

She'd thought the worst of him for so long. She'd believed that he was as shiftless and irresponsible as the tabloids painted him to be.

But that wasn't so. He was honorable. Proud.

He cared deeply for Angyra.

If only he cared for her as well.

CHAPTER SEVEN

MORNING came and went, with Vasos delivering a tray of *bougatsa* and steaming *elliniko café*. But, though she savored every drop of the thick Greek coffee, she took no more than a few bites of the scrumptious pastry oozing with rich cream cheese.

Her thoughts had ping-ponged between the scandal that her sister had stirred and erotic images of Kristo taking her in his arms and making slow sweet love to her.

For the first time she understood how he felt toward her, for he was tormented over betraying his sibling while she was the one feeling the sting of that very same thing from her sister. It was a cruel blow to have family deceive you.

And it was equally torturous waiting for word.

She had no idea how the royal lawyers and the council would view this ordeal. Would they deem Kristo unfit? Because her sister could not be circumspect, would they rescind her betrothal contract?

She went still at that possibility. If the council blamed her for this indiscretion, Kristo could set her free.

She could return to Athens, humiliated yet free. She could take part in the upcoming show. She could follow her dream to be a designer and have her heart's desire yet.

Except her heart's desire no longer held the same allure.

But Kristo did.

And what did that say about her? That she was a slave to passion? It was an admission that came hard, but it was her only excuse.

She certainly shouldn't love him. He was far too complicated. Far too arrogant.

No, she would marry for duty, just as she'd promised long ago.

If the council decided the wedding should proceed, the dress would be her swan song in the fashion world. A creation of hers that would be copied. Envied. That would leave no doubt that she could have been a driving force in haute couture.

If the wedding went through.

She bit her lower lip and wandered aimlessly around her apartment. Her future was up to the council and the royal lawyers. Along with Kristo, they'd decide whether to go on with the wedding. With her.

She couldn't imagine them turning on Kristo. He was their King. Even though he'd erred as well, it was as he'd said.

She'd betrayed the Crown Prince. She'd turned a blind eye to her betrothal vows.

No, they'd not turn their backs on royal blood. But she was a different matter entirely. She was simply the chosen bride for a King. The woman who might be carrying the royal heir now—and wouldn't that be ironic if she was banned from the kingdom?

She crossed to the wedding gown. Ivory silk draped over the form in the beginnings of her creation.

This was her dream gown, the one that was uniquely her.

But this wasn't her dream wedding.

Before her betrothal she'd imagined meeting one special man. Falling in love. Of wearing this gown on her wedding day and seeing appreciation and desire flare in her groom's eyes.

But she wouldn't have had that with Gregor. And all she'd ever have with Kristo was red-hot passion.

The wedding gown that would be her signature creation would symbolize a loveless marriage for the rest of her days. Bound to the one man who made her thrill to his touch, who made her want him even when she was furious with him!

She moved to the window and stared out at the water glittering like diamonds. What was taking the council so long to decide?

Demetria pressed her hands to her head and let out a frustrated groan. If she didn't busy herself she'd surely lose her mind just waiting. She turned back to the dress form and the temptation of finishing this gorgeous gown.

Soon she lost herself in work, and didn't stop until Vasos returned midday with a tray bearing lunch. "Do you require anything else?"

"No. But have you heard from the King?"

Vasos shook his head. "He is still in session with the council and the royal lawyers."

That didn't bode well for her or Kristo.

"If you don't need anything…?"

"I'm fine." Which was a lie. She was a bundle of nerves.

With a slight bow, he left the room.

She threw herself back into work. Whether she was deemed worthy to be the Queen or not, she had to complete the gown.

She was creating a masterpiece with every tuck, every ruching of silk, every cut, that would make the royal bride stand out from all other nobility.

She would be a vision to behold, the envy of all women. Nobody would know the angst roiling within her. How each stitch she'd made was bittersweet, for this gown should have symbolized her love for her husband.

By the time dusk fell her back ached and her fingertips

were sore. But, except for adding embellishments, the royal wedding gown was finished.

She stretched her arms overhead and moaned, her body protesting at the long hours of work on the heels of the passionate interlude she'd shared with Kristo. *Kristo.* Eight hours had passed and still no word from him.

She walked to the chaise and curled up, her mind plagued with worry while her body simply craved a moment's rest. This was by far the most tedious day of her life. How much longer would she have to wait before she knew her fate?

Kristo slipped into Demetria's suite just as night fully settled over Angyra. She'd been in his thoughts all day, but the need to see her had intensified the second the gruelling meeting with the council ended.

Now the fire of anger from that confrontation was doused as he stared down at Demetria's sleeping form. Her feet were bare, the toenails painted a shocking pink.

A gold chain encircled one slender ankle, and a small gold heart rested against skin that would be warm and smooth to his questing hands and mouth.

The delicate ankle bracelet wasn't an expensive piece of jewelry, yet on her it looked elegant. Classy.

His gaze lifted to the gown artfully arranged on the dress form. The design was simple, and as yet lacked the beading she'd depicted in her sketch. But the classic shape and clean lines screamed sophistication.

He could only imagine the breathtaking image she'd present, with the priceless crown jewels set in rare Rhoda gold lying against her light olive skin. How the large pearl pendant would rest between her full breasts, complementing the luminescent quality of the ivory silk.

She would be absolutely stunning in her wedding attire.

And positively breathtaking wearing nothing but the jewels on her wedding night.

A rueful smile tugged at his mouth. He readily admitted the desire she stoked in him, but he was loath to own up to those other sensations that were too new to examine closely. That he simply couldn't trust yet.

He stared down at the woman who would soon be his Queen. His wife. The mother of his children.

She looked small and vulnerable, yet sexy in a very earthy way. And exhausted.

He tipped his head back and heaved a sigh. He'd come straight here to break the news to her, but he hated to disturb her sleep now. When her father made good his threat she'd have enough sleepless nights ahead of her.

He turned to leave, though he ached to gather her close, to kiss her, thrust into her and narrow their world to just them. Just now.

"Kristo?"

Her voice reached out to him on a velvet echo, stroking his senses like a caress, pulling him back to her and the longings he couldn't deny.

He wanted to strip her bare and take her right here and now, on the narrow chaise that was ill-suited for all the desire pent up inside him. He was desperate to ease this longing that throbbed hot and heavy within him.

"I'm sorry I woke you," he said, still thinking to be noble, to walk out and leave her to her dreams if just for a few more hours.

"Don't be. How was the meeting with the council?"

"Hellish." He turned to face her, seeing no reason to delay telling her now.

She sat up, and one strap of her fuchsia tank top slid down her arm. The neckline drooped to reveal the smooth upper globes of breasts that were full and firm.

He ached to reach out and tug her top down a bit more to expose her bosom. To glide his fingers over every inch of her silken skin, then let his mouth follow the same path.

"Kristo, you're scaring me," she said. "What was decided?"

That he'd acted irresponsibly. That he was as much to blame as her, for if he'd been in attendance the preceding years when she'd visited, as had been expected of him, then he and Demetria would have known each other.

This dishonor would have been avoided.

"As we feared, every tabloid and gossip magazine has made us front-page news." He grimaced, for he'd had the displeasure of reading every one, all of which basically recounted the same story with a collage of snapshots of Gregor, Demetria and Kristo.

Most were superimposed. But the average person wouldn't know that.

"Gregor will have heard, then," she said. "This is awful!"

He nodded, certain that his elder brother *had* seen and felt the slap of betrayal by now. That both brothers had lost respect for him when news had reached them.

But neither Mikhael nor Gregor had rung him, and he'd been too busy haggling over the best course of action to surmount this scandal to ring them. Once they'd decided what to do, the royal lawyers had thought it prudent that they contact Gregor and advise him how to handle the reporters that were sure to haunt him.

The confrontation with his brothers would come later, and he didn't look forward to their censure at all. Because of his past exploits, it was the council's worry that the people would see this as a battle of siblings over the title and a woman.

A Greek tragedy come to life.

But while the people might view this as a love triangle, he

refused to feed that lie to save face. His pride would not let him pretend something that wasn't, no matter that it would be the easier road to take.

"The council, the royal lawyers and I have agreed that the best way to handle this situation is to issue a public statement. Once you and I publicly deem this matter as petty lies, we will personally tour Angyra and speak with the people directly. That is the swiftest way to regain their support."

"When do we make this announcement?" she asked.

"Tomorrow morning," he said. "I trust you will wear something demure."

Her cheeks turned crimson. "Of course."

This time brittle silence stretched between them. He sighed, aware he was handling this badly.

He should leave. Seek his room. But all he longed for was the comfort of her embrace.

Since he'd left her bed yesterday her exotic scent had tormented him to the point where he'd caught himself thinking of her during the meeting.

She'd been a virgin.

She certainly wasn't the harlot the tabloids painted her to be. But these weren't feudal times. He couldn't wave a sheet from the palace window to prove her innocence.

Yet he wanted to stand up for her, even though he was angry that she'd let him seduce her. His anger failed to hold its sting for long, for the thought of her lying in his arms, of him sinking into her, of knowing no man had ever touched her, kept replaying in his mind.

No woman had ever commanded so much of his thoughts. No woman had ever left him feeling so conflicted. No woman had ever sated his needs like she had.

He held no illusions that would ever change. He was only sure of one thing.

"I want you, Demetria. I need you now."

Her soft lips parted, and undeniable passion blazed in her eyes. "I want you as well."

"Come."

He extended his hand to her, his eyes on hers, his heart beating so frantically he was sure she could hear it. Her throat worked as she laid her hand in his much larger one.

That contact of skin on skin sent an electric current through him that staggered him. He tugged her to him and groaned his pleasure as she molded against him.

"I have waited all day for this moment," he said.

"Me too."

That admission tugged a smile from him.

He led her into her bedroom, noting the covers were smooth. The thought of her dark luscious hair spread over rumpled sheets doubled the heavy ache in his groin.

His mouth swooped down on hers, demanding and possessive, silencing any protest she might make. She hesitated, frozen for a guarded second like a statue captured for all time. Then, with a sweet moan that sang through his veins, she scraped her fingers through his hair and held his head tight, kissing him with the same demanding need.

He'd known Demetria was capable of deep passion, but he'd not expected she'd exhibit such primal lust. This was the earthy sex he'd expect of a mistress, not the woman he was to marry.

With a savage growl, he slid his thumbs under the thin straps of her top and shrugged them off her shoulders. Still it wasn't enough, for he wanted her naked. Wanted her under him now, begging for his possession.

He pulled from her on an oath, and tugged the cotton from her. For the longest moment he just stared at her, awed by the perfectly shaped breasts and rose-tipped nipples that were hard and begging for his touch.

"Beautiful," he murmured, his palms sliding over her firm

pert breasts, and he had the satisfaction of feeling her arch into his hands on a purr that shot a bolt of longing to his sex.

His thumbs scraped over the hardened tips again and again.

The hands clutching his head dropped to his shoulders, the nails digging into his flesh. Her eyes went black.

"It is always this intense for you?" she asked.

He shook his head for, like her, he was tumbling fast into the morass of passion.

"Only with you," he said.

She swayed into him, head lifted and mouth seeking his.

He met her halfway in a kiss that robbed them both of breath, that left no doubt that in this they were well matched, that here there was no arguing, no battle of wills.

He'd never been one to mutter love words with a woman, but with Demetria he felt compelled to openly adore her. It was those little gasps and moans that she made that proved she held back nothing either.

This time he was determined to savor their joining. His hands swept down the graceful arch of her spine to cup the firm globes of her bottom. She strained against him on a moan, and stroked his already engorged shaft against her belly.

"No more waiting," he said.

"No more," she repeated, between kisses that enflamed him more, that matched the need exploding in him.

He couldn't imagine ever tiring of her kisses, her touch.

Her body quaked. And his did as well, for his control was about to explode.

"You're overdressed," she said as she proceeded to undo the buttons on his shirt.

As hot as he was, it was amazing his clothes hadn't burst into flames. He suffered her ministrations for a minute. Then two.

"For a designer, you are ill-suited at removing clothes."

He pulled back enough to grab his shirt and rip it off. Still it seemed to take an eternity for him to shrug off his trousers and shorts.

Chest heaving, he lifted his gaze to hers. Dawn speared through the bank of windows, gilding the room and the shapely curves of her naked body.

No statue in all of Greece could compare to her beauty. None could rival her allure.

She was a goddess to be worshipped. And she was his.

His palms memorized the delicate line of her jaw before he trailed his fingers down her neck, marveling at the silken texture of her skin, the telling rush of color that bloomed in his wake. Though she made no move, the rapid rise and fall of her chest confirmed his effect on her.

"I have dreamed of doing this again," he said, then bent to suckle one pert breast deeply, before doing the same to the other, leaving the buds wet and pebble-hard.

She moaned and arched against him. "I have too."

"And this?" he asked, dropping to his knees as he pressed openmouthed kisses over the flat planes of her midriff and belly, certain he'd never seen skin this firm and yet so soft.

"Yes," she whispered, her nails digging into his back. "Yes."

The womanly scent of her arousal fired his blood, and he fought for control that he'd always taken for granted. His thumbs parted the thatch of dark curls at the apex of her thighs to bare her sweet essence to him. She trembled, gripping his shoulders harder, thrusting her sex closer to him.

He needed no urging. His hands gripped her hips to steady her and he bent to kiss her intimately, deeply.

A sound burst from her, part startled gasp, part sensual moan. It filled him with male satisfaction and left him feeling triumphant.

His tongue showed no mercy, flicking over her womanly folds, thrusting deep into her core that was hot and slick with her own desire. The tight ache in his groin intensified to the point where he broke out in a sheen of sweat.

He'd never felt this way about a woman before. She made him feel young. Desired. Masterful. With her, the feelings swelling within him were all magnified. Larger than life. Much more than he could grasp right now.

Still he pleasured her ruthlessly, stroking the swollen bud until her body trembled. Her legs buckled, her fingers clawing at him now in either desperation or supplication.

But he didn't stop laving the tender flesh, suckling deeply, knowing she was about to shatter in his arms.

That he could give her this much pleasure intensified his own. This went far beyond being a generous lover.

The emotions building inside him were volcanic, unlike any he'd felt before. Being intimate with her felt right.

He didn't want to rush this joining. He wanted to savor every kiss, every caress.

The pain of his need was almost unbearable for him, yet he suffered the wait until she found sweet release. Until she dug her fingers into his shoulders and climaxed.

She came swift and hard, in a tremor that shook her from head to toe. Shaking him in the process.

Her cry echoed in the room in a song that he'd enjoy waking to every morning and falling asleep to every night. At least in this they were compatible. A man in his position couldn't ask for more.

But deep down a voice mocked him, for he'd vowed not to follow in his parents' footsteps.

No choice, he thought. No choice but to forestall a disaster to his country. No other choice that he wanted to consider.

He lifted his head, reality threatening to dim his pleasure.

But that too drifted away on the breeze as she crumbled into his arms, sweet mouth curved in a smile and eyes languorous.

"My God, I never knew it could be like this between a man and a woman." She smiled on a sigh of pleasure that slid over his skin like a heated caress, leaving him trembling with renewed need.

"This is just the beginning, *agapi mou*," he said as he stretched out beside her.

The honeyed taste of her passion lingered on his tongue, an aphrodisiac that sent his senses reeling. Thoughts of duty and revenge foamed like the surf before washing back out to sea.

She was the woman he wanted as his lover. Now and forever.

"You are such a sensuous creature." He grazed a knuckle along her jaw and down the slope of her neck, smiling as her skin pebbled and flushed at this touch.

"You make me sensuous," she said, on a purr that hummed through his veins.

Her words stroked his male ego, but the simple truth that she wasn't experienced thawed the cold that had been buried deep inside him.

He should have realized it that day on the beach. Her hesitation. How she'd followed his lead instead of taking the initiative. How her big innocent eyes had stared up at him in wonder.

Yet he'd turned a blind eye to the obvious. He'd relegated her to the role of a schemer. An unfaithful flirt who'd make his brother's life hell.

He'd been so wrong. He'd wronged her.

"There is so much more to be enjoyed," he said.

A smile of pure pleasure teased her sensual mouth. She pressed a hand over his heart, the small fingers splayed over his skin to set him on fire.

"Show me," she said.

"With pleasure."

Her hands slid over the slope of her pert breasts and he marveled that he couldn't see the sparks that surely crackled in the air from the erotic contact. A nudge of his knees parted her legs without hesitation, yet there was a tenderness to her actions that he'd never experienced before.

It hinted he should take his time to dazzle her with his finesse. He longed to explore every inch of her body, to leave no doubt that she was his. To make love with her all night instead of for a few stolen hours.

His mouth claimed hers in a torrid melding of lips and the parry of tongues. The moist tip of his erection parted her slick swollen folds, the throb reverberating through him in hot urgent pulses that were nearly his undoing.

The needy sounds coming from her left no doubt she was tired of the wait too.

In one powerful surge he sank fully into her, only to pull out just as swiftly. She mewled a protest and arched against him, silken legs wrapped around his waist to pull him back inside her.

He tore his mouth from hers and obliged on a guttural groan. The strain of holding a rein on his raging desire was almost too great for him.

"Please," she whispered, small hands clawing at his arms, his back, before digging into the firm globes of his buttocks.

He needed no other urging.

His hands bracketed her face as he surged into her quivering sheath once more. Her lips parted and her eyelids flickered with the power of her passion.

Again and again their bodies strained in fiery rhythm. He stared into her rapturous eyes, thinking he'd never held anything more precious in his arms.

At that moment he knew she was more priceless to him than all the gold on Angyra. He'd never made love like this before.

And that scared the hell out of him.

Right now he needed to be strong. To think with his head, not his manhood.

With a savage curse, he set a ruthless pace. But even then she moved with him in primal harmony, until he blessedly couldn't think of anything anymore except clutching her close to his heart and finding his own release.

Her back bowed as she reached for nirvana again, his name bursting from her.

He held her tight, his head pounding with the strain of holding back, of letting her savor every second of spent passion.

She collapsed on the bed, the strong muscles of her inner thighs relaxing their hold on his flanks, her hands loosing their tight hold on him.

Only then did he seek his release. His head reared, teeth clenched at the force exploding within him. His blood thundered in his ears, his last coherent thought one of awe at the pleasure flooding him.

He collapsed on her, the valley between her bosom pillowing his head that was too heavy for him to lift. He'd never been this spent.

Or this pleased.

The beginning of a smile twitched at his lips. If only they could hold the world and all the troubles facing them at bay.

CHAPTER EIGHT

DEMETRIA didn't know when Kristo had left her bed, but he returned to her apartment before nine. She had roused earlier, near starving, to find the air filled with the most enticing aromas from the kitchen. A huge dinner must be in order today.

Perhaps this time she would be able to eat.

Or perhaps not.

She didn't look forward to this display today. But she was ready, having chosen a simple silk blouse and a skirt that was classically elegant and not the least bit provocative.

"You look stunning," he said, and bent to kiss her.

"And you are quite handsome." Gorgeous, actually.

He'd have made a sought-after model with his classic good looks and beautifully sculpted body.

Only she noted the deeper lines fanning from his eyes. The tension that kept his shoulders racked tight.

The tolling of bells brought a grim smile from him. "Come. It is time for the announcement."

She was a jumble of nerves by the time they reached the front balcony of the palace—more so because the servants they'd passed had avoided making eye contact with her. It was if they were shunning her. That fear only heaped more guilt on her.

They hate me.

A crowd had gathered below on the street, its silence needling her nerves even more. If Kristo hadn't had such a tight grip on her hand she'd have been tempted to flee back to her room.

He pulled her along with him to the railing. Cameras were raised in the near distance and she forced a smile, knowing she must appear calm when her insides were in knots.

"At present, Demetria Andreou, Prince Gregor and I are the targets of malicious gossip," he said as the paparazzi snapped pictures of them as a couple. "We come to you today to inform you that it is all lies and half-truths. We ask that you remember that my brother is ill, and that by allowing this gossip to flourish we hurt him."

Demi held her breath as murmurs rippled through the crowd, but nobody spouted the questions or curses she'd dreaded to hear. Nobody said anything that could be overheard.

That silence was damning.

Oh, God, the effect her sister's meddling had had on Angyra must be far worse than they'd anticipated.

"And I also ask that you join us as we walk to the cemetery to honor my father on the fortieth day after his death," he said, shocking her with that suggestion.

This time the murmurs became a low rumble. But Kristo didn't tarry on the balcony to hear.

"Náste Kalá!" And with that farewell he turned and led her back into the palace.

"Are you crazy?" she asked as she kept pace beside him.

"Probably, but the people need to see us holding to tradition," he said. "We must show honor to my father now, and invite them as witnesses."

She could only imagine the headache this would cause Vasos and his team of bodyguards. "I wish you would have warned me."

He shrugged. "I told you that we'd be out among the people."

"Yes, but I never dreamed you'd suggest we all walk to the cemetery!"

"It's an old tradition, and it will allow the staff to prepare the area before the palace for the feast."

"Feast?" she said, nearly choking on the word.

He flicked her a rare smile, looking very assured. Very much in control. "Once we have paid our respects at the cemetery I've invited the people to join us for a celebration on the front lawn."

Surely it was unheard-of for a King to go to such lengths? Dangerous lengths. But then it was clear that Kristo was a risk-taker.

That would explain all the enticing aromas she'd smelled this morning. "Did the council suggest all this?"

"They stressed that we should become approachable to the people. The idea was mine."

His hand tightened on hers, their fingers entwining. It was a fine show of solidarity. Affection for the people to observe. Except they were still in the palace.

Her gaze flew to his, questioning. The quick squeeze on her fingers was solely for her benefit. A silent encouragement from him to her.

Trust me, the gesture hinted.

She wanted to. Oh, how she wanted to trust him. But it was still too soon.

He paused at the door to accept a huge bouquet of fresh flowers. Then they left the palace by the open-air corridor, but the perfume from the bougainvillea and jasmine that she'd thought pleasant upon arriving seemed cloying to her now.

Vasos and his men formed a cordon to keep the people at bay. Still they seemed so close she could read the doubt in their eyes, the speculation, the anger.

Kristo gave no indication he'd noticed, but she was sure he had. Very little ever got by him.

So they moved like an army toward the church and adjoining cemetery. The King with his head held high and his features carefully masked of emotion. She quite literally quaking, with a horrendous case of nerves and guilt.

Talk was absent, which was a blessing—for she wouldn't have been able to speak coherently. The people pressed around them, but the only sounds were the pounding of feet on the cobblestones and the drumming of her heart.

More people crowded around a cemetery that couldn't possibly hold a fourth of them. So they clustered by the walls and watched.

Kristo stopped beside an ornate tombstone, and Demetria tried her best not to lean into his strength. But when he dropped to a knee before the grave of his father and laid the bouquet on the ground a hush of respect fell over those gathered.

Again he looked invincible. A man in control of himself and his world. But she felt the tremor rocket from him to her. She sensed the grief he silently suffered.

Her eyes filled with tears and she tried desperately to hold them back. But the actions of this proud man touched her as nothing else had. The tears fell in silent rivers and she swiped them away the best she could. She hadn't even thought to grab a tissue.

A scuffle at her right caught her attention. An older woman was doing her best to catch her attention around the burly guard.

"It's for Her Highness," the woman said, loud enough for Demetria to hear this time. In her gnarled hand she held a handkerchief.

"Let her through," Demetria said.

The guard remained unmoved, so Demi pulled her hand

from Kristo's and crossed to the woman. "Thank you," she said to the lady, and took the offered handkerchief to dab the tears from her eyes.

"The gods shined on us the day that the King in his wisdom chose you as future Queen," the old woman said as she executed a bow.

And the reporters who were always present captured the moment on film.

The thought struck Demi that maybe now a new headline would grace the tabloids before nightfall. A picture that commanded respect, with an accompanying story that might make the earlier one stand for what it was—vicious gossip.

Kristo had been right. Her sister had acted cruelly. She hoped that she'd learned her lesson now. That she and Kristo could move forward without more trouble. That in time they would find something more than duty to bind them together.

She felt Kristo beside her long before he took her free hand in his again. She spared him a quick glance, only to find that his devastatingly handsome smile was being given to the older woman.

"Efharisto," he said to the lady, taking her gnarled hand and placing a kiss on the thin wrinkled skin. "You are most kind to come to my future Queen's aid."

"O Theos mazi sou," the older woman wailed, bowing so deeply Demi feared she'd topple over.

That simple blessing from an old woman to the King seemed to break the ice that surrounded the people. Some sobbed. Many coughed to clear their throats.

He turned to Demi and smiled then, and any misgiving she held in her heart instantly thawed. This wasn't an act on his part, to garner sympathy from the people. This was real.

Before her stood a man in control of his emotions. A man

who didn't toss praise or words of endearment out at whim. A man who wasn't afraid to take chances.

Yet winning his love wouldn't be easy. Maybe impossible.

"This has been a troubled few months for the Royal House of Stanrakis," he said, his voice ringing loud and clear. "From the loss of our beloved King, *o sinhoremenos*, to my brother's grave illness. To all of you, *na tous cherese*."

Echoes of good wishes came from those surrounding them, one by one. She felt some of the tension leave Kristo, felt her heart swell with pride at the manner in which he'd opened himself up to the people.

And that was crucial—for they didn't know him, only his jaded reputation. "That was beautiful," she told him.

He smiled, and she nearly forgot how to breathe. "No, *you* are beautiful."

Before she could savor that compliment, Kristo addressed the crowd. "Please join us at the palace. A feast has been prepared in my father's honor. Enjoy!"

With that, he clasped her hand in his and strode from the cemetery. Back to the palace. Back to the place she would forever call home. And maybe there was a chance they could actually make it one—if Kristo opened up to her, if he gave her a chance to win his heart.

Kristo smiled when they returned to the palace and were greeted by music. Loud. Boisterous. And purely Greek.

Never in his life had he seen the palace lawn turned over to the populace. His father would surely turn over in his grave, but perhaps that was a good thing too.

His family had ruled with a strong hand, but that didn't mean they couldn't have the occasional throwback to earlier times. Especially now, when he needed to feel the pulse of the people. To know if they were on his side or waiting to stab him in the back!

"This is beyond belief," Demetria said as he guided her to a table set apart for them, the council and other dignitaries of Angyra. "Whose idea was this?"

"Mine. I remembered Father saying that death should be celebrated." He glanced at the tables laden with food. Wine and ouzo flowed freely. "I believe he'd approve."

But, whether he would or not, it was obvious that the people were enjoying this side of their royals. It was a bold step to take, and the council and the lawyers had warned him it could backfire, but it worked.

Though he hoped he'd gain the people's favor, or at the very least their interest, it was clear that they were entranced by Demetria. She'd regained their support. Their respect.

And though that came well before his own slow rise in popularity, he found himself smiling as well. She'd charmed them as she did him.

The morning turned to afternoon, and the crowd grew more boisterous. As he and Demetria were dancing the *hassapiko* with five other people, Kristo caught the guarded look on Vasos's face and knew their time at the celebration was over.

To stay would be dangerous—for him and Demetria.

"It is time for us to take our leave," he told her when the dance ended. "Come."

She hesitated for a moment, glancing back at the crowd. He saw the longing in her eyes. Knew that she realized this would be the last time she was able to freely dance and celebrate with the people.

In a few days she'd be royalty.

"I hate to see it end," she said.

"It won't for them." He ran a knuckle along her cheek. "Or for us either, if you don't mind a very private party."

A slow smile played over her kissable mouth, her face flushed from dancing, her eyes sparkling with happiness. "I'd love it."

In moments they'd slipped back inside the palace. They paused in the hall to kiss—a long, hot kiss that fired their blood.

He'd intended to take her to his room, but hers was closer. As it was they barely made to the bedroom before they fell into each other's arms in a frenzy to make love.

Much later, as she lay curled against his side, Kristo tried to wrap his mind around the events of this day. For the first time since he'd gained the crown he felt in control.

With Demetria he simply felt relaxed. Whole. Happy?

A smile teased his mouth. He'd never believed it could be true, but he enjoyed being with her. And not just for sex!

Today among the people it had been nothing short of magical. And tonight...

Tonight he planned to enjoy a quiet dinner with her. After he woke her with a kiss. After he made love with her again.

The trill of his mobile echoed sharply in the velvet twilight. He swore as he rifled through his discarded clothes for it. The number in the display made his blood run cold. His brother.

He answered with a clipped, *"Éla."*

"Gregor is failing quickly," Mikhael said. "There is nothing more that can be done."

It was the worst possible timing, and yet he had no choice but to show a united front—especially in light of the scandal.

"I'll be there as soon as possible."

No more needed to be said.

He ended the call and placed one to his pilot, aware that Demetria had stirred beside him. "Ready the plane. I must leave immediately."

"What's wrong?" she asked, when he dropped the mobile on the table and heaved a frustrated sigh.

"Gregor is dying," he said, the strained emotions making his voice sound rougher than usual. "I must go to him."

"Of course."

She sat up beside him, drawing the sheet around her, looking sad. Nervous.

He rolled from the bed and the temptation her nearness stirred, dressing quickly. It would be so easy to take her in his arms. Hold her. Take the comfort she was clearly ready to give him. But that was how a playboy would behave. Not a King.

"When do we leave?" she asked.

He cut her a frown, surprised she'd assume he was taking her with him. "We? You won't accompany me in this."

"Why? I was betrothed to him since I was twelve."

"You are also the woman who betrayed him with me," he said, annoyed that she seemed eager to flaunt what they'd done before his dying brother.

"He's certain to have heard about this scandal by now. We could tell him the truth together," she said, biting her lower lip, as if uncertain how to go on with this horrible idea. "We could explain how we—"

"No! We will not team up against my brother."

"I wasn't suggesting we do that," she said, her voice holding a quaver of frustration now. "But I'm the woman Gregor was betrothed to for ten years."

"Which is why you will not be there," he said. "You betrayed him, Demetria. There is no explanation for that."

She reeled back against the headboard of the bed, eyes wide and stark, face far too pale. "I disagree. I want to see him."

In three steps he was at the bedside and had pulled her up against him. Mistake!

He realized it as the sheet fell from her, as her lush breasts molded against his chest and the flames of desire licked over them. That was not what he wished to be tormented with when he faced his dying brother!

He narrowed his gaze on her too luminous eyes, angry she had this power over him. "Why? What possible explanation can you give a dying man? That you fell into lust with me?"

"If you're honest with yourself, you'll admit there was a magnetic pull that we couldn't resist."

"We will not flaunt our lust in front of my brothers. Don't press me on this again."

"Dammit, Kristo! It was more than that!"

"What? Surely you won't claim that you fell in love?"

"Of course not! That would be the last thing I would feel for you," she said, shoving her fists between them and breaking his hold.

He glared at her, chest heaving with annoyance while his heart ached with worry. Again he was handling this wrong with her, but he didn't have time to explain his feelings to her now.

"I'll keep you informed," he said.

She gave a jerky nod, but didn't look at him.

That was the image of her that stayed with him as he raced to the airport.

Thirty minutes later Kristo stood at his brother's bedside and executed a deep bow of respect. "I came as quickly as I could."

Yet the flight from Angyra to Athens had never seemed to long or so fraught with anxiety. He'd had no idea what he'd walk into, yet he was determined to meet his fate without complaint.

Gregor's lips pulled in a weak smile and his glazed eyes lifted to his. "Thank you, my King. Though I told Mikhael not to trouble you."

"I wouldn't have forgiven him if he hadn't called me," Kristo said, flicking his younger brother the barest smile of gratitude.

But the greeting wasn't returned. Mikhael simply stared at him with cool dark eyes. *He knew.* Kristo was certain Mikhael was aware of the brewing scandal. Gregor as well?

The answer came a heartbeat later. "I see we have made headlines in all the gossip rags," Gregor said. "Is there any truth to it?"

He could lie. Save his brother hurt. But he'd hate anyone to do that to him.

And so he told his brother with an economy of words exactly what had happened that day on the beach, leaving out details of their intimacy.

"It is hard to tell who was more shocked that night at the palace when we realized each other's identity," Kristo said. "I never intended to betray you, nor did she. It just happened."

His brothers fell silent. A brooding silence for Mikhael. With Gregor he couldn't tell. Like their father, he was adept at cloaking his emotions.

"Did you sleep with her?" Gregor asked at last.

"Not while she was betrothed to you."

Gregor gave a clipped nod. "It is good, then, that you are the one who will marry her."

"Enough about my indiscretion. What of your condition?" he asked Gregor. "I can't accept that nothing more can be done to help you. That we gather around your bed and wait."

"I've brought in the leading authorities on his condition," Mikhael said, his expression grim. "It is out of our hands."

He'd known it the moment he'd walked into the room, yet conceding defeat left a sour taste on his tongue. He had lost his father forty days ago. He didn't want to lose his brother too.

The brother he'd betrayed. That would always be his cross to bear.

The anger he heaped on Demetria for betraying Gregor was twofold on himself. In his heart, he knew he didn't deserve the crown.

Gregor gasped, teeth clearly clenched in pain for an agonizing moment. When it ended his complexion had turned a cooler gray.

"Forgive me. I didn't want to die before the wedding," Gregor said, gasping for breath again. "I wanted to see my playboy brother claim his royal bride. To see Angyra celebrate its King and Queen."

"I will endeavor to do my best for our country," Kristo said. "But in light of your failing health I should postpone the wedding."

"No," Gregor said, his tone authoritative and yet so weak. "Do not mourn me. Angyra has suffered enough through Father's death. They do not need another one so soon afterward."

"You know that you are still much favored in Angyra."

"That doesn't matter," he said, his voice barely a whisper now. "You are the King. I believe you will be a far better one than I, for you know how to make Angyra stronger."

He hoped his brother was right. Hoped he'd make a strong leader and a fair one.

"Rest, Gregor," he ordered.

"I will soon. The doctors tell me that I have only hours, not days left to live."

Kristo had known that before he came here, yet hearing it, seeing the proof of his brother's decline, tore at his heart. His family could buy anything they wished. Demand that a kingdom bow to their will. Yet they were helpless against this.

"Go home, my King," Gregor said. "Marry as planned. *Nása kalá!*"

Those words hung in the brittle air as Gregor succumbed

to the inevitable. A nurse rushed forward to check his vitals, then quietly unplugged the monitors and left the room.

Left him and Mikhael flanking the bed where their dead brother lay. Kristo coughed to clear the emotion clogging his throat, knowing he'd lost the chance to gain forgiveness or damnation from Gregor.

Mikhael heaved a sigh. "So what do we do with our brother now?"

"The only thing we can do without regret. Return to Angyra with him and hold a state funeral."

CHAPTER NINE

THE loud steady thud of hammering brought Demetria out of a sound sleep. She sat up and gathered the bedclothes to her bare bosom, realizing that the sound was coming from outside.

Yesterday seemed like a lifetime away now. Had they really danced on the lawn with the people of Angyra, acting like children? Acting free? Had they made love the whole afternoon?

Had she irrevocably lost her heart to Kristo?

It was all true. The memories flooding back to her were very real, as was the tenderness in her breasts and between her legs.

Yet tempering her pleasure was the extreme sadness that came from Gregor's death. Kristo had rung her late last night, saying only that his brother's struggle was over and that they'd return home today.

She dragged herself into the shower. Moments later, as she donned capris and a T-shirt, she heard voices in the salon. She padded to the connecting door and yanked it open, thinking Kristo had returned.

Instead she found Vasos and the maid, surrounded by garment bags and boxes.

Demetria poked her head out her bedroom door, her curiosity too great to remain hidden. "What's going on?"

The maid whirled toward her, a smile wreathing her round face. "The remainder of the wedding finery has arrived."

Demi's questioning gaze lifted to Vasos. Though she'd designed the royal wedding gown, there were a few accessories that needed to be provided. But this array of boxes and garment bags went far beyond the need for satin pumps and undergarments.

"The King has asked that you select your trousseau," he said.

She caught the names emblazoned on the boxes and bags and knew there was a small fortune in clothing here. All top designers that she'd studied with envy.

The *crème de la crème* of those she admired professionally and had hoped to emulate one day. Kristo couldn't have known that, though, for she'd never been able to afford anything made by them.

She forced a smile, even though this order felt like salt being rubbed into a wound. He hadn't done this because he cared for her and wanted to gift her with the best. No, this was part of her new role. The future Queen *must* present herself in only the best.

Still, he could have asked her opinion.

"Fine. Leave them and I'll look through them later," she said, her toner sharper then she'd intended.

Vasos inclined his head. "As you wish. Is there anything you require?"

She shook her head. "What's all the commotion outside?"

"Preparations are under way for the royal wedding."

The moment Vasos took his leave, she crossed to the French doors and watched the small army of workers below. Gardeners were planting a row of roses along the perimeter wall, and the breeze from the sea brought their spicy scent to her.

Other workers were setting up an altar at the edge of the garden wall, their hammering remaining steady. It was a perfect location for a wedding.

Beyond the wall the ground dropped off sharply, to leave a stunning view of the azure sea and the city below. This wedding would be photographed and talked about for eons.

She couldn't think of a more lovely place to hold the ceremony. She'd always wanted to have a garden wedding. Always known that the ivory gown of her heart would glow warmly under a full sun.

And now it would. The fairy-tale wedding, right down to a handsome King at her side.

Her heart ached. Except he didn't love her.

She glanced at the designer garments the maid was carefully removing from the boxes. They could wait. She had one small detail to complete on her wedding gown first.

Kristo stepped inside Demetria's suite to find the maid returning a stack of garments to boxes. He guessed these were the ones Demetria didn't want—which seemed to be most of them.

"Your Majesty," the maid said, and bowed, flicking nervous glances to the bedroom and then back at him.

He gave her an impatient smile and canted his head to the door. "I need a moment of privacy with the lady."

Without a word, the maid scurried from the room.

"What was that?" Demetria said as she strode from the bedroom.

She froze in a pool of sunlight that transformed the gown into a glistening ivory cloud. She looked more luminous than a pearl, a vision that no man would ever forget.

He certainly wouldn't.

"Oh!"

She grabbed a multicolored shawl off the divan and held

it in front of her. But the image of her in her wedding gown was already branded on his mind.

He'd never seen a more beautiful woman in his life, even with the bright drape concealing her. Her tanned skin glowed warmly and her eyes were huge and filled with the same desire that pounded in his veins.

In this they were well matched. He'd never tire of her. Never cease to be awed by her beauty.

Without a doubt nobody would be able to tear their gazes from her at the wedding. She'd simply be the most raved about bride in all of the Mediterranean.

And she'd be his.

He never took his eyes off her radiant face, wondering again why his brother had never been enamored of her. Had it been because of his ill health? Or was it chemistry?

"It's bad luck for you to see the bride in her gown," she said as she backed toward the bedroom.

"Perhaps we've already reached our quota of ill fate."

A flush skimmed across her high cheekbones and strands of her glorious hair escaped the band at her nape to dance around her bare shoulders. The vivid memory of that hair teasing his bare heated flesh tormented him, and he wanted nothing more than to strip them both naked again and lose himself in her willowy arms.

"I don't care to take that chance," she said. "Did you just return?"

"About thirty minutes ago. I've not told the people about Gregor yet." He snorted. "Gregor didn't want me to tell them at all!"

"They should know."

His gaze fixed on hers, and he caught the sheen of moisture and knew its cause. Sorrow. "You realize this means a change in the wedding plans?"

"I suspected as much," she said, her voice solemn. Resigned. "We've no choice."

Choice. He'd given her damned little. And seeing her now in her finery, knowing she'd created something so magnificent, boggled his mind.

"I've arranged to make the announcement of Gregor's death at six," he said. "I'll come for you thirty minutes before."

"I'll be ready."

Again that unnerving spate of silence.

"Would you send the maid in?" she said at last.

"She's gone," he said. "I sent her away."

"What? I need her to help me get out of the gown."

He smiled, thinking that was a task he'd take great pleasure in doing. "I can do that."

"The buttons are tiny."

He lifted one dark eyebrow. "Do you doubt my agility?"

"No, but that means you'll have to see me in the gown again." Her frustrated sigh echoed around him. "Please, will you call the maid in?"

He shook his head and crossed to her bedroom, surprised that she clung to such superstition. He stopped at the door. "No. I'll close my eyes. All you have to do is present your back to me."

"You promise not to look?" she asked.

"Yes." He closed his eyes, agreeing to open them only when she was out of that gown and feeling like a child playing a game.

"All right."

He felt the swish of her skirt against his legs and sucked in a breath at the heightened charge of desire not seeing her created. All his senses were suddenly more attuned, and thoughts of a child's game vanished in a heartbeat.

Her jasmine scent was more provocative. The silken wisps of her hair were softer than the expensive cloth.

Just brushing his fingertips against the smooth curve of her spine as he worked the tiny buttons free awakened his desire. In his mind's eye he saw that wedge of creamy skin that was slowly revealed with each slip of a button.

"Lovely," he said, when he'd slipped the last button free.

"Thank you."

Before she could move away, he skimmed both palms up her spine, parting the gown in his wake. She gasped and he opened his eyes then, looking not at the silk that barely clung to her but at the tanned flesh arrowing to her waist.

Desire roared through his veins, hot and needy. Without a word he pushed the garment off her.

She caught it and stepped free of the skirt, facing him with the silk clutched in her hands, giving him more than a teasing peek of her full bare breasts. "I'll be a moment getting dressed."

"Don't." He followed her into the bedroom.

He lowered his face to hers and grazed her lips once, twice. The third time she strained upward to meet him, losing her grip on the gown to slip her arms around his neck.

Their lips melded in a frisson of fiery need that roared through his blood in a flood of need. His tongue stroked hers with bold intent. He was desperate to keep a hold on his control but it was a losing effort, for he was weary of this constant standoff. Of being her adversary when all he wanted to be was her lover. Her only lover.

She gripped his shirtfront and treated him to the same erotic kisses, the sweet sensuous assault dragging a groan from the depths of his soul.

"You are a vixen," he said against her lips.

She splayed her fingers on his face in a possessive caress. "Only with you, Kristo."

It didn't matter if that was the truth, or if she was just telling him that to appease him. She was his now. The perfect match for him in bed, for she challenged him there as well. And he was ready to prove that point right now.

She smiled against his lips. "How interesting that you had no trouble getting me out of the gown."

"That's because I prefer you naked."

His hands cupped her shoulders to push her from him, just enough so he could appreciate her beauty. The blush tips of her bared breasts thrust upward, begging him to sample. A very sexy red satin thong just barely hid the secrets he longed to explore again at leisure.

"That is a pleasant surprise any groom would appreciate," he said.

She blushed, and again he was struck with the anomaly of her coyness. "It wasn't intentional."

He couldn't care less if she'd planned it or not. Another need roared through him now, demanding satisfaction. Demanding release.

He tore off his shirt and swept her into his arms. Long determined strides carried her to the bed.

She gave him a teasing smile.

He made quick work of stripping off his clothes, trying to find the words that she'd long to hear. All the while her wide luminous eyes caressed him, causing his blood to boil and his lungs to burn with want of her.

Seeing her lying there with her ripe body begging for his mouth and questing hands fogged his reasoning. When his gaze lowered to that tiny scrap of red satin between her legs logic evaporated like sea mist.

His fingers grasped her slender ankles and spread her legs wide. "I have dreamed of this all day," he said as he stretched out between her creamy thighs.

He skimmed his hands up her long legs to the red thong, gliding his thumbs under the edge to stroke her moist swollen flesh. An arrogantly pleased smile touched his mouth. She was ready for him. She was always ready for him.

"So sexy," he said as he pressed a kiss on the transparent satin.

Her fingers dove through his hair and held fast. "Please..."

"Whatever the lady wants," he said.

He tugged the scrap of satin aside and kissed her, lightly at first. Then his tongue plundered. Using the lacy thong as a sensual torment. Taking all she had to give. Forcing her to give more. Testing his own limits as he'd never done before.

She bucked and let out a needy moan, rocking against him in a fast rhythm that made the pain of waiting almost unbearable. Such sweet torture!

Sweat beaded his brow from his effort to hold his desire in check. Still he kept up his ruthless seduction, for he'd never received such joy from watching a woman climax.

Never felt this warmth that expanded in his heart.

She arched her back and cried out her release and he smiled, pleased that he'd given her such pleasure.

Heart pounding a savage beat, he slid his thumbs under the satin triangle to hook the lace band. He dragged it down her legs and tossed it aside, his breathing labored as if he'd run uphill.

"Beautiful," he said as he stroked the creamy skin of her inner thighs.

She reached for him, her fingers closing around his length in sweet torment. "So are you."

He smiled at that, for while lovers had touted his prowess none had ever dared to call a prince beautiful. But Demetria dared that and more.

Her boldness in that regard drew him as surely as the passionate promise glowing in her eyes.

He sprawled atop her quivering body. Their lips met in a crush of raw desire.

"My God," she whispered against his mouth as she scraped her fingernails along his jaw.

The sensual jolt shot through him like a lightning strike. "How do you do it?" he asked, his voice raw as his emotions.

Passion-dazed eyes lifted to his. "Do what?"

"Drive me wild with wanting you."

He didn't wait for her answer. He couldn't wait another second to make her his, to bind them together once more.

She clawed at his back, as if trying to crawl under his skin. And wasn't she there already?

The thought came and went as need consumed him like a firestorm. They moved as one, this time as special as the first time, as exciting as the one that would follow.

But he made love with her as if it would be the last time. And deep in his heart he acknowledged that it very well might be.

Demetria clung to his sweat-slicked body, knowing he'd dozed off, knowing she only had to shove him to get him off her. But the weight of his powerful body was a welcome blanket after the intensity of their mating.

Her thoughts tumbled into a conflicting whirl of sensations. The incredible freedom she'd felt dancing with the people. Making love to Kristo deep into the night. And the simple pleasures like holding his hand.

She could easily delude herself into thinking he loved her. But he didn't.

He'd been honest about that from the start. He wasn't "victim" to that particular emotion.

She still didn't know why he shied away from love. Why he couldn't give her more than sex.

"Who soured you on love?" she asked, but her only answer was his breathing that had finally evened out in sleep.

But she was wide awake, her mind troubled. She'd tried hard to deny what she was feeling. But she couldn't any longer.

The depth of emotions rocketing through her were far beyond anything she'd experienced. More powerful than anything she'd ever dreamed of having.

This was more than sex. Much, much more. And that made it more horrible to bear, for what she felt would not be returned.

Love. She hadn't wanted this consuming need that left her fearing she'd die if she lost him. As if she only felt whole when she was with him. This feeling reduced her to a needy woman who tried to convince herself that she could be content with just his physical love.

It was a lie. She needed more than that from him. She needed his heart. His trust.

But she knew she'd get neither. Knew she was in for heartache because she loved him. Deeply. More deeply than any woman should love a man.

"Damn you, I didn't want this to happen," she whispered, tears stinging her eyes as she glided her hands down the muscles in his back that had finally lost their steel. "But it did."

CHAPTER TEN

KRISTO pushed inside Demetria's suite promptly at a quarter till six, wondering if she'd be ready, as he'd asked. If all went as planned the church bells would begin ringing fifteen minutes from now. The last time they'd tolled was when Gregor had had to gather the people to announce that the King had died.

To his surprise, she stood by the open balcony door wearing a royal blue dress that hugged her curves and ended in a swirl just above her knees. It was fashionable, yet sophisticated.

Her glorious hair hung in loose curls, and he couldn't think of a more fitting crown for such beauty. If only she wasn't frowning.

He strode to her and wished that circumstances had been different. Being at crossed swords with his bride was not the way to start a marriage.

His hand grasped hers and she trembled as if shocked. He felt the electrical charge arc into him like a lightning bolt and set fire to the desire that never truly banked.

Touching her was dangerous, for it narrowed his thoughts to one thing—pleasuring her. But he couldn't stop himself. He, who always remained cool, had discovered his weakness. Her!

He lifted her hand and dropped a kiss on the silken skin.

She couldn't contain her whispered moan. He just managed to still his answering groan.

Amazing how a private moment with her could fast escalate out of control. How all he could think of was taking her back to bed.

He stared at the delicate hand resting in his and marveled at the nimble fingers that created such beauty with beads and lace and silk. Slender fingers that had played over his flesh in long lusty strokes to the point where he'd been nearly mad with wanting her.

With a muttered oath directed at himself, he shook off the carnal images that had his blood roaring in his veins and focused on the task at hand. Within the hour, the Royal House of Stanrakis would officially be in mourning again.

Their marriage would be postponed. His personal life put on hold. But before that happened there was one thing he'd neglected to do for her. And that was causing him more anxiety than he'd believed possible.

"You're scaring me, Kristo," she said, her hands tightening on his when he stood before her, staring.

He was scaring himself, for he'd never traveled this road before. God willing, he would never have to do so again.

He managed a smile and looked into eyes that were wide with concern. "I am honored and pleased that you will be my bride. My Queen," he said, and slid a ring on her finger.

The fit was perfect. She was perfect.

"It's beautiful," she said.

It was priceless, but it paled in comparison to her beauty. "It was commissioned for your wedding."

Her gaze jerked to his. "This is the ring Gregor was to give me?"

"Technically, yes, though he never ordered it made or saw it once it was completed."

"I don't understand."

"Gregor asked me to handle this very personal task for him, claiming he had no talent for such things." So, without knowing the likes and dislikes of their future Queen, just remembering the passion she'd exuded, he'd had the ring designed for her.

That had been a horrendous task, for at the time he'd thought the very worst of her. Still, guilt made a man do the impossible at times.

He'd chosen a three-carat blue diamond surrounded by smaller brilliants because it was spectacular. He'd commissioned the ring to be set in Rhoda gold and platinum as well, to symbolize two of the richest ores on earth. The combination was striking. Just as she was too beautiful for words.

But he'd not known until now that the fire in the blue diamond would match the glow of passion in her eyes before she climaxed. Or that the bands of gold and platinum would bring out the warmth in her light olive skin.

"Do you like it?" he asked, for if she hated it he'd have another one created.

Her lips trembled. Firmed. "It's more than lovely."

She blinked away the sudden moisture that seemed intent on filling her eyes, but it was a useless battle.

"Why tears over something so small?" he asked, uneasy around her when she was like this.

She sniffled, and dabbed at her eyes with the tissue he handed her, looking small and miserable. "Don't you see? It's not the ring. It's all of it together that makes this so heartbreaking."

"All of what? You're making no sense."

"Of course you wouldn't understand. You have seen that I have the gown of my dreams. A garden wedding that is picture-book perfect. I have a devastatingly handsome King as my groom, and now this—a magnificent engagement ring." Though her crying had stopped, two tears slipped from her big sad eyes. "And it's all show. I've gone from being the chosen fiancé of your brother to yours. There's no love."

He heaved a sigh. Love again.

"That's it, then? You would be happy if I professed my undying affection?"

She shook her head. "I wouldn't believe you, for you would only be telling me what I want to hear."

He couldn't deny it, though he was tempted to.

"I wanted you since the first day I met you on the beach," he said, and managed a tight smile when she blinked in surprise.

"Wanted me? As in desired me as a sexual partner? Lusted after me? Is that it?"

"Yes, and if you are honest with yourself you will admit that you are just as desirous of me."

She jerked her gaze from his—as if the truth stung, as if the sight of him sickened her. "How can you be so cold?"

"It is honesty, Demetria. In my position I can't afford to be a victim of emotions."

He didn't understand the sense of loss that settled over him. He sure as hell didn't *want* this weakness, so he shoved those troubling emotions to the back of his mind.

He was the King. He had to make tough decisions for the good of Angyra. He couldn't let one small woman disrupt his life and his kingdom.

Their plans had been made and they would abide by them. *Even if he hated what he was about to do.*

His fingers closed around hers and he ground his teeth when she stiffened. "Come. It's time to make the announcement."

She nodded and fell into step beside him, looking regal and composed, yet far too aloof. Still, that electric thrill shot through him just at having her beside him.

But this time he sensed a wall going up between them. A barrier that might not be as easy to breach.

The moment they reached the main hallway leading to the balcony she abruptly stopped, forcing him to do the same. Much of the staff stood along the walls in a show of support.

"Your Majesty," Vasos said, and bent in a courtly bow.

Both lines of servants followed suit.

He nodded, momentarily regretting that when he'd taken the crown the familiarity he'd shared with these people all his life had changed. This was not the life he wanted, yet he was surprised that accepting the burden no longer angered him.

He guided her toward the door that glowed in the late-afternoon sun.

"Your father will arrive late tomorrow for the funeral," he said, and swore under his breath when she stiffened.

"I don't look forward to that visit," she said in an undertone.

"Nor do I, but protocol demands it."

They'd reached the front balcony, and the cluster of guards and staff made further talk impossible. The doors were opened wide and a roar went up from the crowd that extended from the cobbled lane in front of the palace down to the harbor.

The bells were nearly deafening here, but he knew they'd stop soon. Knew that once he stepped out on that balcony and made the announcement his life would take another huge change.

Finally the tolling stopped, but its echo vibrated off the verdant hills for long minutes. Before the last reverberation died, he grasped Demetria's hand in his and walked out on the balcony.

A large crowd had gathered to throw up a shout of welcome. The enormity of the moment wasn't lost on Kristo.

He'd stood back all his life while his father had come out here to speak to the people first. Always after state and family deaths. Always for national celebrations.

Gregor had stood by their father's side, and Kristo had been content to be in their shadow. He'd had the life he ached to pursue, and being the second son had afforded him that luxury.

Now he was King. Duty came first.

"Marry for love," his mother had told him.

Yet here he stood with his chosen bride, poised to start their marriage with animosity instead of affection.

He glanced at her, and his heart lurched with an empathy that had never been strong in his gene pool. She stared unseeing at the sea of cheering people, their din so loud he could barely hear himself think.

This was just another burden his title carried. He hoped she realized now that they'd always be on display with the people. That the celebration the other day had been a fluke.

He bent close to her ear. "Smile, Demetria. You look like I have a gun in your back."

"In a way you do," she quipped, but the inviting bow of her lips curved into a smile, albeit a tense one.

He swore under his breath and knew there was no help for it. Even if he could find the words there was no time for them right now.

With a hand raised for silence, he stepped to the railing with Demetria by his side. "The Royal House of Stanrakis is grateful for your patience and respect these past few troubled weeks. I deeply appreciate that you joined us in celebrating my father's death."

And now Gregor was gone. His chest tightened at the thought of his brother slipping into obscurity, as he'd wished.

He stared at the gathering. Their silence was palpable. Then, like the tide rolling to the shore, the low rumble of rapid conversation came from those gathered. A few clapped their hands, the applause slow but building.

"Hail to the future King and Queen of Angyra," a man in the crowd shouted, and soon others joined in with well wishes.

If there were any detractors—and he was sure there were those who found this turn of events unsatisfactory—they wisely kept their opinions to themselves.

"Wave and smile as if you are thrilled beyond words, for it's clear they hold you in high regard," said Kristo.

He felt a tremor go through Demetria as she lifted a hand and waved. Not the cursory movement he'd seen some royals make. But a genuine greeting. One that she'd give to a friend across the street.

"I'm the same person I was yesterday, when I was dancing with them," she said.

But that wasn't true. Up here she was the future Queen.

"As you all are aware, the royal wedding was to take place in the formal garden next Saturday," he said, pausing to let a ripple of agreement go through those gathered. "Unfortunately tragedy has struck the Royal House of Stanrakis again and the wedding must be postponed. Prince Gregor, my beloved brother, is dead."

Behind him, Mikhael's low voice reached him as he comforted an elderly aunt. Women wept. Men moaned.

Demetria stood quietly at his side. His comfort.

Kristo stood tall and firm, his heart clenched with grief. He had done what duty decreed, even though it went against Gregor's wishes.

This was the right thing to do for Angyra. For him and Demetria as well? Only time would tell.

He wanted the people to accept her. To forget that she'd been Gregor's betrothed. To love her as much as he did.

That admission gave him pause. Was that why he thought

of her every second? Why he had to touch her if he was near her? Why she haunted his sleep with her beguiling smile?

Had he fallen in love with her?

CHAPTER ELEVEN

THE dinner was more elegant than she could have imagined, and far more somber than any meal should be. Demetria sat at the opposite end of a lacquered dining table from Kristo, wishing she knew the workings of his mind. But he'd said nothing to her, leaving her to feel like one of the pieces of art on display.

She wished she knew what was troubling him. Wished she could have had a moment alone to speak with Kristo. But since the announcement his family, friends and royal dignitaries had demanded his attention. She had been pushed aside, forgotten or ignored—she wasn't sure which.

Even now, at the long dining table, a dozen of his cousins and close family members carried on hushed conversations that she failed to grasp. His brother Mikhael sat at her left, far more reserved than she remembered him being.

An elegant young woman who was the daughter of a council member had taken the chair on Kristo's left and captured his attention with soulful looks, softly spoken words that forced him to bend close to her, and repeatedly touched his hand in a gesture of sympathy that lingered far too long.

The last troubled her, for it was blatantly clear that the woman had eyes only for Kristo. Thankfully none of the other guests had seemed to notice but her.

"I was convinced that you were a gold digger, but I have

been proved wrong," Mikhael said, his voice a rich purr that was pleasing but lacked the sensual quality of Kristo's. "I was also certain you hated my brother, but I can see that isn't the case."

Demetria glared at him, which gained her his rogue's smile, and chose to ignore the first remark. "I do hate him at times."

Mikhael arched a dark brow, clearly not believing her.

He leaned so close she could smell the brandy on his breath. "I know a jealous woman when I see one, and you, Demetria, are jealous."

"Rubbish," she said, and took a sip of her wine in what she hoped was a nonchalant manner.

He gave a careless shrug. "Deny it all you wish, but it is the truth."

He was right. She loved Kristo. She was jealous. Furiously jealous of him, and simply furious with the woman seated beside him for her blatant flirtation.

"Of course he is the same," Mikhael said.

She glanced at him over her wineglass. "He's possessive. That is not the same thing."

"I shall prove you wrong." Mikhael pushed to his feet and instantly garnered everyone's attention. "It is too beautiful an evening to spend inside cloaked in grief. So I have invited my future sister-in-law to join me for a walk in the garden."

He extended a hand to her, his smile utter charm. The guests were so quiet she was sure they could hear her heart race like the wind.

She was caught between insulting him by refusing his offer in front of his family, or leaving the woman and Kristo alone. Neither option appealed to her.

Truthfully, she wanted to get away, because the past two hours had been a dreadful strain to endure. She had never been so besieged by such a torrent of opposing emotions.

"What a splendid idea," the woman at Kristo's right said, breaking the silence.

Demi's gaze fixed on the woman's smug smile. Like a volcano, anger boiled inside her again and threatened to spew.

Getting out of here was her only option. If she stayed, she'd surely make a scene.

She laid her linen aside and rose, hoping a walk in the fresh air would clear her head and cool her temper. "I agree."

"As do I," Kristo said, on his feet and striding toward Demi before she could place her hand on Mikhael's arm. "Come, *agapi mou.*"

Upon hearing him voice that endearment in public one of his elderly aunts bobbed her head and let out a pleased sigh.

If only the words held meaning for him. The fierce gleam in his dark eyes was deep and troubled. Yes, he was possessive, but there was some other emotion there that she'd not seen before—something primal and fathomless.

"Shall we?" Kristo asked.

She inclined her head, for truly she didn't trust herself to speak right now. Kristo pressed his hand to the small of her back and she burned with need.

Being alone with him would lead to the bedroom. It always did. For the life of her she couldn't think of a reason to refuse him. It was a shameful admission to make in the wake of Gregor's death, but she couldn't deny it.

"Thank you all for coming, and for your support," he told the guests. "Now, if you'll excuse us?"

All of the guests smiled and demurred to their King and future Queen. All but the woman next to Kristo, whose eyes snapped with anger.

Demetria looked away, relieved when Kristo escorted her from the palace. The balmy night air carried the salty tang of the sea and the spicy scent of jasmine and bougainvillea.

But tension held her in its grip as the day's events played over and over in her mind, leaving her chilled in spirit.

Lights from the various shops along the cliff cast swaths of color over the dark water, making it appear as if a rainbow of ribbons had been unfurled. But the spectacular vista afforded her failed to capture her interest as Kristo slid his arms around her and pulled her close.

Her world narrowed to him and her. She splayed her palms over his warm broad chest and the taut planes of muscle that she'd explored at leisure last night. It would be so easy to cuddle against him.

"I never realized you had such a large family," she said. "That will take getting used to."

"Those are the close ones. There are three times that many with distant cousins." He nudged her chin up with his fingers, his eyes near black in the diffused light. Deep. Mysterious. "What of your family? All you've mentioned is your father and sister."

For good reason! She was loath to admit she came from a dysfunctional family. "That's about it. My father was an only child, and his parents are both dead," she said. "My stepmother was adopted, and after she passed we never heard from her family again."

"What of your mother's people?"

"They disowned her, and subsequently me."

"Because of the scandal?"

She nodded, feeling oddly relieved that she'd finally told someone about her past. It was a very bitter pill to swallow, knowing that your family wanted no part of you, even though you'd done nothing wrong.

"They are fools," he said, and she smiled at the heat in his tone.

"My grandfather was of noble Greek blood, and his daughter's actions were unforgivable. To know she'd given herself to an Italian, especially a married man, when she was betrothed to another noble Greek brought great shame on their family."

"Yet they married her off to your father," he said, proving he remembered the scandal.

"Father said that only my mother's father attended the wedding," she said. "After that day they never heard from her family again."

"Even when your mother died?"

She shook her head. "Not a word. For to them she'd been dead for a year. As for me—Father suspected they believed I was the bastard child of her lover."

But she wasn't, and it shamed her to admit that there had been times when she'd wished it were so—that she was anyone's daughter other than Sandros Andreou's.

"It is unfathomable that they've never been a presence in your life," he said.

"Well, I was told that my grandfather left a trust fund for me. But I can't touch it until I marry and produce an heir." She grimaced. "A Greek heir."

"Yes, very traditional."

She didn't bother to add that she didn't want her grandfather's money. He hadn't wanted her when she was a child in need of love. He was not welcome in her life now.

Kristo's beautiful mouth pulled into a tight, disagreeable line again. "Did you know that a wedding invitation has been sent to them?"

"No. But then I was never consulted about the guest list," she said, wanting to be angry at him over this slight, but simply not finding the energy to fight it any longer. "I know. Protocol demands that you invite them."

He made a gruff sound and nudged her chin up, eyes glittering with an emotion she'd not seen before. "Very true. But remember one thing, *agapi mou*. After we are married, they will bow to you."

"I don't care if they do," she said.

"I do," he said, pressing a fierce kiss on her mouth that stunned as well as warmed her. "You'll be my Queen, and as such you'll command respect."

She managed a small smile, knowing he'd never understand that respect was the last thing she wanted.

Love.

That was what she wanted most from him.

"Do you know you've never told me about *your* childhood or your mother?" she said, hoping he would now.

He heaved a sigh and pulled her down beside him on a bench. "It wasn't a typical childhood, but it was all we knew. Mother was busy with her duties, and so was Father, so we were basically raised by nannies."

"I can imagine you giving them a merry chase in this huge palace," she said.

He laughed, the sound so rare she just stared at him. "We were boisterous when we were young, with all the energy boys can hold, but after Gregor turned eight he was pretty much segregated from us."

"Why?"

"He was the Crown Prince," he said, as if that explained it all. "Father made sure that his duties were pounded into him. So for the most part it was just Mikhael and me."

How sad that Gregor had lost that closeness with his siblings, that he'd been denied a childhood because of the order of his birth. "So what was it like growing up here for you and your younger brother?"

"I wanted for nothing, and neither did Mikhael. We had a huge playroom to ourselves, and a nanny who fussed after us. When I turned eight I was sent away to boarding school in Greece," he said.

And she thought she'd had a wretched childhood! "That's too young to be sent away! And, while I can understand the need for a nanny, what of your parents? What role did they play in your life?"

He shrugged, an abrupt movement that screamed of pent-up tension. This was not a subject he cared to discuss!

"My parents were the King and Queen," he said. "We didn't have a close relationship with our parents. They were simply too busy for that."

"People who are too busy with their own lives shouldn't have children."

He was silent for a long moment. "You'd give up your career or duty for your family?"

"Yes! Children need to know that their parents love them, support them, in order to thrive," she said.

"How can you say that after you've admitted that you were little more than your stepmother's helper? That your father was so greedy that he used you, his daughter, to further himself?"

She reeled back, stung by the venom in his tone. It would be easy to cave in. To leave him to his delusions. But pride refused to turn a blind eye to his assumptions.

"My father is many things—brutal, greedy and at times obnoxiously loud—but I never doubted he loved me, that he believed he was doing the best for me by securing my marriage to the Crown Prince," she said.

He snorted, as if discounting her words as nothing. "And your sister's mother? Would you have me believe that she treated you the same as her own flesh and blood?"

"Believe what you will," she said. "The truth is that she was the one who taught me to sew, who nurtured my feeble attempts to create something by myself. Because of her encouragement when I was young, and her praise when I succeeded, I rushed through my studies at university to begin my career, well aware that time was short before I'd be forced to honor my duty to your crown."

His fingers entwined with hers, and for the first time she didn't feel any jolt of passion. Instead of that sizzle of desire she'd come to dread and crave in turn, she felt incredibly sad that he'd never experienced the love she had.

"You put too much stock in love," he said.

"And you put none in it."

He didn't deny it, and that made her heart ache all the more for him. For a brief moment she glimpsed the little boy who'd craved affection. Then in a blink he reverted to the arrogant man who denied the need for love.

"It's been a very long day," he said, and rose, dragging her up as well. "It's time we returned to the palace."

And bed? She assumed so as he led her to the palace in silence. Each step closer made her dread the night more, for though she longed to make love with him she knew she'd never win his heart.

At the door to her suite, he nudged her chin up and pressed an achingly tender kiss on her lips that brought tears to her eyes. "Get some rest, Demetria. The next few days will be hectic."

Then he turned and walked away. She stood there a moment, torn between letting him go and calling out to him, calling him back to her arms, to her bed.

She choked back a sob. Swiped trembling hands over her now wet cheeks, and stepped inside her lonely suite.

Love shouldn't hurt like this.

Demetria didn't see Kristo at all the next week. The following Saturday, the day that was to have been their wedding, was the funeral for Prince Gregor.

Like everything else Greek, the ceremony was laden with ritual and seemed endless. Demetria, wearing a black cashmere Donna Karan sheath, sat beside Kristo, who was resplendent in a black suit, black shirt and tie, with the royal sash stretched across his broad chest.

He was regal and unapproachable.

By the time the service was over and Prince Gregor had been buried in the royal family plot, she was exhausted in body and spirit. Still, she was obliged to stay until the guests left. Until the palace grew quiet.

Kristo had disappeared again, likely dealing with more state business, more duty that required his immediate attention. Her father and her unusually sedate sister had also left, so she had nobody to talk to. No one to share her thoughts with.

But, considering how troubled they were, perhaps that was for the best too.

She sought out her room, to get a few moments' peace and quiet. But she found little serenity there either.

The palace gardens were still in a state of half-readiness for the wedding. Her ivory gown hung on the form out of the light, ready for her to step into it. But when would that be?

The Royal House of Stanrakis would be in mourning for thirty days. A month to grieve. To wait to marry.

She didn't look forward to biding her time in the palace, where she'd have absolutely nothing to do. She wouldn't have any official duties until she married. It would be the longest month of her life.

Her door opened and Kristo strode in—tall, handsome and still formidable. But at least he'd come to her. At least now they could have some private time together.

"I trust you don't mind that I returned here to my suite?" she said. "I would have told you myself, but I didn't know where you'd gone."

"I had pressing business to attend to."

"That's what I thought." Tension pulsed between them,

leaving her more unsettled than before. "Is something wrong?" The resolute expression planted on his handsome face filled her with alarm.

"I've given this much thought. There is no reason for you to stay in residence through the period of mourning."

She stared at him, unable to believe he was sending her away. "You want me to leave Angyra for a month?"

He loosed an impatient shrug. "This is a good time to reevaluate what we have here."

"What?"

"You said it yourself. You want to marry for love." He stalked to the French doors and stared out, his expression brooding. "Of course if you're with child we will proceed with the wedding."

"What about the betrothal contract?"

"As King, I can alter such things."

She dropped onto the nearest chair, knowing her shaky legs wouldn't support her another moment. "Are you saying you'll only marry me now if I'm pregnant?"

He faced her then, and she'd never seen him look so remote. His lips pulled into a thin, disagreeable line. His magnetic eyes were closed to all emotion.

"There will be no bastards in the Royal House of Stanrakis."

"Don't you mean there will be no *more* bastards, for you are certainly acting the part now," she lashed out, hurt that he really cared so little for her.

"Think what you will. Unless you carry my heir, we are free to walk away from each other now if we wish."

If we wish... Her eyes and the back of her throat burned, for leaving him was the last thing she wanted to do. And yet pride wouldn't let her plead her point.

He'd made his wishes clear. There was no love between

them, just passion that would one day fade. Perhaps it already had. He would marry her only to legitimize an heir.

"If you leave today, you will be able to attend the Athens show."

"Yes." But the excitement that had once kept her awake at nights failed to materialize.

Her partner would have finished the designs. All would be in order, ready for the show. All except her.

How ironic that she'd once thought of nothing but pursuing that dream. Now that Kristo was letting her go, her heart simply wasn't in it. Her heart belonged here, with Kristo. But telling him that would change nothing.

He didn't love her.

He'd never love her.

"My jet will be ready to depart when you wish," he said, again in a cold, dismissive manner. "You'll let me know if you're pregnant?"

"Yes," she hissed, knowing that he'd likely have her watched, that she'd not be able to hide a child from him.

All the passion they'd shared was for naught. He'd likely begun to tire of her already, and without love there was nothing to keep them together. Nothing but duty. And he was willing to release her from that unless she was carrying his heir.

Tears stung her eyes, but she refused to cry. She'd leave with her head high, pride intact. Heart shattered.

She lifted her chin and faked a calm she was far from feeling. "I'd like to leave within the hour."

He gave a curt nod, his face wiped clean of emotion. "I'll inform the pilot. Vasos will see you to the airport."

"Thank you." She bit her lip, thinking this was all too abrupt, too cruel.

He stared at her. His gaze dropped to her mouth, lingered, setting off that low heat inside her again. She was sure he'd take her in his arms. That he'd give her a kiss that would blaze hot in her memory for the next month.

She hoped he'd at least tell her he'd miss her.

But he did neither.

King Kristo turned on his heel and strode from the room.

And in the awful quiet that settled around her she stopped trying to hold back the flood of burning tears.

Kristo sat in the dark in the royal office, a glass of ouzo in his hand and a half-empty bottle on the desk. For two days he'd racked his brain over his decision.

He'd rehearsed how to tell her.

He'd expected shocked surprise. A bit of anger, even. But he hadn't thought she'd tremble like a leaf caught in the wind. Hadn't thought those big eyes would swim with tears and hurt.

Seeing that had nearly toppled his resolve.

For a tense moment he'd struggled to regain control, fought the urge to drag her into his arms and give them both what they wanted. Sex.

Ah, but that was the problem, not the solution.

She wanted love.

He wanted sex.

There was no middle ground. No way this could ever be resolved unless she settled for his terms of marriage.

And that realization was what had finally gotten through to him. If he forced her to marry him he'd ultimately crush her spirit. She'd come to resent him for what he'd taken from her. What he could never give her.

Yes, this separation would do them both good. She could delve into the work she longed to pursue, and he would systematically purge this unacceptable craving for her from his system.

He'd done the right thing by letting her go.

So why the hell did he feel as if he'd made the biggest mistake of his life?

CHAPTER TWELVE

Six weeks later, Demetria sat at the drafting table in her flat in Athens. The show had been a success—so much so that she'd been invited to participate in an exclusive exhibition in London next week.

But the creativity that had never failed her before had yet to resurrect itself. Nothing new had come to mind. Nothing even remotely innovative.

No, all her thoughts centered around Kristo. Over a month had passed and he'd yet to contact her. News out of Angyra had been ominously absent since Gregor's funeral.

Not so the paparazzi. They hounded her every move, robbing her of sleep and keeping her on edge. She'd become a prisoner in her own flat, for she couldn't keep ignoring their questions. Had Kristo set a new date for the wedding? Had she spoken with him? Was the wedding off? Whose decision had it been to cancel it? Had Kristo tired of her? Had she jilted the King of Angyra for her career as a designer?

On and on the questions would go, until she wanted to crawl in a hole and hide forever. Which was pretty much what she'd done. Stayed in her flat and moped.

"You can't go on like this," her partner Yannis said, his thin face showing grave concern. "Phone him."

Her fingers tightened around her pencil, her insides clenching with the misery that just wouldn't let go. "I did yesterday morning, but the line was busy."

Always busy. For the same thing had happened the day before. And the day before that.

She refused to leave a message informing Kristo that she was pregnant. That she was carrying the royal baby in her womb. That he'd be obliged to marry her now.

So she'd abruptly hung up—for what else could she say except that she was miserable? That she missed him dreadfully?

Pride wouldn't let her do that.

"I was thinking that your name should be on our label instead of mine," she said.

"Changing the subject will not make it go away," said Yannis.

Damn him for being right, for knowing her so well. "I'm serious. I feel guilty that you didn't get the credit you deserved at the show."

He spread his arms wide. "My time will come."

"Soon, I would wager."

She glanced at the new garments he'd designed, in awe of his originality.

Now was her chance to shine. What she'd always wanted was in her grasp. But all she could think of was Kristo. Of their baby. Of the loveless future that awaited them.

Could her heart break any more than it already had? Could she possibly get more despondent?

Yannis was right. It was time to get on with her life. She had a baby to think of, to raise. To love.

Kristo's baby.

Time was supposedly the great healer, but her heart ached when she thought of losing Kristo. If she closed her eyes she could almost feel his hands and mouth on her, hear his heart beating in tandem with hers.

"Enough is enough. You need a diversion, and the upcoming exhibition in London will be ideal," Yannis said.

She was shaking her head before he'd finished. "I'm not up to being thrust in the limelight."

He jabbed a thumb at the window. "You're happy to stay here like a prisoner, with the paparazzi camped outside your door? Hoping he'll call?"

"No! But attending the exhibition means I'll have to face publicity head-on, and I'm not ready for that." Not nearly strong enough to field questions about her relationship with one arrogant King.

"The sponsors will have security, so you won't be hounded." Yannis knelt before her and took her cold hands in his. "Demetria, come to London. You need to get away."

She took a breath. Nodded. "All right."

Kristo paused at the rear of the large hall and gave a dismissive glance at the rail-thin models gliding down the catwalk under the swaths of strobe lights. The crush of the audience was as displeasing as the accompanying music that throbbed in the auditorium.

The only thing more distasteful than this chaos was the swarm of paparazzi clustered outside on the Strand. But these same gossipmongers in London were the ones who'd advertised the fact that Demetria had been specially invited to present her creations at this elite show for five new designers.

A phone call to the promoter of the event—a gentleman who was a fellow conservationist as well as a shrewd gambler—had secured him backstage passage. But he was painfully aware that wouldn't guarantee Demetria being pleased to see him.

So be it. He'd suffered six long weeks of misery without her, though he'd been slow to realize why. How strange that it had taken a bottle of Lesvos ouzo and an aged royal gardener to clear the fog from his mind.

"Your Majesty," a stout man said as he hurried toward him, his worried gaze flicking from Vasos to Kristo. "Please, if you'll come this way I'll show you backstage. Unless of course you wish to watch the remainder of the show here?"

"Backstage is fine."

"Very well." The man set a fast pace down the corridor and he followed, with Vasos trailing him.

He had no desire to be a part of the audience—especially when every nerve in his body had gone tight at the promise of seeing Demetria again. Why the hell had he let her go?

Pride. He wouldn't delve into the new feelings tormenting him. Guilt over the way he'd treated her—for she wasn't a chattel to be handed from one lord to the other: she was a beautiful, desirable woman. *Innocent* woman. Stupidity for thinking for one moment that he could live without her.

He couldn't.

Angyra couldn't.

They expected a royal wedding any day. They expected the bride to be Demetria, the woman they adored.

He adored.

If he hadn't been so stubbornly blind he'd have realized that six weeks ago. No, longer ago than that.

Over a year ago, when they'd first met on the beach. He'd known then down deep that she was unlike any woman he'd ever met before. Known she was perfect for him.

But again he'd let pride and jealousy blind him. He should have gone to Gregor immediately. He should have seen the truth in her innocence and fought for her hand then.

Ah, he had made so many mistakes with her. Would she grant him absolution now? Or would he forever be thrust into this personal hell of wanting her from afar?

The questions and doubts hammered away at him as the

man led them past the guards into the dimly lit backstage area. The spacious area was crowded like the Grand Bazaar in Istanbul, with sections partitioned off with stark white sheets.

He followed the man through the labyrinth. Past the impromptu studios that teemed with frantic designers and models in all stages of dress to the last tented room.

The letter *delta* was painted on the billowing sheet that served as a door. *D* for Demetria?

"This is her staging area, Your Majesty." The man managed a clumsy bow and disappeared.

Kristo pushed the curtain aside and stepped into her domain. Impatience pounded in his veins as he looked beyond the crush of models and artisans who made up the design team for a sign of Demetria. But all he saw were strangers.

The sharp clap of hands brought everyone's head up. "Ten minutes, ladies. Let's be ready. Ari! Do something about the neckline on this dress," a man barked, and then moved on to the next model, who stood there in a scrap of a bra and panties, waiting to be dressed like a child.

Kristo narrowed his eyes on the man issuing orders. If anyone knew where she was, it would be this abrupt man.

He crossed to the man in an economy of movement. "Where is Demetria?"

The man's head snapped up, light brown eyes flashing with annoyance. Then came the slightest widening of his eyes before they snapped back to match his scowl.

"So you choose now to finally show up?" the man said, foregoing any respect for the crown and Kristo was sure for himself as well.

He muttered a curse. "Why I am here is none of your business."

"On the contrary. I'm Demi's partner and her friend," the

man said. "You ruined her debut in Athens. Now, stay out of sight and out of the way and let her have this moment."

The truth was the slap in the face that he deserved, for he hadn't let her go until the very eve of the Athens show. She couldn't possibly have been prepared for it.

He gave a curt nod and moved behind a screen to stand and watch and wait when he longed to find Demetria. To hold her. Kiss her. Make love to her.

His heart gave an odd thud the second he saw her hurry toward a model draped in a muted floral gown. Seeing her again was a punch to his gut, bringing back memories that had never left him, reminding him of days at the palace. Of nights in her arms.

She moved away from the throng of models and he immediately noted the changes in her. She'd lost weight, and there were obvious lines of stress marring her beautiful face.

He ached to go to her, to take her in his arms, to take her away from here. Back to Angyra. To the palace and his bed. He wanted her so badly he could savor the satin of her skin against his lips, feel the comfort of her arms around him, the rightness of her body as he sank into her.

He wanted her more than he ever had before. Wanted her now. But her partner was right. This was *her* moment, not his.

She gave the model's abbreviated skirt a final adjustment and smiled. "Walk down the runway like you own the world."

As soon as the girl did as she was bid, Demetria turned back to the next model in line. Only the person behind her was him.

She went still, and stared at him a long moment, the air around them charged with desire, need and another emotion he had just recently come to grips with.

It still scared him to admit how he felt, for it made him

look at the man he'd been in a whole new light. He hadn't liked what he'd seen. Hadn't liked the man he'd become. Domineering. Aloof. Alone.

He was like Angyra—adrift in the sea.

His mother had told him to marry for love. His brother had simply said a man should love his wife.

Love. What did they know that he didn't? Why was this emotion so difficult for him to understand?

Now he knew. Now he hoped to hell he wasn't too late.

She stepped toward him and stopped, staring hard, as if trying to decide if he were real or imagined. "Kristo?"

He allowed a brief smile as his hungry gaze swept over her thin form again. There was nothing to indicate she was with child. Nothing binding them now. Nothing that would make this easy.

His jaw clenched. He didn't deserve easy. He needed to put effort into this—as much as with any deal he'd ever made or more. For his future hinged on this moment. On her.

Yet even now that would have to wait. People were watching them. Listening.

He noted Yannis was looking for her, looking frantic when he spotted them together. "Go on with what you are doing," Kristo said. "I'll wait here until the show is over."

He would wait forever for her if he must.

She hesitated a long moment, as if unsure what to do, as if not trusting he'd stay. But then what had he ever done to instill trust in her?

"Demi," her partner said. "They want you onstage."

"Coming." She turned and hurried back to the designer and the nervous models clustered just offstage, back to her world.

Kristo listened to Demetria's credentials and the short list of her styles presented today. Applause rang in the hall. Her partner motioned her to take the stage, but she balked.

"We both know this is your show," she said to Yannis, surprising Kristo, who'd inched forward to watch, to admire her in action. In control. "If not for you and Ari I wouldn't have been invited to this showing."

"We just held things together until you returned," Yannis said, and all but pushed her out on the stage. "Go. Accept the honor and praise you deserve."

Kristo bunched his hands at his sides as she took hesitant steps out onto the stage. She looked so small out there. So alone. So removed from him.

I could lose her right now. Forever.

That possibility clutched at his heart, paining him as nothing else had. Losing her would devastate him. Leave a scar that would never heal.

"Thank you for your enthusiastic applause," Demetria said to the crowd, her voice surprisingly strong. "But much of the credit goes to my partner, Yannis Petropoulos."

The audience clapped, but before the applause had fully died down, before she'd exited the stage, a man called out, "Miss Andreou? Will you give up designing if you marry the King of Angyra?"

"Is the wedding still on?" another shouted.

An immediate hush fell over the hall, followed by a ripple of nervous whispers. Instead of answering, Demetria simply waved and returned backstage.

It was then that he noticed the tears glistening in her eyes. She stopped to exchange one fierce hug with her partner, but her gaze remained on Kristo.

His heart started thundering as she pulled away and walked toward him. She stopped just out of arm's reach, eyes now dry but wary. "Why did you come?"

Because he couldn't sleep, couldn't eat for wanting her. Because without her his life simply wasn't the same.

But he wasn't about to tell her that here—not with so many

eyes watching them. "That should be obvious," he said, and when she frowned, he huffed out a sigh. "Please. I have a limo waiting outside. We can talk there in private."

Her solemn eyes, with dark lashes still spiked with moisture, searched Kristo's face—questioning. Sad.

He wondered about her thoughts. Wondered if she'd refuse. Wondered if anything or anyone could drag her away from this exciting world.

"This sounds serious," she said, her voice barely above a whisper.

He couldn't begin to tell her how much. How he was barely able to draw a breath for fear that she'd refuse him.

"Extremely so." He extended his hand to her, when he longed to sweep her into his arms and storm out of here.

Her luminous gaze flicked from his palm to his face. The slender column of her throat worked. Then to his relief the hesitation in her eyes slowly ebbed away.

"Very well. I'll go with you."

Slowly, hesitantly, she placed her hand in his. And for the first time in hours he was able to breathe.

"Are you happy, *agapi mou*?"

She was miserable, moody, weepy. Heartsick from wanting him. From longing for the love he'd denied her.

"It's been trying, with the paparazzi watching my every move," she said instead, still desperately clinging to what remained of her pride.

"The world waits to see what you will create. You are an up-and-coming high fashion designer," he said. "You will dazzle the world."

Exactly what she'd dreamed of doing for years. Yet now that the possibility of success loomed on her horizon she'd lost the passion to pour her heart and soul into her art.

All because she'd been swept up in the turmoil that

surrounded this demanding man. Because the weeks since leaving Angyra had been utter hell. Because the royal heir was nestled in her womb, and that sealed her fate.

"What is troubling you, *agapi mou*?" he asked, grasping her hand and entwining their fingers.

The strong, steady pulse of him vibrated into her, drawing her into him, muddling her senses. She took a breath, then another, yet still felt as if her world was about to spin out of control.

Tell him! Spit it out and end this torture!

"You," she said. "I don't know whether to be happy to see you again, or to dread the outcome of this visit."

Silence throbbed between them as she waited for him to say something correct. Something that would put an end to this turmoil, this hoping that he'd come for her.

He huffed out a rough sigh. "We are our own worst enemies. Always at odds. Hesitant to trust."

Her throat was thick with tears and her eyes burned. Sitting beside him, holding his hand and feeling that strong sensual pull ribbon around her, was tearing her apart inside.

"When you sent me away, you hurt me more than I ever thought possible," she admitted, and felt him go deathly still beside her. "But I never stopped loving you. I couldn't even when I tried. And now that I'm...I'm..."

"Shh," he soothed, pulling her into his arms, where she'd ached to be for so long. "I'm a bastard for putting you through this emotional hell when all you asked for was my heart. Do you know why I couldn't give that to you, *agapi mou*?"

She shook her head on a choked sob, afraid to guess why.

"Because I didn't know what love was. Because I'd forgotten the wisdom passed down to me from a wise old man."

"The King?" she guessed.

"No. Someone far wiser than my austere father," he said.

"When I was six years old I saw our old gardener on the cliff path with his wife, walking hand in hand. I'd never seen a man and woman do that before, and I asked him why they did it. He told me that he'd given his heart to her when he was a young man and that their love had never dimmed for one day."

"How beautiful," she said, blinking back the sting of tears, envious of the old couple and yet deeply touched that such love existed.

The oddest smile curved Kristo's sensuous mouth. "I never saw my parents touch each other, though it is obvious my mother did her duty and gave my father three sons. But there was no tenderness between them. No passion." His hand tightened on hers. Warm. Strong. "No holding hands."

She thought back to her own childhood and sighed. "There was no hand-holding between my father and stepmother either, though there were many bouts of raised voices and arguments."

She'd hated the turmoil. Hated the constant upheaval in their lives that had kept her and her sister cowering.

He cleared his throat and stroked her thumb with his. "I vowed then that if I ever married it would be to a woman who'd captured my heart. When I first met you on the beach I was instantly attracted to you. I wanted you more than I'd ever wanted a woman, and those stolen kisses and caresses only left me wanting you more," he said.

"Until you discovered who I was," she said, her voice small.

"Exactly. I hated my brother for being the man to have won you. I hated you for allowing me such liberties."

Heat burned her cheeks, but a new warmth stirred in her at his admission. If only it hadn't been lust that drew them together…

She gave a shuddering sigh. "I hated myself for betraying

Gregor, but I, too, was powerless to walk away from you. But you know that already."

And it had made no difference to how he felt about her. She'd always be the woman who had betrayed the Crown Prince.

"It is time we move forward with our lives," he said, and she felt her breath seize, fearing the farewell that was sure to come.

She couldn't let him voice that final goodbye—not before she told him about their love-child. "We can't—"

"You will let me finish," he said, and pressed two fingers against her lips. But it was the fierce look in his eyes that silenced her.

"I have done many things wrong with you," he said. "But this time it will be done right. I love you, *agapi mou*."

She blinked, stunned to hear the words she'd feared he'd never voice.

Was she dreaming? "You do?"

He gathered her close and kissed her so tenderly that tears spilled down her cheeks. "Will you forgive me for being an arrogant fool? Will you marry me? Will you be the woman I give my heart to, who'll walk in the garden with me hand in hand when we are both old?"

"Yes." She lifted her face to his, gazing into dark eyes that showed the depth of his love, that proved to her this was not a dream.

This was real. And this was right.

"Yes," she said, this time from her heart. "I'll love you now, when we are old, with my last breath and through eternity."

"To the airport," he told his driver, his voice gruff with emotion. "To Angyra and our future."

She took his right hand and placed it over her still-flat stomach. "To our baby."

His dark eyes flickered with surprise. With joy. "You're pregnant?"

"Yes," she said. "I tried to tell you earlier, but you kept interrupting me."

He flashed her a smile that was deliciously wicked. "Which is what I am going to do again, now that you have made me the happiest man on earth."

Then he pulled her close to his heart, as if she were his most valued treasure, and kissed her deeply, leaving no doubt that their love would last a lifetime and beyond.

* * * * *

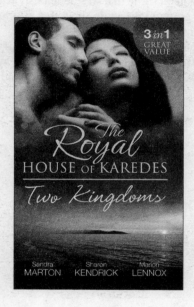

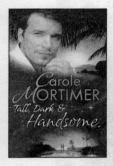
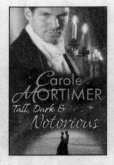
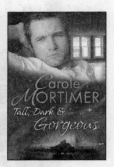
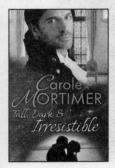

A new line of sexy, contemporary eBooks
featuring fun, fearless women who know what
they want from their lives, their careers
and their lovers!

Brought to you by
Cosmopolitan magazine and Mills & Boon

Visit:
www.millsandboon.co.uk/cosmo

The World of Mills & Boon®

There's a Mills & Boon® series that's perfect for you. We publish ten series and, with new titles every month, you never have to wait long for your favourite to come along.

Blaze
Scorching hot, sexy reads
4 new stories every month

By Request
Relive the romance with the best of the best
9 new stories every month

Cherish™
Romance to melt the heart every time
12 new stories every month

Desire™
Passionate and dramatic love stories
8 new stories every month